Praise for Ali Smith and

Like

"Beautifully written in precise, poetic prose."

—*The Observer*

"Ingenious, shimmering fiction, written with a poetic grace that subtly illuminates the tensions between hope and desire, between past and present." —*Scotland on Sunday*

"There are few writers on the world stage who are producing fiction this offbeat and alluring." —*The New York Times*

"You finish an Ali Smith book . . . certain that you have been in the presence of an artist who rarely sounds like anyone else."

—*The New Yorker*

"It is remarkable to be alive at the same time as Scottish writer Ali Smith." —*Los Angeles Times*

Like

Ali Smith

Like

Ali Smith is the author of many works of fiction, including, most recently, *Autumn*, *Winter*, *Spring*, *Summer*, *Public library and other stories*, and *How to be both*, which won the Baileys Women's Prize for Fiction, the Goldsmiths Prize, and the Costa Novel Award. Her work has four times been short-listed for the Man Booker Prize. Most recently, she won the Orwell Prize for Political Fiction for *Summer*. Born in Inverness, Scotland, she lives in Cambridge, England.

Books by Ali Smith

Like

Ali Smith

Vintage Books
A Division of Penguin Random House LLC
New York

FIRST VINTAGE BOOKS EDITION 2024

Further Acknowledgements on p. 305 constitute an extension of this copyright page.

The Library of Congress has cataloged the Vintage Books edition as follows:
Names: Smith, Ali, [date] author.
Title: Like / Ali Smith.
Description: First Vintage Books edition. | New York : Vintage Books, 2024.
Identifiers: LCCN 2023053658 (print) | LCCN 2023053659 (ebook)
Subjects: LCGFT: Novels.
Classification: LCC PR6069.M4213 L54 2024 (print) | LCC PR6069.M4213 (ebook) | DDC 823/.914—dc23
LC record available at https://lccn.loc.gov/2023053658
LC ebook record available at https://lccn.loc.gov/2023053659

Vintage Books Trade Paperback ISBN: 978-0-593-68798-7
eBook ISBN: 978-0-593-68799-4

vintagebooks.com

Printed in the United States of America
10 9 8 7 6 5 4 3 2 1

For Sarah Wood
with all my art

and for Don Smith
wishing him all the big fish

What is straight? A line can be straight,
or a street, but the human heart, oh, no,
it's curved like a road through mountains.

Tennessee Williams

My story has a moral—
I have a missing friend—

Emily Dickinson

Exegi this, *exegi* that. Let's say
I am in love, crushed under the weight
of it or elated under the hush of it.
Let's not just say. I actually am.
Hordes, posterities, judges vainly cram
the space my love and I left yesterday.

Edwin Morgan

Budding trees, autumn leaves,
a snowflake or two—
all kinds of everything
remind me of you.

Dana

All archetypes are spurious,
but some are more spurious than others.

Angela Carter

Amy

AMY is standing at the edge of the platform and looking down at the rails. They are clean and silver; it must be the wheels of the passing fast trains that keep them gleaming like that. Dull wood sleepers are spaced between the rails like the rungs of a ladder. Above her head sparrows are fighting in the rafters of the station roof. Woodsmoke is in the air, or someone is burning leaves somewhere.

This is the best kind of town. Trains don't always stop here. A train can run straight through and straight past without even slowing up, so fast that the voice on the speakers has to warn people to keep well clear of the edge or they'd be pulled into the wake.

She turns her head one way along the platform and watches how the distance extends like it's going into the sky. She turns the other way and the distance stretches in the opposite direction, it makes a straight line of light and space that slices through the built up edges of the town. She imagines the tunnel of space running clear past the flats and houses and the new office buildings all made out of window, through the derelict industrial estate with its smell of burning tyres and out into shabby open country.

She is standing at the edge with her feet as much over it as possible. She rocks on her heels, testing herself. But people are looking at her now, and just in case someone recognises her, for Kate's sake, she pretends to be looking over the edge for something she has dropped or lost. No, can't see it. Is that it? No, oh well, it's gone. She steps back, resigned, and leaves the station beneath the old Victorian clock that hangs above the automatic doors to the entrance hall. Look at the time. She mustn't be late for Kate. This has got to stop.

Amy Shone. A surname like that will haunt your life. Everything becomes something you did better then, before, in the shining days. But not if you don't let it.

Amy Shone and Kate Shone. When Amy has to sign things it looks like she's written Amy Shore. These are the only words that Kate has ever seen Amy write, and she thinks it's very funny now that they live right next to the sea. Kate likes being called Shone. Kate Shone, Kathleen Shone, Kate Shone, she repeats. (More like Kathleen the Hooligan, Amy says, jabbing her in the ribs with the packet of cotton buds, drying her after her shower.) Kate Shone is like the words from a story, Kate tells her. It's like there's a moment in a story, she says, where I come into a room full of people and the person who's telling the story has to say these words because they can't think of anything that could say it better.

Because he or she can't, not they, Amy corrects her, combing out her wet hair. Not that it really matters, she adds. It doesn't matter at all, not really.

All the people looked round, Kate says, as the door opened.

Kate Shone. She shone for the whole night. The light that came out of her was so bright that you could see by it, it lit up the palace so that people who lived miles away wondered what it was, and birds that were asleep in their nests miles away woke up and thought it was daytime and began to sing. She shone because she was in a very beautiful ballgown, the most beautiful in the whole ballroom.

At the moment Kate is obsessed with ballrooms and ballgowns. Last week she saw Disney's *Cinderella* at a friend's house, and now when Amy looks out of the caravan window and sees Kate playing by herself in and out of the dunes, she can guess that one of the games is Cinderella and that Kate is surrounded by benevolent animals who are making her a beautiful dress from bits and pieces they've found on the beach.

Kate's latest joke is: Why was Cinderella thrown out of the football team? Because she ran away from the ball. She heard it at school. She likes this school much better than the one she went to last, when they lived in the basement of the hotel Amy was working in and the damp made ferny shapes on the wall above the bed. The others in her class have begun to forget to taunt her about her accent and about living in a caravan and not a real house; a couple of them have even started to come round and make muffled knocking noises on the bottom half of the door for Kate to come out to play. *Kate adapts well. Kate has taken very well to this subject. Kate has improved significantly. Kate is a very promising child.* They have lived here long enough for consecutive school reports, pieces of paper Amy folds up and stores in the cupboard after Kate has read them out to her. More, Kate's voice is already becoming markedly rounded, purer about the vowels, more Scottish-sounding. A couple of weeks ago she dragged Amy to the main post office to show her one of the postcards, a postcard of the play-park near the beach, and although you can't really see who it is because it's too far away, it does look a little like them, like Amy (dark hair) pushing Kate (light hair) on one of the swings. They bought a copy of the card and stuck it with sellotape to the wardrobe door in the caravan bedroom.

Amy calls the caravan the stroke of luck. When they arrived here they did what they usually did in a new place, checked out the caravan site, always good for borrowing useful things from: rope, or water in plastic containers, or clothes off makeshift lines. They passed the site office just at the moment that Angus was pinning up the notice. Kate spelled it out so Amy could work out what it said. Assistant Wanted. Amy asked Kate if she liked it here. Then she sent her over the road to the beach and stood for a moment. She crossed behind the office and looked all round her. She carefully worked with her fingers at the washer on one of the outside taps until cold water welled below the spout and ran down into the drain. She put her head through the open hatch at the front of the office. The man who'd been sitting at his desk, Angus, stood up startled, pushed his chair back; it nearly fell over. Excuse me, she said. One of your taps is leaking a little over there. If you happen to have a spanner I'm sure I can fix it for you.

The good thing about the job was somewhere free to live, the stroke of luck, even through the winter when the site's closed, when Amy still has to keep an eye on the site and the other old static vans for weather damage or vandalism, and reply to messages on the office answer-phone from people making bookings for next season; Angus takes care of any letters. It is the easiest work Amy has had for years, and comes complete with two big furnished rooms, a bedroom and a kitchen/dining-room/lounge. There is electricity and gas, though they have to have baths and showers in the toilet block opposite. In the summer it's hard to get a shower or a washing machine when you want one. Winter last year was cold, but it warms up quickly in there with the calor gas heaters. Kate likes the heaters, they smell warm and orange.

On Christmas day last year they were the only people on their beach all afternoon and until it got too dark to see they drew pictures in the sand with driftwood all the way from the pier to the rocks, and when it got dark they walked the whole length of the sand singing all the Christmas carols they could remember. When they couldn't remember the words Amy made them up. We three kings of Orient are. We're too fat to get in a car. All day long we try and try. But never do we get in, o-oh. Cars so thin, so thin, so thin. They're so thin we can't get in.

Kate comes in out of the wind, bringing a cold blast of air with her. She trails sand across the shards of carpet from the door to the breakfast bar. Amy suggests she go and shake herself outside. Even after this her clothes and her hair parting are still flecked with sand. Tiny glitters of it are stuck to her face.

Amy is frying bacon and boiling potatoes and green beans.

Yuch, Kate says.

You'll eat it, Kate. It's all I could get, Amy says.

Kate throws herself on to the couch, dislodging a lump of driftwood, and languidly draws fresh faces on top of the old faces in the condensation.

Amy, she says. What's our postcode?

I don't know, Amy says. You'll have to ask Angus.

We were just playing Ancient Burials, Kate says.

I don't think I know that one. You and who? Amy says.

Roddy and Catriona, Kate says. She hooks her heel on the old book propping the table steady under its wonky leg. The book has a long word in gold on the back. Her A Clit Us. It looks like too nice and old a book to be putting your feet on.

You know Miss Rose? Kate says. You know how we're getting Skara Brae at school?

The bacon spits. Getting what? Amy says.

It's this place in Orkney where all the sand was blown away in a storm, and you know what, the archaeologists found this thing, they found a whole ancient village that had just been lying there under it.

Kate breathes the word archaeologists to herself, checking she has said it properly, before she goes on.

You know how we're doing our project about what it must have been like to be alive then?

A place in Orkney, yes, I think I knew about it once, Amy says.

Well anyway, Kate says at the window where she's been drawing swoopy lines, birds above the faces. With Ancient Burials what you do is. You lie down on the sand and you have to keep yourself really really flat, as flat as if there's like a ton of sand on top of you and you can't move. And then, you're lying there and this storm comes and blows all the sand off you and you wake up on the beach where you fell asleep and you get up and you're in a new place that you've never even seen before even though it's the same place you went to sleep in and you've been there all along. And then you explore the place. Amy?

The fact that Kate calls Amy by her first name when she's talking to her in the street or in the shops, or talking about her in the school playground, is one of the reasons some people round here aren't too keen on their children having anything to do with Kate Shone, who even though she doesn't sound like a tink is after all living no better than them.

For instance, did you know that four hundred different kinds of insects or living creatures can be supported by living on just the one tree? Kate says, and she says the word supported as if it's a very important word, one she's just learned. And did you know that just the one tree can make enough air for, I think it's ten people, but for a whole year? she says. And Amy?

Yes, what? Amy says.

Kate has been thinking about asking this question all afternoon. Can we get a cat? she says.

Not yet, Amy says.

Kate knows what this means. She pushes her green beans round her plate with her fork. It isn't fair. She likes it here.

What do you want to do after supper? Amy asks her. Do you want to go for a walk?

I hate going for walks in the dark, Kate says, sullen. I'm going to Angela's to watch *Byker Grove*. Everyone has a tv. Angela even has a tv in her own room.

The smell of autumn is in Kate's hair. Up here you can actually smell the changes in the seasons. Amy can't really remember being able to do that before.

There was one time when, it must be about three years ago now, round about this time of year, she left her standing in the street outside one of the big department stores, British Home Stores, by the Christmas display in the window, was it in Birmingham? she's not sure. When she came back four hours later, just to see, just in case, all the shopping crowds had gone and Kate was still there curled in her fleecy anorak on the ground in the doorway of the shut shop.

The sea moves black and huge, coiling its froth in and away at her feet. She can see small lights far out in the dark. She found Kate still in the doorway, a small pile of coinage at her feet. Smiling, sleepy with the cold, opening her cold hand above the silver and the coppers, I told them I wasn't wanting any money, she said. I told them we've enough money.

That was the last time she left her anywhere. The first time, when Kate was very small, when she still cried maddeningly and couldn't speak, once when she was asleep, she'd put her down and left her on the grass opposite a police station under a tree by a litter bin, and she'd sat on one of the benches to watch. A woman stopped. She looked like she would do. She poked at Kate with her foot. Before the woman had even pushed the door of the police station open they were gone. They were gone before the woman was even halfway across the road.

The sea, like it is tonight, thick and dark and salt, rolling the rubbish and the shingle into smoothed layers. The hard edges of the rock dig through her clothes into her skin. Amy can feel the scratches on the rock beneath her fingers, an illegible graffiti.

She has caught herself doing the aimless things again. The very top of the multi-storey car park, out of breath from the concrete stairs, four floors up where the stairs come to an end in open air. Look down and the air rushes to your head. The small spread of town beyond you, the mountains to the north. Sitting on a hump of hard earth in the gorse and the tall yellow grass, in the rubble and refuse of an abandoned building site behind a row of houses and some shops, boarded up, paint-sprayed. Three small girls watching from a safe distance. One of them swiping at the grass with a stick calling, you all right lady? You lie down on your back in the grass. Gorse above you against the grey sky. Concentrate on it.

Outside the shopping centre, watching the time change from second to second and the temperature stay the same, 8C, on the digital display in the building society window. Letting your head fall backwards on to the back of the seat, cold metal at your neck, people looking at you as they go past. Standing at the station looking over the platform at the rails. All the people there because they're meeting someone or going somewhere, their tickets in their hands, in their pockets, in their bags. You have no ticket. That's your secret.

She thinks of the three girls staring at her, the tall one mouthing to her friends words that look like mad and fuck. She thinks of the roof of the deserted car park. She could always go further north. The peaks of those mountains are already sheathed in snow.

Or under water. She could walk straight into the sea and feel the ground gladly shift beneath her, the cold wrap her round till she can't feel it then the surface close over her as if nothing has happened.

Nobody would come and find you there.

Then she laughs, and hears her own laugh against the noise of the sea. Kate coming banging in through the door saying, it's so windy, it's windier than anything; pointing out of the window at the trees between the site and the main road and saying, look at them, see, every time they shake those leaves the wind comes again. If those trees would just *stop* shaking their branches like that. *Then* the wind would stop blowing so hard. Kate watching a mist falling over the hills when they first arrived here, and running to tell her, it's history, to come and see history.

Always something there to remind me
always something there to remind me
I was born
to love you
and I will ne
ver be free
you'll alwaysbe apart of me
The words go round and round with the same cracks of space between them. The lines tack themselves round like crockery being smashed. Amy is exasperated, then helplessly amused. The vulgarity of it. The needle stuck in her head.

Kate is excited about something, has run off in front as they go back to the site from Angela's house. Angela McEchnie is the rather bland-faced child from her class to whom Kate seems to have taken a liking. This, Amy reckons, may well have something to do with the fact that they have satellite tv in Angela's house. She is having to get used to lengthening periods without Kate in the evenings.

Angela McEchnie's mother isn't at all sure about Kate Shone.

She's not sure that she likes her coming round all the time, this is what she tells her husband after the Shones leave. They live on a caravan site. There's no father anywhere in the equation. They're so English-sounding. Though to be fair they're not English like the troupe with the goats that moved into the Patersons' farm are English, and do the juggling and the massage and talk to their vegetables.

And there's Angela now, asking all sorts of questions that obviously come from being with the Shone girl. Like why do they go to church on Sundays, what good does it do. And why do people live in houses when they could live in a caravan and go wherever they want to. They've got tickets for the circus that's coming to town next week. Mrs. McEchnie used to love the circus when she was Angela's age. She used to beg her brothers to take her. The lions and seals and everything. Now Angela says she doesn't want to go because guess who's told her that circuses are a shame for the animals.

They pick up the most amazing things from one another, don't they? is what she said when Amy came to the door to collect Kate.

Amy offered Mrs. McEchnie an open smile.

I mean, the other day, Angela's mother went on. The other day Angela told me that Kate told her that there were two kinds of shopping centre. There was one kind that was the ordinary kind, with the shops and the plants and the escalators, and there was a special kind that was half shops, half horses.

Amy looked confused. Then she laughed. Oh, I get it, she said. Shopping centaur. I get it.

Oh, ha ha, of course, Mrs. McEchnie said blankly.

Kate and Angela were sitting watching Angela's father splayed out in his armchair flicking channels. A sixties music programme stayed on the screen for slightly longer than the other channels;

he was looking for his cigarettes down the sides of the chair. Kate and Angela laughed at the singer's hair being so high on her head. They mimicked the way she threw her arms out dramatically with each change of phrasing in the song. Soon both of them were helpless with laughter on the floor.

You might laugh now, you two, Angela's mother said, but it used to be the height of fashion to have your hair like that. You'll probably both be the same when you get a bit older.

I won't, Kate said.

Me neither, Angela said.

Now I used to love to get my hair up like that when I was a girl, Angela's mother said. Probably your mother did too, Kate.

No way, Kate said.

Mrs. McEchnie looked over at her husband. Then she looked at Amy. That one gets more like her mother every day, she said out loud with a smile.

Yes, Amy said, yes, she does. She does, she thought. It still took her unawares, was always a surprise. She fixed her eyes on the television screen; Sandie Shaw was walking barefoot down a platform above the heads of the swaying teenagers. She stopped at the edge, was about to begin a song.

No, you're probably too young for this, Mrs. Shone, Angela's mother said pleasantly. You were probably all green hair and safety pins, eh, whatever the fashion was.

Amy smiled politely, made a polite noise. Come on Kate, she said, pulling her by the collar of her jumper. Where's your coat?

She didn't bring one. I said when she came, didn't I Kate, it's an awful cold night to be out without a coat, Mrs. McEchnie said.

I'm not cold. I don't need a coat, Kate said.

Thank you for putting up with her, Amy said, she's a rogue.

Well at least she picks the child up, Angela's mother says to her sleeping husband after they leave. At least the girl doesn't have to walk home along that sea road by herself in the dark, I'll give her that. Eh Stuart. Eh.

Snow is a good idea. Snow will cover everything, that's its grace. Lie quietly everywhere, quieten everything, cool everything to a standstill, blow into the barky crevices of trees, fill the spaces between the light low blades of the grasses, bend and hold them down, settle without question over anything cold enough left in the open. Good dry snow will fall without sound and leave everything white. Up here it can cling for days to the sides of houses and along the tops of walls and fences, depending on the direction of the wind.

It's not cold enough for snow yet. Amy switches the light off, moves to the window. The moon is up. On nights like this one you can see the surface of the ocean light up and pulse beyond the car park and the dunes.

Two beads of condensation slide slowly down the inside of the glass; before they reach the sill she stops one with her finger so the other runs into it. She sits back on the couch and dries her wet finger off on the travel rug, cheap tartan, garish blue intersecting over red and yellow and white and black like the map of a nightmare city. There are small lines of sand in the rucks of the rug like beaches or saharas on the map.

It is very late, far too late for Kate to be awake. Amy gets up when she hears, waits by the bedroom door, peeks through the narrow gap where the door and the doorframe don't quite meet. The bedroom is dark, lit for only a moment by the lights of a car reversing out of the car park, the place people from the town tend to come to steam the windows of their cars up with love.

In the swerve of the moment the light crosses Kate, lying on her back with her arms above the covers and her hands in the air.

She seems to be playing a counting game. She counts on her fingers as she recites something in a low murmur. Amy can't quite make out what it is she's saying. It sounds rhythmic, like times tables or a poem.

She leans on the door, careful, silent, pushes into the room. Kate is saying the names of streets and towns and cities. One after the other she is listing the places where they have lived. When she gets to where they live now she goes back to the beginning and goes through the list all over again.

Kathleen Shone, you should be asleep, Amy says gently. She sits on the bed. Kate pushes her head into her lap. What story would you like tonight? Amy says, settling the covers round them.

The one about the girl who escapes from the inside of the hill, you know the one I mean, Kate says sleepily into Amy's cardigan.

All right, Amy says. That one goes like this. There was once a girl who went for a walk round the other side of the hill, where she thought the brambles would be sweeter and the world would be full of wonders different from the ones on the side of the hill where she lived. But she walked and she walked, and she couldn't tell where her side of the hill finished and the other side of the hill began. She sat on a stone to rest and to wipe her forehead with her handkerchief, and to eat the sandwiches she'd brought. And the hill opened beneath her, the grass and the soil split open and swallowed her up, and closed above her, and when she opened her eyes she found she was trapped in a dim damp chamber deep inside the hill, and the walls of it were made of stone and earth and rock so thick that she couldn't hear a bird or a footstep or anything, she couldn't hear a sound.

Amy doesn't need to look down to know that Kate, warm in her arms, is asleep.

White all the way from this coast to the other, from east to west, and all the way north and all the way south. White all the way to where the page ends. Down at the edge of the paper, at the corner of the page, scrawled in all the colours in rough crayoned lines, a flat square house with four windows and a chimney. Smoke rising from the chimney in a spiral of orange. Flowers in the garden that are nearly the same height as the house. A garden path, a fence, a gate. Green for grass. A red front door, a black cat. Above the house, in thick yellow shining wax, smiling, the sun.

ROLL over you great big indolent vole.

If you can remember that then you can remember the right order of the colours. Kate's favourite is indigo. Though when she tries she can't think what colour indigo is, exactly. Her favourite colour *word* is indigo but her favourite colour is turquoise. Indigo. Indian. Turquoise. Porpoise. Miss Rose wrote the thing about the vole on the board. Indolent means lazy. Billy Jamieson said had it anything to do with being on the dole. Miss Rose pretended she wasn't laughing and said absolutely not. Then she taught them all the rainbow thing. Red then orange then yellow, then green then blue then indigo then violet.

The Ladies' toilet block on the site smells damp and of disinfectant round the door. In the summer when it was really hot it had the smell of the insides of the spongebags of the mothers and the old ladies, who left footprints across the grass in the dew with the slippers or shoes peeking out below their dressing-gowns; it had the smell of all the different toothpastes. Aquafresh is the one she and Amy get, it tastes the nicest. The Men's block always smells of disinfectant whether it's summer or not.

Once in the summer this thing happened. Rachel and Nicky were waving out of the back of their car when their mother and father were driving them and their caravan away home, and she was waving goodbye and then there was this other family driving in at the same time and it was that boy Sandy from Dundee in the back of the car that she met afterwards up at the souvenir shop, and when their car drove in he started waving because he thought she was waving to him! But these were summer friends so you didn't see them again after they left. It was really horrible that time with Rachel and Nicky on the field when the big girls had come across from the estate and one pushed Rachel on to the stones and the really tough one, Jackie Robertson at school's big sister, said they were going to make them all eat the green stuff. Go on. If you don't you'll get a slap. Go on. It's nice, it's what they make polos out of. Eat it you, and she pushed Kate in the shoulder and Nicky was crying so Kate just stood there and stared right back and when the girl put the stuff in her mouth she still just stood there staring back, then one of their mothers was calling for them for their dinner and the other one, not Jackie's sister, shoved Nicky and they said you'd better be here when we get back right or you're getting battered, and she and Rachel and Nicky all ran back and hid behind the Ladies' toilet block, but they were safe because those girls wouldn't dare come on the site, and Kate had that horrible green taste in her mouth for the whole afternoon. But maybe you could think that was just the taste that green has. If that was the taste of green then blue would taste of salt like the sea. But the real sea was kind of grey. White would taste of cream or milk. But white wasn't a real colour. Orange would taste of oranges. What would indigo taste like? Amy'll know. In the summer this year it was so hot that things in the distance went wavy when you looked at them. That was called a heat haze, an optical illusion. That boy Sandy sent that postcard with the castle on. He stayed for ages, nearly two weeks. Angus brought the postcard over from the office. It said: We are staying at Fort William now and it has the shows there.

Kate climbs the shut site gate, jumps off the top and runs across the road and down to the beach. Where the big bonfire was the night before there is a blackened ring out of reach of the tide. There are burnt-out fireworks lying all round on the sand, it is still early, no one else has found them yet. Kate feels very lucky. Quick, she picks one up, and another. They still smell burnt though they're damp and cold from having been there all night. She shakes the sand off one, black round the hole where the colours and sparks came out, the paper coloured where it isn't burnt and flaking. The black stuff comes off on her fingers.

She darts down and picks up the one by her foot. She throws it into the air and watches it fall. She throws another up over her head, watches it thud back on to the sand. She stuffs the least blackened ones down the front of her dress and jumper, and she looks round. A man with a dog off its lead miles down the beach; some boys on a bike down by the edge of the water, she can hear them shouting and fighting. She puts her head down, holding the dead fireworks with her chin and arms, and runs across the sand up to the rocks and the rock pools, trying not to make any sound.

You can still tell what the names are on most of the fireworks. Blossoming Something. Happy Birds. Roman Glory. Venus Vase. Volcano. Shooting Star. Rocket To The Moon. Kate lines them up against the big rock. Roman Glory, Rocket To The Moon and Shooting Star have plastic spikes so you can stick them in the ground; she sticks them upright in the sand. Then she climbs up and leans over the big rock into the crack. The plastic bag is still there; careful, she edges it out.

The sea can't reach as far as the big rock and the plastic bag has kept the library book dry, and the animals. She reaches in, feels for the kangaroo. It is the one she likes best of the animals that she's taken. Down at the rock pool she dips its nose in the water. She lies on her stomach on the drier sand and presses kangaroo tracks into the sand with its long legs and tail.

In the bag there's also the Clydesdale horse with the holes in its sides and the plastic wagon whose harness clips into these holes, and the lion cub, and the sheepdog fixed in the crouching position with its ears up. The lion cub is much bigger than all the other animals, bigger than the carthorse even, its tail alone is almost the length of the horse. Kate stands them all up together at the edge of the water. Then she sits the sheepdog up high on one of the rock ledges. She stands the kangaroo in the horse's wagon and rolls a path as far round the pool as she can reach. She unhooks the horse and pushes the kangaroo into its place in the harness, and the kangaroo tows the horse back round to where they started. The lion cub floats on its side, its head and one huge paw above the surface. Kate picks it out. With its paw she tries to prise the limpets off the slippery rocks under the water.

She has her other animals back at the caravan, but these ones are the ones that matter. Each of them has travelled the secret journey back to the rocks in her dark pocket and nobody knows. Each of them has been sneaked into her pocket during morning prayers, silently snatched from the narrow window ledge lined with zoo animals and farm animals next to Kate's shoulder in the classroom. Kate can shut her eyes and still see out of them through a tiny crack, this way she can check that none of the others is watching and that Miss Rose is looking elsewhere, usually out of the window, while the voices say the words. You just have to wait for the right moment. You just have to reach over. Later in the day Kate is always careful to rearrange the spaces between the animals that are left so no one will notice. She is only going to do the bad thing once more. Out of all the animals on the ledge there's just the monkey left that she really wants.

She knows she shouldn't have taken them. Other children in the class might like them too and want to enjoy them. She knows that, even so, she wants them more than they do. And it's because she's not meant to have them all to herself, that's what made her reach for the orange kangaroo in the first place. But sometimes when she is still awake at night she feels bad in her stomach when she thinks of the animals. It's stealing, it's like telling lies or hurting other people. You shouldn't do it.

Roddy tells lies all the time. Not to the teacher or to any other adults but if you're out playing with him. He's always telling stories, is what Angela calls it. His father is away on a fishing trip at sea. Or his father is the skipper of a new boat and has had to go to New Zealand. Or his father has gone to Aberdeen to buy a new trailer and he'll be back at Christmas in a brand new car, a silver Vauxhall Designed For The Next Millennium. Everybody knows his father was on the fishing boat, some others in classes above and below them had fathers and brothers who were drowned too. Amy says what Roddy says isn't hurting anyone. Is my father dead as well? Kate asked her. Amy said, I don't know, I don't know whether he's alive or not, Kate, I don't even know who he is, does it matter? So Kate said the next time, Roddy, it doesn't matter about not having a father. Then Roddy went home crying and wouldn't speak to Kate and wouldn't come out to play or anything, but now they're kind of best friends, even better than Angela, though Roddy's mother won't have Kate in the house now, not to play on the computer, not even just to watch the tv, so Kate has to go to Angela's to do that.

Before there was such a thing as tv and radios, and in other centuries when there were no thermometers or when they were rare and only rich people had them, people like ministers and lords used to write down what the weather was, in special weather diaries. They would write when the crops were ready, and the really hot or really frosty days, and keep a note of how long snow lay on the ground for. Miss Rose says the earth is getting hotter and that this year the summer was the fifth hottest ever, or maybe not ever but the fifth since people started writing it down. At school Kate sits between Catriona and Angela now and at Catriona's house there is a huge collection of dolls but they belong to Catriona's mother and Catriona and her friends aren't allowed to touch them. Some of them have never even been out of their boxes and some are standing in a big glass case in the lounge. The lounge. Kate says the word out loud, feels her mouth go round it. She wonders what it would be like if she and Amy had a lounge, a lounge and a living-room and a kitchen that were all different rooms. For instance, it must be really good to have your own bedroom. In Angela's house the living-room and lounge are one big room because Angela's father knocked down a wall. The walls in the caravan are really thin, it wouldn't take long to knock one down. On windy nights things fall off the shelves and out of the cupboards in the caravan. It's a good game to try and run and catch them before they hit the ground. On Friday Kate finished her project early and she could have gone and sat in the Gold area and started a new project sheet, or she could have helped Angela finish hers. But then Catriona and Gemma would have seen that Angela was really far behind, and so Kate got this book off the library shelves and read it to herself instead.

She sits on the sand and looks at the front cover of the book. *One Hundred And One Great Wonders Of The World*. The book is full of black and white and colour photographs. Kate sees The Pyramids, and The Sphinx; underneath the picture of The Sphinx the words tell her that its nose was shot off by French soldiers who used it for target practice. She flicks the pages. There is an artist's impression of a place called Atlantis under the sea, with the fish and bits of plant in the broken walls, and another artist's impression of some gardens in ancient history. A photograph of a huge wall. Kate reads that it's a water dam they used for electricity. A crater in a desert, as big as twenty football pitches, the writing says. It has been made by a small meteor. There is the first telephone, next to a photo of drawings by cavemen. There are pictures of mountains. One looks like a giant back tooth. The Matterhorn, The Alps, Switzerland. 14,688. The mountain is black and massive, sheer cliffs with snow tucked neatly under them and cloud hooked round its peak.

Why do people clim b mountains? the writing says. *Ever since human ex ist ence began, men have long ed with all their hearts to con quer the natural world. Perhaps the Eng lis h po et Rud yard Kip ling knew the ans wer when he wrote:*
Something hid den—go and find it;
Go and look behind the Ran ges,
Something lost behind the Ran ges,
Lost and waiting for you—Go!
She puts a twist of hair in her mouth, wipes sand from her hand off the page, holds the book up so she can blow the sand out of the crack between the pages. You can see mountains not far from here. Rud. Yard. She wonders if it is only men who do that long thing with all their hearts. It can't be. There were children on the news in the summer who had a mother who was a mountain climber and got lost up one in the snow. Kate and her class had said prayers, and for the girl and boy she had, when nobody could find her any more. But it wasn't this mountain in the picture that she went up. The it doesn't Matterhorn. Kate laughs at her own joke.

Or it could maybe be said Rude yard. It is funny the sounds that some words make, sometimes they're so different from what they look like. It's funny how the letters that make up words can look like people. They can look like different people depending on what book they're in or what sign they're on, depending on how they're written or painted. In this book the small a's look sort of like small nice people with fat stomachs. The other way of doing a's, the round way, makes them look like they have long faces. The capital M on Matterhorn looks like it's had its points sharpened ready for a fight. Some e's can look smiley but usually they look like they do here, mean, like they're laughing at something horrible. Small d's always look like they're wide awake. Small g's like they're holding out a hand to shake it, or if they have loops underneath, like they're looking at you with their mouths open.

Kate likes to stand in the book section at the back of the newsagent's shop, where you can smell the paper of the pages of the thick paperbacks. She thinks it might be nice to be locked in overnight at the newsagent's. Amy sometimes uses the pages out of books to fill holes in the caravan lining or the roof or the door, or to help light fires on the beach, and when they go to a new place she wraps the small things that might break in the pages out of books. Kate is always very careful to hide the books she's reading from Amy, who might easily just throw them away. If it's schoolbooks then you have to explain to someone where they've gone or why you haven't got a page that everyone else has got. And if Amy knew the good things that books said then she wouldn't throw them away. But Amy can't even read the words on the fronts of shops or buses, she peers hard at the shapes of them and shakes her head and has to ask Kate. She can't read a story out of a book. She says she doesn't need to, that she knows enough about things without looking at words or pictures in books. That's true, because Amy knows thousands and thousands of things. Amy says you can carry more things in your head than you could ever hope to carry on your back, so you have to work out what's worth carrying and what to leave by the side of the road.

But even so, Kate doesn't leave books lying around in the caravan if she's not there. *One Hundred And One Great Wonders Of The World* will be safest kept in the safe place at the beach, or in the drawer under her own side of the bed where Amy never looks.

She holds the picture of the mountain up close to her face. It looks as if the Matterhorn has just breathed out, left its breath in the freezing sky.

Down among the rocks there are all the good hiding places. Kate shuts the book and jumps up. She shakes the Clydesdale horse to get the water out of the holes, rubs each of the animals dry on her sleeve and the edge of her jumper, and puts them back in the plastic bag. She puts the empty fireworks in the bag too, and rolls it up and pushes it back inside the rocks. She shoves the book, big and square, up her jumper. With difficulty she scuffs the sand over her own footprints, shuffling backwards dragging one foot, until she reaches where the rocks meet the rest of the beach and the footprints meet all the other footprints and don't make any difference any more. Whistling, hugging her book to her, she starts to run, speeds like the gulls through the clear cold air.

Angus stretches on his back, his hands behind his head. His pyjama top is open. He contemplates his chest. Downstairs Avril is making his coffee and clinking cups and plates. He turns, sighs, stretches again. Far at the back of his head a church bell is ringing.

Angus, dour Angus is here, how are you man? Donnie slung his arm round Angus's neck, winked at Linda behind the bar. A drink for dour Angus here please Linda. It's his ancestry, he told Bill and Willie and Hughie in the packed Saturday pub, he can't help it, Donnie went on, it's those teuchter voices calling to him across the centuries, up through the clay of the earth, eh man Angus, is that no right? Donnie slapped his cash on the bar, put on a west coast voice. Be dour now Angus Mhor, he whined, it's in the family, it's in the bloodline, it's the motto, Dour till the Death. Wha dour meddle wi him? Donnie said, and they all laughed. But Angus made them all laugh even more by keeping his face straight and long and saying, well Donnie, me and my northern ancestry, we thank you for the compliment, there's at least three hundred years' worth of ancestors here with me in spirit tonight and we'll all of us have a short and a half each and thank you very politely too, thank you very much.

A rare thing, one up on Donnie, a rare enough thing that.

Then swaying the hazy long way home past the harbour Angus saw how the boats sat, like big horses nosing at each other, in the slight wash of the tide. Up past the chip shop, past the garage, careful navigation through the cars parked side to side and bonnet to bumper, then over the road and the grass, along the site fence and the dark space bulked with the shapes of the hire caravans. He stopped at the gate. He held the cold padlock in his hand. He pulled to test the strength of the chain.

I have to come by and check, he was thinking. Anyway I can just stand here. I can stand here as long as I like. I can stand here looking all night if I want. It's my right. It's my site.

He leaned over the gate, stared into the dark. He couldn't see anything. The wind sang through the wire fence. He pushed himself off the gate and off to where he should be, towards the houses over the park with the lit squares of their windows, the winter-shut site lying rich and quiet and dark behind him.

Angus rolls over again when Avril comes in. She looks tired. She is starting to look like her mother. Downstairs on the cabinet there is the photo of them all outside the church. His collar is big and floppy, his shirt with the ruffly frill down the front tucked into the kilt, it didn't seem pooftery then, they all wore them. His hair was the Kevin Keegan look. Her hair, what would you have called it, full-blown, like someone had inflated it with a bicycle pump.

He sits up in bed, picks up his cup. He watches her turning the ends of her hair in neatly with her hairbrush.

What's it called, he says, that style your hair was when we got married?

What? she says.

What's the style your hair used to be? I can't remember the name of the style, Angus says.

Feathered, do you mean? Avril says, busy at the mirror.

Angus shifts down the bed again, stares up at the light fitting in the ceiling.

Funny, isn't it, he says, to see yourself like you were then. Stuck in time like an old Cortina.

Avril buttons herself into something smart. She sucks air in through her teeth.

I'll not tell you again, she says. We've to be there by lunchtime.

Now Angus has just nipped out quickly to get the papers before they go. But he takes the long way round, through the park along the beach road. Down by the rocks he sees Kate, at least he thinks it's Kate, it looks like her. He scans all round but there's no one else, there's no one with her. When he glances back to where she is she's gone and he has to look all along the shore to track her again, there she is now, sprinting away towards the water.

At the gate he puts his foot on one of the spars and swings himself heavily over. There are just a couple of things he has to check. He'll just check them. It'll not take a minute. He unlocks the office and goes in, leaves the door standing open behind him. There are no messages on the answerphone. He stands for a moment. Then he locks the door again, looks across to her caravan. He looks at his watch. He walks over, brisk, business, and raps twice on the door, and stands, and waits.

When he eventually finds her she is in the laundry building unloading washing from a machine into a washing basket. She has her back to him, bending in front of the machine, then bending to pick up the basket of wet clothes.

I'll do that, he says, don't you be lifting it.

Oh! she says, you made me jump. No, I can do it—

But Angus has already swung the load away from her, and from one end of the room to the other, from the washing machines to the dryers.

Amy smiles. Thanks, she says.

Angus stands, shifts his weight. Right, he says. He passes close by her on his way to the door. Everything all right with you? he says.

Yes, perfectly. Thank you, Amy says.

No problem, Angus says. Any time. If you need anything, you know, just ask.

I will, thanks, Amy says, turning away, pushing the change into the machine. Angus hears it falling through the slot as he leaves.

At the gate again he puts his hand on the top spar and vaults it in one, lands squarely, a little painfully, on his feet. There, he says to himself. He has always been able to do that, since he was a boy.

On the way to the paper shop he is thinking how some English people can be quite nice, when you get to know them individually. Not that he knows her. In fact it is just amazing how you can be working with someone for more than a year and still not know them at all, more than that they like their pay in cash, and they don't like that much milk in their tea, and they don't want to be bothered with a lot of questions and the like. Her favourite is the red one with the ice-cream inside, he bought her it and he even managed to persuade her to put her purse away for once, that she didn't have to give him the 57p for it, he didn't want it. 57p, for God's sake. It's strange how you can not know someone but still know they're not like anyone else. Angus takes the letters and papers from her, he says, don't you worry about those, I'll do those, Amy. He likes to say her name. He tries not to say it too often so that when he does it really feels like it means something. He is sure she's run away from some man, some man who was beating her about, her or her girl. He's sure of it. Some man who lifted his fist to her just once too often, now that would make anybody take to the road. Or some man who took all her money, something. Or maybe she took all his money. She's got her reasons anyway, whatever they are. Sometimes Angus imagines a suave English smooth-dressed smooth-talker at the site gate, sometimes he's a balding stocky thug, built like a boxer, who asks whether she's there. He says something ungracious about her in his East End accent, or his posh water-resistant surface of a posh restaurant voice. Angus looks him up and down, feels his nostrils flare and sneer as he coils his arm back and punches him hard, knocks him to the ground, both of them, the thug and the smooth bastard, on the ground feeling their jaws as Angus flexes his fist. Don't be letting me hear you speak about the lady like that again, he says. And if I catch you hanging around anywhere near her. If I catch you anywhere near her again.

Hughie in the pub last year: See you've a new helper up at the site now Angus.

Donnie: English, is she no? Stuck up, is she?

Hughie: No yet, but she soon will be! eh Angus? eh Donnie? eh?

Angus, looking at the bar, looking at the smoke uncoiling into the air from the cigarette in his hand, saying nothing.

When he gets to the paper shop and takes his hand out of his jacket pocket he is surprised to find, crumpled in his palm, a small white sock, damp and warm. A child's school sock, he stares at it in amazement. He smooths the creases out of it. He sorts through the damp change for the girl behind the counter, and he folds the sock up even smaller and lets it fall into the inside pocket of his jacket. He chooses a packet of the mints Avril particularly likes. He jogs home, takes the short cut, singing to himself under his breath.

Amy opens the door into a place that has been scorched black. The door swings back behind her and thuds against its frame, both the frame and the door have been buckled by heat. At least there is still a door. Everything that was here in this room before has become rubble, brittle, nothing. She steps forward. She can't go very far into it because the floor is broken open, if she looks down she can see right through to another place below. There is a hole above her head too, burnt through the roof. The walls are charred black all round her. She steps carefully back to where she was, puts her hand on the door to balance herself. The varnish on it is cracked and blistered. When she takes her hand away her fingers are smudged with soot, so that the creases in her skin stand out white.

She can't think where she is. She can't think what it can mean. It is like the inside of her head has been blasted with the same sudden heat and left porous and buckled, smoke still hanging, as sky smashes through the soft top of her skull.

Amy Amy Amy.

Kate wakes her, calling from the other room.

What? Amy shouts, what? what?

She looks down at what's in her hands, a jumper, needle, wool. She pushes the needle in the direction it seems to want to go in, from one side of the tear in the wool to the other.

Did you know this thing, shouts Kate, that we're just made of water and rock, I mean our bodies? Did you know that we eat rocks all the time?

Yes, Amy shouts, I knew that. I'm sending you out to the beach later to pick up a bucket of stones. I thought you'd like them for your supper tonight.

She can hear Kate laughing through the wall. She laughs too. Will you want them fried or roasted? she shouts. Baked might be nice. Or how about chips? If someone will lend us a chisel.

Oh, Kate calls through. Wait, I forgot to tell you. What kind of mountain—no. Wait. What mountain doesn't matter? Do you give up?

I give up, says Amy.

The Matterhorn!—no, that's wrong. What do you call a mountain that doesn't matter?

I think you've given it away, Amy shouts. Aren't you cold through there? Stop shouting. Come through.

Kate comes through. She flops down by Amy's feet and opens a big book.

The doesn't Matterhorn, she says. Do you get it? Do you get it?

Here's your jumper back, Amy says. It's filthy. I'll have to wash it. It looks like you've been carrying coal inside it.

She looks down at Kate. Come here, she says. Stand up, come here. What did you do to get your neck so black?

She wets her finger in her mouth, scrapes at Kate's collarbone above her dress.

Can I write a diary? Kate asks.

A diary? Amy says.

I'll write the weather in it, Kate says. Today it was sunny *and* rainy.

She picks up her jumper and examines the darning Amy's done. It is quite good, the wool is nearly the same colour as the jumper.

Miss Rose says it's getting colder and colder in the winters, and the summers are getting hotter and hotter, says Kate. There are new insects and everything, new spiders coming because of it.

As long as you don't bring any of them home, Amy says. The water pump must be broken again; Amy is pouring water out of the big plastic container into the sink.

There are all new plants too, Kate says. There is this new kind of green stuff on ponds and rivers, and dogs if they swim in it can get poisoned and even die.

Pull that jumper off, Kate, Amy says.

But I just put it on, Kate says.

And find me your flannel, Amy says.

Kate leaves the book with its pages splayed open on the floor and comes over to the sink. She stands still while Amy rubs at her neck. Do you think, maybe, do you think that people could get poisoned by the green stuff? Kate says.

I can't get this black off you, Amy says. It's like you've been rolling in oil. Wait—

Ow, Kate says.

There, Amy says. That's a bit better. Then she says, Kate, look at this, it's all down the inside of your dress. Where have you been?

Just down at the beach, Kate says.

Take it off, I'll have to soak it. And I've just done a washing. You liability, Amy says. I know exactly where you've been.

Where? Kate says. She wonders what the word liability means, if it's anything to do with being able to tell lies. She thinks of the plastic bag with the animals in it, tucked in the rocks in the dark. I wasn't there, she says.

You've been up the inside of a chimney, Amy says. You've been playing Roll In The Grimiest Place So Amy Has To Wash Everything.

Kate cringes away from the cold flannel. But if I'd been up a chimney, she says, the black would be on the outside not the inside of my clothes.

You turned them inside out on purpose, to fool me, Amy says, flicking the flannel. Then you told the coalman he had a new girl helper. You've ruined this dress. I'm never going to get this out.

She tosses the dress into the dirty washing corner. What's a coal man? Kate says. She squats down on the floor by the gas heater in her vest and pants; she cradles herself inside her book. She sings, it doesn't matter horn, it doesn't matter horn.

Amy rakes through the wardrobe, pulls out the green dress.

What about wearing your favourite? she says.

Kate looks down at the book again. No, I don't want to wear that one today, she says.

Usually it is a special treat for Kate to wear this dress. They found it in a second hand shop in Aberdeen; a dress some child wore to a wedding or a special family occasion, like a miniature evening gown, fancy, thick satin green and flouncy in all the right places, lovingly hand-made. Amy is surprised. Not this one? she says. You can. You can if you want.

Kate doesn't raise her head. The last time I was wearing it, she says, some boys said about me wearing it.

Amy can see Kate in the long door mirror, picking at something on the floor. Some boys said what? she says.

Well, Kate says, I was playing Best Man Dead on the beach—

By yourself? Amy says.

Yes, Kate says, if you do it yourself you get to decide how to die, and you always win. And some boys came past—

Which boys? Amy says.

I don't know them, they were quite big boys, maybe in primary six, Kate says, and one said to me, you must be going to a party, you're going to get into trouble, you've got sand all over your party dress. And I said no I wasn't going to one. And then they laughed at me and one said she's wearing a stupid party dress and she's not even going to a party.

Oh, Amy says. I see.

She shuts the wardrobe door, comes over and sits on the couch.

Come here, she says, and get warm.

Kate takes her book and pushes under Amy's arm, hooks it

round her and presses into her side. She opens the book at the mountain section and reads about them again, silently spelling out the difficult words.

Is that the doesn't Matterhorn? Amy asks, glancing down at the page.

Yes, Kate says, squirming in closer. This one.

There are several pictures of mountains; she points to the one in the cloud. Read about it to me, Amy says.

As Kate is reading out the words and the poem she feels Amy's arm stiffen uncomfortably round her neck. Amy's whole body seems to stiffen. Kate looks up. Amy is staring at the book.

Kate turns the page.

No, wait, Amy says. Turn it back.

Kate flicks the page back over.

Is that—Vesuvius? Amy asks, her voice small.

Kate looks to see what the writing says. She spells it out to herself. Yes, she says, that one, and she points to the colour photograph of the green hill with the split in its peak high above a city and the sea.

No, Amy says.

Amy puts her finger on the page opposite, on the writing, on a word.

Yes, says Kate, amazed. Yes. She points to another word. Can you read that? she says.

Amy doesn't say anything.

Kate points to another. Can you say that one?

Amy stands up.

Well how can you read only the one word? Kate says. If you can read one word then you can know the other words too. You must be able to.

Amy walks over to the big window and stares out. She walks back over to the couch. She takes the book from Kate and stares hard at the page again.

If you can read some letters you must be able to read others, Kate says. She scowls. When Amy gives her back the book she turns it the right way up and reads what the writing says: *In August 79* AD *in (hard word) south ern It a ly the ground started to shake and the sea round Mount Ve su vi us began to boil. On 24 August the volcano erup ted and the top of the mountain split and blew right off. Burning stones and smoke and red hot lava were throw n high into the air and fell for miles around, complete ly cover ing the towns of (hard word) and (hard word).*

Do you want me to read it out, what it says? she asks Amy.

Amy is still pacing up and down, now her hands are both covering her face. No, no, she says. She turns, and when she takes her hands away from her eyes her face is wild-looking.

Listen, Amy says. Get all the things together that you'll need and put them in the big blue holdall.

Kate feels cold all over. She shuts the book slowly. She looks at the cover. It is made up of pictures of wonders of the world. She traces with a finger the lines of space between the pictures, from the top of the book to the bottom, and from one side to the other. Now Amy is rummaging about in the other room. Kate holds the book hard against her chest. It is big enough to reach all the way from under her chin to her stomach.

Amy comes clattering through. She has the blue holdall. She goes to the wardrobe and begins taking things out and pushing them into the bag. Come on, Kate, she says.

When she looks to see what Kate is doing, she stops, puts the bag down. She comes over and crouches down to Kate's level. She pulls her hand up inside her cardigan sleeve and uses the cuff to wipe Kate's face.

We're not leaving here, she says. It's all right.

Kate chokes a wailing noise in her throat, sore, shuts her eyes. Aren't we? she says.

No, Amy says. Now listen. I have a question for you.

Kate sniffs wetly, opens her eyes.

If you wanted something, Amy says, if you really wanted something, but you didn't know how to get it. If you needed something, but, say, you didn't have enough money to pay for it. What would you do?

Kate doesn't know how to answer this. It sounds like a trick question.

What would be the best thing to do? Amy asks. Under the circumstances?

Kate wipes her nose on her sleeve, forgets she's crying. Could you just take the thing you needed? she asks.

Amy laughs. No, she says. Not this time. What would you do?

Kate thinks hard. She can only think of one answer. I'd ask you, she says.

Right, Amy says, jumping up. Right.

The right answer; Kate is relieved. Amy goes to the wardrobe, takes out Kate's favourite dress again. She holds it up and it shimmers on its hanger. Wear this one, she says.

Kate looks at the floor. Where are we going to go? she asks.

We're going on a holiday, Amy says.

A what? Kate says.

I'll be back in a minute, Amy says.

What about school? Kate is saying as the door clicks shut. She tries to see out of the window where it is that Amy is going, but it's too dark outside to make anything out.

There's school tomorrow, Kate hears herself say.

She sits in the new silence, still holding the book.

KATE closes her eyes and opens them, closes her eyes and opens them, closes her eyes and opens them. What she can see out of the window is different every time she opens them. When they're closed she can hear even louder the sound of the train, and the voices of the people, and most of all she can smell the food; almost everybody in the carriage is eating though it's nowhere near lunchtime yet. When she has her eyes open she doesn't notice the smell so much or the way the train throws her slightly from side to side in the seat. Racing away from her, fearful sheep. Then an empty field. Then cows, standing. Then trees. Then fields and hills. Then the wet tangle of bushes banked up next to the track. The closer it all is to the window, the faster away it goes. Only the mountains and sky at the back of it all seem to be moving with her, in the same direction.

She shuts her eyes and puts her hands over her ears. You could be sitting still and still be moving, like now. But it's better when you're sitting still and not moving at all, like at home. But even so, even when you think you're sitting completely still at home, you're still moving because the earth is always actually moving even though you don't notice it.

Beneath her hands she can hear the people. She can feel the speed, smell the breathed crisps and burgers. Something lightly touches her head; she opens her eyes. When she sees it's Amy's hand, even though it feels quite nice, she ducks away from under it and closes her eyes again, puts her fists over them and her head down on the table. Sitting still. Still moving. She wants to ask Amy about the word and how it can mean both those things. But she wants to keep her eyes closed like this as well, and not say anything at all to Amy.

Amy lightly lays her hand on Kate's head again, lightly scratches with one finger. Kate pushes her fists deeper into the pits of her eyes, but this time she doesn't move her head away.

They'll be doing maths now, she says. We were starting a new module today.

I thought you hated maths, Amy says.

If you push your fists into your eyes you can almost make yourself cry. Kate feels the tears coming, keeps them in with her fists.

I do, she says. I really hate it.

When she opens one eye again over the wet knuckles, the whole world is wavering under water with all its separate things running together, the sky and the land, the window and the outside, and everything moving and changing. Kate gives in. She turns and pushes her head under Amy's arm, wipes her eyes on Amy's jumper. Now all she can see are the fine hairs of black jumper wool raising their thin curled necks, stretched across the surface of Amy's chest and stomach. She decides they are a crop in a wide black field. There are small animals living at the roots of the hairs. A fieldmouse and its family, asleep in their nest. Small wild rabbits like the ones you get in the grass banks at the far end of the beach, grazing, each with one woolled ear stuck in the air listening for the kestrels.

Today Amy is able to make out some more words. She can read a word in the headline of a newspaper that someone has left folded on the table opposite. PEACE. She can make out some words in the sub-heading. PROCESS JEOPARDY. When she leans over, easing Kate with her, some of the words in the blocks of swimming black print detach themselves and flash into her head, theatre political loss the Israel. They surface out of the jumble so suddenly, so randomly and clearly that it's painful, like too much light entering at the eye. She looks away, down into the dark below the table. There is a discarded food wrapper on the ground by her foot; too tempting; she tries to read what it says. She can make none of its words out. It's coming back, she thinks, and the thought fills her with excitement, and numb fear. It has been a long time. She has been puzzling at the lost shapes of words, gratefully taking their loss for granted, for the best part of eight years now, a short lifetime.

One of the seats across from Amy and Kate is broken, so no one is sitting there. The woman in the window seat opposite Kate is reading a tabloid, holding the pages up spread open in front of them. Another word, clear and hard, breaks open in Amy's head. WEST. She says it out loud by mistake.

Where? Kate grunts, lifting her head.

No, Amy says. I was just talking to myself. But the real change, the real challenge, she thinks, will be when the words start to appear in relation to each other again, when a whole sentence shows itself. Maybe even a phrase, just a phrase.

The west is where they built that bridge, Kate thinks, the one the people who live there don't even want, and now they have to pay to go across it. It's where you can get a McDonald's in Gaelic. If Amy would ever let you eat at McDonald's.

Is that where we're going, west? she says.

No, Amy says, we're going south today.

South in Scotland? Kate asks.

South further than Scotland, Amy says. South out of Scotland.

Kate puts her head down on the table. I don't want to go out of Scotland very much, she says. I don't want to go to England again very much. I like it better now in Scotland.

Oh but we're not just going to England, Amy says. We're not just going to any boring old country. We're going much further than that. We—and she leans down and whispers near Kate's ear so that only she will hear—are on a train that's travelling back into the mists of time.

Kate looks out of the window. There's no mist, she says.

You can't see it because we're going through it so fast, Amy says. As she speaks the train shoots smoothly through a station. Kate tries to read the name of it but the signs go past too quickly.

See? Amy whispers. Did you see those people we passed, standing on the platform back there? Well, we couldn't see their faces, not just because we're going so fast, but because we're actually moving in a different time cycle from them. All they will ever see of you and me in their whole lives is one moment, one fraction of a fraction of a second of our time. And see all the people round us? They look real enough. But actually, in reality, they're all nothing but the thin shadows of people, hurling through time at hundreds of miles an hour.

Kate is interested in spite of herself. What do you mean? she says.

I mean, Amy says. This is a ghost train.

Amy points with her eyes for Kate at the newspaper the woman is holding up across the table. See behind that paper? she says into Kate's ear. Well, there's no one there. Those hands holding it up are ghost hands.

Don't, it's a lady, Kate whispers.

It looks like a lady when we can see it. But behind there now there's nothing but air, Amy says under her breath.

There's no such thing as ghosts, Kate says. She knows it's one of Amy's stories, meant to stop her being sulky. She knows it's a joke. But she can't help looking over at the hands and the paper, just in case. The hands are shaking their newspaper into shape, holding it firmly up over whatever's behind it.

Amy turns her head, nods discreetly across the aisle at a bullet-headed boy asleep on his bag. If you were to touch him, she says, your hand would go right through. That would happen if you were to touch any of the people on this train. Except us, of course, she adds.

Further down the train a baby has been crying occasionally, when the train shifts between unsteady speeds. Even that baby? Kate says.

Even that baby, Amy says.

Now that she has Kate interested, Amy closes her eyes and settles down to doze. Kate sits right up in her chair so she can see as far as possible down the carriage. The sleeping boy. The woman who has the baby, a baby smelling of sweet milky sick, she can smell it even right back here. Two ladies talking. Some people eating with plastic spoons, steam coming out of their plastic food containers.

Behind Kate a girl with long black hair and a fringe is reading a magazine and biting the skin at the sides of her fingers. She uses her wet fingers to help turn the pages. Across from the girl a man in a suit is eating a sandwich and talking with his mouth full into a mobile phone. Yeah, he says, we've just passed through there. He shakes his phone and speaks into it even louder. Hello? he says, then he shakes it, and presses buttons on it which make a beeping noise. Hello, that was a tunnel, he says. Can you hear me? I lost you. Yes, we've just passed through there and then we went through a tunnel.

Kate sits back down in her seat. Under the table, below the hands holding the newspaper, she can see legs with thick tights on and feet in shoes.

She gets herself into position and stamps down hard on the shoes.

The yelp makes Amy open her eyes. She sees the woman opposite crush her newspaper in one hand as she bends to feel under the table.

She stood on my foot, the woman says. Your child. Stood on my foot. She looks at Amy, her face all shock and indignation; she acts as if Kate isn't there at all.

I'm so very sorry. I'm so dreadfully sorry, Amy says. Kate, apologise to the lady. What a terrible accident. Say you're sorry.

I'm awful sorry, Kate says. I didn't mean it to be that sore.

The woman rearranges her big legs under the table, rattling the paper up over her face again. Amy looks sternly at Kate and turns away. She thinks about the woman's face, come alive with surprise. Soon her shoulders are shaking with her silent laughter.

Kate rests her head on her arms. She watches her own reflection in the window as the trees and the sky pass through it. She keeps her legs tucked well under her seat, well out of the way.

We were starting long division, she thinks to herself.

Angus came stomping fast across the grass at ten past nine in the morning. He stood breathless at the caravan door. Amy opened the top half, leaned out above him.

I got two months' worth out for you in the end, he said when he'd caught his breath. The machine wasn't working, I was waiting for them to open, they opened late. Would you believe that! Are you late for your train? Will two months' worth be enough? Aye but if you'll take my advice. It's better to have more than you need. You're not to worry about it, it's long term, I was thinking, we'll work it out. You'll not be short. A tenner off a month, I was thinking, something like that. If that would suit, only if that would suit, like. Now are you needing a lift to anywhere? I've the car at the gate. I could give you a lift to the station. I could give you a lift as far as the city if you were needing one.

He stopped, took a breath. Whew, he said smiling, he couldn't help smiling.

A lift to the station would be a very great help, thank you, she said. She took the banknotes and folded them in her hand, put her hand in her warm pocket.

Right, Angus said. Right. I'll be waiting in the car.

He tidied the things off the passenger seat, stuffed the things from off the floor into the glove compartment and wound the window down. Who was that? Avril had asked last night after the phone went.

Nobody, Angus said. The girl Amy from the site.

He lifted up the receiver, listened to the dialling tone, hung up again. He felt wonderful.

Everything all right? Avril asked. She was watching a tv programme where two couples wearing matching sweatshirts were racing against the clock round a huge antiques market trying to buy the most auctionable piece for the least amount of money.

Yes, yes, everything's fine. Nothing to worry about, Angus said. He went through to the kitchen and opened the back door and stood in the sharp dark.

So what did she want? Avril called through.

Angus paced the small square of back garden then went and stood in the shed, his heart exploding and exploding in his chest. He didn't put the light on in case Avril came to the kitchen window and looked out and could see the things he was letting himself think.

The next morning he drove her and her girl to the station and every question that came into his head was one he was careful not to ask. Where is it you're going. What are you going there for. How long will you be away. When will you be coming back.

When the car doors had slammed shut, when the waving was over and he couldn't see her at the ticket office through the big window any more, he turned the car and drove away. But when he had driven half a mile down the road he found he wasn't sure where he was going, so he pulled the car into the kerb and switched the engine off. The day lay stretched ahead of him, full of nothing. He sat in the parked car and watched the keys sway in the ignition. When he looked up some minutes later small spots of rain had begun to spatter the windscreen.

Angus is in love with me, Amy thinks idly.

She turns to watch Kate, who is playing a game on the dirt-edged table, walking her fingers across the surface and speaking to herself in a quiet range of voices. The game is incomprehensible to Amy. Kate has insisted on wearing her school clothes to travel in. Amy pretends to be fixing the collar of Kate's shirt, runs her finger over the fair smooth-haired skin of Kate's neck. She tugs the back tufts of Kate's hair.

I'll need to trim this soon, Amy says. You're beginning to look like a wild child.

Amy, what do you get, Kate says without looking up, when you tip a tin of Heinz Beans over a ghost?

I give up, Amy says.

No, do the whole thing, Kate says.

I give up, what do you get when you tip a tin of Heinz Beans over a ghost? Amy says.

Beans on ghost, Kate says. She concentrates on her fingers moving back and fore between the sticky marks left on the table by the coffee and the Danish pastry and the rest of the paper woman's lunch.

People are still eating, though now it's well after lunchtime, it's nearly four o clock. People beat a steady trail through the carriage to the buffet, to buy the things the man whose voice comes out of the speakers tells them about. Amy says they haven't enough money to have anything from there. I promise you we'll get something when we get off, she says.

Kate watches the people coming back through the carriage with their small paper carriers bulging with food. She watches to see what they take out of their carriers. She thinks about what it would be like to choose things at the buffet. It is nearly dark and all she can see in the window is the reflection of the inside of the train. The voices round them sound mostly English now. Scotland is gone, left by the sea somewhere far behind. Scotland was just about gone when they got to Edinburgh. After Edinburgh Kate watched out of the window for the border; the last time they crossed it she was too young to know. This time, though she looked and looked, she couldn't see it. She couldn't see anything like it, and then when she asked Amy, Amy said she thought they must have crossed it already. Kate was dismayed. She had been looking out of the window at England as if it was still Scotland.

At Darlington Kate and Amy have to move seats, the seats they've been sitting in are reserved. Because the train is so busy they sit on seats that fold off the wall by the toilets and the litter bin outside the carriage door. They sit in the smell of toilets and food. One of the toilets is out of order. People walk past them with bags of food the whole time.

I told the school you had mumps, Amy says.

Who did you tell, did you tell my teacher, did you speak to Miss Rose? Kate asks.

I spoke to a lady, Amy says, I don't know who she was, the secretary I suppose. I said you had mumps and that the doctor said you'd be back in two or three weeks. She went into a terrible flap, she wanted to know what class you were in and all sorts of details.

If it's Mrs. MacInnes the secretary, Billy MacInnes is in my class, Kate says. She cheers up. Amy has never phoned with an explanation to a school they've left before, not that Kate can remember. Two or three weeks, she tells herself. That's fourteen days. Or that's twenty-one days.

Amy thinks of the fear of mumps spreading like germs from room to room in the school, and from house to house at lunchtime all the way through the neighbourhood.

Have I had mumps? Kate asks.

Yes, Amy says.

Where were we living then? Kate asks.

From where they are sitting they can see the same small baby who was crying earlier. Now the baby is asleep, held in its mother's arms. Its mother is asleep too, her head rocking down and down until she suddenly jerks awake and checks on her child, then blearily tries to stay awake, closes her eyes again with her head going down.

Tell me about when I was that small, Kate says.

No, Amy says.

Tell me about when I was born, Kate says.

You weren't born, Amy says. I found you.

Everybody gets born, Kate says.

You didn't. I found you under a gooseberry bush, Amy says. I found you one day, you were tucked in at the bottom of my bed.

That's not true, Kate says.

No, you're right, Amy says, that's not true. The truth is, I fished you out of a loch.

When Amy says loch it sounds like lock. No you didn't, Kate says. Tell me the real truth.

A big white bird flew over my head and dropped something out of its beak, and I caught it, and it was you, Amy says. I opened my eyes one morning and there you were. I looked inside myself and you were curled up in there, holding your hands out in front of you like you were sniffing a rose.

Kate gets up off the chair and presses her nose against the window in the door, trying to see out into the dark.

I went into the big white room where you were with all the other new babies. I had to see which one you were. I could tell straight away, just by looking at you. Then I just picked you up and you came home with me.

Kate's name around her ankle and on the card at the end of her perspex cot. The last written words to mean anything.

Kate is running her hand over the plastic buttons, the ones you press to open and close the door. Amy is unsure what she has thought in her head and what she has said out loud. Kate, she says, and it sounds very loud. That's a little dangerous. What if the door opened and you fell out? Then where would we be?

Then where would we be, Kate says at the same time. I'd be on the outside and you'd be on the inside. It's all right, because they're not switched on or anything.

But she does as she's told, comes back over to the seat and folds it down, sits half on and half off. When I'm an adult, she says, I'm going to invent this machine that does this thing. You wear it in your shoes and then wherever you go, if you switch this machine on, it can actually tell you where you've been. So that if you go to a place, you'll be able to see your footprints sort of light up in the ground if you've been there before.

Ingenious, Amy says. So if you fell out of the train, I'd be able to follow the steps and find you?

Oh no, Kate says, nobody would be able to see other people's footprints, just their own.

I see. And what would be the point of that? Amy asks.

Well, then you'd know, whether you'd been there or not. Because you'd be able to look down, Kate says, and tell if you'd been on this train before because you'd be able to see your own footprints on it, on the carpet.

But this is a new train, Amy says. We've never been on one like this before.

Yes, but say this was the way back *up,* Kate says, exasperated, flapping her arms. We could *know* if it was the same train we were on that we'd already been on.

Two stops later Amy lets Kate press the lit button, and they get off. In the station, before she takes Kate for something to eat, Amy stops at a photo booth and looks in the mirror on its outside, runs her hand through her hair. She calls Kate into the booth to scramble on to her knee for two of the photos.

The photos slide shining out of the slot and Amy waves them in the air to dry them before she will let Kate touch them. Hold them by the sides, she says. At supper she folds the bottom of the strip back and fore and tears a photo off, gives it to Kate. Kate is delighted. She has never had a photo of herself before with Amy in it too. She holds the photo by its sides, props it up on her dessert spoon. She is careful all the way through her supper not to splash spaghetti sauce anywhere near it.

Say you took a small child, and you buried it in the dirt and leaves, and it fell asleep, or died, whatever. Say it lay covered through the autumn months of sun and damp and frost, and more leaves fell on the place, and the small animals and insects which had laid their eggs in the fallen apples or the late flowering plants or the cold corners of sheds died, like they're supposed to, emptying their one summer into the crisp shells of empty matter. Say the apples shrivelled and the leaves dried and froze and broke, and the child froze like a hard winter stone or a hard sealed nut deep below the surface. Then the snow fell, and sleet, and sun came out, dazzling, no heat in it; say the earth was so cold after the too-warm autumn that the frog which had spawned in the watering can in October, taking October for a spring that was still half a year away, found itself trapped in ice, unable to move its legs as the water hardened into rock round its cold heart. The telegraph poles, furred in ice, and the telephone lines strung between them, frozen then snapped under the weight of snow, grass snapping like twigs underfoot, and the stunted branches of stripped plants and trees, static, probing the air, covered in spikes of ice.

Say the child under the ground, under the skeletal frameworks of the leaves, under the thaw and the mulchings of leaves, the gradual widening of the sky and the still cold air and the wet leaves rotting, cracks open, and out of its fingers, and its toes, out of its eyes, mouth, nose, and from under its arms and behind its knees, through its small stomach and its tough guileless genitals, tendrils stretch, blind, inch the old rotted soil aside and reach the surface and break the surface pushing eyelessly up and up in the search for it, driven by it, the promise of it, warmth.

It is coming back, Amy thinks. It is all about coming back.

Did you hear about the witch who lost her bus fare? She had to witch-hike home. What kind of music do ghosts like most? Haunting melodies. What do ghosts ask for in restaurants? Ghoul-ash. Why was the skeleton always scared? Because he had no guts. What did the skeleton come home with after his holiday? A skeletan. Why is the graveyard always noisy? Because of all the coffin. What do ghosts put on their roast beef? Grave-y.

I used to be a ghost but I'm all right nowhooooooo. Kate tramps along the narrow verge kicking the leaves, holding Amy's hand and telling terrible jokes in the darkness.

Kate, Amy says, save your breath. You'll need it if I make you carry this heavy bag. Then she says, I say I say I say.

This is the way that people used to tell jokes. What do you say what do you say what do you say? Kate says.

Who was the first prehistoric novelist? Amy says.

I give up, Kate says, who was the first prehistoric—something?

Charlotte Brontesaurus, Amy says.

It sounds funny, but it is probably about one of the things Kate doesn't know about yet. Are we nearly there? she asks.

Nearly, Amy says.

Down this dark road there is hardly any traffic, though the occasional fast car swishes past them lighting up the road ahead and the trees above, or blinds them with its headlights so that they have to stop and look away for a moment.

Are we nearly there now? Kate says.

Kate, if you ask me that one more time I'll murder you, Amy says.

It is funny how Amy is speaking in a new sort of way, Kate thinks. Kate first noticed this in the place where they had their supper, and then again at the place they tried to catch the bus that doesn't run any more. The lady behind the computer said most people have cars, that the bus company stopped running the bus they needed when it was changed five years ago. Amy talked for a while to the lady and Kate could hear, she sounded like she was putting on a voice. Kate can't decide whether it's a more posh voice or a less posh voice. It sounds sort of harder. Catriona at school says that her big sister Cheryl puts on a voice like Amy's, like Kate's used to be, when she wants to pretend she's a snob or she's very rich, for a joke. After she told Kate this, Kate listened very carefully to hear if Amy sounded like Catriona said. But Amy just sounded like Amy. Some days it's good that Amy sounds so different from all the other mothers. Some days it isn't so good.

Right at this moment Amy isn't saying anything at all, and when Kate asks her if this lit-up village is the place they're going to, she doesn't answer.

They pass along a street of small cottages. There is nobody on this street, though there are lights in some of the houses and there are cars parked outside them. They pass a shut post office and a shut shop. They look like they've maybe been shut for years.

Some of the houses have thatched roofs, like pretend houses or houses in a film. Where the streetlights stop, the wide gates and metal entrances start, with the signs that Kate can read in the moonlight. WARNING: ALARM SYSTEM. PRIVATE. A picture of an Alsatian on one gate has the words I LIVE HERE! in angry letters next to it.

Kate thinks about how, at home, the mad Mackays have that horse that wanders about all over the road, stands with its nose at the grass on the Mackays' front lawn, how they don't have a gate or fence on their field for it. That's why everybody calls them the mad Mackays, though people say it like they're proud the Mackays do that with their horse, and like it's really good that the horse doesn't just run away. Roddy says they're mad because of in breeding and that the horse will get hit by a car. Kate has been meaning to ask Amy what in breeding is. This is not really a good time to ask her. She thinks about the time when the policeman came to the school and all the classes had to sit in the hall so they could see the film about stealing and the policeman gave them the talk about how they had to tell their parents, and especially any older grandparents if you had them, to shut and lock gates and doors and windows at night in case of criminals.

She is finding it harder to keep up. Amy takes her hand and they cross a road. Halfway down a tree-lined grass path, too narrow for cars, Amy stops, and they stand in the dark outside a tall door. The door is in a stone wall that is too high to see over or climb over. Amy tries the door.

See that lion on the pillar? she says to Kate. I'm going to lift you up, and I want you to feel round under it with your hands.

She bends down until Kate can sit on her shoulders. Kate balances herself against the wall on the way up until she is level with a damp lump of stone; it flakes where she touches it. She wonders if this is meant to be the lion.

Feel round the back, where its tail is, there should be a kind of ledge, Amy says, muffled under Kate's anorak.

Kate finds something sharp under a ridge, edges it out and lifts it, holds it tightly in her hand as she feels her way down the wall. On the ground again she opens her hand to look and gives the key to Amy.

Amy has to work the key for a long time before the lock will give. Both she and Kate push hard to move the door. It is as if they are pushing against overgrown bushes, though there are none there behind the door when they go through and push it shut again. They climb a grassy bank and cross what feels like a lawn until they come to a gravel path. The gravel crunches under their feet like a too-thick carpet, hard to walk on. Kate can't ask any of the things that come into her head in case she makes Amy angry. Her hand smells and tastes metallic; she rubs her fingers against her palm.

There, Amy says.

They have crunched across the stones to the edge of another smooth black lawn. In front of them is the shape of a house against the sky, a shape that seems as big as Kate's whole school. One window is lit up, light held between its curtains in the dark like a screen or a stage. A woman crosses from one side to the other. On the way she carries a vase full of flowers. The other way, she carries the same vase back again.

At the front door Amy stands behind Kate. Can you reach that bell? she asks.

Kate reaches up and presses hard, but she can't hear anything.

I don't think it worked, she says.

It worked, Amy says.

Inside, far away, a door opens. The outside light comes on suddenly, too bright. Kate looks down at her hand; she sees that rust from the key from under the damp stone has left her hand all brown grit; she wipes it quickly on her leg. Someone is pulling back a bolt in the big door. When it opens, the woman they saw in the window is standing there. She looks them up and down. She looks angry, she takes a breath as if to blow them fiercely away. Then she shuts her eyes, and opens them again. Her mouth falls open as if she's seen a ghost.

Amy has her hands on Kate's shoulders. Kate, she says. This lady is my mother. Say hello.

COME in, Amy's mother says, throwing the door wide open. What a fright you gave me. I thought for a moment you were—what I mean is, there are protesters protesting, well, they would, wouldn't they? being protesters—about British Rail or whatever they're called now cutting down all the trees and bushes by the bridge, I thought you were them, only as it's getting colder some of them have actually believe it or not been putting up their tents in people's gardens, I was about to lecture you about private property. They come round with their children, it's most manip-ulative. I thought you'd got into the garden somehow and come to the door to ask me for money.

Amy's mother, Patricia Shone, says it all in long laughing breaths as she throws the door wide. Come in at once out of the terrific cold, she says, though they already have, they're already halfway along the hall.

(When Patricia Shone was a girl, when she was still Patricia

Williams and was ten years old and was staying with her mother and father in an outhouse on the grounds of her grandfather's farm, one autumn the boy who did odd jobs and drove the tractor round to feed the pigs shut himself in one of the barns, put the cold metal end of a double-barrelled shotgun under his chin and shot himself. It was rumoured he had shot his whole face off. It was rumoured, she heard, listening when she shouldn't be, hiding behind the kitchen door while her father and her grandfather were talking, that he'd been caught doing something unspeakable with another man, an older man, an officer from the barracks. He had had to use a thorned walking stick to reach the trigger; he was seventeen and quite a small-boned boy. The shot had reverberated round the farm, unsettling the horses, lifting the ravens momentarily out of their trees into a round of complaining caws as they circled and landed again. The voices of her grandfather and her father, murmurous and knowing, seemed to be in agreement that he had done the right thing, the boy, Tom, who had laughed as he lifted Patricia Williams high into the air and swung her round and set her on the wide smooth seat of the tractor and let her hold the wheel, had lifted her up and sat her firmly in his lap with one arm round her, letting her take the wheel of the tractor and steer it round the yard.

Why she is thinking of this now, standing in the doorway, why it has flashed into her mind after all these years, she doesn't know. A raven lands back in the tree, knocks loose an old dead branch that shifts, falls, catches dryly through the other branches and drops down to land in the grass by the big old gnarled roots; Amy, this stranger, her daughter, has appeared again out of the nowhere she has been, bringing the smell of leaves and damp into the house with her as she brushes lightly past. Amy as a child passes neatly into her head, home for the summer and standing on the lawn, quietly reciting for all the world as if it is a test, a litany of the Latin names of all the species of flower she can see.

She is standing by the wall of the walled garden, and already she is staring past the camera as if there is no one behind it at all.

How are you, Amy? You could ask her, how are you? like your child is a vague acquaintance you meet on the street, or see again after some time at drinks before dinner at someone's house. How are you, how have you been? How very like her, closed, cool child that she is, to walk in after eight years of nothing. How like her, to disappear so callously in the first place, and how like her, now, to turn up as if nothing has happened, to turn from a collection of photographs, a closed book on the bedside table, a question you've finally just about stopped asking yourself, into this person real enough again to leave a trail of mud from the garden across your floor. Patricia Shone tries looking away, but when she looks back to see if Amy is still there, more, there is this new child too, staring with wide open eyes. Unkempt, they both are; their clothes are unkempt, their hair and skin unkempt. The girl's clothes are too small for her, her hands come out so far below the cuffs that it's almost rude. None of this is what you'd expect of Amy. And yet, how like her, to defy you, to be so unlike herself.

Patricia Shone has been to a class where a young woman called Michelle, terribly thin, with terrible acne, told her and twenty others how to deal with things. The Three Rs of Emotional Well-being, it said in the pamphlet. Michelle scratched the words on the board in green felt tip: Repressing Releasing Resolving = Well-being. Underneath, in brackets, (Relevant Scenario—Reimagine). Imagine something all pent up, she said, then imagine letting it go, imagine it released. Choose a Relevant Scenario in your own life and Reimagine it, but so that it happens the way you'd like it to be when you're at your most angry. Personally, Michelle said, I always imagine really losing it, really shouting my head off at a room full of women on plastic chairs. Just a joke! she said; everybody laughed nervously.

Patricia Shone only went to the class that first week, but the technique must have been good, it has stayed with her. She imagines the crew in her kitchen carefully filming her hands (some tv chefs actually use hand doubles, but never she, her hands are an ingredient without which the recipe would be incomplete) as she chops things up with her characteristic precision and with a very sharp knife indeed, and puts them in the blender. She quarters the beetroot and pours boiling water over the tomatoes in the pot. Always skin them, she says to camera, then says it again, always skin them, as they film her hands pouring more water with the steam rising. She waits for the tomatoes to soften, telling the lens, always measure for the right amount, no underdoing, no overdoing, that's the only way in the world to enhance taste. She splits and skins the tomatoes, and slices them into rough cubes, puts them in the blender. She takes the top off the puree and squirts it in, squeezing her hand down the whole length of the tube and the obscene red worms out; she does the same with another tube while they film from behind her. A sizeable lump of raw stewing steak diced and seasoned. She chops a red pepper, slides it in and adds half a cup of sherry, pouring herself a little glass as she does so, aperitif, of course, she says brightly, holding it up and sipping it, making an mmm face as the camera circles her. She prises the top off a jar of grainy mustard, holds it to her nose to smell it, and spoons a generous dollop in. A thinly sliced red chilli. A teaspoon of cayenne pepper. A dessertspoon of sugar. Wholemeal flour, she says, two tablespoons, to thicken. And now the secret ingredient, she says, and takes the napkin off the bowl of strawberries. Then she says it again for the other angle. And now the secret ingredient. That looks terribly good already, she says, pouring them whole into the blender. Salt and pepper to taste, and a dash of Tabasco. She imagines it all at fast-forward speed as she fits the lid to the blender and presses the on button, watching it spin till she jerks the top off in mid-motion and the red flies everywhere, spirals out of the blender to smash and spatter on the shiny surfaces and up the walls and all over the cupboard doors and the hanging pans and the mugs on hooks, and the equipment and the lights and the clothes and the hair of the crew, and herself and her face and her hair and her clothes. The machine stops. Time stops. The sound girl is picking, in slow motion, in disbelief, at the drenched fluff on her mike. The cameraman is staring, his lips moving, no sound coming out. The blonde girl producer has nothing to say for once, her clipboard is unreadable and her little French suit is ruined, she stands with her hands and arms held out away from herself. The camera, covered in dripping red, is still running. She looks into its eye, licks round her mouth. Delicious, she says, and does her camera smile, holds it for just the right length of time. Then she stops smiling, turns and says to the producer: Sally, would you like me to do that again?

Sweet and hot and disgusting, and people all over the country writing it down or videoing it to copy it later in their own kitchens. Throughout suburban England people's kitchens dripping with gore all over the Laura Ashley borders, all down the lemon matt walls. Sometimes she thinks it would be best to do it on her own, preserve it so that nobody else would know how to, prepare it and blend it and cover the kitchen and herself in it and then sit in it with nobody knowing, lifting her hands to her mouth to taste it, licking it off her sleeve, sucking it off her collar, then getting up, leaving her footprints in it across to the telephone and phoning Wendy to come and clean it up, hello Wendy, I've quite a little challenge for you this week, then going upstairs to shower, watch it running off her hair and skin and disappearing with the water down the drain until the water runs clear at her feet again.

Of course, blenders won't let you do that kind of thing. But just to do it, uncontainable, joy.
You've come home, and I've missed you so very much.
You've come home, I always knew you would.

You must never go away again.

You must always know you can confide in us.

You must always know we will be here for you.

You must never be afraid to bring home someone you like, you can always have the spare room, we are tolerant people, you know that.

You must know how proud we are of you.

You must know.

You have never known.

You have never wanted to know.

You have never loved me.

You have never shown me the slightest respect.

You have made me old.

You have made me ill ever since the moment you were conceived.

You think you can come back, just like that.

You think you have changed, but you haven't, you haven't changed.

You think you're different, but you're just the very same as you ever were.

Patricia Shone—achieved tv personality of four series of *Supper With Shone*, aired first on terrestrial tv then on respectable cable channels Europe wide, achieved author of bestselling supermarket large format paperbacks *Summer Shone* and *Seasonal Shone*, now working hard on the new *VegitariShone*, happily married to one of the world's leading academics in his field and living in one of the most beautifully restored and converted (smallish, or rather, comfortable) sixteenth century houses and grounds in the south of England, about whom and about which there have been several magazine articles and daytime tv exclusives—is a small girl standing by a door behind which the world has changed, beyond which there is something she is not supposed to know, something she is never going to be allowed to understand.

None of this is said. None of it has even reached her mouth, her eyes; it has all taken a moment only. Patricia Shone is still holding the door, holding herself and her voice in the shape of the woman who was about to answer it to people she could politely have sympathised with and politely have asked to leave.)

I do hope you'll be able to stay for dinner, she says.

Come in, Amy's mother says. I thought you'd come to the door to ask me for money.

I have, Amy says.

Come in at once out of the terrific cold. How are you? How have you been? I do hope you'll be able to stay for dinner, Amy's mother says.

Actually we'll be staying for three or four days, Amy says.

She drops the blue holdall on the floor in the hall and helps Kate take her coat off, hangs it on the hallstand with her own and guides Kate through to the kitchen. She leans down to speak by Kate's ear. Do you remember, she says, the time when we came here before?

No, Kate says.

What a sweet child, Amy's mother says. Sweet little eyes, sweet face. What does she like to eat? I don't think I have any of the food in, that children of her age tend to like to eat.

I didn't think you would, Amy says, you were just a tiny baby. You were only just born.

She pulls one of the tall chairs out from under the edge of the big new worktop in the centre of the kitchen and helps Kate up on to it. On her way up, Kate scuffs the white underside of the worktop with her shoe. She looks at Amy, her eyes full of alarm. Amy smiles and shrugs, shakes her head.

Kate has already eaten, she says. I'll have something with you later, though, if you're both at dinner; I have to talk to you both anyway.

Her mother is saying something, but Amy doesn't hear what. The kitchen has been gutted since. Where the hob was has gone, all bricked up as if nothing had been there at all. Where the way through to her father's study used to be there is now nothing but white wall. Amy goes across, traces with her eyes the line still there above the old door where the arch was. She taps her fingers where there used to be space and listens to the sound of thin plaster.

We had it done about three years ago, her mother says. It's sympathetic to the house's original design. We had it verified. It's warmer this way. Your father has his half of the house and I have mine.

Amy turns towards her mother, looks at her for the first time.

We prefer it this way, her mother says. We both do. It's really quite amicable. It is possible, Amy, though I don't expect you to understand this. It is possible to remain faithful and gracious to an idea of someone even if you choose not to have to look at the same profile over every routine meal you'll ever have.

No, I think that's easily comprehensible, Amy says, and she allows herself to smile.

Her mother looks younger than she had expected, she looks younger, even, than Amy remembers. Now her mother is blushing like she may at any moment burst into tears; immediately Amy regrets having said anything that might be construed as nice. She comes back across to see to Kate, who is sitting perfectly still and good and needs no looking after. From here Amy can see Kate's coat hung by its hood on the hallstand, its sleeves still rounded, holding the creased empty shapes of her small arms.

I'll answer all your questions at dinner, she says to her mother, her back turned on her. Where can Kate sleep? I'll put her to bed first. She's tired out.

I'm not tired out, Kate says. I'm fine.

Kate can sleep in the guest room, Amy's mother says. You'll find your own room is ready for you. Dinner will be in one hour. I'll call your father.

She picks up the telephone.

He's still at work, Amy says.

He's over in his half of the house, Amy's mother corrects her, pressing the buttons on the phone.

Upstairs Amy reads the words Guest and Room on the plaque screwed to the door of the spare room. Halfway down the hall another whitened wall makes a dead end new to her eye; the other half of the hall and the other rooms must be in her father's half of the house. She unzips the bag on one of the beds, then she leaves it sagging open and sits down on the quilt. Her hands fall, useless, to her sides. Her clothes are stuck with sudden sweat to her shoulders and her back.

Come and see this room I've found, Kate says. It's really fantastic. Wait till you see it.

Amy's, and Room. The plaques with the writing are new, but across the hall Amy's room smells the same, is the same as if it were just yesterday, just this morning, that she had used her thumb to press into the wall the drawing pin holding up the cutout picture of the actress dressed in a nun's habit; the half of a Christmas card, its angel holding a rose in the rose garden; the black and white postcard, someone from fifty years ago or more, dressed up as Joan of Arc. In a moment, if she is not careful, it will all surge back into her head, who the actress is, which medieval artist painted each minute gold scale on the wings of the angel, who has dressed up as St. Joan, and when, and why. Her head and eyes and shoulders are tired already from just these three; there are all the hundreds more. She blurs the wall, focuses on nothing. She can't help still being able to see that the pictures cut out of newspaper have yellowed and curled, and the bed waits with its sheet over its blanket in the sweet high smell of woodpolish. Hairbrushes on the dressing table sit stolid, where they should. Leaves are moving silently just beyond the window. She shuts her eyes.

Can I sleep in here? Kate wants to know. There she is, staring at the books all up the wall, then turning to gape at the collage.

No, Amy says, it's too dusty. It's too damp.

Then, in the corner on the chair, below the large white stuffed toy cat with the discreet zip in its stomach for nightclothes, Amy sees the pile of letters. She lifts the hollow cat and drops it on the floor; she brings their envelopes close to her face. She peers at the postmarks on a couple of them, lets them fall back on to the chair unopened with the rest.

On the floor, under some small packages she has discarded, is a large taped box. She rips the tape off the top and pulls the flap open. She puts her hand down inside the gap between the books inside it and fishes the letter out, rips it open. She holds the signature close to her face. Then she holds the letter away at arm's length to see it properly.

She folds it up again, crushing it into its envelope, dropping the envelope back into the box. She takes the top book out, turns it over in her hand, runs her hand across the familiar cover. She opens it, holds it open, puts her nose to the pages. Dry and sharp, the smell of old paper, nothing else.

She closes the book with one hand. She fits it back inside the box and closes its cardboard flap. She does it all with the resolution, the emotional panache, of someone who is being watched by an audience quiet in their dark plush seats below the edge of the stage, though there is no audience, there is only Kate, who hasn't noticed, who is sitting up on the bed now and moving from picture to picture pinned on the wall, moving her lips and touching each of them in turn.

If Kate sleeps in here, Amy thinks, then I won't have to.

Downstairs there is nobody in the dining room, but the table is covered in dishes piled with food that steams and gleams. When she sits down in her old place, there are two large books by her hand, gleaming like the food. Shining lists of words and photographs of immaculate glossy food catch the light in colours selected to please the eye.

Her mother flits in and out of the room with more dishes of things to eat. You see, I have been busy since you were away, she says. I haven't exactly been idle, have I? she says. You know all about it now, don't you, now that you've had your own; when I was pregnant with you I felt so dreadful I couldn't eat at all, she says. Six months into the pregnancy I actually weighed less than I did before it began, your father was delighted, he had had the good taste to marry the only woman in the world who didn't get thick ankles, who managed to look elegant and uncommon at eight months gone, her voice wafts in from the kitchen. Perhaps while you're here, she says over Amy's shoulder, you could run your eye over my ideas for the vegetarian edition, it's for vegetarians, are you still vegetarian? I remember you were. Perhaps you could check the proofs, if you feel so inclined, it would be an enormous help.

Amy passes from page to page of tastefully arranged colours; she shuts the book and sits in the rich smells of the real food tastefully arranged round her. Her throat closes. I'm not really that hungry, thank you, she thinks. I won't be able to check your proofs; I have been unable to read now for a long time, she thinks. Reading words is like reading hieroglyphics on the walls of dark tombs. No doubt you could find me a therapist who'd sort me out in six quick sessions, but I have opted for the slow way round. I have different ambitions now, thank you, she thinks. And neither of you is anything to do with Kate. She is nothing to do with either of you.

It is only when her mother sits at the table, rests her head on her hand and tells her to start eating, not to wait, that her father won't be coming for dinner this evening, that Amy says anything at all. What's the number? she asks her mother, and when she pushes the numbers on the phone in the kitchen she can hear another phone ringing somewhere through the wall.

Hello, it's Amy, Amy says. I have some things I need to ask both you and Patricia.

In her ear she can hear her father breathing.

This is what I need, she says, and looks to make sure her mother is listening too.

I need you to give me a little money. Not very much, I want to take a holiday and I haven't enough. In particular, I need you to telephone your friend at the passport office, the jovial man with the beard, I can't remember his name, with whom you were at college in the good old days. I have a child with me, but I have no birth certificate for her, and we need a passport. A British Visitor's passport will do. I have photographs. And the quicker the better; we would like to go in the next few days, as soon as we can arrange a flight.

There is silence at the other end of the line. Then the line disconnects with a click.

She puts the receiver down and waits for her mother to ask. Yes, she has imagined herself saying, that's right, Kate's birth was never recorded. No, I never recorded Kate's birth. No, because I never recorded it she hasn't got one. No, it has never really been a problem, we have always got round it one way or another. Because I didn't feel like recording it. I want to take her abroad. Because she has never been. A couple of weeks, or a week, I don't know. Well, we live very happily. No, we don't need much. No, I don't want to tell you where we live.

She sits and waits for the questions. The perfect food across the table between them grows cold.

Then her mother stands up. Well, she says, I don't know about you. But I'm quite tired out.

Her mother starts to clear the dishes into the kitchen. She tells

Amy that she needs no help, she hopes she will sleep well, not to worry about getting up, and that they'll see each other in the morning, won't they.

Now the house is silent. The central heating has switched itself off. Amy is lying on the guest bed looking at the dark. The tasteful bareness of the spare room magnifies the sound round her when she turns over.

She has practically given herself away, and nothing has happened.

She stares at the dark. Soon Kate will come through. Kate doesn't like to sleep alone, she doesn't like the dark and she's bound to be afraid in this new place. She'll stumble out of the bed in Amy's old room and she'll cross the landing still almost asleep, with one eye closed and the heel of her fist in her other eye, smelling of warmth she'll sense her way in like an animal too young yet to be able to see, push under the blankets by Amy and be asleep immediately as if she'd been there all night. She won't want to be alone in the middle of the night in a house she doesn't know.

The house creaks, then settles. Beyond the double glazing there is a mild muted noise, it could be dry leaves rattling on the gravel or the grass, or random rain on dry leaves. Dark in the room, dark that arcs over the roof of the house and fills the village, floods its grass tracks and its pathways and small roads, streetlights and motorway lights pushing the dark back a fraction, but above them nothing but dark for miles and miles, hardly disturbed by the small lights of big cities far below. Dark over the country, over the coasts, over the other countries massed beyond this one. The old story, the surface of the world slurring round again through dark that will always be there, turning half through dark, half through light, until light edges back into dark again.

Amy deciphers the shapes of the furniture in the room. She

lies on the bed and waits. Soon the universe will act, surely soon the moral universe will come into play. It is ironic, she thinks, I have left all the clues. I have left my prints at the scene of the crime, and now I have practically handed myself over. And there's nothing. No hand on the shoulder to say no, or stop, or caught in the act. Nothing but empty middle-class plot, middle-class dilemma. Nothing is going to happen to me. Nobody is going to say a word.

For a moment this is exhilarating, this is free-fall, breathless, enervating. After the moment, Amy wonders whether there will be nothing to stop the fall, nothing but endless space and empty air to fall through. Then it seems that all there is in the world is the dark, and the racketing noise in her ears that turns out to be the jolting of her own heart, keeping her awake, saying its word over and over like a hammer hitting rock.

She lies in the dark and waits.

She wonders when she will come.

Come in! the lady says. The lady is Amy's mother. She looks very pleased and she is still holding the vase full of tall flowers. They sway about in front of her as she speaks and laughs. Heat surges out of the front door at Kate and Amy like it does when you stand at the doors of some shops in Aberdeen.

The lady is still laughing. She has her hair cut short like a helmet round her head. She sounds a bit like Amy when she's speaking. To make sure, Kate checks quietly with Amy as they go into the big house.

Is the lady a granny? she asks quietly. I mean, is she mine?

Amy smiles over Kate's head. If you like, she says.

It is unbelievably hot in the house, which is sort of like a hotel. Kate can still feel the brown grainy stuff prickling on her hand. She keeps her fist closed. Amy tells her they have been here before, but Kate can't remember. The granny, the grandmother, carries the flowers in front of them into the kitchen, which is bigger than Angela's house's kitchen even, and has logs of wood in the roof. She seems very nice. She is quite like a lady from the television, on adverts for things. Up on the white table top there is a machine like the ones on the adverts on Angela's tv that go on for ages between the programmes. It is one of those machines for putting things in plastic bags. On the tv an American lady (not like the grandmother) puts her strawberries in the bag then puts the bag in the machine and the machine sucks all the air out of it and seals it so that it is air tight. The lady on the tv also seals soup and chicken and even clothes in her bags.

Kate's grandmother smiles at her. Kate smiles politely back. She wants to know what Kate would like to eat. She puts the flowers down and opens the fridge, which is taller than she is. Inside, Kate can see the sealed things.

Below the ledge of the table she uncoils her fingers and glances down. The brown-orange stain is all over the inside of her hand. She doesn't want to put her hand near the table because the table is so white. But she doesn't want to wipe her hand on her school skirt either. She closes her hand again and places it carefully on her leg.

Where can Kate sleep? She's tired out, Amy says.

I'm not tired out. I'm fine, Kate says. If she has to go to bed she'll miss what happens when you let the air back into one of those bags. Or they might play games without her; at Angela's granny's house they play Pick Up Sticks by the fire, Angela has to go there when her mother is working afternoons and Kate has been once; they had scones. But this grandmother is not much like Angela's one, or even Roddy's one, though her hair is quite greyish. Kate watches her grandmother go from one side of the huge kitchen to the other, carrying the flowers, the big yellow kind that have sort of tongues and on the tongues they have bright orange pollen that bees collect, and that can stain.

Kate's hand on her leg is getting sore now from being a fist.

When she looks at Amy she can see from her face that there is no chance of getting to stay up. She gets ready to say goodnight, but her grandmother goes into another room. While Amy is sorting out the bag in the hall, Kate licks the whole inside of her hand. The taste is like when you put your fingers in your mouth after you sit on the big metal bollards they loop the boat ropes round at the harbour; it is a horrible taste. She pushes her wet hand inside the pocket of her coat and wipes it hard on the lining. When she takes it out again, most of the brown stuff has come off.

The stairs are small and wooden; she goes up them two at a time behind Amy. It makes her stretch until her legs hurt. These are her grandmother's stairs. This is her grandmother's house, and she didn't even know she had a grandmother. Granny. Grandmother. For instance, granny sounds more friendly than grandmother, but grandmother sounds like a better thing to have.

Was the lady here when we were here before? Kate asks Amy's back.

No, Amy says, there was nobody here but us. They were away in America.

Kate doesn't say it but she thinks it, that there is also a grandfather.

Amy has pushed the door of a room open; Kate looks round the room, then goes further up the hall and puts her nose through the partly open door of the one at the end. It has a big white bed in it, and has mirrors all along the walls. Back down the hall she turns the handle on another door.

She calls Amy through.

There are more things in this room than in a shop. There are nearly as many books as in the newsagent's. Their backs reach all up one wall, all different colours. Even better, this room has a slanting roof, and most of the slant has pictures stuck all over it, all the way up and all the way to the ground and round on to the next wall behind the bed, like a wall frieze that the person who made couldn't stop. She climbs on to the bed to look. There are black and white pictures and colour ones. There are pictures of birds and some of flowers, and a really nice big one, big like the middle two pages out of a magazine, of a huge tree. One of a lady lying on her back beside a picnic hamper, a lady on a horse, a lady with a lot of lipstick on and with a crystal ball with a rose inside it. Some people on bikes. A lady in a knight's uniform, a picture of someone drawing a picture of someone flying through the air, and one of some tigers lying round a lady who has hair that shoots out round her head like it is on fire. One of an old lady with the skull of a sheep or something dead like that above her head. Some girls are playing cricket on a beach, wearing old fashioned bathing suits. A girl is holding a book and putting a pen in her mouth, the picture looks very old, like some of it has flaked off, like historical pictures. It is not the actual old picture, but a picture of it. There is one of the girl from the film about the wizard and the scarecrow, one of a line of ladies wearing cowboy hats. Every time Kate moves her eyes she sees a picture she hasn't seen before. Some of them are postcards, some of them look like they've come off Christmas cards, especially the angel ones. Some have been cut out of newspapers or magazines, and round them, in the gaps between them, are the scrapbook stickers that look like they are a hundred years old but that you can still buy. There is one picture that is actually a real photograph, of two girls under a statue. The statue has a dog, and she has her hand up like she is shielding her eyes from the sun so she can see better. The two girls are really small below the statue. One of them looks a bit like Amy. Kate puts her nose close to the wall, but even if your eye is almost on the photograph you can't really see, it's quite far away.

There's no dust, Kate says. There isn't even dust behind the bed. *Please* can I sleep in here?

Amy sighs. She is looking at letters and things over by the window. All along the edge of the window sill are beautiful delicate thin china cups on saucers. Amy comes over and puts her hand inside the bedclothes to test for damp.

You can if you get ready for bed right now, she says.

It is like magic. This room used to be Amy's own room. Amy's name is on the door even. When Amy was small she used to sleep here. (Whenever I *was* here, that is, Amy says.) The bedrooms even have their own sinks. Kate turns one of the taps on, then off, then on again. When she is brushing her teeth she sees the row of watches on the wall under the sink, hung by their straps on a row of nails. One hangs from a chain, a pocket watch kind, but the others all look as if they are for wrists, they have straps that are different colours. There are five altogether and they have their hands stopped at different times. The pocket watch says quarter past seven. The red strap one says XI to V. The two brown ones say eleven twenty-five and ten past eight, and the small one with the gold face says five to eight.

Can I have a watch? Kate asks Amy, who is tucking her in. The bed is blankets not duvet, and Kate's arms are trapped tight at the sides of her body.

No, Amy says, sitting on the side of the bed, but you can have a story. Which story would you like?

I think I'd like a new story tonight, Kate says.

All right, Amy says. What kind of new story?

One I haven't had before, Kate says. She has pulled the covers loose and wriggled round to lie on her front. What is this a photo of? she says, seeing again, just by her head, the two girls and the statue.

Amy bends to look.

71

That, she says. She sits down again on the side of the bed and smooths the covers back over Kate. That's a photo of your mother and her friend, she says.

Kate turns over again. I'd like the story of that, please, she says.

What about this one? Amy points at the woman on the horse dressed up as the knight, with the lance with the streamers on it, and the people behind her taking photographs of her. That would make a good story, she says. Or this one? She points to something else Kate can't see.

Can I not have the first one? Kate asks.

The first one, Amy says, the first one. Well. Now. Wait, I need to think. Right. Are you ready? How about something like this? Once there was a girl who went into the woods on a beautiful day in spring. She came to a river, and sat down at the side of it, and looked down into the water.

And she saw herself in the water, her reflection, Kate says.

Well, yes, she did, that's right. But that's not all she saw. Below her reflection she could see something moving. It was a fish, a silver and gold one shining and gliding in the water. She was hungry, the girl, and she thought she'd like to catch that pretty little fish and take it home and have it for her dinner. So she pulled a thread out of her jumper, and she tied it firmly to a berry that she reached up and broke off the branch of a tree that was hanging above her head, and she cast it into the water and she caught the fish. But when she pulled it out of the water, when she pulled it out on to the land, it flapped on the banks and changed before her eyes into a beautiful shining girl standing there smiling in the long grass. The fisher girl didn't know what to do. And while she was worrying about what to do, the other took the berry out of her mouth, glimmered in the light from the river, and do you know what?

What? Kate says.

She disappeared, Amy says. Thin air was all that was left of her. The girl was left by the side of the river alone.

Then what happened? Kate says.

Well. She looked behind the grassy banks. She looked all round her. She looked everywhere. She even put her face in the water and got her hair all wet looking below the surface of the river. But she couldn't find her. So she put the berry in her pocket, and she rolled the wet thread round her finger, tied it in a knot, and swore on the knot that she would search her whole life, if it took that long, until she found the one she'd caught again.

What for? Kate says.

I don't know. To take her home for dinner, I suppose, Amy says.

Couldn't she just have thrown the berry in again and caught another one? Kate asks.

No, Amy says.

Why? Kate asks.

She was like you. She wanted the first one, Amy says, and uncurls her legs, gets up off the side of the bed.

That's not the end, Kate says. It didn't have an end! Anyway what about the statue? What about the photo? It wasn't the story I was wanting.

Well it's the only story you're going to get, Amy says, and pulls the blankets tight again, kisses Kate on the side of the head, switches the light out and pulls the door over, leaving a crack of light from the hall.

It is funny, there is no sound of the sea. It is the first time that she can ever remember getting to go to sleep by herself in her own room. In what light there is she can see the dark lines of wood along the edges of the roof and the way the pictures shine all up the slant. It is very hot. It is so hot it is quite hard to breathe. She squeezes out of bed. Careful not to disturb the cups arranged on the sill she stretches up and picks at the catch on the window. But when she has opened it there is another window on the outside of it that can't be opened.

She doesn't dare touch the cups, balanced so thin on their saucers that just the thought of touching them might make them break into pieces. She looks inside the wardrobe to see if the clothes are in sealed bags, but they're all hanging up. She bends by the sink and tries to see the faces of the watches. She wonders if any of them work. She wonders what would happen if you tried to wind them. She hears a noise, and clambers back on to the bed, shoves back down into the warm space she's made. She shuts her eyes. She will pretend she is asleep until it is quiet.

When she opens them it's light; the pictures are all lit up; through the curtains a few birds are singing beyond the glass. It is very early, and very hot in the room again.

Kate sneezes and something comes out of her nose on to her hand. She doesn't know where to put it. She holds it on her finger. She thinks about putting it in her mouth. But all the things watching her in the new room make her decide not to. There is black in it; that must be from the train, you get that sometimes when you go on trains or buses. You can also get it from fires on the beach if people are burning tyres or the rubbish that comes off the boats, if there's plastic in it. Once the keyboard of a computer was washed up, with a cable off the back of it like a tail. It was really heavy with the water, and full of sand so none of the letters would press down.

It would be awful if the thing went on the bed, and so she squirms up out of the covers without untucking them and turns on the tap at the sink, so that only a little water comes out, enough to wash the thing down the drain.

Breathing is something that when you think about doing it you almost can't do it any more. She can feel more stuff inside her nose needing to come out. She can feel it when she breathes. It is like the stuff that comes out of her ears when Amy cleans them, stuff you would never know was there, and tastes horrible, and the stuff that comes between your toes, though that has a smell that you want to keep on smelling sometimes.

Kate uses one of the brushes to brush her hair. Amy used to use this brush when she was little. The brush must be really old. She pushes her arms into her school shirt again. It is too hot for the sweatshirt. Amy has folded her clothes on top of a box, and one of her socks has fallen down the back of it.

Under the flap of the box there are books. Kate takes one out. It is quite big and heavy, like a notebook or a thick jotter with a really nice cover that looks like it has been dipped in oily colours. Inside the book there is someone's writing. It is like a diary. She takes the next book out. It has a green cover with more oil swirls on it in pink and light blue. Inside there is more of the writing. The pages in this one are bent into, the person must have been leaning on their pen like when you try very hard to write neatly. They stick to each other, she has to pull a little to open them.

Kate's sock falls out of her hand into the box. Down inside between the two piles of books her hand fishes out a piece of paper or card, a card sticking out of an envelope. The envelope has Amy's name on it and the card has black lines round the edges. It says: *We are return ing this prop er ty found stored and already ad dress ed at the house of our father, Ken net h William Mc Car thy, rec ent (recent) ly dec ease d. If you know of the where a bouts of our sister Ai A is A is ling (hard word) McCar-thy we would be very grate ful if you would con tact us so we can*

Kate needs to blow her nose. She drops the letter back into the box. On her way back from the bathroom along the wooden hall she can see her grandmother asleep in the mirrors of the big bedroom. Her head is turned the other way, but Kate can hear her breathing. Kate steps from board to board until her bare feet reach the rug at the side of the bed and her toes sink into its red colour. Perhaps her grandmother can't afford a whole carpet.

She runs a finger over the carved bedside table; a wooden bird, wooden leaves with stem things curling out of them. On the table there are some bottles from the chemist's and some magazines and a book. She reads what it says up the backs of the magazines. *December 1995 I'll be lie ve it when I see it in Good House keep ing November 1995 Vog ue A Con de Nast Pub lic at ion Woman and Home December 1995 The Mag az ine You Always Want ed.*

The book has Kate's second name on its side in gold lettering. *Shone.* She picks it carefully up. On its front the words say: *The Pa in and the Ple a sure of The Text A Shone.* Text, like Teletext on tv, that you get when you press TV/MIX on the remote. She opens the book and some photographs flap out on to the rug. Kate freezes, but her grandmother doesn't waken. She bends to pick them up; they are both of a child in a garden, they look old, from the time when colours used to be faded like that, before she was born. She puts the book back where it was, on top of the magazines, leaning on the clock that is also a radio. That is a good idea, to have a clock that is a radio too.

Her grandmother's mouth is open and she is making a noise in her throat. If Kate stands on her tiptoes she can see her top teeth. They are very white. Catriona's granny has false teeth that she can push out with her tongue. Kate has never seen this, but she has heard about it. These teeth look like they're still real. Kate's grandmother has lines round the sides of her eyes and a line across her forehead above the top of her nose, as if someone drew it there. Her eyelids are twitching like her eyes are moving behind them.

Down in the kitchen Kate turns the metal lock until the door opens. What was darkness last night is now a lawn that doesn't have an end. The sun is out. A mist is rising off the lawn. Whenever Kate tries to catch up with the mist it has gone, is behind her or ahead of her. When she turns round to look, she sees footprints curving after her in the wet grass.

It is like having a whole school field to yourself. Kate does a somersault like they do on the school field and a leaf sticks to her face. There are leaves everywhere. She kicks through them and some of them stick to her bare feet so it looks like she is wearing boots made of leaves. Round a corner the lawn turns into shrubs and bushes with little paths through them. Kate sees a squirrel. When she tries to follow it, it runs up the trunk of a tree and she can't see where it has gone.

Then there is a room of glass stuck to the side of the house. Kate stands on the lawn, stares at the garden and herself reflected in the glass and the low sunlight. The glass isn't a greenhouse, there are no plants. She picks her way across the gravel and puts her face against the glass.

Books. Nothing but books. More than the school library, more than the library that used to be in the town before it got shut. More books than ten libraries, so many books that she had never thought there were that many in the world. The room behind the glass is made of books instead of having walls like a normal room.

One of the windows goes dark and turns into a door which opens. A quite old-looking man is staring at Kate. He has a beard and he is nearly bald, except for some long bits of hair that hang down one side of his face. He sees her looking at them and sweeps them up over the top of his head.

Kate steps back on to the gravel. It hurts her feet. The man is looking at her as if she has done something wrong.

There was a squirrel, she says. I didn't touch anything. I was only looking.

The man is scowling at her.

You're. I think you're meant to be my grandfather, she says.

Oh, the man says, breath coming out of his mouth like smoke in the cold. Is that what I'm meant to be?

I think so, Kate says. I was running in the grass. My feet got wet.

The man doesn't say anything. He is wearing socks. His trousers are open and his shirt collar is bent all wrong.

I'm Kathleen Shone, Kate says.

It's *shown,* not *shon,* the man says. You say *shown.*

We say shon, Kate says.

Oh, we do, do we? the man says.

It smells of cigarettes in the room. The table in the middle of it is messy with books and paper and ashtrays. Above the fire there is a big painting of a man and a dragon; the man has his lance stuck right into the dragon's nostril. When Kate looks up further she sees that the room is like two rooms on top of each other, twice as tall as a normal room. There is a staircase so that you can walk round beside the highest books. Under the staircase there is a tank full of fish. Three angel fish as big as Kate's hands, dark-eyed and flat like skimmers when they turn in the water at the same time, float through the hordes of small white fish and small golden ones with a red stripe through them. At the bottom of the tank there are black catfish with whiskers and fangs, whipping themselves round in circles.

The big fish like to eat the small ones, the man calls over to Kate.

I know, Kate says.

They eat them alive, the man says. Those angel fish, they'd even eat each other, apparently, never mind their offspring, if it came to a question of territory.

Kate is watching a tiny completely see-through creature walking unsteadily on the stones at the bottom of the tank.

You can get coloured gravel for tanks where we live, she says. You can get plastic skulls and they can swim through its eyes, the small ones could anyway. There's a plastic diver you can get and you can even get bubbles coming out of his helmet like he's breathing air.

The man is lying with his feet up on the couch. There is a

sheet and blankets crumpled on the floor next to the couch. He is staring up at the ceiling, or maybe at the very highest books. He blows smoke up over his head. On the floor by him, balanced on a pile of uneven books, there is an ashtray full of smoked cigarettes.

Did you know it was bad for your health to smoke? Kate says.

Well now Kathleen *Shon*, he says. Where could it be in the world that one can buy the diver and the skull, the gravel of many colours?

One what? Kate says.

What I mean is, where could someone buy these wondrous things? the man says.

We have them at the pet shop at home, Kate says. But they're quite expensive.

And where might that be? the man says.

In Scotland, Kate says. We don't have a fish tank, Amy says we don't need a tank because you can see seals right from the caravan window.

In Scotland, the man says. A caravan in Scotland, how very close to nature.

Yes, Kate says, and sometimes there are dolphins, if you watch long enough.

Dolphins, the man says. Kate can't tell if he means it to sound amazed or bored. And who is it, who lives in this caravan?

We do, Kate says. Me and Amy. Your daughter, she adds.

And you are Kathleen, he says. He is still looking at the ceiling, watching his own smoke rise and fade.

Yes, but mostly I get called Kate, she says. I'm nearly eight. I was born on twentieth February 1988. Next year I'll be eight, in four months, no, three months time.

I, the man says, am sixty-three. My birthday is in April. In April I'll be sixty-four years gone, Kate who is eight.

Kate sits on the dirty rug by the vase. She has already looked inside the vase, where there are more cigarette ends. She counts on her fingers. You're eight times older than me, she says to the man, her grandfather. My star sign is the fish one. Which is your star sign?

The bull, the man says. Then he makes a bellowing noise. It is supposed to be funny. Kate laughs.

Do you know that story, she says, about the fish that turned into a girl?

The man doesn't say anything. His eyes are closed.

Do you know the one about the twenty cats who all come into this room where the man is asleep, right, and he wakes up and sees them there and they're all warming their paws in front of his fire, and then one of them goes to the window and says Hooray for England, right, and—no, one of them is wearing a hat and it's the one that goes out of the window and says Hooray for England and it throws its hat to the other cats and one picks it up and puts it on and jumps out of the window and shouts Hooray for England too, and they all do it, till the last one, and it does it too, and throws the hat on to the floor so the man gets off the bed and puts the hat on and shouts Hooray for England and jumps out the window, and when he opens his eyes he's in England, and he's on a, those things, where they hang people—

A giblet, the man says.

Yes, a giblet, and they're putting this rope round his neck because they're going to hang him, so he asks for a last request, he says he wants to wear his hat again before he dies, so they let him and he puts it on and says really really quickly really loud Hooray for Scotland, and he opens his eyes and he's in his own room again in his own bed in his house and all his friends are there because they were wondering where he went and they're really surprised when he appears from nowhere. Do you know that one?

The man is staring at her again.

I really like that one, Kate says.

So, the man says, as if he hasn't heard. Piscean Kate who's eight, who lives in a caravan, in Scotland, apparently, with Amy my daughter.

Yes, Kate says. Perhaps the man is a bit stupid. Perhaps he doesn't know about Scotland, perhaps he has never been. Do you not know about it? she says. It has the highlands and the lowlands. It has mountains and its own songs and everything.

She explains about how it is a completely different place and for instance there is the border, which has been there since history and could make it a completely separate island when they vote to dig it so that the sea can run in. This is going to happen soon, she tells him.

The man puts his hand out blindly, feeling in the air for where the ashtray is. He taps his cigarette and a column of ash smashes open on the floor.

I'll take you home again Kathleen, he sings. Then he says, do you know, Kathleen, Kate, that even at night, when there is no noise, no noise at all, I can't get any sleep?

Kate looks sorry but the man doesn't see.

Do you know, that when I eat, I can't taste anything any more? And at night, when I close my eyes and try to sleep, my ears fill up with the sound of telephones ringing and a noise like a whole city full of cars all blaring their horns?

Kate glances up the walls of the high smoky room. I suppose it's a good thing that you own all these books then, she says.

The man stares at her. Then he bursts out laughing.

Probably he has that book about the mountains here. Probably her grandfather has some books, in among all of these ones, that tell you about the other great wonders they couldn't fit into the one book about it that Kate has read.

Do you have that book with the pictures, about the one hundred and one great wonders of the world? Kate asks.

No, the man says, still laughing. I don't think I have that one. But tell me, Kate, Kate the great. The great Scot, the hundred and second great wonder of the world, are you hungry? Would you like breakfast, would a little toast and marmalade do? Good, then it will do for us both, what do you say?

Yes please. Thank you very much, is what Kate says.

When he has gone she goes straight over to the open fire. It is low and warm, spitting and smoothing through the wood with the soft looking red colour like glowing feathers below it. She reaches up and feels along the edge of the mantelpiece until her hand closes on the box of matches, rough on the sides. Kitchen Matches. She opens the box. It is full of them, waiting with brown painted heads.

She throws a single match into the flames and watches its small explosion, watches the water fizz along it as the flame eats the length of it and it blackens and dies. She throws another one in. Then she turns to make sure that there is no one watching. She throws the whole box in.

In a moment, when the fire has burned through the outsides, all the insides will flare up hissing and sparking as if they're alive. She strains to hear if anyone is coming back yet, then she bends over the fire with her hands on her knees, tensed, holding her breath, for the special colour of what she's just done, the flash of light of it about to happen.

SAY you took a child. Say you just took a child.

Go on. Say it.

Amy has taken Kate right to the edge of the crater. They are watching the smoke dribbling up the volcano's insides. All the way along the red-brown rubbly track hewn round the volcano for tourists to walk on, the cloud closed them in so that they couldn't see anything, they couldn't even see that they were walking on a curve, nothing but the path and cloud below them, cloud above them, until the raw mouth of the place opened in front of them and there was nowhere left to go.

Now the sun has broken through, burning off the cloud. It hangs, dissolving, drifts like smoke. The air is dead and pure, pleasantly sulphurous. A lone wasp sways between the shrubs and a few clumps of moss on the edge; other than this there is almost stillness; no sound but the small noise of the wasp, the drone of a far-off aeroplane, the faint exchanges and camera clicks of the two English men further round the path.

There is hardly anyone here, just Amy and Kate and the two young men holding each other's arms, visibly disgruntled at not being alone on this particular top of the world. Is late for tourist, the taxi driver said who took them from Ercolano station as far up the mountain as cars can go. They want to go to the top. So what's new? There is nothing new in the world, he said in Italian to the people who own the restaurant at the car park, stopping to speak to them sitting outside at one of the bar tables. He spoke in English to Amy. Very sheep. Very sheep, he said again, holding out his old hand for more after Amy had given him the sum they'd agreed. I wait, he said. You have forty-five minute.

Amy warns Kate that if she goes under the safety rope again there will be trouble. Then Amy puts her head beyond the rope so she can see too. Down inside the crater a few trees are growing out of the different layers of rock. They look tiny; it is impossible to tell how big or small they are. It is impossible to judge the scale of any of it, though there it is, plain, in front of your eyes. Vesuvius. Amy crouches down, sifts some of the red rubble, the brittle dregs of a great heat at her feet, lets it fall through her fingers. Dust with sharp edges. Vesuvius, she sifts the word through her head. The word and the thing it means, the barbed dark between the word and the world; nothing but a rope bridge hanging by knots across a ravine, dropping loose slats as soon as you put your weight on it. A path around a chasm, that's all there is.

From down there, from most of the coast, it seems like Vesuvius is everywhere you look. It dominates the town they're staying in, blue-black, unthreatening, as if out at sea; catching at cloud right in the middle of the view from their hotel room where the line drawings on the walls are all of views of Vesuvius. When you get close to the actual mountain you can see how green it is. Greenery creeps up round it as far as it can, almost to the summit. The shadows of clouds moving on its sides, Vesuvius is always ahead of them or behind them in the windows as the train circles towards it, away from it. And now here we are, about to turn and go down again, and that's that, Amy thinks, that will be that, that's Vesuvius, done.

At home their caravan is locked and empty with its curtains drawn, with the iron step and the mat inside behind the door. Maybe it is raining, windy, cold; rain drumming on the roof, patterning the skylight. She stands up. The cloud has cleared completely. Below she can see the miniature network of small towns and roads leading into Naples, spread messily next to a sea whose surface is all light, like a sheet of precious metal. A small group of tourists arrives, bedraggled and elderly, out of breath after the climb. Their guide explains to them in French about the historic site they're visiting. Amy looks round for Kate, who has disappeared.

Kate is right on the edge of the crater beyond the safety rope. She has her chin in her hand, the other hand holding a stone up to the light.

Kate, Amy says. Come away from the edge right now. I won't warn you again.

What language are those people speaking? Kate asks.

French. Come away from the edge, Amy says.

You know what we are? And those boys are? And all those French people are? Kate says.

Kate, Amy says again, packing years of practised final threat into the one syllable.

We're all lava louts, Kate says.

Amy can't help it; she laughs out loud. Kate looks pleased. She scrambles back to safety under the rope, over the crumbling rocks.

They have come to see the real Vesuvius, not just the one in the book. The real Vesuvius is a bit boring. It is like looking at a quarry except without any diggers. There is nothing but old hard lava and although there is still some smoke from its insides, there isn't even very much smoke; the middle where the lava should be coming out is all filled in with stones. It is dormant now. It means like sleeping. Dormouse. Apparently the last time it erupted it broke and fell in on itself and filled itself in, and now the stones have been there so long they even have grass and moss over some of them. You can't go in it, it is too far down, though it doesn't look like it is. You could walk right round the edge of it. There is a path. But Amy won't let you because you have to go in a minute in case the taxi driver goes back to the town without you.

Kate sits down. Her shoes are full of stones, little bits of lava, powdery and red. The stones smell of earth. In fact, there is a damp kind of smell everywhere. Amy has explained to Kate how volcanoes erupt: there are kinds of plates in the earth that rub and push against each other and pressure builds up underneath until it explodes, throwing lava which is melted rocks from the centre of the earth up into the air and down the sides. This volcano once erupted and covered two whole towns full of people who were all killed, like the lady from Scotland on the bus told them. But today, for instance, it is like nothing ever really happened here. It is like it is just a big damp mountain with a hole in the top. It could be anywhere. This is Italy. But it could be Scotland, if it was hot in Scotland, if it was sunny in Scotland in November.

She is collecting the different colours of stone at the edge of the crater. The red kind has holes in it and is light to hold. It is quite like the bits of bone dogs leave in the field at home, or the insides of old chicken bones. She wonders if it is like the insides of her own bones. She looks at her hand. There are bones inside it. You can't see them though you can imagine them. At her grandparents' house there was a thing on the news on the television in the kitchen when nobody was watching it but Kate, about a child who was buried in the garden of a house when she was only small. It was just her bones, apparently, that the police took away in a bag. It was a skeleton. There were a lot of skeletons buried there, but only one child. Kate has been worrying since she saw it, about the police maybe mixing up the bones of the different skeletons all together. What if someone else's bones got in with yours? But this isn't bone, it's just stone. There is a grey kind, a pinkish kind, a red kind and a white kind. The white kind is like concrete. Vesuvius. The good thing is, the next time she sees the picture of Vesuvius in the book, she will know that she has been up it. If one of those aeroplanes was taking a picture now, for instance, for a book, she would be actually in it, in the picture *and* in the book.

On the way back down the steep path there is nothing to hold on to except Amy. It would be really easy to fall down the side, you could roll all the way to the ground. Amy won't let Kate walk on the side you could fall off. They sing the song about the bear going over the mountain, and seeing another mountain, and climbing the other mountain, and seeing another mountain. When they get down the side of the volcano to where the trees and plants are, there are butterflies everywhere.

The hotel they are staying in is cut out of a cliff, down in the town where the dock is, where the hydrofoil goes to some islands that look like they're just rocks that have been dropped into the sea. Amy says they can go on the hydrofoil later in the week. There is a church cut into the cliff right next to the hotel, as if it is part of the same building. There is a statue of Mary outside it and they sell statues of her in some of the shops up in the town too, you can plug them in and their haloes light up. It is the first time that Kate has ever stayed in a hotel that she wasn't living in. There is always too much food at supper; first they give you soup, then they give you spaghetti and then there is even another plate of food, you don't have to ask, they just bring it, and after that you get fruit or ice cream. The waiter is nice. The man who owns the hotel is nice; he keeps wanting Amy to eat at his restaurant at lunchtime too because of its fish, but Amy says that you have to pay if you eat there at lunchtime. There is no beach, just rocks that are too sloped to sit on and too big to walk over. There are these three dogs who live at the dock. They don't seem to belong to anyone. They smell of fish. Kate's hand smelled of it too after she patted one of them, so now she talks to them but doesn't pat them. There is one dog who came with her and Amy all the way up the stairs on the side of the cliff to the shops and the town. The lady in one shop came out to tell them, that is Vena, she said, she is a very nice dog. Another one of the dogs, the small brown one, has this game it plays on the road. It waits on the stairs and watches for when cars are going to come, then chooses which car will be good to chase. Then it runs out alongside it barking and biting at the wheels.

You can walk up the stairs to the town and the shops or you can walk up the road. The road is a bit dangerous to walk up, especially in the dark. The cars come down it really fast. The stairs smell of toilets. People just hang their washing out of their windows here. They don't have gardens and the windows have shutters. Amy says that abroad, like here, there is so much sun that they have to shut it out. In the toilet in the airport there were red ants on the floor breaking a peanut to pieces. They were climbing all over it. Kate saw them carry pieces of it between her feet and away under the door. Gatwick airport wasn't like it is at the Italian airport. It was the first time that Kate has been to an airport. There was a shop about cartoons, a shop for star signs, places to eat where you could get anything, spaghetti or sandwiches or Kentucky Fried Chicken. It was like a shopping centre that you could fly all over the world from. There was a place where you could get Virtual Reality.

Up the stairs, in the town, there are postcards of in the past when Vesuvius was erupting. A lot of them are in black and white but some of them are in colour. The smoke on the colour ones is really bright colours like orange and pink, you can actually see the lava on fire going down it though Amy says the colour has been added on afterwards. Some of the black and white ones are from before the insides fell in. *Napoli Vesuvio in eruzione 1944*. That is the Italian language. The words are nearly the same but not quite. Naples Vesuvius in eruption 1944. On the postcard you can see the wing of the old fashioned kind of plane that the photographer is taking the picture from, and you can see that inside the volcano it is like another smaller volcano and that is what is erupting. She is going to send this picture to Roddy, and the colour one to her grandfather and grandmother in England. She also got one to send to Angela because she thought it was a cartoon. But when they sat down to have a drink of something in the cafe and took the cards out of the paper bag they saw it was a picture of a man with a really big sticking up willy and horns, beside a lady who has what looks like a mushroom or a cloud coming out of her head, but it is supposed to be leaves. Amy read the back. It is good that Amy can read now, and she can even read things like what the Italian language means. She says the picture is Pan the god trying uselessly to rape a lady who has turned into a tree. In the picture the god is holding its beard and watching. Its legs are really hairy. The legs of the lady are turning into the trunk of a tree. Amy says it is from a myth. A myth is like a legend. There is that book called *Myths and Legends of Ancient Greece,* and there is a person on the soap about Australians who was raped. The picture of the God is all made of really small stones or tiles. It is a mosaic. Amy says Angela's mother won't like it so Kate can't send it to Angela. Amy can't think who Kate could send it to. She says Kate shouldn't be sending postcards anyway if she's supposed to have mumps. She buys Kate a coffee that is almost all made of milk and that looked like it would taste really nice. It is nicer than usual coffee but still a bit horrible. Amy says I told you you wouldn't like it, she says Kate will get to like coffee when she is older, but Kate doesn't think she ever will. Amy buys her a milk shake instead, but they don't need any food or anything, because they already get so much of it free at the hotel.

Amy is drowning out the words, filling the space they have made in her head with other things. Italian dust. Italian rust. Coffee, steam off the foamed top of it, postcards stacked on racks in the background, smoke coming off the rims of their volcanoes. It is hot, but winter is coming; the leaves on the trees are old and over, near dead, ready to drop.

She watches the people passing. People in Italy are handsome. Almost all the men are handsome. Bus drivers, men outside shops or on stalls, men digging ditches in the road by the hospital, or ditches in Pompeii, men chipping at the towering sheer mud wall in Herculaneum. Potbellied small men, dark with curled hair round their eyes, working to catch her eye, boyish and polite when they see she has a child with her but no man, smiling and companionable like the dogs she and Kate keep meeting in the town, no common language more persuasive than the friendly willingness to accompany. Amy smiles politely, enjoys the sun, keeps her eyes shaded and distant. The night they arrived the man who drove their bus to the hotel had seemed too small to wield the big wheel of it; small and muscle-compact, smoking gracefully outside the bus, he leaned against it, one hand on his hip, with the other drivers before they set off. Think about that. Amy lifts Kate's glass of coffee to her mouth. Italian coffee. She wonders whether Italian people, arriving in England, say, will find English people attractive like that simply because new and strange, because something different.

Two teenage girls on a moped putt past, one with her chin on the shoulder of the other in front, her arms loosely round the waist of her friend. The girls, the women are beautiful. Yesterday when they sat on the wall by the harbour Amy watched the people meeting people off the boats. A man came off the pier. A girl, small and dark and pretty, had come to meet him on a tiny Vespa, and when he sat on it and drove them away he dwarfed both her and the bike; she leaned her cheek on his leather back. By the cafe now a girl has just met a friend; the girl she has met swings without a word on to the back of her Honda. Mouth close to ear as they speed past, both looking ahead.

On the wall of the road tunnel on the first night the bus headlights lit up the huge white letters painted in a scrawl across it. LAURA AMORE MIO OSCAR. She could read them. She is finding she can read most things now that meet her eyes. There was a Glaswegian tour guide on the bus, this had excited Kate, who asked her where in Scotland she was from and told her where they were from. The guide sat at the front of the bus and recited to them over a speaker system about how Vesuvius had shrunk from twelve thousand feet to three thousand feet, splitting in two, when it erupted on that famous day in August 79 AD. It split so it became two mountains, she told them, and it became two mountains with approximately three times the force of the atom bomb dropped on Hiroshima. There are towns under there that are still not excavated. There may even be some towns that no one knows about yet. But the famous ones are Herculaneum, which was drowned in mud, and Pompeii, which was buried in ash and burning lava.

Ash, the guide said again. Volcanoes are fertile, she was saying now, because of potassium. This area, which as you probably know is known as Campania, is famous for its fruits and flowers thanks to the volcano. There is an observation post, she said, where scientists can give a week's notice of eruptions, and have detailed plans for evacuation on constant standby.

And this is the coastline where the greatest of all seductions took place—that's right, that of Ulysses, also known as Odysseus, and the Sirens, who, as you probably know sang men to their deaths by tricking them off course in their boats with their beautiful songs. So if you go down the Amalfi coast in a boat in your week here, just make sure you're with a friend who can tie you to the mast!

The bus was full of old people on their winter holidays; they all laughed. No, but really, the guide said into the echoey microphone, it is reputed that the world famous Siren song was really the noise the goatherds used to make when they were calling the goats off the cliffs at night. So don't be fooled if you hear beautiful songs, because in actuality they're not for you at all, they're more likely to be for the goats.

The hotel they have been allocated is like most hotels; everyone is very pleasant until it comes to money. The grandmother, sitting by the tv with her lottery ticket in her hand; the wife, grey and tired with being nice all year to people she doesn't know and doesn't care about; the owner, with his proprietorial stomach, his big moustache, his silent insistence that you do as he suggests. At dinner on the first night Amy and Kate shared a table with a middle-aged couple. The woman had an old face and child-hair; she introduced herself and her husband. I'm Thelma and this is Clifford. She was charmed by Kate. She thought Kate a beautiful child. She thought Kate could probably make it in show business, looking like that. Thelma had been a singer and a dancer when she was that age, round all the theatres and concert halls of the north of England. You're a quiet one, you don't say much, do you? Thelma leaned across and said to Amy. When Amy spoke back and she caught Amy's accent Thelma's face hardened, she became determined and deferential, she repeated how her own daughter, grown up now mind you, had a degree, a university degree, a good university, not one of these new ones, in drama and philosophy. Her daughter is her pride, just her pride, but she doesn't seem to want to do it any more, even though she has acted with some very famous actors, including one famous one, so very goodlooking, whose name Thelma can't remember, he's always on the BBC in serials, he has a long jaw, you'd know him if you saw him, and when Thelma went to see the dress rehearsals this actor had come up to her in the stalls and said that her daughter was one of the best Ophelias he had ever played with. But she just doesn't want to do it any more. She's not doing anything now, she just stays in bed all morning. Thelma shook her head. Her fringe shook a fraction of a second later. She just couldn't understand it, she said. She told them about how she and Clifford had moved to the Isle of Man from Accrington, and now Thelma had a buzz in her ear all the time—not here, not in Italy, and not in England, but *there*. And you can't get good reception for your tv or your radio. And it's queer—there are always things going missing, and you just had to put up with it, and believe it or not, this is true, girls—Clifford was speaking now, the only time he did speak, a big man, handsome and gruff and vehement in all his gold, with his wristlet slipping up and down as he wagged his finger and the thick gold chain rolling and settling its links in the hairs of his chest inside the open neck of his shirt, which was silk—this is true, he said. If you don't shout hello to them bloody fairies when you go over the bridge, I'm not joking, you'll have a bad day that day, guaranteed.

Kate was more interested in Thelma's buzzing ear. Your father has that ear thing, she told Amy back in their room afterwards. Your father, I mean my grandfather.

Amy had not known that Kate had even seen her father.

Where? she said. When? What did he say to you?

He is a nice man, Kate said. But he is quite old. He is the sign the bull is. We made toast in his room.

Amy thinks of her father's room and she is standing on the

wire spiral stair; below her, her father is reading a book. She knows not to ask him anything while he is reading. With one finger she is tipping a book out towards herself. It is summer, and she is reading her way through her father's books one after the other. She is making good progress. She is almost a quarter of the way round the room. She is looking forward to saying to him: I have reached the letter J. One day she will write a book and her father will be made to read it.

Now Kate is kicking her legs against the chair; her milk shake is finished; she is bored. A butterfly with wings the colour of stained parchment flies drunkenly across the square over the open-air cafe. Amy watches it until it disappears among the people and the traffic.

I could take Kate to the museum, she thinks. In that big garden there they have those fruit trees. We could pick some oranges, if nobody is watching.

Or, if they have time, they could go back to Pompeii again for the afternoon. Think of that. Nothing but the empty shells of you left, nothing but the air where you were. The shape you made last, by chance, the shape you'll end up keeping. When the excavators poured plaster into the air pockets they kept finding in the lava, the plaster hardened and made doorknobs, doors, furniture, wooden embellishments, and people. The wood and the bodies had decomposed and left their shapes behind them, spaces in air. In rooms round the Gladiators' Court they found eighteen bodies, seventeen of them big men, and one elderly woman covered in jewels. Seventeen gladiators couldn't save her.

Amy asks Kate which she'd rather do. She asks the waiter what time it is. The waiter points at the sky. It will rain, he says.

She shrugs and smiles, puts the money in the saucer. The waiters behind the counter look up at the sky, watch the woman and the girl cross the road towards the station, shake their heads at where they were sitting, and at all the empty chairs in the cafe. A storm is coming. Anyone can see that.

Though the main museum, where most of the plaster casts are kept, is shut for renovation at Pompeii, there are other casts strategically placed round the site for tourists to see. In the Grain Stores one small man lies like the stone figure on a tomb, except that his toga is all caught up round his waist where he fell. His hair has fallen back off his forehead. He looks like he is asleep. Behind him, in among the clutter of found things, another man sits with his knees comfortably before him and his head in his hands, as if he casually stopped for a moment to sit on the ground and think about something. Sitting in there with the amphorae and clay bottles and bits of broken statue, the man has become a statue too.

You expect it to be sad here, Amy thinks, but it isn't. If anything is sad about it, it's the hands, raised above heads, or resting on stomachs, or clenched on the ground, or cupped hopelessly over faces to keep the poisonous gases out. The public baths are beautiful; their walls are decorated with the delicate shapes of stars and etched with the carvings of fine-bodied men and horses with powerful haunches; light falls through well-placed skylights and makes the room golden. There are two bodies here, in dusty glass cases. One has his hand poised just above the flat place where the plaster encases what would have been his genitals. His face is split in agony. He looks like he is smiling.

Amy sits on a wall by some pillar stumps and watches Kate playing in the grass of what used to be the main room of a fine town house whose walls are patched with yellow and red. A cheerful place, really, where gracious people lived, and painted their houses those bright colours, filled their lives with pictures of dolphins and boars and bears and mythical creatures with wings, and people with wings; a place where they painted versions of their happy families straight on to the walls of their homes; gracious women, gracious children, gracious men, looking into the light now all over again after centuries of darkness, their ancient eyes staring calmly out at the workmen putting their houses back together. A lively, cultured city, the pretty materials of civilisation, of rich people who honoured their gods, had mosaics of fierce dogs put at their front doors to ward off thieves, warded off evil with paintings of men with phalli so large that they couldn't have walked with them, erect or not, they'd have fallen over; there's a kind of optimism in that too, she thinks.

The temples here are truly pagan now, overgrown with trees and bushes and flowers, their altars grassed over. Kate is playing under a palm tree in the House of the Faun. She is lifting up one of its huge fallen leaves, twice as big as herself, leaves that have been pushed out of the top of the tree by new leaves already sprouting. She waves the big dry leaf in the air like a giant fan.

The House of the Lovers is shut. The Brothel and the House of Venus are shut too. In the Amphitheatre, where buttercups and herbs are growing in the rows of stone where the audience sat, a boy much younger than Amy drops his rucksack near her and sits down beside her. This is a very beautiful place, he says in German. We could perhaps enjoy it together. You might perhaps like to come to my hotel with me? It is not very far. Do you not like me? Am I not the type of man you like? What type of man do you like? Where are you from? Why will you not speak to me? Do you not know German? It does not make me a bad person, you know. I did not do all those terrible things. It is not my history. Why should I be made to feel guilt for some things which I did not do? You are very nice. I have in my hotel room some condoms. I am safe. It is not necessary to fuck, we could just chat. It is good to be on holiday but it is also a little lonely. It is not necessary for us to be alone on holiday. You have beautiful hair.

Luckily it starts to rain. Amy pretends she hasn't understood, and when the boy reaches to touch her hair she smiles her incomprehension, stands up, holds her hand out to show how it is raining, mimes goodbye.

Kate has collected a stray dog, and for a while they shelter with the dog inside one of the entrance arcades. The rain turns heavier. Thunder crosses the sky and rain pounds on the streets, sluicing along the ruts left in the stone by the wheels of carts that vanished thousands of years ago. Workmen call to Amy and Kate to come and take cover in one of the houses, but Amy smiles and waves, carries on walking. Kate has her tee-shirt up over her head, she is looking out of the neck hole. The dog she has befriended is still following her, drenched and bony in the rain, rain running off the end of its tail. When they come to a nondescript crossroads, the dog stops and stands, wags its tail, won't come any further.

It is getting dark now. They walk past the Forum again, its floor blackened by rain. They walk blindly down a road lined with structures that look like tombs. At the bottom there is a lit window, a small warm office with nobody in it, where they stand out of the rain by a heater until a man comes through and shows them kindly back out into the rain again, pointing to another building further up the road. They join four other tourists and wander in the dark along parapets on the mud, from room to empty room. A man in a wet cap stands behind Amy and the rain stops above her head; he is holding a big umbrella over her. He has a torch with him, and in Italian he tells them to follow him; he leads them through the maze of rooms and corridors, he steps over a chain, there to keep tourists out of a room, and he stands in the middle of it in the dark and glances torchlight off the room's red walls. Life-size figures appear and disappear round the walls of the room. Amy knows where she is. She has seen these paintings before. She knows them well. She has studied them, knows them by heart. This place is the House of the Mysteries.

The other tourists have tailed off. The old man with the torch is delighted that Amy can speak Italian; he shows just her and Kate round the rest of the building. He takes them to see the corpses found in the house. One of them is more grotesque than Amy has yet seen, its clay torso twisted in pain. Not the mistress, he says, the mistress of the house was not found here, it is thought she went to live somewhere else before the disaster. Many people left the city before the disaster. Only the porters were left here, the mistress had other villas like this one perhaps.

He smiles a special smile at Amy as if he is about to show them something nobody else gets to see, and he unlocks a door. Inside, the small room is painted to seem as if there are further rooms beyond its wall. See? he says. See? He takes them out to the yard again where he shows them a huge press, for oil or grapes, he says. It is not the real one, he says, but a genuine copy of it. This is how it would have been.

Outside by the postcard booth a puppy is fussing over Kate, leaving muddy paw scratches all over her bare arms. Amy gives the old man some money; he looks pleased and shy. She asks him the way to the station. A moment, the man says. From behind the counter in the booth he gives her a plastic wallet full of postcards.

Amy opens the wallet at the station; she peels the cards out with her cold hands. In Amy's wet jacket, under one of Amy's arms, Kate, drenched and cold with her hair smelling of wet earth, has tucked herself in to wait for the train.

What are they? Kate asks.

They're pictures of the fresco in that red room; the one we couldn't see properly because it was so dark, Amy says.

What are they of, though? Kate wants to know. She goes from one picture to the next, leaving wet smudges from her fingers on each one, though Amy can see she is trying to be careful. I can't understand it, she says. Is it like a puzzle?

They're pictures of what probably happened in the room. It was a room where people were taken by other people to be taught about things, Amy says.

What things? Kate asks.

Mysteries, Amy says.

Kate looks through the cards again. I like the animals in it, she says finally, giving them back to Amy.

Amy turns the cards over in her hands. They were painted by a local painter in the first century BC, they form a cycle, and one small part of the fresco is missing. A story circles the walls of the room. A woman arrives at a door, met by a serious-faced naked child, a boy, who is reading a rite. Another woman carries food on a tray to some others who are busy unveiling a hidden sacrifice. A satyr breastfeeds a faun while some others play music, and a woman, perhaps the same woman who arrived at the door, turns as if to run in fear from something she can see ahead of her. Some men feast and drink round a figure who represents Dionysus, and a woman, kneeling in humility, unveils the sexual organ of a hermaphrodite angel (Hermaphrodite, from the child of Hermes, god of the arts, eloquence, thievery, and Aphrodite, goddess of love, who merged himself with a nymph called Salmacis and became one person, two genders). The erect angel is blandly whipping a woman who hides her head in the lap of another woman; a nude next to them dances a fetching dance holding two small cymbals above her head, as the first woman is dressed and readied for initiation while some cupids watch, coy, waiting, holding up a mirror in which she sees herself. Last of all, guarding the door, the mistress of the house sits comfortably, watches languidly. She knows it all already, she has seen it all before. For two thousand years now she has been watching what happens; for two thousand years the people in these paintings have gone round and round the walls of this red room in this suburban house, hidden, buried, dug up again, damp and dark and empty.

Amy packs the cards back into the plastic wallet. She puts the wallet down on the seat beside her. Then she picks it up again and drops it into the litter bin next to the seat.

Do you not want them? Kate says.

No, not really, Amy says. I've had enough of civilisation for today. Why? Did you want them?

No. Well. Only the one with the small deer in it, Kate says.

Amy picks through the crisp packets and cans to find them; she flicks through the cards for the one with the fauns. It is also the picture of the terrified woman, her cape flying up round her head as she gets ready to run, her hand held out in front of her in fear. Amy rips the postcard, tears round the part with the fauns in it and drops the rest back into the bin. She puts the torn picture in her jacket pocket for Kate, reaches in under the jacket, and takes Kate's hand in hers.

A fragment of the card sticks to the damp concrete under the bench. It is a ripped-up part of the woman's body, one of her feet. It is painted as if in a sandal, like the kind of sandal people still wear. It is very like a real foot. It is so like a real foot that Amy is shocked. She bends down, scrapes it up off the floor with her nail. She knows this panel of the wall quite well. She has studied it in dim libraries, she has read books about it, and articles, she has even written a lengthy paper on it and used slides of it in lectures in shaded lecture halls. Not until now, until she has seen it like this, ripped apart from itself on the wet floor of a noisy station as she sits with a headache surfacing because of the thunder and with a soaked cold child slowly growing warm again under her arm, has it ever struck her, how painfully like a foot the painter has taken the care to make it.

———

Pisces means the two fish. That is what Kate is. Amy is the one that carries water. Pompeii is a good place. It is nearly two thousand years old which is almost all of AD. You spell it with two i's. First it was covered by a layer of what is called lapilli, it says in the book. Then there was a layer of white pumice stone, then one of grey stone, then green stone, then sand, then lapilli again, then sand and ash, then more ash on the top. They had to dig through all that to get to the town and the people again. It is still all ash on the roads and the paths, like black sand. In one house there was a picture of a man dressed as a soldier whose willy was so big he had to hold it up with a kind of scales as if he was weighing it. There was one of a man with two willies, one in each hand. There was a better picture, of Hercules when he was a baby, when he strangled two snakes. They even found a plate of food that was nearly two thousand years old, it was pasta and beans. The first time they went, Kate made Amy buy a book from a stall outside the station and the lady gave them a free picture of someone, a saint. The book is full of pictures. There are some of the bodies they made out of plaster that were gone but were really there all along, but mostly it is pictures of paintings and buildings.

At Herculaneum, a different thing happened. Herculaneum, Hercules. They thought that everyone had escaped but then they found a smashed up boat and a lot of skeletons in the mud. They found a lot of jewellery and rings. Herculaneum used to be a kind of seaside place for rich people. The man told them that the horses had to wear special socks so as not to upset the rich people who lived there with the noise from their feet. No poor people were allowed. There is still a lot of it that hasn't been dug up yet, because there are living people who have their houses on top of the old place. There was even real glass from nearly two thousand years ago still in the window of one place, and the man who showed them round took them into one house and let them touch a bed and a door, though the door was inside a glass sheet. One time a wasp landed on Amy's chest and the man lifted it off with his fingers, not even with a piece of wood or anything, and let it fly away. The bed that they saw was very small. People were smaller in those days than they are now.

One of the dead people in Pompeii has bones sticking out of his plaster hand so that you can see them. The second time they go, Kate slips back inside to see the bones again. It is like his hand ends in bones instead of fingers. She is not sure whether the top of his head is skull or plaster. She decides to think it is plaster. She looks at the hand again. It is like the man has claws.

In the Amphitheatre, where the people used to do sports, a dog comes bounding up to Kate. It is huge, and it puts its paws up on her legs and leans all its weight against her. It is a female dog, it is all nipples underneath, and its feet are like bird's feet. The dogs here are really brilliant. The last time they came, a dog showed them a house with paintings in it; it went under the rope and led them both into a garden they weren't supposed to go into where there were paintings of people from myths. Kate gave it a drink from one of the taps and it drank the water out of her hand with its tongue.

It pours with rain the second time they go, so that you have to use the big stepping stones across the middles of the streets to keep out of the wet. It isn't so good to take photos in the rain, but Kate takes some anyway to see what they will turn out like. Amy has bought her a camera, the kind that when it's finished, you take the whole thing into the shop and they give you back just your photos, not the camera you took them with, because it is recyclable, that is a good thing. Kodak FUN Camera. Camera is the word the other man uses in the really dark place they go, when he opens the door on the room with the pretend other room painted on it. Camera doesn't mean camera in Italian, Amy says it means room or bedroom. There are frescoes there. Frescoes rhymes with Tescos. The House of the Mysteries is a very boring place, it is so dark you can't see anything. The plaster people there are more horrible than the other ones Kate has seen.

Amy, Kate says as they leave the House of the Mysteries in the rain. Why did God not stop the lava killing the people?

I don't know, Kate, Amy says. Anyway, she says, our God, the one you say prayers to in school, isn't the same god as most of the people here said prayers to. They had several other gods.

Yes, but those gods are just kinds of story, Kate says.

The one you're talking about is a kind of story too, Amy says.

Kate walks in the rain. She is so wet now that it doesn't matter whether she walks through the puddles or not, so she does, splashing through the pools at the side of the ashy pavement.

Besides, Amy says above her. If it hadn't happened, we wouldn't have been able to come and see it. We wouldn't be able to know what it was like to be alive then.

At the postcard place where Kate had been playing with the man's puppy, there had been a card of a dog that died, a plaster dog now, all curled up on itself as if someone was hitting it. Kate tries not to think about that picture. God is a story, God is a story, she thinks the words through her head so she won't think of anything else, the words over and over again in a kind of rhythm, kicking the water as she walks.

The next day is their second last day in Italy, and they get to go on the hydrofoil. It moves like it is bouncing on the waves. Amy says that that is exactly what it is doing. She says it makes her feel sick. They go to a place where a lot of rich people live, and they go up a special kind of train to get high up it to a house that Amy says it will be good to visit. Funicular means it can go right up the side of the rock. The man at the bottom who runs the funicular asks Kate where she comes from. He laughs. I am Otto, he says. I am Otto and you are Scotto. He lets Amy and Kate get on free. Amy makes a good joke, she says they have got on Scot-free.

They have to walk even further up a hill and wait on a wall outside the house, which is a kind of museum, because there are already people inside it visiting it and only some are allowed in at one time. In the bush next to Kate's hand as they wait, there is a funny high pitched noise. When she looks to see what it is, it stops. She can see a spider wrapping up a bee in its web, twirling it round with its feet. The bee must have been making the noise. When Kate looks again the spider has taken the bee away to eat it.

Kate wonders if this rock is alive too, like Vesuvius. She is going to ask Amy but she forgets because then they get to go inside the house. The house is full of statues and art things, and they walk right through it and outside into its garden and round the edge of the garden which is actually the edge of the rock itself, with the sea and some boats miles below it. If you fell off here you would die. Your bones would all break inside you. Amy is walking ahead and up; the path goes up and up and ends in a wooden hut with a glass roof.

You would think there would be something good in the hut, because of having to go all the way up and round to see it. But it is just a collection of dead butterflies in glass cases. It is stupid to kill butterflies when you can see them alive. If you have the light on in the summer they will spread their wings against the window, though those ones are moths really, and not the same as butterflies. Kate walks round the cases, and then goes outside and walks slowly, with small steps, round the whole garden again, and when she comes back Amy is still looking at the dead insects.

Kate reads a bit of what it says about the butterflies; there is one place where the writing is in English. *Butterflies of Cá pri Butterflies are one of the most diver se insect group s. There are more than (number) spec ies de scrib ed in the world. Of these about (number) fly dur ing the day time, the others are noc turn al. They feed them selves on nec tar and plant jui juices. The in ac ces sib il*

She stares at the nearest butterflies. One has markings like eyes on its wings, and the wings' edges are shaped as if little bites have been taken out of them. The pin is stuck right through its middle. That is the most horrible thing. You can't see its feet. That is how butterflies taste. It would be really good if people could taste with their feet. Then you would know what Italy tasted like, and if it tasted different from Scotland and England, just by walking about in it. Or if you could with your hands. You could know what everything tasted of just by touching it.

Can we go now? Kate says. Are we going in a minute? Will we go back on the funicular? Do we go on the hydrofoil again?

Amy calls her over. Look at this, she says.

I've already looked at that one, Kate says.

No, look properly, Amy says. Look really closely. If you do, you can see where the colours come from.

Kate does an impatient dance and makes a face showing her bottom teeth. Then she leans up over the glass case to look again. Amy is right. If she looks really closely and carefully, she can see that the colours on the wings of the pinned-down butterfly are made out of the thinnest strands of hair, so thin you almost can't see them, and it is like the colour is a kind of dust balanced on the hairs, coating the outsides of them.

Can you see? Amy says.

Yes I saw, Kate says. *Now* can we go?

AT midnight, at hundreds of miles an hour, at thirty-seven thousand feet up above the Alps, three hundred people are hanging in the sky, watching an advert for Schweppes. Above the newspaper she is holding Amy sees the top explode off the bottle, its insides frothing soundlessly out and over its neck and sides. She folds the newspaper. She loosens her own seatbelt then loosens Kate's for her; the turbulence has stopped. First the plane, then the morning train, and by suppertime tomorrow they will be home. The word, home. It has casually attached itself to the end of her sentence, waiting quietly there like a line of familiar horizon. For instance (as Kate would say), there is a scent in the caravan that belongs only to Kate and her, one Amy can still catch in Kate's clothes or her own; you can tell its absence or its presence alongside the more recent scents of her parents' house, of the hotel. For instance, maybe that's what home is, your own smell, as basic and uncomplicated as that; the smell you share with others close to you, or the condensation that forms from your own breath on the windows you look through every day. All of the people on this flight are going somewhere, maybe home, like they are. Each of these people will know a special smell of home.

Now there is a cartoon on all the screens, where a bull is out-witting every bullfighter in Spain except the cartoon rabbit. A hundred cartoon bulls in unison up and down the plane chalk the tips of their horns with billiard cue cubes and get ready for the charge. Kate is watching with her mouth slightly open and one of the earphones in; she is nearly asleep, determination to stay awake etched round her eyes. A thin stream of squeaks, the music of the cartoon, comes from the loose earphone at her throat. The air hostess laughed politely when Kate asked her the one about air ghostesses. What job did the ghost get on the aero-plane? That's a good one, she said charmingly, and gave Amy her free newspaper with a smile. Amy has read it from front to back, missing nothing out. There is a scandal over the govern-ment selling weapons to a country it subsequently went to war with. Princess Diana has appeared on television saying she will fight on. A jury is still out over a series of gruesome murders in a terraced house in an English town. Uneasy peace in Bosnia. Uneasy peace in Russia. Uneasy peace in Israel, uneasy peace in Northern Ireland. A panther has been sighted. Some neighbours are suing each other over the size of a hedge. Cars, shares, health care, and pension plans are for sale. Now that she has finished reading it her eyes are sore, her head hurts and she is exhausted. There, she thinks as she folds it again and puts it on her knee. I don't have to do that again for a long time.

The paper slips down between her and Kate. Amy presses the button in her seat and pushes it into recline position which isn't very different from upright position. As she leans back she can feel her keys shift in her pocket with what's left of the Italian change. Home. Safe. She could have left the caravan door open, she thinks. She could have left the door wide open, it's not as if there's anything worth stealing there. She has everything that's worth having here, with her. She looks down at the top of Kate's head, sees skin, pale through the messy parting. Her stomach contracts at the fragility of it.

Kate is still awake, holding the newspaper, following a line of newsprint with her finger. Amy leans down to be level with her, where she can't see the top of Kate's head any more.

This time tomorrow, Amy says, you'll be back home, in bed, asleep.

Kate turns in her seat. What does this word mean? she asks. She spells it out, then remembers that Amy can read now, and holds the paper up with her finger on the word.

Lift your finger. That word is desecrate, not de-secret, Amy says. Kate has been reading the article about the vandalising of Jewish cemeteries in London and the north of England. It means to do something you shouldn't, Amy says. She tries to think how else to explain it. Here, she says, it means these vandals have done something they shouldn't to a place of memory.

Like what? Kate says. Like taking things that aren't theirs from a place?

No, Amy says, it's a different kind of wrong from that, it's more abstract. It doesn't hurt so much in a physical way or a material way, it hurts most in a mental way. More like if you were to, to, I don't know. Amy racks her brain. If you were to carve your name in someone's furniture, she says. Or spit into his or her tea. Or like if you were to disturb someone's grave. That's what these people have done.

Kate looks baffled.

These people, Amy says, messed up the graves of dead people who were a different religion from them. It doesn't hurt the dead people, but it offends their memory. And it will have upset and hurt and frightened other people who are related to them, or who are the same religion.

Why, though? Kate says.

Well, because—Amy says, and stops. History looms large in her head. She has no idea how or where to start.

Look, she says instead. If you push this button your seat goes back. Push it. Now push with your feet, can you reach the ground with them?

Kate slithers down to push.

That's it, Amy says. It's more comfortable that way, isn't it?

Yes, Kate says.

Try and have a sleep, Amy says. Tomorrow by now we'll be home in the caravan, in bed. Back in Scotland. You can go back to school on Thursday, if you like.

Amy thinks the word again, Scotland, and the same strange thing happens inside her. It must be nostalgia. It must be homesickness, this must be what it feels like, she has caught it from Kate. It comes on her like a kind of relief, like giving in, like the moment you know a germ has taken hold in your body, a comfortable cold sweat, an unspecific itch inside the torso somewhere around the lungs or the digestive tract.

People all round them suddenly laugh out loud for what seems like no reason. Kate is looking up at the nearest tv screen, which is playing a funny film about a coloured bobsleigh team from Jamaica who have entered the Winter Olympics. When she turns to Amy again her face is screwed up, incredulous.

Why would anyone want to spit in anyone else's tea? she asks. Why would anyone ever want to do that?

When she goes into the site office on her first day back there are two surprises waiting for Amy. One is a substantial heap of letters and parcels addressed to her. From the writing she can see that her mother has forwarded them up the country. She must have wormed the address out of Kate. The other surprise is that Angus has decided to make her redundant, as of today.

It's not because I had some mail delivered, is it? she says, and smiles.

Angus doesn't smile. He pulls on his coat and pretends he is on his way out. He won't look at her. He looks instead at the desk and at the floor and then out of the window as he shoves his arms into his coat sleeves. One of the sleeves is caught up in itself, half inside out, and he has to struggle to push his arm through. She can feel his embarrassment rising in the room like heat.

It's just that we don't need anyone extra any more at this moment in time, that's all, he says. He thrusts his arm hard into the sleeve and jerks the coat on to his shoulders.

But we were really busy this year, Amy says. Busier than last. And another thing. I have no problem with reading any more. I can read again now, I used to be able to, and it's come back. Next spring I could easily take on all the things you had to do.

Angus puts his hand on the door handle. There'll be no next spring, he says. There's no job here any more, there'll not be one for you here in the spring neither. Nothing in the foreseeable future. That's it finished, it's finished, when I say finished I mean finished. And if you could find somewhere else to live as soon as you can. I've got, there's this, someone else for that particular van. They'd like to move in within the week. A fortnight at the most is what I told them.

Oh, Amy says. I see.

Angus is about to leave. What about the money I owe you? she says.

We'll keep that between just you and me, he says. We'll call it our arrangement. To help you with your moving on from here.

He stops and turns, still not looking at her. But don't be telling anyone I did that now. Do you hear? he says.

He closes the door after him.

Amy sighs. She shuts her eyes and opens them, shakes her head. She sits down, leafs through the meaningless letters and packets. She rests her foot on the box, on the floor under the table. It is just the right height.

There is a letter for Amy from her mother. There is a separate parcel for Kate in Amy's mother's handwriting too; she weighs its lightness in her hand, wonders what it is her mother wants Kate to have. There is a postcard for Kate, in her father's scrawl. *Kate—you reprobate—how about this one? Q: Why did the Cyclops give up teaching? A: Because he only had one pupil. (Look up the word Cyclops.) Come and stay again soon. With lots of love from your (new) old Gfthr.* She turns the postcard over. It is a picture of where her father works; ivy eating away at the front of the old building. Outside it has hardly lightened today, and in a couple of hours it will be dark again. Bleak November, bleak Scottish winter has set in. Out of the windows on the train yesterday there had been the interplay of the frost and the black winter-burnt land, grey frost dusting the landscape, leaving the trees beautiful, bare. Amy thinks about the winter trees. She opens each letter, scans it briefly, drops it in the wastepaper basket. She folds the cheque her mother has sent to her, puts it back inside the envelope it came in, crosses out her own address and circles the sender's address on the back. She sticks one of Angus's stamps from the drawer on to it and reseals it. She gets 25 pence out of her pocket and puts it in the tin Angus keeps in the drawer.

When all the letters are dealt with she switches off the wall heater. She buttons her cardigan and pulls the heavy box out from under the table, balances the things addressed to Kate on the top of it, opens the office door, locks it behind her and posts the key through. It falls with a dainty thud on to the linoleum.

Outside the caravan she drops the box where the grass has been worn away by Kate's and her own feet. She puts her hand up to open the door; already the door looks different, shabby like the grass, irrelevant. She sits down on the box, outside in the cold. The side of the box has been strengthened with sellotape. She imagines her mother stretching and ripping and stretching and ripping tape off a roll and lining it precisely along the weak spots of the box. She picks at the tape with her nail. Kate will be home any minute. There is no food in.

At the Spar Amy buys things for supper. She has about half an hour before Kate gets home from school. When Kate gets home they will go for a walk along the beach and decide what to do. At the cash desk Amy has no small change, only a twenty pound note, one of the few left on the roll in her pocket. The girl behind the counter looks bored, unsmiling as usual; she holds the note perfunctorily up to the light, then she scribbles over it with a pen to check it isn't fake. But when she gives Amy her change she reaches across the counter and takes Amy's hand, and cups it in her own so that none of the change will fall.

Angus says there's a call for you! Angus says there's a call for you!

Kate comes swooping across the grass and shouts up through the window to Amy, who is trying to open a can of sweetcorn with the blunt tin opener.

It's on the phone, she says. It's someone on the phone for you. Right now. He says could you hurry, and he doesn't know who it is.

There's a call for you, Angus says, still not looking at her, nodding at the receiver on its side on the table. He gets up. I hope you'll not be long, he says on his way out. I'm expecting some calls myself.

Amy puts the phone to her ear.

Is that Dr. Amy Shone? The voice is high, an English voice, a woman. She tells Amy her name, which Amy immediately forgets. She tells her the name of the Sunday newspaper she works for. I found you via your famous mother, she says. I swear by her books, honestly I do, I must tell you, they're terrific. You always know, don't you, that what you make will be suitable, and light, and that it will taste all right too, do you know what I mean? Of course you do, you'll have grown up on Shone recipes.

Oh, right, Amy says. If this is about my mother—

No, it's Tamsin, my researcher, the journalist says.

She says Tamsin's second name, it sounds like Bleagh.

No, I don't think I know anyone of that, I don't think I know—Amy says.

No, you see, Tamsin was at college at the same time as you, the journalist says, she remembers you well, you've such a reputation.

Amy holds the receiver away from herself, lets it hover above the rest of the phone, about to hang up. The woman is still speaking. A piece of luck, she bleats into Amy's hand. Coincidence. Amy puts the receiver back against her head, takes a deep breath.

—when you consider it, pretty amazing, I'm thinking we should do a full feature on the brilliant shining Shones some time soon, now that we've tracked you down, the woman is saying.

Can I ask you what it is that you actually want? Amy says.

And it was Tamsin who gave me the lead for this one as I say quite by chance, she's a clever little thing, she says she remembers you were friends, the woman continues almost as if Amy isn't there.

I'm terribly sorry, but I really honestly and truly haven't a clue who Tamsin is, Amy says.

No, not friends with *her*, I mean friends with Aisling McCarthy, the woman's insubstantial voice says, miles away, thin and sharp and distorted by lines of electricity, lines of a power which suddenly pierces Amy so that it is as if her whole body jolts. She stands, and breathes. She says something, but no sound comes out of her mouth.

You know? the woman is saying. Aisling McCarthy? I'm doing our weekly series on What Happened To, it's a weekly colour spread, if you haven't seen it, so far we've done oh loads of people, we've done Lynn Paul from The New Seekers, the blonde one, and Kenneth Kendall, and—the idea is to pick someone who's fallen out of the public eye and follow them up and see What Happened To them, you know, find out where they are now, tell their story, and we hadn't done anyone Scottish yet so we thought either Clare Grogan or Aisling McCarthy, but Clare Grogan's still on tv quite a lot, so we thought Aisling McCarthy'd be perfect. Not mind you that I had actually heard of either of them until Tamsin put me right.

You know where she is? Amy hears herself say.

Well no, I was hoping *you* would, the woman says, and laughs a peal of social laughter. I tell you, this column can be a perfect nightmare. Last week, we had Mike Holoway from Flintlock, do you remember him? We had the most horrendous time tracking down What Happened To him. He was in *The Tomorrow People*, remember?

You don't know where she is, Amy says. She sits down.

—how they all used to touch their belts, the woman is saying, and beam themselves into new places, and they all used to sit round in their spaceship and ask that computer thing in the ceiling questions, and it would tell them anything they needed to know, we could have done with that computer here in the office to tell us where he'd beamed himself off to, jaunted, they called it—

I really must go, I'm afraid, Amy says.

The woman slips straight into her serious work voice.

Well I do need to check some things with you Dr. Shone, if you'd be so patient. Now, we've already spoken to Simone Weaver at the Royal Court, she doesn't know where she is either needless to say, and I spoke to some school friends of hers, an American who's in charge of replanting areas of forestry in the north of

Scotland, quite near you, and a woman who wrote a piece for the *Guardian* women's page a couple of years ago when the film had its network premiere, an extraordinary piece, actually, about before Aisling McCarthy was anybody—

Before she was anybody, yes, I see, Amy says.

—yes, when she apparently fainted outside this woman's house and she brought her in and fed her biscuits to revive her.

That's made up, Amy says. She'd never have done that. She never fainted in her life.

And we've spoken to others who knew her when you were both students, the woman says, we've got all the stuff about her starred first and her many roles at the Arts Theatre.

That's made up too. She didn't get a starred first. She wasn't even a student, Amy says.

I think you'll find you're wrong there, Dr. Shone, the journalist says, since there's a college photograph of her with the rest of her year, in fact we're using it in our feature. We've got some great pictures, we've just this minute, literally half an hour ago, I'm very pleased with myself, sorted the rights to those culty ones she did naked and pregnant and all long before the fuss about Demi Moore doing it which suits the piece we're doing just fine as we're concentrating on the originality of coming from the north. Her own brother doesn't even know where she is, you know. You live quite near him too, do you know him? Plenty of colourful rumours as to where she is, actually it's almost better if we don't know What Happened To her, really, we can run it as mystery. I heard somewhere in California with her child and its father, and Tamsin dug up someone who says she was living at this spiritual centre in the American south with the Ku Klux Klan threatening to burn them out, I've been phoning a number in Hartsville South Carolina but they say there's nobody like her there, and last time Tamsin called they hung up on her, which I personally thought wasn't at all a spiritual way to treat one.

I see, Amy says. How interesting. It should make a very readable piece for you. Is that—are those all the stories there are about where she might be?

Oh she could be anywhere, the woman says, anywhere in the world. But what I especially wanted to ask you, Dr. Shone, is about the time you were arrested with Aisling McCarthy.

The time I was what? Amy says.

My researcher Tamsin remembers a scurrilous little tale going round, the woman says, about you and Aisling McCarthy being held in the cells overnight for some interesting misdemeanour or other?

In the cells? Amy says. I was never in a cell, or arrested, in my—

Then she stops mid-sentence as the memory unearths itself, and she laughs. No, no, we weren't arrested. Not arrested exactly. She wanted to take me to visit a place, the place in a T S Eliot poem if I remember rightly, she must have been humouring me for some reason, so we got on a train and then we walked for miles along roads that seemed to be going nowhere at all, and when we got to the place we were trying to find it wasn't a beauty spot at all, it was an army or navy base, it was all chain link fences and barbed wire, and we were thinking about turning round and going home again when all of a sudden out of nowhere these landrovers came speeding towards us from different directions, men in sunglasses, and an American man in a steel helmet pushed us into the back of the car and they drove us inside the base and threw us into a room with no furniture in it, nothing at all, they locked the door. Then late, when it was dark, they put us in another car and drove us to somewhere in the middle of the fens, dumped us in the middle of nowhere. We hadn't a clue where we were. I remember I was terrified, I was terrified because they'd taken our names, and I was terribly afraid someone at the college I was a member of would find out and think me irresponsible, or worse, left-wing, and I wouldn't get the fellowship I'd been promised. But it was warm, it was midsummer, I slept in a ditch that night, it was very exciting, I'd never done anything like it in my life before, I say night, but it was only dark for a couple of hours—

Hello? Dr. Shone? the woman interrupts. Hello? Hello, Dr. Shone, are you still there? the woman says.

Amy is relieved. She hasn't said any of it, not a word. Yes, hello, she says out loud.

The journalist has stopped tapping at her keys some minutes ago. Thank you very much for your help, Dr. Shone, she says. I think that's everything we need. Now. You work up there now, yes? Can I ask what you're working on? And do you live alone?

I'm working on what to have for tonight's supper. And I live here with Kathleen, who is now nearly eight. Did you get that? Amy says.

. . . Ha ha . . . eight. And one more thing, if I may, just a small thing. Of course you'll understand we'd like to concentrate just a touch on Aisling McCarthy as a symbol, so we'd like to look briefly at her sexual preferences, in good taste I assure you but I'm sure you'll agree it is important to clarify these things, so do you mind if I just ask you? Because you were close, weren't you?

She was my friend, Amy says. We were friends. And we weren't arrested, or anything like that. That's not what happened.

Tap tap tap. Amy puts the phone down. Her head is full of the smell of sun-warm skin. Out by the door Angus is standing glaring at his watch. Finished with the phone now, *Doctor* Shone? he says quietly, his face all annoyed and ashamed. Amy ignores him, crosses the grass. She thinks about how newspapers get read all over the world, and of how, when she and Kate walked down the middle aisle to leave the plane in the early hours of the morning at Gatwick, pages of newspapers were strewn all over the seats and floor. She thinks of how newspapers get thrown away, in fact how the whole point of them is that they don't last, they get thrown away, get used to wrap fish in at the fish shop, or chips, or how pages of old news, whatever happens to be printed on them, will end up round old oily tools in someone's shed or garage or rolled into spills for lighting the fire. Chips, they could have chips for supper, eat them out of the newspaper, Kate would like that. She feels decidedly light. She could be walking on air, not grass, or ground, or earth at all.

Who was it? Kate says, bounding up to her. Was it my grandmother? Was it my grandfather? Was it the school? Who was it?

It wasn't anybody we know, Amy says.

As they cross the road to the chip shop a car passes behind them with music pulsing so loud that it is as if it is beating against the car's insides.

The story has taken a new twist. She could be anywhere, Amy thinks. Anywhere in the world. Any minute now.

It is very cold tonight; the sea is howling and crashing up at the edge of the rocks, right up, it seems, against the side of the caravan. Amy has wheeled the calor gas heater into the bedroom and left all three of its meshes lit even though they are both in bed. She is taking care not to fall asleep with it still turned on. She will turn it off in a moment, but not yet. It throws an orange glow all up one side of the room.

Amy has the pillow between herself and the thin wall, and her coat over her shoulders. Kate is asleep. One arm is flung across her head, the other is caught by the fingers in the crocheted wool holes of the underblanket. The caravan still smells of chips. Kate ate hers without her hands to see if she could. She ate them by picking them up out of the paper with her mouth and tongue. It is late; she is completely asleep. The way the blankets fall about her shoulders in this light makes them look like marble, carved art.

Kate, Amy says quietly.

Kate doesn't move.

Whose child are you? mm? Kate? Whose girl are you?

Amy leans over Kate, pushes gently alongside her, close to her, breathes into her ear. Kate stirs.

Did you hear me? Whose girl are you, Kate? Whose are you?

The sea and sky roar and fall outside the room. Amy waits to hear the word, waits for Kate to move and turn towards her, to give the answer across the murky slurred distance of sleep.

Yours, she says, like she always does, and sighs, swallows in her sleep, curls in on herself like a shell, an unborn child.

Kate is by herself, playing by the side of the road. The road is not too busy because it's Saturday but when cars do go past they go past quite fast. She is playing by the drain. She has taken the plastic kangaroo out with her. It is the only one left of the animals now. She has put the others in the wheelie bins outside the fronts of the houses on her way to school. She has put them all in different wheelie bins, including the horse and its separate cart. She made sure that the animals fell down the sides of the rubbish bags inside the bins, or people might have found them if they looked in. Even if someone did find one, they probably won't have found the others. The bin men come on Fridays and that was yesterday so now the animals will be at the dump and will probably be being buried or burned. But she kept the kangaroo. It is the one she likes the best.

She jumps the kangaroo along the spars of the drain cover, and up on to the kerb, and down on to the drain cover again. There is a crack in the side of the kerb by her leg; she pokes into it with the kangaroo's long tail and scrapes out some brown stuff and grit. She wipes it off the tail on to the side of the kerb further along, far enough along so that she won't sit on it by mistake.

Usually on Saturday mornings and sometimes on Saturday afternoons too she goes to Angela's and watches children's tv or a film, but today Angela has been taken to visit her auntie and uncle in Dundee and to go Christmas shopping although it isn't Christmas for a month yet. One week when she was at Angela's there was a film on in the afternoon where these two ladies were twins, and a man with a moustache kissed one of them and the other one could feel it. Even though she was in another room and nowhere near them the lady closed her eyes and was smiling like she could feel it too. Then they did this dance and song with their arms and legs all tangled, one was the right way up and the other was upside down and they made a kind of somersault together all round the barn. It was in black and white. Angela's father doesn't like the black and white ones, he always flicks them off, but he wasn't there the time this film was on. Angela says she doesn't like black and white either because it's boring. She didn't see the film because she was in the kitchen helping her mother put buttons on her father's shirt. But soon Kate will be moving away again, so she won't be doing that on Saturdays any more. She can't really think what she will be doing on Saturdays, or where she will be doing it.

There are all old sweet papers caught down the drain, and a crushed cigarette packet and a bleached-looking bit of a packet of Ringos. The water in there is black and has gritty stuff floating on the top of it, like oil or spit, and black muddy thick stuff covering other things that might be sweet papers, and some lumpy things that might be anything, dead things, could be anything. You can never know what is under the ground. You can't tell how deep the drain water here might be, it might be really deep. A dead person couldn't get down the drain, not really. Not even if the person was quite small. A dead bird maybe. A dead bird couldn't get through the gaps in the metal of the cover, though, the gaps are too small. Kate can only just get half of her hand through one without touching the sides if she keeps it flat.

Her grandmother sent her a really good thing. She sent a big envelope with a Native American head-dress in it, not a bought one, but one she had made herself by sewing the feathers off real birds on to a bit of material. She wrote in her letter to Kate that she found all the feathers in her garden and in the wood near their house. Amy says she can write back and say thank you. Amy says it's Native American that you say, not Indian. She says the birds almost definitely weren't dead that the feathers came off, that birds that are alive lose their feathers when they drop out just from flapping their wings and it doesn't hurt. Birds would have really small narrow bones. The stiff bit up the middle of the feathers isn't actually bone. Her grandfather sent her a postcard. Reprobate means bad person, but Amy says her grandfather is making a kind of joke calling her it, like he is fond of her. He sent a joke about the Cyclops on it. That is the monster that only has one eye and gets killed when the man escapes from his cave. It is a good story, about the man tricking the Cyclops by not telling him who he is. Kate found the book about it at school and Amy read it out to her. It is good now that Amy can read. But it is not as good as before, when Amy couldn't read but Kate could. Now they get letters and everything, and even people they don't know on the phone, which is maybe why they are moving again. And as well, Angus doesn't need them to live at the site any more. Amy says that it is good that she can read again but that she doesn't know what to read. There are a lot of books that came in a box, the big box that was in England that they've got at the caravan. They are Amy's diaries from a long time ago. Amy says they aren't worth reading. Kate has opened the box and looked at them again. They are pretty, but they are a bit boring and it is hard to read the writing.

Kate balances the kangaroo on the edge of the kerb and watches it stand there. She pushes it forward on its long hind legs. She pushes it a little further, and a little more, until it tips and falls over the edge and she has to catch it. She thinks about how there is a book in that box that isn't like all the other books. The writing inside it is different, it is a bit more difficult to read. The cover isn't hard or coloured like the others. It isn't beautiful on the outside like they are. She found the book when Amy was out and looked in it and read a good thing about some friends who go camping in the countryside in a tent, and they woke up one night and looked out of the door of the tent and saw all these deer eating grass outside right up near their tent. But then one girl sneezed and all the deer were scared and ran away, the writing said the deer were like birds when they ran away like that, that is a funny thing to say, like in a poem, like the deer changed into birds and could fly away when something scared them, that is a good idea, that is what birds can do.

The kangaroo has a smile by mistake, where the dot of black paint that is supposed to be its nose has smudged into the groove in the plastic that is its mouth. She stands it on one of the bits of metal on the cover over the drain. It could easily fall, almost by itself, through the gap into the black mud. If you poked at the sides of the drain cover with its tail the black horrible stuff you could scrape out has probably been in there for ages, maybe years, all caked together. You could never know, you could never find out, where all the dirt and grime and grit and germs and things that have got stuck in there had come from in the first place.

Kate looks at the pavement, at how the small bits of stone have been melted and cemented into it, probably by a huge machine like a steamroller. The kangaroo waits on the drain, ready to jump. She gently inches it over with her finger until it is right on the edge, until it falls. It falls through the drain cover and down into the black water with a dull noise. When she looks down inside, the kangaroo is gone. It has been completely swallowed up inside the drain.

There is no one at the bus shelter. There is no one in the street. In the distance she can hear a dog barking, but there is no one watching, nobody to hear. She leans over the top of the drain until her mouth is quite close to the metal grate.

That's for you, she tells the dead girl who lives in the drain. That kangaroo's for you to have. You can have it.

AMY strikes the match away from herself. She crouches down in the snow and sand and shelters its bead of flame in her hands, angles it so that the flame will stay lit but won't grow too fast, won't come too close to her fingers. She lights the newspaper on both sides of the woodpile and drops the burnt match in. The colour of flame catches and spreads and the wetter wood begins to hiss. Already the fire, small as it is, is sending out visible waves of heat. Already it has eaten a hole of light in the dusk.

Kate looks disgruntled. I wanted to light it, she says.

You can do things like that when you're big, Amy says.

It's freezing, Kate says, it's really really freezing. She slaps her sides and front with her arms like she has seen people do on television. She spins with her arms out and her head back. She goes round and round till she falls over in the snow and lies there on her back, out of breath.

Amy imagines the grey sky and the fire wheeling inside Kate's head, churning on the surfaces of her eyes.

Once, Amy said, *there were four brothers and a sister who lived in the Peruvian mountains.*

Amy had her new glasses on. They made her look different. Kate was lying across Amy's knees, stretched over the armchair with *The Big Book Of Myths And Legends II,* holding the book open so that Amy could read it out loud over her shoulder.

The eldest of the brothers decided it was time he showed his family he was also the strongest, Amy read. *So he climbed to the top of the highest of the mountains and he threw four stones, as far as he could. They flew through the air for miles before they landed, one to the north, one to the south, one to the east and one to the west. "I own all this land that I have marked with these boulders," he said.*

What about the north east and the north west and the south west and the south east? Kate said.

Quiet, Amy said. You're the one who wanted this story. *"I own all this land that I have marked with these boulders," he said.*

Boulders or borders? Kate said. She shifted and fidgeted on Amy's knees. Amy shut the book. Kate stopped fidgeting. Amy opened the book again.

His other three brothers were jealous. They wanted the land for themselves. The youngest of the four brothers was by far the cleverest, and he hatched a cunning plan. "Come into this cave," he said to the eldest, "and see what I have made for you. As a special gift, and to honour my brotherly love for you, I have worked hard on many beautiful, detailed maps of the lands you now own," he said.

It's a trap, Kate said.

I think you're right, Amy said. Yes, you are. *When his brother went inside the cave, the youngest, with all his might, rolled a huge stone in front of the opening and left his brother to perish there.*

Well, couldn't he just push the stone away and get out? Kate said.

That's not what it says here, Amy said.

When does the sister come into it? Kate asked.

I don't know, Amy said. *This act of imprisoning his brother gave the youngest of the brothers magical powers. He went straight up to the second oldest brother and changed him into a rock, which he picked up and tossed off the side of a cliff. When the last remaining brother saw this, he fled.*

I thought it said they had a sister too, Kate said.

It did, Amy said.

She flicked the pages over. No, she said. I can't find her, she isn't mentioned again. But—and Amy shut the book and put it down the side of the chair—but what the sister did was this. Are you listening?

Yes, Kate said.

After she had sat there for a while, watching all the squabbling about who owned what and who was stronger or better than whom, she stood up, stretched, packed a bag and left them fighting. She set out walking. She walked all the way to the other end of the country, where there was nobody who knew her. She threw a rope up into the branches of two trees that stood near each other at the foot of a very picturesque mountain, and she made a roof of their leaves and she sheltered there for the night, and the next morning she decided she liked it so much that she would settle down and live there. And there she lived, under the two trees, quietly watching the sun go down every night. Quite soon after, she realised that she could hear something or someone moving around on the other side of the mountain.

How could she hear something that was that far away? Kate said.

Be quiet. She just could, Amy said. She called out. Hello? Is anyone there? Hello! a voice called back, far away. Soon they were both calling out good night to each other before they went to sleep and good morning to each other when they woke up again. One evening, as she called out her usual good night, the girl under the two trees added something extra. Isn't the sun beautiful going down tonight? she called. The voice from the other side of the mountain called back. Sun going down? Don't you mean the moon coming up?

No, the girl called, indignant. It's the sun that's setting. Maybe it looks like the moon from the *back* end of the mountain, but from the front it's definitely the sun setting.

But *I* live at the front, the voice called back, annoyed. It's *you* that live at the back. And from here, at the front, it's absolutely definitely without a doubt the moon rising.

All that night the girl couldn't sleep. She woke, she tossed and turned, she woke again. All that week she couldn't sleep, because all that week, as the sun went down, she would have the same argument with the voice, and she would go to bed with it still ringing in her head. At the end of a week without any sleep she was so tired and angry that, as she shouted hoarsely one more time, it's the SUN, I tell you, the SUN, without really thinking what she was doing she picked up a rock off the side of the mountain and flung it angrily over the top.

Silence. Nothing. Then, through the half light of the sunset, something whistled through the air, flew down and bounced hard and sore on her head. She picked it up. It was a big rough stone. She turned it over and over in her hands. I don't believe it, she said to herself. Look what she just threw at me. Look what she dared to throw at me. This stone could have left me seriously injured.

And she bent down and picked up another larger sharp-edged rock and hurled it back over the summit of the mountain.

Ouch! the voice said on the other side.

A huge lump of boulder, about the size of a small house, soared back at her through the air, landing dangerously close to her feet. It made a great hole in the ground and sent rabbits scuttling and night birds shrieking away.

The girl waited until the dust settled. Then she shouted: Missed! Ha ha!

Kate laughed. She turned with her feet over the arm of the chair, her head on Amy's shoulder.

So all night, believe it or not, Amy said, they threw rocks and pebbles and stones and great big boulders and branches and lumps of tree trunk and turf and moss at each other in the dark, hurting each other and missing each other. At last, the morning came. The girl, exhausted, with her hands all cuts and gashes from ripping things out of the ground to throw and from protecting herself from flying rocks, with blood running like sweat down her neck and forehead and bruises changing their colours all over her body, looked up from the ground, where she had been trying to find something else to throw. This is what she saw. The whole mountain was gone. There wasn't any more mountain left to throw. In front of her now, instead of a mountain, was someone she'd never seen before, someone scanning the ground, weighing stones in her hands, dropping the ones that were too small. She looked behind her. Behind her was a tall messy heap of thrown stones and rocks. Ahead of her, behind the other, was another hill of stones. Behind her, the moon was going down. Ahead, the sun was coming up. They stood facing each other, eyeing each other in the morning light with the rubble of the night all round them, still with stones held in their hands just in case.

Amy stopped. Kate opened her eyes.

The end, Amy said.

They all lived happily ever after, Kate said.

Maybe, Amy said nodding, who knows? Anyway, she said, sliding Kate off as she stood up, stretched her shoulders and back and arms, straightened the cushions in this new place. All the best stories end like that.

Like what? Kate said. She lifted her feet carefully off the cloth thing pinned to the arm of the chair. The story had made her forget she didn't like the feel of the chair. Yawning, tired suddenly, she set off towards the bathroom, going the wrong way at first until she remembered where the door was.

In the middle like that, like all true stories, Amy said. Your pyjamas are in the House of Fraser carrier bag. Brush your teeth, remember, they'll fall out if you don't. Wipe round the sink when you've finished.

Kate shut the door behind her. Outside the door, in the ticking, strange-smelling quiet of the hall, she put her fingers in her mouth and pulled hard at her top teeth, then her bottom ones, and the ones at the back. None of them was loose. There was no way they could fall out, not tonight anyway. Amy was lying.

She went up the stairs on the wooden bits at the edge of the carpet. She got all the way to the top without touching the carpet, and she stood at the top of the stairs trying to think which door was the bathroom one. Q: What happened to the girl who slept with a fifty pound note under her pillow? A: The fairies took away all her teeth. Kate laughed. But imagine if you really woke up and found you had no teeth left. Kate stopped laughing. Imagine if there was nothing in your mouth but holes and blood.

Downstairs in the unfamiliar house, hearing Kate's laugh come from somewhere above her, Amy stood in the musty room and looked at the ceiling, wondered what the joke was.

The books have caught fire. You can see them, falling into each other now that the side of the box has burned away.

Amy and Kate are burning the things they don't need to keep any more. Amy says it is as good a way to celebrate Christmas as any. Because it is Christmas there is nobody on the beach but them. The beach looks different; there is snow everywhere. This year has been one of the sunniest ever on record, Kate says, and, when it isn't the school holidays, Miss Rose is keeping a record of daily temperatures to see if the winter will be one of the coldest. There is so much snow you can't see where the beach ends and the rocks begin, though you can guess from where the sea curves in. They have had to clear a patch in the sand to build their fire.

The wind whips the fire through the wood. They have been drying out driftwood for weeks especially for this fire, in the tiled fireplace of the front room next to the electric bar heater. Kate likes living in a house. At first she didn't like the smell of it, but now she seems to have forgotten about it. She is delighted to have her own room, even though it is small. I think we'll stay, Amy has told her. I think we'll live here for a while, see what happens.

Does that mean we can get a cat? Kate wanted to know.

Not yet, Amy said.

Angus has been round to the house several times, ringing the doorbell, tapping at the window if nobody answers the door. When Amy opens the door he stands on the mat, shifting his feet and picking at his fingernails. I want to apologise, he says. I want to make amends. He has found out where Amy works now and has come in to try to talk to her over the counter while she puts cups on saucers, runs her fingers over the buttons on the till with her eye on the door whenever someone comes in.

I can't talk now, Angus, she says, I'm busy.

The last time he came he looked panicked, forlorn. He leaned across the top of the coffee machine and told her through the columns of crockery that he had seen *Brief Encounter* on the tv, that it had made him cry. Amy burst out laughing, almost dropped the pot she was filling with boiling water all over her own feet. She put the pot carefully down and leaned forward as if to tell him a secret. He strained his head towards her to hear what she'd say.

Listen Angus, Amy said gently, you've got it all wrong. I was never going to seduce you, or fuck you, or even touch you. I'm just not like that.

Angus stepped back, looked at her with eyes that were shocked and hurt; Amy couldn't decide whether it was because she'd told him the truth, or because in her best *Brief Encounter* accent she'd said a swear word. Either way it was successful, Angus hasn't been back yet, to her work or to the house. When he does come padding round again Amy will try once more to give him back the money she owes him. She has opened a bank account and taken out an overdraft so that she can do this. So far, Angus has refused to take a cheque from her at the front door, and he hasn't cashed the one she sent to the caravan site. When the one she sent expires, she has decided, she will go round and push the money, in cash, through the office letterbox. Debts can take over a life.

Kate is skipping round the fire singing a made-up song. Freezing cold, very cold, very cold indeed; cold warm very warm, hot hot boiling, she sings. She stops and holds her hands over her eyes after the wind sends the smoke at her. Last week they finally took her holiday camera to the chemist's, and when the photographs came back they were almost all of dogs. A dog by the sea. A dog standing outside a shop. A dog's back legs. Two dogs lying down. A dog in a garden. A dog in the rain. Kate hasn't seen the photos yet; as an extra Christmas present Amy has had the best ones fixed inside a big frame and has had the words *Kate's Italy* screwed on to the frame on a plaque. The picture is wrapped up at the house. Kate's other present is a camera, a real one this time. Amy also owes this to her overdraft. She has calculated that she will have to work reasonably steadily for three years and seven months to pay this plus the rent deposit off. Kate doesn't know about the camera yet.

She shoves her head under Amy's arm. Amy looks down at her. Ash all over her. Her face, her hair, her mouth, her eyes.

Did you take that other book out of the box? Kate asks, pulling away.

What other book? Amy says.

The other, different book, Kate says.

What different book? Amy says. She watches waves of light move and change through the paper as it burns. Light wavers as if breathing through the layers of pages. Points of light rise in the air above the fire, there, gone.

Of course, it is perversely exciting, to burn books. Not with quite the force of perversity, though, as using books as a kind of power tool was, eating and sleeping with them, living by the book, you might say; still, this burning brings its own particular frisson of foulness, and Amy is not surprised at how much she enjoys the idea of what she's doing. Kate was stubborn about it. You shouldn't burn diaries in case they were important for history, she said. Amy explained; they're like when you draw something or write it for the first time and it's not what you wanted, so you throw it away and start all over again.

But we could recycle them, Kate said. They're paper.

We could, Amy said. But they're very private. And this way we can light up the whole coast with them.

Even Kate had been persuaded, when it was put like that. As they stand by the fire, the pure and burning space of it in the snow, Amy gets her attention, keeps her far enough away from the edge of the flames by telling her a story about the Greek man who wrote books about tragedy, comedy, ethics—

Like an ethic minority? Kate says.

Eth*ics*, Amy corrects.

What's an ethic when it's at home? Kate wants to know.

Like a study of rules or a set of rules for how people behave, Amy says. But listen. He believed that the only real colours in the world were the colours white and gold, gold for the earth and the sun, white for the air and the water and everything else.

White isn't a colour, Kate says.

He thought, Amy says, that all the other colours there are were nothing but a kind of dye, and that you could remove this by burning things.

How? Kate says.

Well, Amy says, what he said was that everything goes back to its original colour when you burn it, it goes back to being white.

That's stupid. Burning makes things go black, Kate says.

Amy laughs. That's right, she says. She catches Kate under the arms and pushes her over backwards in the snow, tells her that if she flaps her arms up and down then stands up carefully she can see what shape she has made.

While Kate makes the shapes of birds or angels in the light of the fire, Amy waits with what's left of her burning words. The fire is collapsing in on itself now. Soon, Amy thinks, there will be nothing left of it. Ash, that's all. Nothing else.

Ash

SO I'm home, and I haven't a clue where I am.

Well, that's not totally true. The town's the same, a little big-ger, a little uglier. Spread out like it always has been below the bens, lying in wait for the nothing that's happening round the Firth. The air's still clear, smells of firs and pines from the bed-and-breakfast house gardens. Seagulls with their hooky beaks still squealing on the roofs. Nothing's changed, and everything has. Home, this old house, my father's house, new to me. It smells different in this house, like someone old lived here and died and the smell hasn't gone away yet. This is it, you're home, I keep telling myself, opening the doors into strange rooms.

He's boxed up all my books and things and put them in the garage. No room for all that, he said. But he's gone and filled the house with the most amazing stuff, all the junk he must have found in the loft when he moved. All over the place, and all out of place, the things I remember, the bits and pieces. From as far back as when my mother was still alive and I was too small to see much over the window-sill, standing at eye level to the ornaments on the sill and gingerly fingering what I knew I wasn't to touch. The china jug that says Boston USA and the glass duck we got in Scarborough covered in grainy chemical stuff to make it change colour, pink for bad weather, blue for good. Grey-orange now, I wonder what that means. Don't touch it too much, the lady in the Lucky Duck shop said, you'll make it lose its magic if you do.

The two pottery rabbits tucked into their pottery bed. Shabby, stupid, cheap-looking, lost. All this stuff, as strange and familiar as it would be if I were walking around on the moon and were suddenly to see it there. The paintings. They're terrible. Loch Ness and the castle, the little cottages in the snow, the road that goes nowhere, the wildcat, the stoat. Even the things you'd think would fit in anywhere, the chairs, the sideboard, the video machine. It's all just so much nameless junk when you see it like this, adrift.

Look at the photos on the mantelpiece. The people who grew up with these things, all moved on now to collecting their own. My father out just now collecting widows and women neighbours up and down his new street, who think he's just charming and let him put his hand on their thigh, not too high of course, a friendly touch, while he sits in their kitchens with a bowl of their soup or a cup of their tea and tells them the story of his life, and watches out of the corner of his eye their daughter out in the back garden stretching up to hang out the washing. Some things don't change. The old rogue. He's been chasing pretty young women all his life. It's about the only thing we have in common.

Yesterday at the station I bought this notebook, this morning I dragged the folding table up the stepladder, no mean feat. But here. This place was a good find. Cool and unpapered, I'm pretty sure nobody's ever lived up here. Storage space with nothing in it, rough roof walls, the wood still bare. Dust particles turning suspended in the light, and the sound of my arm moving across the table, the sound of my own breath. Still and quiet, though I can hear the birds, and the ambulances grinding in and out of the hospital over the way with its smoking tower of a chimney. The same hills in the background, covered with houses that weren't there the last time I was home. If I lean out of the skylight and look directly down I can see the sun on the sheds, the back gardens of other people's homes, the pale square of lawn that belongs to here, small, like it's been washed and shrunk, its old rose bushes with their root-hearts showing above the soil. No trees in the garden of this new home.

Monday the 6th April 1987. Dear Diary. Actually this is not going to be a diary, diary is the wrong word for it. I have been suspicious of diaries anyway, since I stole Amy's and read them on the roof. Amy, mon âme, my aim, my friend Amy. It was very shocking to read her version of things. No, diaries are stupid. Diaries are all lies. Diaries, they're so self-indulgent.

But we live in self-indulgent times, after all, and for once I want my own twist of it. And if you write something down, it goes away. I've been carrying it around with me now for so long it's taken on a kind of life of its own, I can feel it breathing against me inside my rib-cage, feeding off me, taking all the goodness out of what I eat, all the calcium out of my teeth. I want rid of it.

And what a story it could be. What a beautiful, what a romantic, what a passionate story. Not a story for here, not for small town Scotland, not then, not ever, never here in the decent, upright, capital of the Highlands, where when I was still at school there was an unholy row in the newspapers and in the council chambers because someone thought that something like the teaching of drama on the school syllabus would be nothing less than the work of the devil. Land of my soul and my formation, the Highlands. Where the Brahan Seer, ancient highland magician of the greatest of powers, once foretold that if there were too many bridges over the River Ness, or if there were too many women in power in the nation, then terrible dire chaos would follow. I read in a book once that they halted work on the fifth bridge when word came that Hitler had invaded Poland. The Second World War, all because some people in the north of Scotland started putting together that one-too-many bridge.

Pity nobody thought about the warnings before they voted Thatcher back in again. Poor old Seer, foreseeing the black rain, the sheep, the bloodshed at Culloden, think of him, before he had time to announce the demolition in just two terms of government of a welfare state it took two world wars to make, he was rolled to his death down a hill nailed in a blazing barrel of tar, set alight and set rolling by the wife of his patron. It was his own fault, he'd been stupid enough to tell her out loud what he'd seen through the hole in his magic little stone, that her husband was having an affair. He got his own back, of course, cursed her noble family before he died, and they all grew up idiotic or died in carriage crashes and falls from horses.

But the truth brings terrible things to bear, I suppose that's the good Presbyterian lesson to learn there. Imagine the scandal, imagine the curse, there's no guessing the chaos we'd have brought upon the world, two girls falling together in the streets of the beautiful decent Highlands of Scotland where a whistling woman was still as unnatural as a crowing hen. Though very few people kept hens by then, only those mad English incomers trying to get back to the natural life. Let's face it, we're not talking about very long ago.

And if we had, if we had fallen so clearly, so loudly, so out-in-the-openly, at the ripe young age we were at, somebody would have seen and, too soon, everybody would have known that the McCarthy girl was, you know, a bit funny, *like that*. And eventually, depending on how bold our falling had been, my father would have got the looks in the street and less work coming his way, and my brothers would have had the snide comments and the jeers and maybe the threats in pubs, and my mother would have been being turned in her grave at a dizzying rate, and perhaps I'd even have found it harder to get a summer job than I did, in a liberal age, in a small town.

All along I always knew the rules, I knew them innately. I had somehow learned them even before I knew what the word meant, the silent mouthed word for it that some kind and knowing anonymous seer had scrawled like a scar on my science folder at school when I was eleven or twelve, I picked my folder out of the pile and the word branded itself inside my head. The word that meant that later, when I wanted to burn my fingers, burn through the hearts of other girls instead of the boys I was supposed to, then I'd better respect the small town etiquette. At least until I was clear of the place. No wonder I didn't know what to make of Amy, crashing in on my greengage summer like she did, giving me that special something to work towards. My true Ame.

Not that I knew what a greengage was. Not that I tasted one, or very much summer fruit, until I had left Scotland far behind and gone south, to the land of summer fruit, where there were puddings made of it, where the supermarket fruit shelves were stacked with tropicana, and strawberries and satsumas all year round, and the open market stalls were cheap and plentiful and loaded down with fruit even through the winter. But even up here, even where all the things I felt were kept boxed and still and dark and ripening, I had always known that I liked girls. I liked boys too, but I certainly liked girls more. The summer I first met Amy I was deeply infatuated with the American girl who'd come to our school the January before. Now that I come to think about it, of course I fell for an American the year love first hit my body with that coiled hard fist and I found out late at night in bed by myself what you could let loose when you followed up those first twinges of interest beneath the covers.

I was a late developer. I was fifteen. I remember I was just beginning to wonder what my mother must have been like; not to wonder in that offhand, accepting, guardian angel way I had since childhood, but with an obsessiveness that left me peering for hours at colour faded photographs of her, holding them up in front of my angle poise lamp and shining a hundred watts through them to light up things I maybe hadn't noticed before. There were some things I knew well. She came from Boston but her parents had been Irish. That's why she had called me my Irish name, because she loved Ireland so much. We went on a family holiday there the year before she died. There's the photograph of me on her knee, we're sitting on the Giant's Causeway. I'm wearing a dress with a cherry pattern round the hem and two red pompoms like cherries on a string near the neck. She's wearing light blue trousers with little straps that come under her feet inside her shoes, and a white turtleneck sweater, and sixties glasses, and the sky above our heads is blue streaked with white. The Giant's Causeway, made of the big flat stones which Finn the Giant had used to try to fling a path across the sea. In the photograph we're both looking off to the left at something, I'd hold the photograph against the lightbulb and strain to work out what.

Your mother has gone to the angels. Your mother had to go away, she's gone into the sky. She hugged me goodbye, warm and sweet-smelling, and then stood with her arms by her sides, and then there was a great roaring, and fire came out of her feet, out of the soles of her shoes, and she shot into the clouds. Bits of her clothes, the strap off her vanity case, flaked down after her, singeing in the heat haze she left behind.

It always happened in black and white, it still does, I probably picked it up from the moon landings. *Your mother had your name ready and waiting for you to slip into it for years before you were born. You were so small the neighbours didn't even know your mother was pregnant until she came back from the hospital with you. She's gone into the sky, to help God with all the dancing they do in Heaven.* I never asked my father for any more than those few things he repeatedly told me. When I did want to know more, well, she was so many women behind for him by then. I asked James and Patrick instead, all sorts of questions, but I could never be sure they weren't just making things up about her; at night calling softly to each other from their bunk beds, or down in the unmown part of the garden lying in the long grass in the summer, they'd do what they always did, what maybe all twins do, talking to each other in their special way, agreeing with each other's version of it, *first she put on the red cape (like Wondermouse, yeah like Wondermouse) yeah like Wondermouse and then she could fly (yeah she could fly and they hadn't a chance, she'd special powers and a gun that could zap even the things she couldn't see) yeah, and the gun was a real magic gun and you could see the future and the past in it (and yeah, she could see us with it and you know, you know when there were, like, snails and worms and the bad things coming to get us if they were, in the dark, (yeah, she'd zap them easy) yeah 'cause she could see (she could see and she'd watch over us) yeah, both of us, she'd be watching. And Ash too (yeah, you too Ash).* Me, small and nodding, trying to look like them, a stalk of grass in my teeth like they had. But I knew it was made up, I didn't believe a word of it, not even when we were older and the stories they told were more utilitarian.

No, there were facts, I held on to them, they had their own special rhythm for me. She married my father in 1958, she died in October 1968. She was a dancer, and she died of cancer. She was thirty-five. That meant she was born in 1933. Later I used to imagine that American people on tv programmes were her. The ones who talked like her, shockingly like her. The pretty blonde woman in *Bewitched* who also had a little girl with a funny name. The mother in *The Partridge Family*, so jaunty that she made my stomach hurt, and the yellow-haired glamorous woman in *Star Trek*, my hair was nearly that colour. June Allyson, she had the same first name, and in *Little Women* she kept the whole family in bright Technicolor even after Beth's death. The woman who rode her grey pony beside Clark Gable in *Across the Wide Missouri*, which I watched with my father one Sunday afternoon. Though she was dark and foreign she was pretty and tough, and she led the way across the snowy wastes of the mountains, the only one brave enough, whooping and shouting at the men too scared to follow her in the snow. And she did die, and she did leave him with a small child, like I had been left (though it was a boy and it didn't have brothers. Well, all the better). And sometimes my father did look a little like Clark Gable, especially at the weekend when he didn't bother to shave.

The American girl who came to our school was the first real other American I had ever known. Her name was Jenny Timberberg and she was from Texas, her family had come to the back of beyond because her father worked with the oil company. She didn't act like a girl, she spoke up in class. She didn't mind what people thought of her, she told the teacher the answer in her beautiful nasal voice, and ignored the boys who copied her accent. She talked about God as if He was a personal friend. She was light brown and freckly and athletic from years in the sun, and she went around the playing field at break with her arm through the arm of whichever friend she was talking to. One day she stood up in class and spoke for a full five minutes about how much she loved the mountains of Scotland, how inspirational they were. After that I looked out of the window at the snow-topped mountains in the distance and I knew for the first time that they weren't just the boring backdrops to life I'd always mistaken them for, the places where careless people got lost and had to be rescued at New Year. After that I understood what all the Wordsworth stuff was about. The Solitary Reaper—my book had been vandalised, someone had scratched out the first e in Reaper with a pen— look past that, look closely, it was Jenny Timberberg single in the field, breaking the silence of the seas, whistling the opening bars of Don't It Make My Brown Eyes Blue with her hands in her blazer pockets leaning against the maths hut.

Though since Jenny Timberberg had arrived, my schoolwork had suffered. It had never been very lively in any case, and I must have scraped my way into good classes by grace of luck and intu- ition, voracious lonely reading late into the night, early into the morning, when it was too late for television. Now that I spent most of my time watching the back of her head for the minute changes in the movement of her hair as she paid attention to the board or drew earnest curlicues on her jotter cover, even the passive learn- ing I usually did was gone and I hadn't a clue what was happening in history, maths, German, whatever. Calculus could have been a Roman god for all I cared; Jenny Timberberg's back was full of hidden little muscles and I was watching for every one of them.

But it was more than a physical thing. In fact it wasn't really physical at all. Mostly I just wanted a friend, it's what I'd always wanted. I had friends, of course, lots of them, I was never short of someone to hang around with and talk about which boys we liked and which we didn't and who was getting off with whom, how embarrassing it was to have to take communal showers after gym and what we thought about the new Blondie single or Kate Bush being number one. But what I wanted was different. Someone who would push her arm through mine in front of all the others, someone who'd sling her arm round my shoulders and walk off into the sunset with me. A friend like people had in books, on television, friends like men had in all the films, friends you could trust with your life when the Germans were coming to root you out or the law had your house surrounded.

Jenny Timberberg was different. She was different from every-body else in the whole school, the whole town. There were other Americans in the school, from other oil families, but Jenny was the only girl who'd come all the way from America. She was the one. We had something in common. I had only spoken to her once, she didn't even know who I was, but I knew we were soul mates.

Then it was summer, the beginning of the summer holi-days. I was working in Littlewoods' restaurant, serving on the hotplate, dishing up chops and chips and green peas, steak pie, fish in breadcrumbs. I hated it, I wished I worked on the Bev Point, where you served people through clean hot steam, where when you went home you would smell of coffee instead of gravy and sweat. But hotplate was a promotion from my Saturday job working on clearing tables, because McWilliam had taken a lik-ing to me. I was glad he had. I didn't mind him looking at me like he did. When you came home from clearing tables you could peel a layer an inch thick of stuck trodden food off the soles of your shoes.

Summer. I had a day off and for once the weather was hot and clear, one of those rare, perfect, clear days, even warm enough to take your shoes and socks off; too warm for the jeans I was wearing, I had them rolled up to my knees, I was roaming round the big hot garden, books strewn across the grass, none of them could hold my attention, my head was hot with dreams. School being over had meant the disturbing loss of the small workday miracle of the back of Jenny Timberberg's head. I had been industrious, I had managed to find out the Timberbergs' address, their father's name (Beau) and their phone number, courtesy of James, who was working in the yard office, both he and Patrick were working at the rig yard like everybody else's older brothers and earning big money, a hundred pounds a week.

I was supposed to be cutting the grass, or making the boys' supper, but I had hauled the old wooden bench from the top lawn to the far lawn, all overhung with ancient apple trees from the house backing on to ours. The bench left rut-marks all the way across the lawns and through the vegetables. I knew I'd be in trouble for it later. But I pushed it up against the wall and lay on my back with my head in the shade and the rest of me in the sun.

We could meet by chance on the street. I could wait around somewhere outside her house until she came out, I could shadow her into town or wherever she was going, and I could bump into her by chance. What a surprise, meeting you here, how are you doing, have you, um, started the geography project yet for next year?

I could phone up. I could pluck up the courage to phone up. Hi, it's Aisling. Aisling McCarthy. You know, from school. I sit behind you in French and maths. I was just wondering if you . . . (if you what? I knew nothing about her except that she liked mountains) if you wanted to go up Ben Wyvis for a walk? (far too complicated, we'd need lifts in cars and boots and maybe ropes and icepicks and stuff. Also, I wasn't keen on actually having to *climb* a hill) if you . . . saw that programme about mountains on television the other week? (quite good, feasible at least, but—drawback—I would need to wait for a programme about mountains to come on tv) if you . . .

I could write her a letter. That's what I could do, I decided, I could write her a witty, funny letter. It would be so witty and funny that she'd realise what an entertaining person I was, and she'd phone immediately or better still, she'd write back and we could start up a correspondence, and meet each other every few days to talk about the things we'd written to each other. There would be nothing mundane about our letters, they would be letters full of adventure, discovery, large declarations. Eventually our most secret selves would grow and flourish from letter to letter, and nobody would know but us.

Possible, possible. I knew I'd never do such a thing, I knew it'd never happen, but it was calmingly possible, so I drafted the first of the letters in my head, lying flat on my back looking at the sky through the branches and watching the air shimmer like it hardly ever did, hearing flies and bees drone over the flowers and the old garden rubbish along the wall. A warm day, a rare day, a gift of a day. I must have fallen asleep, and it was a final kind of sleep, now that I remember, because although I didn't know it, after I jolted myself awake again everything in my life was going to be changed.

Then there was Amy, up a tree. There she was when I opened my eyes, looking down at me.

In a voice straight out of every BBC Sunday afternoon classic tv serial I'd ever seen, a voice straight out of every Secret Seven, every Jane Austen, every Virginia Woolf book I'd ever tried to read, she said:

You'll never guess. I just saw the most beautiful thing. There was a butterfly drinking from the corner of your eye just a moment ago. *Nymphalis io*. They're quite rare this far north.

My mouth fell open. I looked at her, hanging balanced above me in the branches of the apple tree. I said, Really? Really and truly?

Promise, she said.

TUESDAY ten a.m.

Dear Diary,

I like this game. Giving a shape to things that didn't actually have a shape at the time, or didn't seem to. Finding the hidden shape, the invisible shape that was there all along. Making the shape up, like it's just a story, like it didn't even have to have happened. Random, meaningless, the things you're left with surfacing inside your head like driftwood jolting on to the surface of the water, floating up and up in the dark and then hitting air and flipping over, lumps of splinter rotted off the dead weight they've left behind. Down on the sea bed the wreck and all the details you'll never see again. The rusting cutlery. The jacket the steward wore. The greying notice screwed on to the wall with the words *No Unauthorised Persons Beyond This Point,* shoals of fish flashing blindly past. The hundreds of things you can't call back. Who knows? Skulls, pearls, old bones. What lies at the bottom of the sea and shivers? A nervous wreck. Joke from the sixties when you could have nineteen nervous breakdowns, they're coming to take me away, ha ha. Patrick's favourite joke. James's was the rude one about the nun in the lift. He told it at school and got cuffed round the ear by Sister Ambrose. Amy knew all about nuns, she knew much more than I did and she'd never even met one.

Things Amy Told Me At One Time Or Another
Nuns are not allowed to give each other presents.
Graveyards are actually very nice places to have picnics.
There are seven St. Katherines altogether and three of them are Italian. Only one of them was martyred, the one on the Catherine wheel. She didn't actually die on the Wheel, but they cut her head off as she knelt with her hands tied behind her back blessing everyone who would remember her, and when they cut it off pure white milk jetted out over her neck.
It must be fascinating to have been brought up a Catholic because Catholicism is so gorgeously theatrical and Catholics are lucky enough to have such a real view of the value of sin.
There is one word in Greek for both butterfly and soul. Psyche. Psyche was the girlfriend of Eros and she had wings with butterfly markings on them. The planet Eros is remarkably close to the earth and was discovered in 1898.
I think you'll like this book, Ash. (I usually did.)
The pelican pecks into her own breast to wound herself and provide blood for her babies to eat. The phoenix lives for 500 years, then burns itself to death so a new phoenix can rise out of the pyre.

There is a glass mosaic of Eve with two tigers, one at her
    knees, one pushing its shoulder lovingly against her
    lower back, hanging in the choir of St. Paul's Cathedral.
When you're ill you have a temperature because your body
    is working so hard to fight the germs that have invaded
    it. Don't worry. (The back of her hand on my forehead
    to test it.)
According to the Aztecs, the world is made out of a god-
    dess who was torn apart by some gods, so that the earth
    is her top half and the sky her bottom half, and trees and
    flowers are her hair, mountains are her shoulders, caves
    are her eyes.
You look like Frankie from *The Member of the Wedding.*

Uncanny, that last one, one of the first things she said to me. As
usual I hadn't the faintest idea what she was talking about. I listened, I couldn't help but always be listening to Amy's voice, precise, clear, quiet, sure, the making of wondrous mad connections
I couldn't understand. She told me that one, about me looking
like Frankie, from up above me in the tree while I was sitting up
dazed, trying to see who was talking to me with the sun in my
eyes.

Her: dark, long dark straight hair. Small, neat, mouth full,
eyes brown, shielded, a cat's. Me: fair, gangling, thin, hair short
and rough and yellow, mouth a line, eyes grey blue, the only thing
about myself I liked, holding my hand up over my lower face and
looking at my eyes in the mirror. Me: taller, no breasts yet, gawky,
hard thin slight body, so like a boy that I had to have my ears
pierced to stop people in shops calling me son. Her: a girl. Really
a girl, girly clothes, the kind of girl I despised, I wouldn't be seen
dead with, the kind who would never vault a gate, who would
never dare climb a tree. Her: always catching me out.

Yes, now, this is what I mean. For instance, how did she ever get up into that tree wearing the long girly skirt kind of thing she always wore? More, how did she ever get down? I must have watched her get down, I mean, I must have seen it. But I don't remember it. I can imagine it easily enough, her balancing, graceful then clumsy then graceful again, shifting between the branches, feet braced and edging down the trunk carefully inch by inch, unpicking her caught sleeve or the fabric of the skirt from the twigs and making those little exasperated noises in her throat.

The slightest shiver of leaves above me.

Like the time I nearly got caught up the tree in the minister's garden. The apples on his tree were famous, good for stealing, almost eaters, the ones you'd find in the grass down the lane past the back of his house were always at least half bitten away before they were dropped. How old was I? nine, and badly wanting to get into the hideout they'd made on the canal banks, and that boy Colin who must have had a cleft palate, had a scar down the soft part under his nose, said girls weren't allowed. (To be a girl, worse fate than death, playing in someone's safe back garden with the other girls, their plastic teasets, the dolls that wet themselves.) Me standing there with my arms by my sides, not moving. James looking at Patrick and Patrick looking at the ground and telling me, yeah, you better get lost Ash, and those other boys waiting and watching, one of them was the boy who always went to the toilet outside, would never go home to do it. Then we heard the ice cream van playing Greensleeves from across the housing estate.

She's allowed if she buys us something from that, Colin said. Where's she supposed to get the money from? James said. I can get us apples for nothing, I said. Patrick looked up and nodded, his forehead cleared. She could even get us apples off Thain's tree, he said.

We were over Thain's fence and I was through the vegetable

patch and halfway up the rough tree before I looked back to see them all scattering and heard Mr. Thain crunching down the gravel, saw him running with his long thin black minister legs down the garden and nearly catching James, nearly had him by the collar, I nearly shouted out loud, I had to push myself further up, far enough up the tree that when Thain passed underneath, swearing under his breath and doubling back to smooth out the footprints in the soil round his potatoes, I could see the top of his bald head, and he didn't think to look up or he'd have caught me hanging there.

I waited at the top of Thain's tree until it was almost dark. I could see all the way across to the garages. I saw Mrs. Taylor go down her back garden, and that boy Hughie who was one of the tough Frasers my brothers kept out of the way of, who had just left school and was working at the train station, met her between two garages, I watched them, they were kissing like they were eating each other's faces, then heaving up against the side of the garage, I was thinking how he'd have splinters in his back and hands, or she would, you always got splinters if you went anywhere near the garages, then she straightened her clothes and he straightened her hair and I think they even shook hands, or he sort of bowed to her like the boys did to the headmaster's sister who gave you the book on the last day at school, and I watched her come back up her garden again swiping at something in her flowerbed on the way, and I heard her back door shutting. And when it was dark enough I filled my pockets with small apples, then I tucked my jumper into my jeans and put as many as I could carry down the neck. I shinned down the tree shaking the branches in the dark. I ran all the way to the canal bank and sat on the flattened grass in their hideout in the bushes and ate one of the apples, it was hard, green and bitter. I pushed my arm through the grass wall to drop the core outside.

It was late, I'd be in terrible trouble, I knew, out in the dark by myself near the canal. So I went where I'd really be leathered for going, up to the canal itself, right to the edge. When I got home my father would be waiting with his belt, and my brothers with scared faces round the back of him, whispering to me afterwards, did Thain get you, did he? I balanced on the rocks above the water and dropped one of the apples in. I liked the noise it made in the dark. I took them out of my pockets and out from under my jumper and let them fall one after the other into the canal. They floated, they made a cluster, clusters of floating apples on the surface of the water.

But when I got home the house was in darkness. I went upstairs on my toes, I could hear my father snoring when I passed his room. I stopped by the boys' room. My brothers were breathing in unison. I could see Patrick, the sheets thrown off him, one arm across his chest, the other hanging over the edge of the bed. In my room I shut the door, deep in my throat the urge swelling and kicking inside me to jump up and knock all the books off the top of the wardrobe, slam the wardrobe doors. I put my hands under my thighs and sat on them hard to stop myself.

Was it then I decided that I would just make someone up? someone who would have seen my arm coming out of the bushy wall of their hut and my hand in the dark dropping the core like it did, and who wouldn't tell; someone who had been sitting on the canal bank and had seen, the same as I had, that black light the moon had made round the apples in the water. I'd look out of my bedroom window at night, any night, and she'd be sitting on the pavement opposite, poking sticks down the grate of the drain. She lasted quite a long time, at least until I exchanged her for the dog I made up instead, who lived under my bed, who protected me from all anxiety like it said at church, and who, I knew, would be there sitting shifting on his paws outside the school gate every single day waiting for me and for the four o'clock bell like the boy and the dog in *Lassie Come Home,* so faithful he didn't need a lead, so well-trained I didn't need to call or whistle, he'd be there, his ears forward, his tail up. I can still see him. Black and white muzzle, black round the eyes like a mask. Black and white back, white legs, black tipped tail. I can still see her too, sitting on the kerb there in my head; she looks just like I used to look when I was that age.

Six, seven years later. Nine, ten years back, and I'm coming in from work, kicking off my shoes at the back door, longing to wrench the tights off and fling them across my room, bath off the smell of the chipsteaks when—Aisling? could you get through here now?—my father calls me. He's in the kitchen, showing the units to another woman. This is Aisling, he tells her, she's my youngest. Oh, she's like you right enough, the woman says, looking me up and down and nodding. The woman is his youngest too, his youngest for ages, recently they've been well into their forties but this one looks early thirties, still pretty, in a way that's starting to wear out, though, so she's probably ready for him. She's looking at me with sympathetic cow eyes which means he's already given her the wife dead left with three we manage but God sometimes it's hard story. I wonder what her name is; already this year we've had a Marjory, a Brenda and a Moira all fingering their wedding rings in our kitchen. Soon she'll start advising him where to buy clothes for me, and it will all last for the next few months or maybe weeks, depending. Sometimes it only lasts as long as it takes to install their new kitchens. I look her up and down back, equally sympathetic, and turn to go.

Here Ash, he says. We call her Ash for short, he explains to the woman. Aye, it's quite a mouthful, her name, I've never heard of it before, the woman says. What's this about you and some doctor? he says to me. There was a man here knocking on the door looking for you. What man? I ask. A doctor something, a man that says you're going travelling with him tomorrow, tweedy sort of a man, with one of those beards, my father puts on an affected voice and the woman giggles stupidly. I shrug and turn.

I hope you don't think you're going anywhere with some man three times your age, my father calls. Because you're not. It's hard with girls, he says to the woman. I don't know if you know what I mean, Marlene, but I always knew what to say to the boys. This one, well. He looks at me sorrowfully. This is Mrs. MacKay, he says, she's come to see our kitchen in action, she'll tell you, it's not safe going off with just anybody. It's not safe at all, Kenny, Mrs. Mackay says, shaking her head.

I give up. It's one of my father's games to trap his prey. I tell him I don't know what he's talking about, and as I head upstairs I can hear them as he shows her the easi-swing hinges on the doors and the rubbish bin hidden away in the false cupboard. I shut my door, turn The Sounds of Silence up very high, lie on my bed and think about Delphine at work. Pretty Delphine who looks like a French film star or something, a French film star with an Invernessian accent, she was in my year at school till she left last Christmas to work there full time; today she was so stoned or drunk at half-past eight in the morning that she was dancing round the kitchen with the brush in her arms singing Some Day My Prince Will Come, and fat Janet the cook who's usually so mean-tempered made her lie down in the office and covered for her to McWilliam.

I'm just out of the shower when the doorbell rings and Patrick answers it. He calls me to the door. There's a woman there with short dark hair, she's smiling inanely, behind her there's a man with a beard, and behind them, leaning over next door's front gate, the weird serious girl from up the tree is playing with the catch, pressing it up and down. I focus back on the woman, who is holding her hand out as if I'm expected to put something in it.

I'm Patricia Shone, I'm so pleased to meet you, the woman says to me. She takes my wet hand and shakes it, then holds it in hers. I'm so glad you're coming with us, she says, it's one of Amy's better ideas, it will be wonderful to have a native of the area show us what we really ought to see. It's terribly nice that you and Amy are friends, and a real stroke of luck for David and myself.

My father comes to the door. What've you done, Ash? he says to me. What's she done?

I'm Patricia Shone, so nice to meet you, you must be Mr.—you must be Amy's friend's father, the woman says. My father looks down at his hand in hers. He grins all over his face. We're staying slap-bang next door to you, she says with a little laugh, a whole week, our first visit to Scotland. It's so kind of you to let your daughter—

Ash, says the girl at the gate, still playing with the catch.

—show us around while we're here, the woman says.

We all stand for a moment and nobody says anything. You'd better come in, my father says. Oh, the woman says, I can't get over how lovely and friendly everyone here is. She and the silent man follow my father inside. The girl runs her hand along the scored wood on the top of the gate. We can hear them all laughing and the sound of my father at the whisky cabinet.

It'll be fun, she says gravely.

You're mad, I say. I can't go anywhere with you and them, I'm *working*. I've got a job, I can't just leave, just like that.

Now James is at the door, and Patrick behind him. Are you not coming in? Patrick says to the girl. What's your name? Would you not like to come in? Who's your friend? James whispers in my ear. He puts his arm round me and blows hot breath through my tee-shirt on to my shoulder, I can smell it, sweet. Patrick puts his arm round me on the other side and says to the girl, we're all twins here, can you tell the difference? He ruffles my wet hair and I duck away from under them. Is your friend not coming in, Ash? Patrick says. My name's James, we're her big brothers, you're from England, aren't you? James says.

The girl looks straight at me as if there's nobody there but me and her. Do you find it very boring where you work? she says. Do you like it very much?

I nod, yes, then I shake my head and say no, I mean no.

Well then, I should think that's argument enough, she says, so quietly I have to strain to hear it. She closes the gate with a click.

Would you not like a cup of tea, whatsyourname? Patrick calls over my shoulder. Her name's Amy, I tell him as she comes up our front path. Do you, would you like a coffee or tea? I say.

What kinds of tea do you have? she asks me.

Kinds of tea? I think, as I'm leading her in, pushing through past my brothers.

I have no idea what she can possibly mean.

My father still asks after Patricia Shone even now, he asked on Sunday when I got home, remember that English lady, the mother of your friend, she was a right nice woman, do you ever see her? The one with the doctor husband. Not the kind of woman who'll fall for your average kitchen units, he said, impressed, after they'd gone back next door. You can go driving with them, he told me, though I'd already made up my mind that I was going regardless, if only out of a sense of confusion; no girl who'd ever been to my house had failed to be charmed by my brothers so singularly as this one had. And if you're short of a summer job afterwards, he called from his chair in front of the tv, you can always come and work for me in the shop. I stood by the door, astounded. I thought our house must have been touched by some sort of magic, and instead of going upstairs I hung about by the door, then sat down and watched tv with him, something with the Marx brothers, Groucho wearing a mortar board and dancing on a table, Harpo in somebody's study shovelling books on to a fire and warming his hands.

That first summer, then. Amy and I in the back of the car, her mother and father in the front. The backs of her parents' heads and their so English voices as they held forth and argued about luxurious things like what they thought about books and what they'd read about them in the Sunday papers; it sounded like they would never dream of reading a book they hadn't read about in the Sunday papers first. Driving on the tourist route roads where the roadside weeds and the cow parsley spilled out on to the tarmac, roads winding round and up and round and down, single-track with passing places, mountains above us and all round us in the distance, forests looming close then the road suddenly splitting away from them again and the sky taking over. Gnarled white birches in the rocky fields on either side of us. Me taking secret glances at Amy, sitting neat and composed, her hands in her lap, her hair long and coiled and her face empty, so much a girl that it made me nervous, like I shouldn't be there, like I was a mistake. Rain streaking the window by my head with long horizontal slashes, the sound of the windscreen wipers working against the classical music in the cassette recorder, the rustle of their cagoules, the smell of peppermint. Her mother sucking carsick tablets and peppermints, pressing them on me (no, *do* take one), talking like she did, smiling all the time, saying anything into the air, turning to me once and leaning over her seat like a child and saying, what do you think Aisling, of my theory that my dear daughter Amy, dear to my heart, my only child, was replaced with a changeling not long after her birth by a race of being that cannot, simply cannot be brought to love its mother, or even to smile once in a while?

I nodded and smiled politely, and then stopped smiling in case smiling would reflect badly on Amy, and quickly looked out of the window.

Amy has no need to smile if she doesn't wish to, her father said. Amy's father, I gathered, gave lectures about books all over the world. He didn't ever say very much; I assumed he must always be thinking very hard, about books. Amy's mother did courses and had just finished doing one on Japanese flower arranging and one about "the poets of that terrible, terrible first war." She was still leaning over the back of the seat, waiting for an answer. I looked at Amy, who was looking blankly out of the window at the rain. Um, ha ha, I said.

I should like to think I were a changeling, Amy said. Anything's possible, after all, even doubtful parentage in the respectable suburban villages of Mother England.

She's so clever, I thought, and tried to think of something to say. There's a song about it, I said, we got taught it at primary school; and though I was too shy to sing it I told them what I could remember of the story, about the mother who leaves her baby while she goes gathering blaeberries and comes back to find the fairies have taken it away, left an ugly goblin child in its place.

Careless woman, Amy sighed, and glanced at me out of the corner of her eye.

It's most likely an explanation for the mentally retarded or physically disabled of the various communities of the time, her father said.

It's a lament, I said.

A lament, how sad, her mother said. How romantic. Call me Patricia, Aisling, she insisted. Call him David. Everyone does. Amy does, and she's our daughter. At least, I think she's our daughter. Aisling, she mused, it's such a strange name. Irish, did you say? Like a little person all made out of ash.

No, Amy said, much more substantial than that. Like a tree.

She looked out of the car window beyond me and then looked back at me. Mountain, Ash, she said, and I was beginning to understand that it meant something when her eyes did that playful thing, though I couldn't be sure whether it was that they were laughing because something was funny, or that they were laughing at me.

We drove all over the place; Doctor Shone stopping the car to take photographs of the views, Mrs. Shone buying postcards of the same views, more views, clan crests, highland cattle. We drove to what was left of the Victorian health spa at Strathpeffer, vile-smelling and derelict. They wandered round it talking in voices so loud that people looked at them. I pretended I wasn't with them. I sat and scratched my name on the wall of one of the buildings covered in graffiti. But when I looked up Amy was behind me, watching, and I was ashamed. She came over and ran her finger over a heart gouged round some initials. It's romantic, isn't it? she said, as if she hadn't even noticed my vandalism, more, as if she were asking a question, as if she really wasn't sure, she really wanted to know.

We went to the wildlife park, where Amy liked the birds of prey best, I think she said they were sweet, and where her mother went into a huff because the baby deer kept running away from her. We did the woodland walk at the Landmark centre and saw the slide show and went to the shop. We did the forestry commission walk round the side of a loch. Doctor Shone stayed in the car most of the time, pursing his lips, reading the dry-looking books about books that he kept in the glove compartment and listening to sonorous violin concertos. In town again, I took them to see all the sights. The crazy golf. The trampolines. The ice rink. The field where the shows came in June and where they held the inter-school sports. The Northern Meeting Park, where The Kilt Is My Delight was performed in open air on summer evenings even in the cold and rain and where the two parachutists tried to land every year at the Tattoo. The canal. The swing bridge, which would stop the traffic in the summer a couple of times a day when it swung open to let the canal cruise boats go through to Loch Ness. I made them wait for over an hour to see that happen. The walk through the Islands, the place I once found a dead salmon, the war memorial, the tennis courts and swings at Bellfield Park. We walked to the castle and I showed them the greeny bronze statue of Flora MacDonald endlessly watching for Bonnie Prince Charlie to come sailing back up the river to her, with her hand stuck in the air over her head like she's about to lash out at somebody, or like she's been frozen in time in the middle of doing a Scottish country dance.

Oh, said Mrs. Shone. When you said we were going to see Flora MacDonald, I thought we were going to meet a school friend of yours, or maybe an old lady who knew about the area, I even imagined her showing us how to use a spinning wheel, how silly of me.

Flora MacDonald, I said, is the heroine who helped Bonnie Prince Charlie escape from the English.

In 1066, wasn't it? Amy said.

It can't have been, her mother said.

It was 1314, I said. She hid him in her house, dressed him up in girl's clothing—

And she dressed in men's clothes, Amy said, nodding—

Yes, I said.

And they went round the town pretending to be a newly married couple to see if they fooled anybody, Amy said.

And when the English regiments came looking for him, I said, and they were hammering on her croft house door, she shouted to the prince to put on her dress again and leave by the back door while she held them off at the front, and she was so brave she put her arm through the latch of the door to keep them out because highland people had been banned from having latches by the English, and they broke her arm when they broke down the door.

How very interesting, said Mrs. Shone. It doesn't say anything about her here, said Doctor Shone, flicking through his guide book.

And she was thrown in prison for aiding and abetting, I said. And she probably didn't ever get her frock back either, Amy said. No, she didn't, I said, and it was her best one. Is there anywhere round here where we can get a cup of tea? Amy's mother said.

I took them across the road to the Castle Snack Bar. That's where I found out where Jenny Timberberg was spending her summer. She served us; she didn't recognise me; her neck was covered in big red weals and she spent most of the time we were there hanging over the table at the back where three boys from fifth year were jostling each other and snorting with laughter. I stared into my glass of flat coke, hardly hearing when Amy's father asked me if I could tell him what The Clearances were.

I think we should go to this battlefield, Doctor Shone said, snapping his shiny book shut. He left a large tip, 75p. I made sure I was the last person out, and slipped it into my pocket. I didn't want Jenny Timberberg to have it.

We were standing in the middle of Culloden Moor in the spitting rain, and Doctor Shone was taking photographs one way, then the other. I was in a very bad mood, and telling them how the Duke of Cumberland, because he was such a little man, had stood his horse up on the Cumberland Stone so he could watch the battle, and how his troops had massacred the highland troops because they knew how to form and close ranks, how to kneel and stand in tight little groups while they shot, reloading their guns while the men in front of them or behind them kept firing so that the shooting at the Jacobites never stopped. I hadn't realised I knew so much about it. I hadn't realised how angry I could get about it. I jingled the 75p in my pocket and pushed facts out of myself like poison. The battle only lasted forty minutes, I said, and it left more than a thousand people dead, and that was only the beginning. I told them about how then the English troops and the treacherous Scottish troops ran wild through the town and the countryside around the town, killing as many people as possible, especially people wearing tartan, and that there was a grave by the river where they lined Jacobites up one in front of the other and shot them, letting them fall where they were into the pit. I told them how the speaking of Gaelic had been banned by the English government, and so had tartan, and that though they'd tried to stamp tartan out altogether there was even a square of it on the moon, now, right now as we spoke, left there by one of the astronauts ten years ago. Amy's parents went muttering past me, quiet for once. I saw Amy's eyes on me, speculative. No, I said, it's true, it really happened, all of it, honest.

We looked at the old stones marked with the names of the clans. A big mass grave, really, Amy's mother said shivering, I should think it's rather creepy round here at night. Not very big on a historical scale of massacre, not really, her father said.

His book told him there were Neolithic burial cairns nearby, so we drove to them and Doctor Shone stood inside one and took photographs of Mrs. Shone smiling over the top of it. I sat on the piny ground under one of the trees and watched Amy examining the places where the bodies had been in each cairn. She came over and stood beside me. Death is so fascinating, she said. I love graveyards. They're so very beautiful.

I had never heard anyone say such a mad thing in my life; I looked at her in disgust. But when I looked away, and around me, the place had suddenly become just that, beautiful. There were her parents scrabbling around on the cairns. The birds were singing over the top of them and over us under the tree as if we weren't even there, nothing had to matter, nothing did. I looked at her again, this time in wonder. She was polishing her glasses. She put them back on and blinked down at me with that blank look. Lemurs sit round the gates of Hell, she said. They're the animal spirits of the underworld, and they shriek high-pitched screams to atone for the lost souls, to persuade God or the gods to have mercy and rescue them from the dark, pluck them out of the flames.

Oh, I said. Right.

We went to the waterfall at Foyers, which Mrs. Shone kept pronouncing wrong in a French way, as if it were the theatre kind. We parked on the road at the top, you could hear the roar of the water getting louder and louder the closer you went down the woodslope, her mother and father slithering ahead, then me, then her, picking her way down delicately between the tree roots. We leaned over the railing and watched the water whitening over the rocks as it fell. Amy put her mouth right next to my ear. If I dared you to jump, would you jump? she said. Oh sure, I yelled back, course I would. She put her hand against my head to shout through it into my ear. One minute you'd still be safe here, she shouted against the noise, the next you'd be nothing but air and movement, the secret of it would flash before your eyes, you'd know it all. Yeah, but then you'd be dead, I shouted back.

In bed that night, for the first time in my life I couldn't get to sleep. I couldn't stop thinking about the noise of the waterfall. It was a noise that would never stop. It would always be roaring, even now it was, in the middle of the night, all the days and all the nights, shattering itself down the sides of the crevasse. It wasn't something you could switch off like you could switch off a light or a hairdryer. Somewhere at the back of my head the thing I could hear, the noise I thought was just silence, was the same roaring noise of the fall in the distance. When eventually I slept, I remember, I dreamed a vivid dream of dead people who lived in round stone houses, herringbone people whose skulls smiled all the time, who were able to lay their skeletons down in their special beds in the wall and sleep through the roaring next to them, because the stones they'd built their houses with in the first place were so thick.

But when I pointed out that blackbird on the lawn, its head cocked sideways, and told her how it was listening for worms, she went into a squirmy panic at the thought that there were worms everywhere under her feet. Still, since she seemed to like dead places so much, I thought, I could always take them to see the cemetery. I went to the library and looked it up in the local history books. I memorised all about it being the Hill of the Yews, how someone called Thomas the Rhymer was sleeping under there, how in ancient times an Irish wizard had made two of every bird and beast walk round the base of it like an Ark, how even the whales got up and walked round the foot of Tomnahurich. I thought how I could show her the graves of the soldiers, and the elaborate white stone angels and draped chalices (she'd love them, they'd be beautiful), the open-bible shaped headstones, and the tomb with the hole in the stone where you could put your hand in if you were brave enough. I knew she wouldn't be brave enough. I thought, if I could get her away from her parents, I might even show her the graves at the top of the hill, the really old ones from the eighteen hundreds and the one that, years ago, I'd secretly chosen to use as a place to visit my own dead.

When I called next door to suggest it, Mrs. Jamieson sent me up to the guest rooms. I knocked on the door with the number 1 screwed on to it. No answer. Number 2's door was a little open. This must be Amy's room. They'd gone out somewhere without me.

I stood in the smell of Persil and air freshener. A cardigan was folded over the back of a chair, I lifted the cuff of a sleeve rounded by her wrist and put it to my nose; the smell of some

166

kind of soap, bland. There were things in the drawers of the bedside table, soft material caught in the pushed-shut drawer, I didn't dare touch. The glass of water had a light film of dust floating on top, barely moving as I came closer. There were novels one on top of the other next to the glass. An aged-looking Hardy, *A Pair of Blue Eyes* (I'd read it already, I thought, pleased with myself), something French underneath, and under that a book with a blank marbled cover, a notebook was it? I pulled it out, let the pages fall open one after the other in my hands, lined with blue handwriting, disconnected words catching the eye, perhaps, the, touched, exquisite, immerse, or immense? raven, or riven? or river? then above the noise in my chest someone was coming up the stairs, or a tap was turned on somewhere, and I closed the book and slipped it back under, quickly carefully lined the spines up again (good at leaving things exactly where they had been from years of secret foraging in my brothers' room), was out of the door and down the stairs, shouting through goodbye to Mrs. Jamieson, not waiting to hear, pulling the front door shut behind me, and when I was back in my own house, in my own room, I opened my hand and looked at what I had stolen, a strip of woven lace, sort of macrame, a bookmark maybe, I'd taken it just to show I could though I didn't even know what it was. I didn't know what to do with it. I hid it under my pillow. Later I went out the back and put it in the dustbin under the top layer of rubbish, same as I'd done earlier in the summer with the copy of *Claudine at School* in case anybody caught me reading it, or, more likely, I caught myself.

I put the dustbin lid firmly down. From then on, I decided, that was that. I wouldn't go anywhere with them. I didn't like them, they were mad, what's more they were embarrassing, and I didn't like her, and they were leaving soon anyway, I'd never have to see her again, it was all all right.

The next day we drove to Loch Ness.

7:15 p.m.

My father's gone fishing. After he went I scraped my share of tonight's supper on to the compost heap. I couldn't swallow it. It smells of here and tastes of here. I got rid of lunch earlier when he answered the phone, gave me the chance or I'd have been sick I think. I put it outside and covered it over with some old pieces of wood. Stew. I haven't eaten stew for years. Not eaten stew.

There is a girl playing the piano downstairs. I don't know who she is. I answered the door and she was there, she looks about fourteen years old, she was holding music books in her arms. I think it's Chopin she's playing now. She's very good. He's had it tuned, I don't think I ever heard our piano sound that good. She said, are you Ash? She made me a cup of coffee in the kitchen, she knew where the cups and spoons were and where the coffee was kept, she sat up on one of the stools and leaned on her elbows on the breakfast bar and said, Mr. McCarthy says you're in films and in plays and things, what's it like, will any of them be on here? We never get good films here, she said, it's such a dump, do you know anybody famous? Nobody from here would know anybody really famous, she said. Her name is Melanie. She said she loves music, she really really loves it. Mozart is really difficult to play because you have to keep it all expressionless, like, kind of flat, you're not allowed to put any of yourself into it. Bach is like having a discussion inside your head where a whole lot of different bits of yourself join in. Her piano teacher says Chopin is like standing in the rain in the Mediterranean, so she wants to go there, have I ever been? She thinks it's like when you've been running really fast for a bus and you miss it anyway, or like when you've eaten something that makes your stomach go funny and you're sick but you feel really good afterwards. But her total total favourite, she told me, is Ravel, it's brilliant, though her piano teacher says she won't be able to play it properly until she's older.

She's trying to learn Ravel's *Pavane pour une infante défante*, do I know it? It's going to take maybe years to learn but it's really moving. She likes the piano being in the hall, she thinks the acoustics are pretty good. What am I doing up in the loft? she said.

Loch Ness, dark and brooding, place of hidden monsters. So deep and murky that nobody knows for sure what's down there. There can be wild and thrashing waters, whole seastorms raging underneath and you can be standing on the pebbles at the edge skimming stones or looking down from the hills at the still reflection or even sailing over it, and you won't know anything is happening; in the cold calm of the surface only the merest rippled wave.

At the Loch Ness Monster Exhibition Centre I was keeping quiet, polite and removed, but nobody had noticed yet how polite and removed I was being. Amy's mother fingered the plastic monster keyrings and sniffed thoughtfully as she turned postcards over in her hand, cards with tartan borders or green cartoon monsters superimposed on real views. Amy's father in his heavy tweed jacket was pushing the buttons on a tank painted to look like a cross-section of the loch, randomly lighting up plastic models. A sunken boat. A Second World War spitfire. A long-necked plastic dinosaur. When the dinosaur lit up he smiled, and when the light went out he pulled his lower lip with his finger and thumb and pressed the buttons again. Two small boys were waiting behind him for their turn.

The books on the book table were all *The Story of Loch Ness*. I opened one and looked over the top of it at where Amy had just been, at the blown-up grainy black and white photograph of the head coming out of the water. I didn't know where she'd gone. Then I saw her out of the corner of my eye, she was sitting in the cafeteria area. I casually put the book down, casually went over, casually sat down opposite her.

Maybe when you get home, you know, to England, maybe we could write to each other, maybe you'll write to me? I got as far as the second maybe before I guttered out, Amy wasn't listening anyway, she was blinking into the air as if I wasn't there. I turned away. I was angry. Talking to her was like talking to stone. Like talking to a rock and expecting it to talk back.

Then she said, that one over there, Ash, she likes you.

I didn't know what she meant, until I turned and saw the girl taking money at the till look away just a little too late. It dawned on me. Amy's eyes were doing that laughing thing again, and I began to laugh, I was shaking my head and laughing, and then Amy was laughing too, out loud, which took me so by surprise that I stopped laughing and watched her, amazed.

I'd very much like a black coffee, Amy said. Here's the money. Choose something for yourself too, won't you?

Well? she said when I came back with the tray. Her name is Donna, I said, and she's at the same school as me, she's in the year below me, she says she knows me though, you know, Amy, God, I don't remember seeing her there ever. She lives out here, she says she hates it, it's really boring.

I looked round and smiled over at Donna, who smiled back, a bit sheepish, a bit shy. Yeah, I'd really hate living out here too, I said to Amy through the steam rising off the plastic cups, and I felt the blush spreading up my neck and the cup in my hand changing shape and proportion with the heat of the coffee inside it.

Fascinating, you have so much in common, Amy said, glinting, removed, polite again.

Sure enough, it wasn't long before Donna and I were friends, and because she lived out of town we spent a lot of time together staying over at each other's, late nights and early mornings watching the sun come up or the clouds lighten, edging closer and closer to each other, arms touching, sides of thighs touching, hand brush-

ing hand, and it wasn't long till we were vowing eternal friendship, and vowing eternal secrecy, not long till we were fumbling at
each other on the river bank at midnight after making ourselves
brave on Woodpecker cider. I stayed out at her house in the October holidays; we had the house to ourselves, we were supposed to
be revising for exams but instead we spent the afternoon digging
up her back garden looking for the dead hamster her younger
brother had buried the month before. We found it; she took the
lid off the Tupperware box, and the hamster was ravaged, crawling with life. That afternoon we made our fevered first love, up in
her bedroom below the posters of Snoopy and The Clash, with
Rita Coolidge singing We're All Alone on the stereo. After that I
would have done anything for her, I didn't even flinch when she
told me that her and her brother's favourite game was to hide
pins in bits of bread and feed the bread to the seagulls on the
lochside and watch what happened.

Amy faded away south on me, and once or twice before I got
too involved with Donna and forgot everything else, I would dare
to stand in my room and imagine being in that room next door
with the strange charged air she'd created in it just by not being
there. That autumn she sent me a letter, but it was in Latin, I
couldn't understand a word of it. Her mother wrote a thankyou
letter to my father, a letter full of delightfuls and so wonderfuls
and we're indebteds. She enclosed a photograph Amy's father
had taken at the war memorial, of me, herself and Amy. I cut
her out of the middle and stuck the two halves of the picture up
on the wall by my bed, me and Amy stuck together out of joint.

Was that the really bad winter, the one with the blizzards,
when all those people died in their cars, caught in a total white-
out on the roads round the town? Falling slowly asleep, asphyxi-
ating inside snow caves, their ignitions on to keep them warm.
I can't remember. There was ice inside the windows of the bus
I used to take down the loch road to Donna's house, I scraped

her name into it, breathed on it, watched it melt. I didn't care about the weather. From what I remember I didn't really notice, my heart was in my mouth all the time, and my mouth was on someone else's often enough to keep me more than happy.

Is that the Ravel she's playing now, that girl? Far too sentimental for me.

Listen to it.

TONIGHT the birds are crossing the sky, singing invisibly in the gardens, calling for mates and calling for more as the dark comes down. I'd forgotten how spring breaks open here. Not like down south and the slow seep of mildness on some days in January even, leaving you a mixture of hopeful and not-trusting, sniffing the air and listening for birds who won't be back for months. Early April with its schoures sweet. Something has given somewhere, it's the season.

I spent the morning in town wandering about, jumpy on old roads with ghosts at my back, catching my reflection in shop windows and thinking for a half second that I was someone I recognised. The record shop's still there, still full of fourteen-year-olds juping off and smoking at the back. The shopping centre, new, at least to me, already pretty grimy-looking, is half full of shops and half empty of them. Benetton, Our Price, This Space For Rent. They've knocked down the place where my father used to have the warehouse, where we found all the deformed seven-leafed clovers, it's a British Rail van park now. There's a Dixons where the shop was.

The second-hand bookshop is still there. The man didn't remember me. He looked just the same. His shop looked just the same. The river looks the same, very high, lots of rain. I walked home past the theatre, went in to get out of a schour. The handles on the toilet doors are still the same. On the way home up the hill at lunchtime I saw two girls of about twelve climbing on to the roof of a bus shelter, school skirts and bags flailing. I shouted up to them to be careful. They shouted down to me to fuck off and mind my own business. When I looked back, a man was passing below them and they were about to drop something on his head, we used to use crisp bags full of puddle water. I could hear the man shouting and them laughing behind me all the way up to the corner. I went home laughing, I should have warned him as he passed me. No, I couldn't have. Everything changes, nothing changes.

My father hanging around the house all day, that's new. The house, small as failure. Too small. I went out to the garage. I found all the pony books and the Laura Ingalls Wilder books. I found the Spike Milligan book that Patrick pulled my hair out for losing. I found a box of things that must have come out of somewhere in the boys' room, old Black Babies certificates with the names below the photos on the dotted lines. Aloysius, Ringo, Dusty; I was touched by how many of the girls were called Aisling. By the time I got to school it was Holy Childhood, not Black Babies, and you couldn't name the child in the picture any more so they had to devise a Holy Childhood Race wallchart with the winner paying in the most money. I found those coins they used to give you with petrol, World Cup coins, Apollo moon coins. Old 45s, I Feel Fine/She's a Woman, I'm an Apeman, Beg, Steal or Borrow, I'm the Urban Spaceman baby, here comes the twist,

I—don't exist. A bag of golf balls, pocked and cracked, grime in the indents, the boys used to collect them off the golf course and sell them back to the golfers who'd lost them. Patrick once showed me how you could pick off all the white stuff and then if you unwound the elastic, unwinding for yards and yards, at the centre of the ball you'd find the poison. The thrill in that, holding the small soft poison sac in the palm of your hand, feeling the liquid shift. The elastic after you unwound it was useless and brittle, you couldn't imagine it ever having made anything bounce that high on the pavement.

Lots of old clothes, theirs and mine, they look like children's clothes to me now, small in the shoulder. All the old catalogues and display books and ledgers from the shop. All the bits and pieces of kitchen he never managed to sell in the end, the gutted insides of the shop. It explains why his kitchen is made up of all those different styles and colours of unit, a red door next to a brown next to a pine, and the handles all at different levels. Like he couldn't make up his mind, like he wanted them all.

All my books. All the books I stole from James and Patrick, all the ones I bought with my pay packet on Saturdays, all the ones I bought down south and sent back up, still in the boxes I sent them in. Old school books. I found the maths jotter with the cover I had to censor with the marker pen, remember, sweating, fearful, scribbling over it in the few seconds before they collected everybody's up to be inspected by the Head when they were investigating old Mrs. Humphries. She wasn't that old, she just looked old; the rumour was she'd got a double first years ago at Oxford and that's why she was always drunk, she was nice, she was just always drunk, and unconscious in one too many classes. I'd censored it well, I couldn't make anything out. What can have been so very terrible about it? I remember I was mortified, I was sure I'd get caught, but I can't remember what for.

I found Amy's journals in a box inside a black bin bag. I put them up on the shelf out of the way. Tucked behind the stacked sections of kitchen unit by the door I found all the board games; something had chewed a hole right through the Colditz box and made a nest in it.

It's like a junkshop paradise in there. He's kept everything; he's put together bits of unused unit to make cupboards along both walls, and stuffed them full of it all. I opened one and a hundred empty Tupperware ice cream cartons fell out spilling their lids. I opened another and found a plastic bag full of half chewed pencils and chewed-up pens, plastic combs and hairbrushes, old ring-pulls and pieces of wire, even, for God's sake, a rubber alligator with the tail chewed off and the teeth bitten out. Behind this though there were two old broken fifties radios, nice, I'd never seen them before. Up on top, a set of stiff blue suitcases. I opened one. Clothes, women's clothes, folded flat and musty. He's kept all her things too. I closed it carefully, clicked the locks, and after that I sat on the floor by the fishing tackle, unsealed a book box and took out the first one that came to hand.

I was leaning against one of the mopeds flicking through it when he knocked on the window. Could you not hear me? he called on the other side of the glass. Are you not freezing to death out here? I might've known you'd found a book. There's a coffee for you in the kitchen. No sugar. I remembered. I didn't put any in.

I sat on the stool at the breakfast bar, flattened the book open. He was staring hard at the free newspaper, looking through it for something.

You know, he said eventually, I got Barbara to hang those curtains in the back room.

Then a moment later: she went to Frasers and chose them specially. She ran them up on her machine and she brought them over and hung them up.

He still hadn't looked up from the paper. Mm, I said.

You know I had her choose the bedding and everything, so I could make the bed up specially for you coming home this week? he said.

Now I understood. I like it up there, I said.

But it's your own bed, it's *your* bed. It's a nice room. It's the same bed you had before, for Christ's sake. It's clean. There's no carpet in the loft. It must be bloody freezing up there.

It's not, it's fine, really, I like it. I prefer it, I said.

A sleeping bag, a bloody sleeping bag, he said, shaking his head. You're a queer one. You always were.

I kept my eye on the page open in my book. Who's Barbara then? I asked. Barbara, *you* know, he said, scanning the paper. She lives across the road, the big white house at the corner.

The big white house, right, I said, none the wiser.

Silence. I lifted up my book. *Journal of the Plague Year,* he said. That's an old one. I read that one in the war.

That made me look up. Because he's never said anything about it, never, at least not to me. I don't remember him ever talking about it. The only reason we knew he'd even been in it was that we were scrounging around in his room once when we were small and one of the boys found a wooden box under the bed that had what looked like a medal in it.

Christ, he said, I remember. There were people who thought they wouldn't catch it if they covered themselves in vinegar. Did you ever hear anything so stupid? And people who drew, what're they called, lucky things on bits of paper and hung them around their necks, like magic words or their star sign. People who wrote out the words of, you know, prayers and that, and went around wearing them. The cart would be going round covered in dead bodies with these bits of paper stuck all over them.

He was laughing at that. Where was it you read it, again? I said.

At sea, we were at sea, he said. But the best thing about it, you know, girl, is that the man who wrote it wasn't even there when the plague was happening like that, he wasn't even there, he made it all up afterwards. You think it's a documentary, you think what you're reading is real, then you find out afterwards it's all, you know, fiction. I don't mean that it's lies or anything, he said. It's real enough, but he made it up. And you'd never know by reading it, would you, eh? He put his cup in the sink and reached for his jacket. Wash your cup out after you when you've finished, he said.

Did you read a lot when you were, when you were at sea? I said.

Christ, yes, we did enough reading, all your Shakespeare and all sorts, he said. There was bugger all else to do. Took your mind off it, and half the time we didn't know where the bloody hell we would end up. I read the lot, all the big Russian books. I hope you haven't mucked my garage about, I've enough to do without putting things back after you.

I found some really nice old radios, I said.

You got as far as the radios, he said. There's serious damage done, then.

It's trendy now, old bakelite like that, I said. You'd get a good price for them.

You like them? he asked. He opened the back door. Well, you can have one. You can have the one that works, he said, and closed the door; I watched him from the window as he trudged over to the greenhouse, the trays of plants held out in front of him.

For a moment he could have been any age, he could have been himself ten years ago, could have been either of my brothers, his back straight like that as he crossed the grass.

Spring. A weekday afternoon, so it must have been the Easter holidays. We were lying in my bedroom on the floor, we were under the bed with the door shut and wedged with the chair, we had our legs twined round each other's legs and our heads just touching in the dark. Donna had her hand up my shirt, she was idly fingering one of my nipples, asking me about my brothers.

But *you* can tell them apart, can't you? she was saying. How? How can you? Is there, like, a special way? She was fascinated by them. I was only flirting so that he won't suspect, she said. I only like Jim because he looks a bit like you.

That was Patrick, I said.

Oh, was it? Well there you go. Same difference, she said.

Donna was staying over at mine for a few days and it was the first time she'd met them, they were home from college for the holidays and hanging dangerously around the house at funny times of the night and day because of the shift work at the site. She'd never seen identical twins so close up before, and she found it deeply exciting to have them both in the same room.

All lunchtime she'd been in flirty giggles at Patrick's stupid jokes, though so had I. He'd been working hard to charm her, and she'd been convinced as soon as he came into the room wearing a pair of underpants on his head for her benefit. I had been proud, prouder still when he made her laugh by putting some of my fish finger into my glass of water making a joke about its original habitat. After lunch he'd asked her did she know how to play fifty-two card pick-up? He'd thrown the pack of cards in the air, and said, right, now you have to pick them up, and we'd both crawled round the room on our stomachs collecting them, eyeing each other in helpless laughter.

She was squirming next to me under the bed. My brother was so funny, she told me. Was Patrick, like, the funny one then? No, I said, James was funny too, only in a different way, but I couldn't think how to explain. And they don't look at all the same, I said, not even from a distance. Their faces are totally different and the way they hold themselves is too, and they both walk in totally different ways, and talk in totally different ways, and even the way they drive. Even if they're just standing there not doing anything it's obvious.

But how? she said.

I tried to think of clues for the uninitiated. Say they came into the room both at once, I said, nine times out of ten it would be Patrick who came in first, you know what I mean? Say they're both sitting there in the room with you. One of them would say something like: do you know what the best ever drink of water would be? It would be the drink of water you were given if you were ever lost in the desert and dying of thirst. The other would say: do you know how cartoons are made? I can show you, go and get some paper.

As usual Donna wasn't really listening. Is it their eyes, can you tell by their eyes? she was saying.

Well, yeah, I suppose, their eyes too, I said. The difference, I was thinking, though I didn't want to say it, was that James would have played that card trick throwing them all round the room, and then, if he'd been there by himself, he would have helped you pick them up afterwards. And it wouldn't have been nearly as hilarious as it had been, after all, with Patrick watching smugly from the chair.

I wouldn't be able to tell even if they were sitting next to me one on either side, even if they were up as close as we are now, Donna said. She'd turned on her side towards me and I could feel her thick breathing; she was asthmatic and the dust under the bed was beginning to take hold. Are they inseparable? she breathed. Like us?

I pulled her further under, shifting on my back until we were right up against the rolled posters and the travel bags, and we listened to see if we could hear anybody anywhere near us in the house before I let her push my shirt up and hook her mouth on to me, running my hand encouragingly up and down her back whenever we'd stop and struggle for breath in what little room we had.

Was that how it was? That's how I remember it anyway. Us crammed into secret places, snatching at each other, trying grimly not to give ourselves away or let anyone hear. Two years of nowhere to go, of always looking for a place to be. The toilets of the pubs we went to under age, the jukebox rasping out Chrissie Hynde and the boys we'd gone there with waiting for us at the bar, girls always go to the toilets in twos. The dark car park at the carpet showroom behind the bus station before her last bus left to take her back home down the loch road.

What were we like? All innocence, all sweetness and lit anarchy. The slightest passing look or touch flaring between us like a struck match, the promise of something bigger, maybe big enough to torch the whole town. What a time. We've only just begun, don't you remember you told me you loved me baby, the Carpenters layered into soaring harmonies, and the jangling harmonies of those Abba hits and A-A-Afternoon Delight, fracturing without warning into X-Ray Specs and black-eyed Siouxsie, the Jam and the Damned, into being sixteen, seventeen, sharp knowing for the first time. All innocence, raw energy, practised irony, all of us. Catherine MacKenzie brought her Carpenters tape to school to prove that Karen Carpenter was singing "the best love songs are written with a broken a-arm." The rich drip drip of her voice, like fat off a roast. That. Is. Why. All the girls in town. Follow you. All around. Just like me. They long to be. The best place was under the stage in the school hall, good for lunchtimes and the half-hour or so after school, you could drag the hatch safely shut after you and nobody knew you were there; the whole drama club costume department to hide behind, the perfect spacious comfortable private dark warm place to set about testing the age of innocence in pure and breathless combining, until Lorraine Burns started going out with Paul Black and Paul knew about under the stage too. That was the first time we were nearly caught, trapped down there for over an hour behind a thin layer of chipboard listening to Lorraine and Paul thumping expertly about, both of us shaking, trying not to move in case they heard us, Donna so scared we'd be found that by the time we got out of there she was crying with fear, hardly able to breath anything more than a thick wheeze, and I had bitten the soft inside of my lip into a bloody mess. For several days after that we avoided each other, not speaking to each other, we didn't even dare look at each other when we passed in the corridor, both so terrified that somehow everybody would suspect, everybody would know, both, I think, just as terrified that we had found each other out, found out something about ourselves that we really didn't want to have to know.

I saw Karen Carpenter on a television show a couple of years ago, an old James Last repeat transmitted very late one night, and there she was, skeletal, smiling, singing a sweet jaunty song about remembering a telephone number; it was shocking to hear that voice, so full and so sure, coming out of the body of someone so very nearly a ghost.

Dear God, please pray for Karen Carpenter and let her into Heaven. When I was small those Russian cosmonauts landed safely back on the earth, but they were dead inside their space machine; they got added to the dear God list along with my mother, my grandparents in America and the other mysterious grandparents he could never be persuaded to tell us about. Dear God please pray for them and let them into Heaven. Though God knows why I thought God should pray for them. Dear God please pray for my mother, my granny and grandpa and my other grandparents, the Russian spacemen, the thirteen people killed on the Sunday in Northern Ireland, the artist Pablo Picasso, the hundred and eighteen people killed in the crash at Heathrow, the hundred and five people killed in Switzerland in the plane that hit the side of a mountain, and the actor who died who spoke through a hole in his throat because of cancer, and let them into Heaven, I put them all on the list, but the list got so long eventually that I had to just say "and all the other people who have died too" after immediate family members because I couldn't hold it all in my head. Then I stopped saying the prayer altogether. There was another air crash, near Paris. I was watching the news when it happened, I was picking at a patch I had ironed on to the thigh of my jeans, it was shaped like a speech bubble and had the word "ouch" written in it. The plane had come down in a place that was popular for picnickers. I wondered what it would be like if the three hundred and forty-four people who had died were all to be in my room that night when I went upstairs. All of them, pushed in together, standing blank and silent in there waiting for me, and, yes, the cosmonauts there too, swaying airlessly among the others, their big glassy space helmets marking them out in the crowd. I put the landing light on before I went upstairs. I checked with a quick look. The room was empty.

I asked one of the teachers at school, where we were taught our prayers and always to tell the truth because lying was wrong and that we were luckier than other people because we had Jesus *and* the Virgin Mary *and* the Pope, I went up to the table when we were supposed to be silent working on The Essentials of English, and said, Miss, if Adam and Eve hadn't sinned like they did and brought death into the world, then would they still be alive today, and all the people ever born all over the world? No no, she said, she went red, flustered, now you know that's not how it was Aisling, she said, but then she didn't go on to tell me how it was, she went back to counting the dinner money and told me to go and sit down. At home I told Patrick about it. He laughed. Ask her about the Big Bang, he said. Ask her about the Dead Sea Scrolls. I asked James instead. He took my hand and flattened out my fingers. Look at your fingernails, he said. Who else gave you fingernails just so you can scratch yourself when you're itchy? Who else gave tiny insects their wings and their digestive systems and their antennae? Stop worrying.

That big chested woman, primary six, mean as stone, posh Edinburgh trapped in backwoods Inverness and hating the snot, the smell of ten-year-olds, she's the one who dragged Bernard and Mary out to the front of the class, hauling him up out of his seat by the shoulder of his jumper and her by the arm, so small her fist went all the way round it. Holding hands! she said. She shook them both in front of the class. Now, she said, you can all have a good laugh at them. That's what they've done, they've gone and made themselves a laughing stock, you can laugh at them as much as you like. So we did, we all did, and when Mary started to laugh too she hit her hard across the back of the head, that'll teach you, she said.

Donna's house had plastic matting down over the carpets in the hall and up the stairs, and you had to take your shoes off if you were going into any room but the kitchen, where there were plastic mats down over the carpet tiles. Her father's butcher's shop was at the back of the house. He wasn't allowed to come in till he had stripped and showered in the yard, even in the winter. Her mother was very suspicious of me after she found out I was Catholic; I never knew why that should make her particularly suspicious, there were plenty of better reasons. Out at hers there was countryside and lochside to be lost in, it was generally safer, good and dark at the bus stop in the winter, good and deserted after the tourist traffic in the summer. We got quite careless, were almost caught a few times, still, that was part of the excitement of it in the end and we were soon pretty wise wherever we were, adept at flying to different sides of the room at the creak of a stair, expert at explaining ourselves away. It's when the thrill of the hiding got more exciting than anything else, that's when I began to get bored with Donna and she began to get fed up with me, that's when it was nearly over, when we had nothing more in common than the same adrenalin and lies.

She hated it when I was reading. She used to knock books out of my hands and send them skimming across the room. Once she took a cigarette lighter and set fire to the bottom of the book I was holding. Once I went to bed one night, opened the book I had by my bed and found she'd scrawled her name over and over in felt pen all up and down the margins of the pages I'd left it open at; it wasn't till I got near the end that I found she'd ripped the last pages out of it too. I shouted at her about it. She thought it was funny. She thought it was funny when I went around sounding off, as she put it, when there was the meltdown scare at the reactor in the States, she said I was beginning to get boring, going on and on about things, as if I could do anything about it anyway just by going on and on till everybody was blue in the face. I was having nightmares about it. She said that was just like me, making myself important with something that was happening millions of miles away and nothing to do with me in the first place.

She's a vet's assistant now. Married too, I don't know who. Donna in the smell of disinfectant, carefully shaving the belly of an unconscious cat, carefully tapping a syringe over the head of a frightened, patient dog, leaning down to tell some child with a scrabbly animal in a cardboard box full of airholes how to grind the tablets up. Probably her own child. Thin and wicked, coming towards me with her wide pretty mouth all mischief and guilt, getting away with it, daring me just as much as I dared her, further, more. Winding it up to breaking point, and still winding. Taunting each other in each other's arms about the boys we were going out with, better at it than you anyway, better than you any day of the week or the month or the year, swinging each other down and over, her nasal breathing in my ear, the mucous sound of first love. I'd know that breathing anywhere.

Like the time we went camping in her tent down the Aviemore road, supposed to be summer but we ended up in the same sleeping bag because we were so cold, keeping each other warm. I woke up cold in the middle of the night and she had her head out of the door of the tent, she heard me behind her and her arm, her hand held up, stopped me speaking, beckoned me to come and see. At first I couldn't make out anything but then I saw the shapes moving in the dark. Deer, all round us, nosing the grass, nosing the air, we could see the one right in front of us moving its jaw gently up and round, the black liquid of its eye calm, and Donna, hayfever, cleared her throat, she had to, and in one movement they were all off, like birds, darting together in different directions. In the morning I was washing in the river, the sun was out but the water was freezing, so cold it made me catch my breath, I remember it was like I was feeling coldness for the first time, I was singing and splashing, birds were singing everywhere above me, I was watching the leaves above me moving in the sun and then I was throwing stones and bits of stick into the water, the noise and the cold of it coming back at me, and I was whirling around, heaving up great heavy rocks and throwing them as far as I could, standing up to my thighs in the water, throwing clear water round and above my head with my arms, Donna there behind me on the shore laughing at me, shouting, you're mad, Ash, you're fucking mad, girl.

But there was that last spring we had when it was so cold that all the flowers were late; the crocuses when they did open were killed off or stunted by the frost. There were white lines round our boots from the wet and the salt on the roads. We were walking along the canal up towards the weir in a freezing fog, we could see the footpath just ahead of us but we couldn't see where we were going or where we'd been, Donna in one of those foul silent moods, her hands shoved in her jacket and her shoulders hunched and round, walking just ahead of me, primed to shatter. I was trying to help, I was saying, still, it's you and me that's it, isn't it, I mean, I like him, and I know you like Ian and everything, but it's you that's real, that really matters, for me I mean, she stopped, she looked at me with white eyes, she turned away and in a split second had turned back and hit me, hard, across the forehead and the eye, she was shouting, you're mad, you're fucking mad, you think the world owes you a living, you're off your head, you've no chance, you fucking cunt, no fucking chance, just shut up, shut up. Me stunned, held in air, then it all speeding up and I was hitting her too, smashing my arm down on the hand coming up to punch me again. I hit her so hard the muscles in her hand and wrist froze, she had to go to casualty to have them checked. We went up to the hospital on the bus, sitting as close together as we could on the front seat at the top, her with her good hand warm in mine inside my duffelcoat. Her mother came to pick her up. She told her mother she'd slipped on ice and landed on her arm. I told her mother someone had hit me with a badminton racquet at PE.

I refused a lift home, I went home by myself in the dark. My father was there for the first time in three days. He was sitting in the living-room, slumped in his chair in the tv light with no other lights on. Good God, he said when he came through to the kitchen. What happened to your eye? He went to touch my head, I flinched.

Someone hit me with. Someone hit me, I said.

He sat down, he was looking at me. I hope you hit him harder, he said.

Her, I said. And I did. I'm not proud of it.

Well, thank God for that, he said.

I caught sight of the worried look on his face, it made me laugh. For what, I said, that I hit her harder or that I'm not proud of it?

He laughed too. Both, he said. What do you want for tea, Ash, I could go down to the Chinese if you want?

Brilliant, I said.

I was feeling a bit better for some reason. I went to look at my eye in the mirror. It was a beauty, she'd hit me a real beauty. I fingered it, impressed, wincing away from my own touch.

Donna's arm was in a bandage for quite a while, my eye was black for nearly a week, and the next time we had the chance to sleep together we were both shaken by how good it was, better than it had ever been, it was all I could do to keep quiet. I found afterwards I'd left teeth marks deep in my own hand.

Spring came, and summer was coming round, and another autumn would come after that, and then it would be winter and the hills would be whited out again. I sat on the window ledge and looked out. All the urgency had gone. The tips of the branches of the trees had lost their swollen points, split into the beginnings of this year's leaves. It was the way of it, I was watching things fall into place. I knew.

I threw my book across the room and scowled at the mirror. My arms dropped by my sides and I hung there in front of myself. The haunting possibilities. I shook my head. Something was beyond me. I couldn't see what it was, how to get to it. Something was slipping past, barely sensed, the vague outline of it gliding down the stairs and through the shut front door, goodbye. Since the day we had clawed so hopelessly at each other in the fog, something wouldn't leave me alone, something or somebody was always at my heels wherever I went, whatever I did, or was it just ahead of me, mocking my moves before I even made them. I sat crosslegged on my bed. The small child with the insolent eyes stared back at me. The girl swinging her legs off the top of the high wall, waiting for me to tell her to jump off, amusement on her face, scorn, of course she'd land on her feet, what was I waiting for? The girl with her eyes over the top of that book I'd hurled against the wall, she'd been there only two minutes ago and already she was lost, fading. That one, crosslegged on the other side of the mirror, silent, frowning, waiting for me to tell her something, anything. All the likenesses. Sometimes when I was alone in the house and it was late, the others, the ones I was really frightened of, would come and settle at the bottom of the bed, the selves that didn't have faces yet or shapes, their eyes trapped and sealed shut inside the skin, small black x's where their mouths should be, like two stitches, one sewn over the other.

Then summer. The exams almost over, grass on the playing field where the mud tracks had been, classes half empty, then hardly any classes, no point in turning up to them so close to the holidays, we took to hanging around in the prefects' room, which is where I was the day Shona was reading the newspaper and saying out loud, as she sat there and the sun was coming in through the skylight and hitting the graffiti scratched into the table we'd painted and Sandra was pushing at her hair with a hairbrush and looking in the mirror and Donna was pouring hot water into a Pot Noodle tub and Ruth was toying with the tuning of her guitar against the noise of the radio and my friend Rory was cleaning under his nails with the end of a teaspoon and Susan was fishing something out of her locker and Jenny was waiting for the kettle so she could make herself a coffee and Neil was building a pyramid of dirty mugs and Lorna was helping him and Alan was writing something on the table and Shirley and some other people I can't remember were all sitting round, like I was, reading—and Shona was rattling the newspaper, holding it up, saying out loud:

God, that's disgusting. That's one of the most revolting things I've ever read. I think I'm going to be sick.

Shona and I, friends since the first day of secondary school. I had been there when her sister had been swinging round the lamp post with her plastic umbrella in the thunderstorm singing I'm singing in the rain, just singing in the rain, and the plastic handle had snapped and her sister had fallen in the puddle.

When Shona had broken her leg on a skiing trip I took her a tray of fruit, when I'd been in hospital for my tonsils she'd brought me one. We'd composed a letter to David Soul together, she'd had a crush on him. I'd written it and she'd drawn the Love Is couple at the top and in the spaces between the paragraphs. In second year we decided we'd be cartoonists together when we grew up, words me, pictures her. For the last couple of years now that we were prefects we'd run a scam where if we didn't want to sit through a particular class we'd come with a "note" from the secretary, please Sir, Aisling McCarthy's/Shona Green's wanted at the office. When she fancied my brothers I'd made sure they were in when she came round. When her mother had been ill in hospital, unconscious with something they couldn't identify, and she was crying in the school corridor, I'd taken her into the toilets and cleaned her up and waited with her. When Robbie took me to that party and then snogged someone else on the stairs she was the one who slapped him across the face for me and took me home, sobering me up before she'd let me go in. Invisible links like these were running between all of the people in the room that day, like they always are, like thin strands of light you couldn't see but you knew were there nevertheless.

What's disgusting? someone said.

This tennis player at Wimbledon's had this relationship with this woman, right? Shona said.

No! said Rory. That's disgusting.

No, it is, though, *she*'s a woman too. I mean, they both are, they're poofs, well, you know, queer. But it's worse than that. It says here they got married and everything.

Through the room the sound of disgust; someone made the sound of being sick, someone else giggled. I didn't look up from my book. The moment passed, we went on with what we were doing. Shona went on reading out the article. I didn't look up from my book. I mean, she said, can you imagine? With another woman? I was staring at my book, not looking up from my book and my ears were burning, I could feel them reddening, and a small voice from somewhere inside my throat before I could stop it was saying, well, maybe, maybe they like each other.

My ears were burning, my whole head was burning with the space I'd made round myself, but nothing had happened, then I wasn't sure I'd said anything, maybe I hadn't, maybe it hadn't been me who'd said it, maybe I'd just imagined it and nobody had said it at all, and Shona said, clear and loud, maybe who likes who, Ash?

I cleared my throat at exactly the same time as Donna across from me was clearing hers, I glanced to see but she was looking down and away, stirring her spoon deep in the plastic tub.

Maybe the tennis player and her friend, the voice said.

Silence. The radio, blurting on. The little sounds of people who are pretending not to listen.

It's perfectly okay for people to like whoever they want to like, the voice went on. It doesn't hurt anything. It doesn't hurt anybody.

Yeah, but it's *perfectly* disgusting, Shona said. Lorna joined in. Yeah, she said, and they got married, yugh, it's ugh, horrible! She was laughing, and Shona was saying, yeah, it's really unnatural, eh?

No it's not, the voice said, and it was coming from me. Not unnatural, I said. Just unexpected. It's just a different kind of natural.

I've never heard such rubbish in all my life, Sandra said, looking into her own eyes at the mirror. You can't have a different kind of natural, there's no such thing. It's, like, either natural or it's not. And it's not. And I think it's *really* disgusting when men do it. It's really violent. I don't even want to think about it. It should be illegal.

Neil was watching me through the piled-up mugs. Does Sandy

know, Ash? he said. I'll have to be telling him, it wouldn't be fair, now, to keep him in the dark about it. Or maybe the two of you have some sort of wee arrangement and there's something Sandy should be telling us about?

Everybody laughing. Alan was saying, I quite fancy it. No, I mean two women, two women, not two blokes. I'm not a fucking poof! Show me two women and I'll show you I'm not a fucking poof.

Laughing. Shona not laughing, her face full of loathing, not looking at me. I think it's really repulsive. It makes me want to be sick to even think about it, her mouth said; she turned the page of her paper; beyond her I could just see, round the side of my book, Donna staring at the floor.

Well, don't think about it then. The voice, not me this time. Jenny Timberberg slammed a cup of something hot down in front of me, squared herself in front of my book so I couldn't not look at her, and went on. You want milk in it, Ash?

She sat down. I'm with Ash, she said, and ignored the faces and the noises Neil was making. She knocked Shona's paper with the flat of her hand. If any rich tennis player who can play like she can play wants to marry me, I don't care what sex she is, she said, and picked up a magazine, fanned through the pages of it, hummed along with something on the radio.

A pause. Then—quiet, reasonable, the last word:

People aren't meant to act like that. Otherwise we wouldn't be made like we are. It's not natural. It's not normal. It's really sick.

That was Donna.

I shut my book. Jenny Timberberg winked at me. My mouth was smiling, I could feel it. I said, I think I'll go outside and get some sun. I could see glances exchanging all round the room, the flicker of a grin, the raising of an eyebrow, Rory smiling a vague embarrassed smile at me. When I shut the door I waited for a moment outside it. Neil's voice. Watch out girls, youse'd better watch your backs. No, I mean, you better watch your fronts. The explosion of laughter. I took my book and my cup of coffee and went to sit on the wall.

My hand was shaking so much I couldn't bring the coffee up to my mouth without spilling it. I shrugged my jacket off and let it fall on to the ground behind me, I rolled up my shirtsleeves, I undid my top buttons, let my head sink back, shut my eyes. When I opened them, Ruth was sitting beside me.

Ruth. I didn't know her very well, we had hardly ever even spoken to each other. Small and dark and pale, like a frail Victorian child in a painting. Her mother and father were born-again Christians; everybody knew she hadn't been allowed to watch David Attenborough's *Life on Earth,* and had been excepted from Section Six at science in first year, the section about the sexual organs of plants. She was good at the guitar, could play Leo Sayer songs and the song about the snowbird, spread your tiny wings and fly away, and take the snow back with you where it came from on that day. She played it when you'd ask her to, and she played her guitar for hymns at the Christian Union meetings. I braced myself, I thought she'd come to tell me the good news, that I could be saved.

Ash, she said, I just wanted to say.

Round brown eyes, doe's eyes, scared and gentle.

I just wanted to say. I agree with you. I mean, I think you were right. To say that. I mean, what you said. That people should be able to like who they want to like. I think that was right. I mean, I think that was really brave. To have said like that.

I smiled. I was shaking and smiling. I let my eyes close again with my head in the sun. God, Ruth, I said, isn't it a really lovely day?

Yeah, it is, she said.

It's such a beautiful day. I love it when it's hot like this, I said.

She sighed. Me too, she said.

Ghosts and ghosts and ghosts. Ghosts and dust, the dust of it all I'm disturbing up here. Sore, like touching dust on the wing. Dust in the head, black dust crossed on the forehead. Remember man that thou art dust and unto dust thou shalt return. Many happy returns. I'm tired. I'll finish this.

School nearly over like it was, the rumour didn't spread as far and as fast as it would have done under normal circumstances. Normal. Though some small boys did throw stones and shout names at me when I was walking home a couple of days later, this may or may not have been connected. A whole group of people stopped talking to me. A whole other group started. Sandy, with whom I'd gone to the pub a couple of times, phoned me and told me he'd always wondered why I was frightened of sex. I told him I wasn't, not that he was ever going to get the chance to find out, and we hung up on each other. I phoned Donna to let her off the hook. She said, hello? I said, it's me, it's okay, it's finished. She said, if you tell anyone, Ash, you're dead. I said, you're dead already Donna, bye bye, and put the phone down. I felt really good for an hour, then I felt terrible, cried myself to sleep. Then I was all right.

And literally the next morning, the next adventure. A car drew up alongside me, a 2CV, inside Miss Carroll, home economics, and Miss Robertson, one of the PE teachers. Miss Carroll called me to the window; she said, would you like a lift into school, Aisling? She reached to open the back door for me.

Tight Miss Robertson in the passenger seat. She liked going out with sixth-year boys, taking her pick every year. She was also well known for coming into the girls' showers on the first day you had to take one, and standing watching; the showers were open plan. On our first day, with her small eyes on us, she had turned a full circle pivoting on her heel, the sneer on her face even more pronounced than usual.

So what're you doing with yourself these days Aisling? she said from the front without turning round. I was hearing something about you the other day.

Nothing much, nothing different, I said.

Yes, different, she said, that's the word, that's something like what I heard.

We were driving past the main gate. Miss Carroll braked suddenly, throwing us all forward. I'll let you off here, Fiona, Miss Carroll said. She drove me to the back gate and reached over her seat to open the door when I couldn't work out which lever to press. I was about to shut it, and she said, um, Aisling, I was wondering. Are you doing anything this summer?

Yes, I think I'm working in my father's shop, Miss, I said, he has the fitted kitchen showroom, you know, McCarthy's Kitchen Ware, on Academy Street.

Oh, right, I know, she said. It's just that, well, I'm doing some work of my own on my cottage this summer, my cottage in Skye, well, for most of July anyway, and I'm actually in the middle of looking for someone to help out, you know, cook and things, and help with the painting, and the garden, that sort of thing, and your name came into my head, but if you're already doing something—

Her face hidden behind her long hair. She looked young suddenly. She was young, she must only have been about the age I am now. Her hand on the door, about to pull it shut. I said quickly, the thing is, you know, Miss, I'm a really terrible cook.

Well now, she said, looking ahead, thoughtful, serious, we could always work on that.

No need to mention it to anyone else or anything, she said, a very informal arrangement. Between you and me. Yes, Miss, I said. I packed my father's *Penguin Cookery Book*. By the end of that summer I had learned how to make almost everything in it. She taught me lobster sauce, pork chops with sage and apples, apple dumplings. Double crusted rabbit pie, pancakes, rock cakes, all sorts of cakes; how to tell when cakes were cooked in the middle, how to make a lot of things with kippers and shrimps. She was from Buckie, Miss Carroll, and she taught me a lot about cooking fish, and a song about what to do with herring bones, of all the fish that live in the sea, the herring it is the fish for me. Green salad, Greek salad, salad with tuna. Tongue salad. How to pressure-cook, all the French cooking terms. By the end of the summer I knew how to fix tiles on the roof and patch leaks, I knew how to repair skirting boards. I knew a lot about spirit levels. I knew the melting method, the rubbing-in method, the creaming method, I knew Miss Carroll's first name, it was Judith. I knew how to make her say mine with the sound of it like the hiss of water hitting red embers. I was getting listless, I was eating too much. I was lying with my eyes wide open at night with Miss Carroll asleep on my rounded stomach and wondering if this was all there was to know.

I remember that summer was wet and humid, its skies low and grey; when it wasn't raining it looked like it was going to. After it there was the prospect of one more school year, or of begging my father for a job, or there were full-time jobs on offer in the Littlewoods cafeteria. At school they said I should stay on, leave next year, go to university, further my education. I should think of something I'd like to do with my life. Autumn, the leaves and the light falling, Miss Carroll throwing me meaningful glances across the car park. I began to walk to school a different way in the mornings. When I'd get there Ruth would be waiting for me, sadness round her like an aura. Autumn, winter, cold.

Then I woke up in the middle of February and there was a thick letter on the mat. The writing on the envelope was fountain pen ink, neat, round, light blue. The paper was rich and rough to the touch.

I know it off by heart.

Ash: ash, n., a well-known timber tree (Fraxinus excelsior, or
  other species) of the olive family; its wood white, tough,
  and hard; an ashen spear-shaft or spear—adj., ashen—
  ash-key, the winged fruit of the ash; ash-plant, an ash
  sapling—mountain ash, the rowan tree; prickly ash, the
  toothache tree (Xanthoxylum); quaking ash, the aspen.
  Aesc, esche, askr. Ash, ash, n., the dust or remains of
  anything burnt; volcanic dust, or a rock composed of it;
  plural, remains of a human body when burnt.

Ground ash, wild ash, mountain ash.

The warlike beech, the ash for nothing ill. (Spenser)
The ash is the greatest and best of all trees. Its branches
  spread over the whole world and even reach above heaven.
  (Mallet's Northern Antiquities*)*
That body, where against
My grained ash an hundred times hath broke
And scarr'd the moon with splinters. (Shakespeare)
The hot ashes commonly set the house on fire. (Lady
  Montagu)
My heart is within me
As an ash in the fire. (Swinburne)
The mortal disappears, Ash to ashes, dust to dust.
  (Tennyson)
Whole Kingdoms laid in Ashes. (Addison)
Al men ar eird ande alse. (the last word means ash, Ash)
Lord, what shall Earth and Ashes do?
We would adore our Maker too. (Wesley)
The sweet blue eyes—the soft, ash-coloured hair. (Arnold)

By ashen roots the violets blow. (Tennyson again)
Wait soul until thine ashen garments fall! (Elizabeth Barrett
   Browning)

volcanic ash, black ash, ashes of roses.

ashling—a young ash sapling or tree.
Aisling—a vision, dream poem.

My grained Ash,
are you running like sparks through the stubble?

I carried it around with me all day. By afternoon I'd decided. I went to Miss Carroll's room, I could hear her through the door, she was teaching a first-year class how to make a full English breakfast. I knocked on the glass rectangle, waved goodbye, was round the corner and down the stairs before she'd have time to get to the door.

My father was at work. I left him a note, DEAR DAD I'M OFF NOW I'LL SEE YOU WHEN I SEE YOU BUT NOT IF YOU SEE ME FIRST I'LL KEEP IN TOUCH. I put a change of clothes in a bag, caught the bus to the bus station, took the bus to Edinburgh and waited in the Edinburgh bus station for the overnight bus that was going to the place on the postmark of her letter.

Dear Dad I'm off now, I'll keep in touch. I left it on the fridge, where I usually left the list of groceries we needed. Block capitals, like the note I wrote, This Message Is From Inverness On June 24 1973, folded up and pushed with a stick into a bottle, the top screwed as tight as I could, thrown as far as I could into the canal. Watching it float to the middle, it was the first day of the summer holidays, the days empty and long, the longest of days stretching ahead, anything could happen. I thought it would maybe reach Russia, America. I thought of someone finding it and me reading about it in a newspaper when I was grown up, in my teens, as old, say, as my brothers were. It's probably still down there somewhere in the rocks on the floor of the canal, with the other sunk things, the broken bits of glass, the rusty skeletons of prams and bikes.

Christ. It's half-past two.

Ink all over my fingers from this pen.

SO over the border, soaring over it in the dark. The axle grinding in the wheel below your seat. The sea, huge, rolling down the coast somewhere out there to the left, swelling in its socket. A new country, invisible round the dim orange light of the bus moving through it, and you in it, the roar of its engine, small firefly buzz between the vast darknesses. Different accents at the service stations giving you your change. All your money in small notes that you have to uncrumple out of your pocket each time. Then the middle of the night again and the grass banks of the motorway, colourless.

The driver looked you over when you got on; is that the only bag you've got? he said when he checked your ticket. Memorising your face, you must have looked like a runaway. Further than you'd ever been by yourself before, you didn't even mind sitting in the smoking section. Your arms hugging your knees, feet drawn up on the seat. A town bypassed, and another. Thinking you were wise to it all, that you knew where you were going, a bit of something broken off and whittled sharp, supple and green, then strung and flying, shot like that and speeding through the air to somewhere, or other.

It's ten past six in the morning. I can't sleep, didn't sleep all night, my skin's pins and needles and my body's all bones. My eyes wouldn't stay closed. I was cursing the dawn chorus, then I thought how stupid it was to do that, like cursing flowers for opening. I got up and watched the night going instead. The crossover point of dark and light is blue. Then, hold your breath, a deep grey, and we're into unspectacular today. Heavy cloud that could go either way, it might rain, it might clear. I can hear my father moving about in the kitchen. I hope I didn't wake him.

It's Thursday. I am already halfway through my time here. Whatever it is I came for, whatever it is I'm waiting for, it hasn't happened yet, at least I don't think it has. All that's happened so far is that my chin has erupted in spots the like of which I haven't seen since I was fifteen. It must be the water. Proof that I'm definitely here, even if all night I've been back there, moving between the places curled and taut on the seat, rain soundless across the windows of the bus and her letter light blue and white in my inside pocket, the stiff end of it tucked under and rubbing against my neck. Her letter, no address, all part of the game I hadn't even realised I was playing. The smiling girl at the circus in the spangling waistcoat, her silver top hat cocked at that raffish Dietrich angle as she douses with a flourish the torch she's used to set the fuse alive to blow the other, still smiling at the crowd from the o of the cannon's mouth, straight into the net. So gorgeously cheap. Here I came, bowling down the coast of the country like it was my own private banister. No fear.

Because in telling me my name like she did, in letting me know what it meant, my friend Amy carved her own name in me like a scar. After that, every time she looked my way, and every time she didn't, though I didn't know or notice, something was branding her deeper into me. If I were to snap open now at an arm, a leg, anywhere on my body, I could look down and there would be the a and the m and the y of her, visceral and elastic, stretching with the flesh; look in the bones, the cross-section of the honey-comb marrow, and there it is again written all through me, sweet and sticky, a souvenir from Amy.

The Frankenstein game. We make something of someone else, then we're surprised when we come home one day and it's gone out by itself for a wander around the neighbourhood. So we lock the door, angry, disappointed, how dare it. Then we get worried. Only we alone know how dangerous our creation is. So we reach for the rifle. After the previews of *Lipstick Prophecies,* after the full houses of people who came to see it, I was freaked, I was saying to Malcolm how weird it was to watch an audience watching you, how weird to see them in the act of peeling the surface off you, I mean, peeling God knows what off you and taking it away with them in their heads. That's what it comes down to, people snatching at surfaces, he said, so nothing, and so all there is.

Frightening. All making it up as we go along, and making up other people too, to fill our own gaps, meet our own needs. Made gothic by it, hanging thinly round the house that's locked us out, tapping little ice-cold hands like branches on the window, calling, it's me, it's me, let me in, I'd lost my way on the moor! Pathetic. I'm too tired to be writing this now, no sense, non sense. Where was I? I was in England.

And not just in England, but the epitome of England. Flags flying off turrets, the land of *Blue Peter* and the Royal Family and *Sunday Times* colour supplement advertisements for glossy Barbours. The south east. The place of learning. The sun was out, it was the middle of February and my jacket was hanging open. The air that morning was as mild as April. The money. The smart clothes. The light. The expensive shops. The bookshops. Bookshop after bookshop, a place where bookshops belonged as if naturally, as if they were a special culture grown there; I lost count of the bookshops on my first walk through the streets. Building after building was etched with beauty against the sky. A flat land, its light and sky spread like it was near the sea; the streets filled with people my age calling to each other like rare birds, I'd never heard anything like it. Tabithas, Ophelias, Justins and Julians, Jocastas and Finolas, books under their arms in the open air, all going somewhere terribly important. I had stepped off the bus on to a different planet; I stood on the cobbles in the middle of the road outside a kind of castle, a palace, or was it a huge church, stained glass like that, and watched the bicycles pass and pass. A Midas town, I was seeing it turn the casual people who touched its streets into gold. I watched them, they glinted past. The virgin shine of the place. I walked across a bridge by a river with no rubbish in it. There were willows. They were weeping. There were signs up saying Keep Out and Members Only. There were cows grazing in the distance by another beautiful bridge. Somewhere a perfect church bell was ringing. I was finding it hard to breathe. The river water looked putrid, but there were ducks on it with fluffed-out ducklings. I held on to the rail, saw my reflection down there wavering between the green.

The place of education. New things for me to learn. Like, that near can actually be further than you ever imagined. That cold can mean hot. Nothing can mean something, something can mean nothing. Even words can mean nothing, and as soon as they're said or thought or written down they can immediately mean the opposite of what they seem to say. There's magic on the borders where the opposites meet, and there's bloody war. The reflection I was looking at, I thought it was just a reflection, the play of light on water, but no. I was here and so was she.

When I finally tracked Amy down I think it was more by fluke than by fate, though it isn't always easy to tell the difference between the two, the meant-to-be, the throw-away. Anyway, Amy was never in the pretty streets I walked along; she never passed by when I sat on cold walls watching for her or hung around in urine-smelling historic passageways waiting for a glimpse of her. It wasn't until I was sitting on the floor of a bookshop late one afternoon, I was keeping warm and the carpet was thick, I was thumbing through the guide books and looking randomly at the pictures of all the different colleges, and I found it near the back of a book, a building that looked like a wedding cake. The photographs of it were all of girls, like it was a big Victorian girls' school, its grounds and gardens carefully arranged round it like a long skirt. A girl was hard at work in a spartan-looking room, two lumpy girls were walking along a path, one wearing an anorak, both carrying books. A girl sat in a library, surrounded in books. Five rows of girls wearing silly fluffy hoods and black capes smiled for the photographer.

I must have made some kind of noise out loud; the man at the cash desk looked down at me as if I had just spat something unpleasant out by his foot. When the man was busy serving someone, I ripped the map out of the back of the book and crushed it into my back pocket, pushed through the doors into the street. Outside I took the map out and tried to work out where I was. It was dark cold, raining. I was dim with hunger. My money had run out three days back.

A Shone. That was Amy's name, wasn't it? I found a wooden door with her name on it, and I knocked.

A door opened to one side of me and a girl came out. I don't think she's in, she said. She would have answered her door by now if she were. You've been knocking for more than ten minutes. I'm trying to work. Do you want to borrow a piece of paper? You could leave her a message.

She was the first person who had spoken to me for over a week, and when I spoke back it was a shock to hear my own throaty voice.

Just a moment, she said, and shut the door.

She opened it again. I was holding on to the wall. Are you all right? she said. You don't look very well.

When I came to, I was in an enormous room on the floor and she was holding half a glass of water above me. My face, my hair, my shoulders were all wet. Are you all right? she said. What college do you come from? Do you want me to phone anyone?

No, no, I said. I scrambled up but the room was swaying. I sat down on the floor again. The girl made me a cup of black coffee. When she saw me looking at the biscuits by her kettle she jumped up and brought them over, putting the packet by my hand then slipping away across to the other side of the room again.

We sat on opposite sides of the room and I ate her biscuits one after the other until the packet was empty, and she watched me with her arms folded and her legs tucked under herself. Strange in her room, there were suitcases with clothes in them spread across the floor, books in boxes like she had just arrived or was just leaving. I asked her; oh no, she said, we can live here for all three years, can't you at your college? I told her I was Amy's sister and that I was making a surprise visit. I'm a first year; she said, the person next door is a second year, I don't know her.

She held the door open for me and gave me the piece of paper to leave the message, but when she had shut me outside again I realised I didn't have a pen. I stood for a long time until I saw that other doors in the corridor had paper pads and pens on strings tied to their doorknobs. I broke the string on one of the pens. But I couldn't think what to write. I was here. Guess what it's me, came to visit you but you were out. In the end I folded the piece of paper, blank, and pushed it under Amy's door.

There was a bathroom and a big kitchen further down the corridor. There was half a loaf on the sideboard and there were two opened tins of beans and some brown sludge in a bowl in the fridge. I locked the door, ran a bath, sat in the steam eating the beans and the brown stuff with my fingers. I hadn't eaten this much for nearly three days. Someone's underwear was drying over the boiler in an airing cupboard; it fitted. I wiped the mirror clean with my hand. The map I had stolen would tell me how to walk to where the motorway started. I'd get my things and hitch back up north again. Or better; I could go to London and make my fortune. I dried myself as well as I could on a bathmat and the roller towel.

Fluke, fate, fate, fluke. Either way, no escape. I was walking shivering through the damp streets at the back of her college, and I saw the notice on the door up the steps. A handwritten sign. I walked past it, then I went back, and stopped, and read it. It said: Katherine Mansfield Women and Literature Seminar 7:30 Carmen's Room (14) all welcome women only. That's it, I thought, that'll be it. My finger on the bell by the number 14, and a wild laughing feeling in my stomach and rising like bile at the back of my throat.

A girl with short orange hair opened the door. She was wearing a knitted cardigan with safety pins holding it together, and she had a safety pin through her ear. Hi! she said, is it for the Katherine Mansfield? It's nearly over but come in anyway, I think there's still some tea in the pot, it should still be warm. We're talking about celibacy tonight, anything to put off reading *Clarissa*, I've got an essay for tomorrow, I mean, it's brilliant, it's all about rape, but I just can't face it, do you know what I mean?

I was looking past her, scanning the room. Dark, small, warm, the window all condensation. Seven or eight people were crammed into it, one of them earnestly reading something aloud from a book, someone else knitting. The others listening and looking into space ahead of them, looking at the floor, looking at the girl reading, except—yes, Amy, who was sliding from the armchair she was in on to the floor and saying with the slightest movement of her wrist and her finger, sit here, shh.

Amy, totally unsurprised. She asked me later in the pub (we always go to the pub afterwards, it's a little reward for being serious, the girl with the orange hair told me on the way, me looking down in alarm at her arm through mine; she bought me a drink when everybody was fumbling with little amounts of change from bags and purses and buying their own and she noticed I wasn't buying one for myself, what would you like? she asked). Amy sitting across from me, the same Amy as before but her hair different, tied somehow, and her clothes different, even neater, all in black, and her eyes different, what was it? and her shape, thinner, smaller than I remembered. Sitting there with the detachment of a cat, asking, and where are you staying? *And* like that at the beginning of her sentence, like we were in the middle of a conversation, like we'd been talking for hours. I told her about how I'd found this great place to live and broken in the back window; her eyes lit up.

There's nobody using it, nobody in it, it's all boarded up, I said. It looks like nobody's been near it for years, it's all rags hanging off rafters, dust, space. I didn't even know where I was, you know, what it was, till I kind of fell on to it, it's so dark in there, I came through a door and there I was in the, wings I suppose is what they are, there was this big space all round me, I got up and I was walking across a huge space, there was nothing in it, I could just make out these sort of curved crescent shapes out ahead of me and then I realised they were, like, the balconies, I was trying to see where I was, and I nearly fell off the end of it, the stage I mean, I was out on it, and Amy it's all echoes, every time you take a step you hear it again in front of you, it's really dark, no wonder I nearly fell off, the next morning there were all these strands of, strings of, just made out of dust caught round my shoes, I had to pull them all off and clean my shoes with grass.

I stopped myself speaking and I took a breath. I could feel my face reddening.

Staying in a theatre, and illicitly, how very like you, she said. Amy's voice sometimes, if a rose could speak, that's its voice, clipped, velvet, deep-tinged red. The intonation that makes things how they are just by saying so, quite, yes, quite. I don't think I'd heard my own voice till then. Rough, coarse, unfeminine, brave and different. I was staying in a theatre, illicitly, it was very like me.

I've just worked it out, you're Scotch! a girl sitting next to me said. She had a perm that made her face look very small, she had been talking about French writers, pronouncing their names with gusto. I was wondering why I couldn't understand what you were saying, she said, and then I worked it out. I love Scotland! I love the people.

Yeah, it's a great place, I said. I turned back to Amy's eyes. I left you a message where you live, I said, I put it under your door.

Thank you, she said.

There's no running water, I said, and there's all this old scenery up against the walls, and there are rats behind it, you can hear them. But I like it, and it's better than the park, I was sleeping in this park for two nights before I found it, it's better than that, eh?

Yes, I should imagine it's much less chilly, she said nodding, then she turned her head away and was talking, preoccupied, to the person next to her about something else, something I couldn't hear.

We go up there every year, the girl sitting next to me said. We go to Gleneagles, it's glorious. My father always calls Scotland his favourite leisure centre, she laughed, and choked on her drink, put it down on the table and put her hand to her throat. Awful, isn't he? she said when she could speak again. He loves it, wonderful for sport. Edinburgh is lovely too, full of such very good places to eat.

The girl with the sullen eyes sitting next to her agreed with her, and they asked me what I had seen at the Festival. Of course probably absolutely everything, coming from up there after all, the perm girl said.

I'm not from Edinburgh, I said.

The girl turned to talk to the one next to her. We go up every year but I still can't understand the Scottish accent, she said. Though I do love it. She beamed vacantly at me. The other looked at me as if something was my fault.

I leaned across the table. Amy was gathering her things together, putting a purse into a bag. I'll take you, I said to her, would you like to come?

She was putting her arms carefully into her coatsleeves. Perhaps not tomorrow, she said, or the next day. I would have to check my diary. But I'd love to see your theatre, yes, thank you for asking me.

Oh, are you in theatre? Brilliant, the girl called Carmen said. Meet me tomorrow at eleven for coffee. I'll be in the buttery.

The buttery. I was feeling dizzy, light-headed again. Where I came from, a buttery was a kind of bread roll.

Carmen's hair was always changing colour; by the next day it was brown, and she looked groomed, glassy, like so many others in the place that I wouldn't have recognised her if she hadn't thrown herself into the seat opposite me, lighting a cigarette with the flame on her lighter shooting so high it nearly caught her fringe. Think of Carmen, always working at three in the morning to finish something, the cleverest girl at her school before she came, she was going to be a famous clarinettist but then she got there and there were so many other people who played it as well as she did that she gave it up. I went to a comprehensive too, she told me, squeezing my arm, that gives us everything in common, Ash. Actually we had nothing in common, but I liked her very much. I stay up working all night most nights, she said, come and see me whenever you're passing. Bright then dark like a lightbulb that's about to blow. I'm spiralling, that's all, I'm just spiralling, she'd be saying through tears when something had to be handed in or some floppy-haired boy she was sleeping with hadn't turned up or had got too boring; two suicide attempts while I knew her, both hushed up by her college, there must be hundreds like that, there always seemed to be girls like Carmen around, so high, shining, brittle. She threw herself off a bridge, broke her ankle when she landed on it, wouldn't answer her door when we came round with flowers. Thank you, you're so kind, I'm so ashamed, she said through the wood. I saw her that first spring, she came running across the road with her arms full of daffodils, so many she could hardly hold them all, they were spilling behind her as she ran. Look, she called to me, you wouldn't believe it, they were about to shut the stall for the night and the woman sold me every last one for just fifty pence! She gave me some of them, quite a lot; I took them to Amy's, we put them in vases all round her room, she was pink with pleasure, she said I wondered if you'd remember. It was her birthday, I hadn't known. I sat in her old armchair chewing the petals of one of the daffodils, with Amy leaning against the chair, curled and reading. Carmen was always doing me inadvertent good turns.

Not just inadvertent good turns. She lent me money when I hadn't any. She knew the people who gave me the job (they actually prefer people who haven't got degrees to work there, she said, her eyes like the dots on exclamation marks), she always seemed to know people with spare rooms in their houses. The onl

7:30 p.m.

I had to stop. My father called me downstairs. When I went into the kitchen he'd made breakfast big enough for five people, bacon, mushrooms, sausages, he was frying eggs. I couldn't eat any of it. But when I was clearing the dishes I tried some of the bacon out of the pan and it was delicious. I was fishing one of the sausages out of the bin and he came in and nearly caught me. He had a pile of videos under his arm. What, eh, what are you going to do today, girl? he said.

He went into a huff, slammed the videos down on the sideboard. You're never out of that loft, he said. You're stopping here in my house and I can hardly even remember what you look like. You may as well be on the aeroplane already and halfway across the bloody world for Christ's sake.

I said, okay, I'd watch one.

They all had John Wayne in them. Eight hours of John Wayne, getting younger as the day went by, from the fat old drunk hero with the eyepatch like a pirate, dragging the girl up out of the snakepit away from the snakes and the bones, to the chiselled young handsome boy, the stagecoach rushing towards him like it can't not. And when he sets fire to his own ranch like he does in the film with James Stewart in it. Can't have the girl, so he doesn't want the house. Stupid thing to do. Made him even more of a hero.

It's been pouring it down since this morning. It still is. It was good to watch films with the rain outside; the musky smell of sitting in all day. The news at lunchtime was depressing; the *Herald of Free Enterprise* that sank and all the bodies in Belgium. It was good to watch John Wayne come through anything and everything on either side of it.

That girl Melanie is here again playing the piano. I think she might be something to do with the Barbara who made the curtains. She said she always comes round when she's over at her grandmother's. Her grandmother has a piano but she complains because she can't hear the television over the top of it and Mr. McCarthy doesn't mind. Tonight she's playing things out of her Cole Porter book. She's going to university if they can afford it, she says, she wants to be a lawyer and she's going to help fund her way through by playing in cafes and bars, and they like things like Cole Porter. I'd lived in London, hadn't I, was that really brilliant? I said it was good, but lonely and dirty and huge, and not so good if you didn't have much money, and the flat I'd stayed in had been a dump and was always getting broken into. Because Mr. McCarthy had said I'd stayed in, was it Oxford? No, it was the other place, I said. Oh, she said, but was it like on *Brideshead Revisited*? she wanted to know, she'd seen that last year, the first time it had been on she'd been too small but now she thought it was really good. Everybody in it was so beautiful, she liked Sebastian, it was so sad when that happened. I said that it was full of much more ordinary people; really, though, it was like everywhere, only concentrated. There were a lot of people who were beautiful or rich and a lot who were both of those things or neither and because of this were just completely off their heads.

Like drunk all the time like Sebastian? she said. No, not really, not usually, I said. More like it was a place for people to think they're special, different, better than other people. So you got a lot of people who were disappointed with themselves there, and at the same time a lot of people who never would be, no matter what.

I told her about one of the times that I'd been the only person on duty in the reading room. First there was the learned man who came up to the desk and showed me a photograph of Princess Diana in the newspaper. Look, he said, you can see right through her clothes. He sounded sensible and reasonable, like politicians sound on Radio Four. She's nothing but a slut, you know, he said, there are better girls than her serving burgers in the Wimpy Bar, you could get a better whore at Kings Cross. I decided I would just pretend he wasn't there. It worked; he began to pretend I wasn't there, that he'd been talking more to everybody in the room than to me. As he was leaving he leaned over the desk and said, I know what you are. I know all about you. I can tell by the way you talk.

No sooner had I got rid of him than I noticed the woman walking round and round the bookshelves, she was pulling telephone directories off the shelves then pushing them back on, she was quite calm but she was talking to herself. She sat down and she started crying into one of the directories, at first it was quiet crying, little sniffs, but it was getting louder and louder, I went over to ask her what the matter was and she said in a whisper, there's a dress I want, it's in Miss Selfridge, but they won't give me any money and I just can't have it. I gave her my handkerchief and suggested she go for a cup of tea, she apologised for making a noise, she was sorry, she said, she didn't mean to disturb anyone. Then a well-groomed boy came in, and when I told him someone else had the book he wanted out on loan he made a scene, slamming his fist down on the desk. I had to phone down for help with him. And when I was finishing, on my way out, there was the man complaining at the front desk because he had seen an Asian woman using the computers, that these facilities weren't provided for the likes of her, and that she was probably too stupid in any case to be able to use them. I tell you, I said to Melanie, it's this beautiful place, like you made up a place in your head, but that day I had had enough of it; I was standing across the road from beautiful chapel windows, light was coming through them sending this rich colour out into the dark, I thought if I went in and sat down I could relax a bit, unwind, forget the afternoon. But they wouldn't let me in to the chapel without paying. So I stood outside it instead. The stone of it. I wanted to take a pick-axe to it.

Melanie, wide-eyed, nodding. I work at B&Q, she said, we're

always getting mad people. People who shout at you because you're just a shop girl and they can. And the homeless people, because we stay open late, she said. They come in when it's cold and the British Rail men throw them out of the station. They're always asking for money. I never know what to do. One time one lady was in the kitchen showroom and she was, like, acting out making supper, pretending she was taking things out of the drawers, only pretending to, cause there wasn't actually anything in there for her to put out. The manager threw her out of the shop.

I didn't tell Melanie about any of the stupid vandalisms I actually did, the time I was staying in that first house where there were the weekly meetings and rotas about whose turn it was to buy things and do things. I lasted two weeks there. Everybody looked the same, I didn't like the food. Though what really did for me was the thing they did on Saturday afternoons, on the rota it was called the Living Together Workshop. Someone had to stand in the middle of the room, everybody else sat on one side calling out the things about her that annoyed or upset them; she had to take a step forwards if she accepted the criticism and a step backwards if she didn't. I was watching this woman doing a backward-forward dance on the carpet. She looked like she was near tears. It came to my turn to say something and I didn't know what to say, my mouth hung open and everybody was looking at me. I rubbed the back of my neck. I said, well, you seem very nice to me, I don't actually *have* any criticisms of you. Someone behind me said, that's so unhelpful, isn't it? The woman in the middle of the room was looking from face to face, she looked more panicked now than before I'd said anything, she was shifting from one foot to the other not knowing which direction to go in. I made an excuse and left the room, phoned Amy's college from the payphone and got someone to fetch her to the call box, asked if I could come over. Yes, why don't you, she said, that'd be nice, but bring something to do with you, I'm reading. I put the phone down, ran upstairs two at a time, packed all the stuff I wanted to keep, left the rest. I'd go and see Amy, she'd make Earl Grey tea in the cracked teapot and give me one of her china cups on its matching saucer, I'd tell her about the afternoon, she'd laugh and laugh. We'd read, or whatever. Then I'd find somewhere else to live.

Night and day, you were the one, something something something moon and under the sun. Amy's scholarly rooms. They were always getting bigger; the last time I was in her room—well, but I'm not ready to write that bit down yet. But the last of them, at least the last of them that I saw, must have been one of the largest in her college—she'd moved to a mixed college by then, it was a much older building, a much more important place. Her room there had ornate cornices, a door half a foot thick, big metal-framed windows as big as doors on a balcony overlooking the rose gardens. I began to understand she was doing well here, she was being rewarded by the people in power. Wherever she was, though, whether it was the room in the 1960s concrete development with the plaque on it saying it had been opened by the Queen and Prince Philip, or this one with its beams in the roof in the oldest, most prestigious part, it was Amy's room, it looked and felt the same, rich prose you're familiar with, somewhere you're sure you've been before.

Her belongings in a neat clutter as if Ibsen or Shaw had written the stage directions. This tray with the set of tea-things placed on a lace drapery here, this fringed lamp in this corner, this low-backed sofa, this Turkish rug thrown over it with a devil-may-care exactness, here. A vase of fresh flowers on the writing bureau. A small elegant glass cabinet with jet inlay placed stage right, visibly filled with notebooks, the kind one might use for journals, and a key poised in the lock. (The General's pistols, off-stage.) Me sitting under the Botticelli reproductions, the golden medieval women whose moon faces told you nothing, I'd be looking across directly at, say, the black and white photograph, the innocent arty back view of two small girls on a tennis court, their frilled skirts high enough for their underwear to be just visible; when Amy was vulgar it was always tastefully, eccentricity always within the bounds of correctness. You'd have afternoon tea in those thin-lipped cups and she'd be showing you her collection of Edwardian pornographic postcards, or if she was showing you her collection of Edwardian pornographic postcards, you'd be having afternoon tea in delicate cups as the cards passed under your nose. My nose, I was honoured and scornful at once. Two girls with sailor-suit tops on and nothing on from the waist down, their pubic hair erased in a photographic fuzz. A girl chained to a tree, fingering her chain, her other arm round her captor, about to kiss. A man with large handlebar moustaches, wearing nothing but a policeman's hat.

Surely, after all, it was only me who knew she was so strange, so mad, so perverse beneath the propriety and the poise of her? The antique cups were cracked at the lip, but I was honoured by that too, they were filled with the rich filth of antiquity. And there were books. An ordered chaos of books on every subject, books about medical conditions of children, books in Greek and Latin, books about Hollywood and ancient Rome, novels piled on novels, English, American, French, German, everything, everything you could imagine (except Scottish, I don't remember anything Scottish), novels that were old and novels that were new and still in hardback, currently gleaming in the shop windows. Almost without exception the books in her room looked like they'd never been read, sometimes never been touched, like nobody had dared finger and bend their spines. But she'd read them, I'd seen her, and she knew them, she knew passages, paragraphs, whole pages from so many of them off by heart.

Round the corner in her bedroom, where the narrow white bed was tucked, neat, nun-like, the wall space was covered almost completely in a claustrophobia of cut-out angels of every imaginable kind, and in among them the pictures of child stars from the movies, Elizabeth Taylor and a blonde little girl in *Jane Eyre*, Margaret O'Brien in *The Secret Garden*, her chest bound down with bandages to keep her looking young enough for the part (Amy told me). Pre-pubescent boys from over the decades, boyish-looking girls from the 1970s, they were all there, all the angels.

I was always out of my element in her rooms, fish out of water, bird submerged, John Wayne, yes, striding towards Helena Bonham Carter in *A Room With a View*, walking into things and breaking the crockery in the dining room, arms and legs too big, stetson knocking a picture frame squint. Enervating, the new element, the real risk of suffocation, and I can see myself now taking a deep breath and striding in regularly like I did, watching where I put myself; after a while I only felt so clumsy and deliberate when I'd some girlfriend or boyfriend on my arm. Always bringing them to her for approval, like a cat with caught birds or like she was my mother or something, look who I'm with now, then, look what I've got now. Amy sitting polite, distantly friendly as always, eyeing me wryly and asking all the right questions of Julia (did English, big glasses, radical, was always going on about how working-class she was), Fiona (from Edinburgh, Law, red hair, nice, but she told me she loved me on our second night out so that was the end), David (worked on the fish stall in the market, very handsome, smelt of fish), Will (very rich, a bit boring, had a sports car, an MG, all the chickens died in the experiment he was doing and he cried, I liked him for that), Simone (lovely Simone, lovely and loving, her mind light and racing, all mischief and adventures, I miss her). Whoever. All jealous of my friend Amy, the girls especially.

I never asked myself how I'd feel if she were to settle on someone, but of course she wouldn't, of course not, though she was always surrounded by insubstantial, admiring, clever boys who did Spanish or German, quoting Lorca and Rilke at her with hope in their eyes as she sipped tea with them in respectable snack bars; all those bespectacled lost boys who'd heard her being so intelligent in their classics seminars insisting, no, no, let me pay, fumbling with their fists in their pockets at the cash desks, sitting explaining Plato to her through the coffee steam, as if she ever needed anything explained, nodding though as if she did, letting them think she did, watching the clock without them noticing, politely taking leave. None of them had touched her, I was sure; but it was me who was polite, nodding, having to ask all the right questions when I swung into her room one day without knocking and found her with her arm fitted around the waist of a thin pale girl.

They jumped apart, until Amy saw it was me and slid herself back round the girl again (disdainful face, was she dark or fair? I've consigned her to forgetfulness, was Amy teaching her? probably, probably everything). I sat down and Amy, as if it were something that happened every day, poured tea in a perfect arc and passed me the cup, I took it, it shook on its saucer. I went home, polite, bereft, even more aware of the arm's length of air between us. Inviolable. The kind of word she'd use. Served me right. The kinds of word I'd use. I phoned her, so nervous that my hand was slippery on the receiver; by now she had her own extension in her room and it rang for a long time before she answered it. I said, who's your friend then? She laughed, she said, *you* are, Ash, you know that.

I told her everything, she told me nothing, that's how it was. She listened, keen, to me telling the story of how Simone smuggled me in after hours; the gate was locked and it was about half-past three, I'd be saying, and we were being extra careful not to wake the night porter, and I was giving her a leg-up over the wall, and then suddenly this bell was ringing somewhere, and the porter was waiting for us on the other side, see, Simone had used the bell-pull as a foothold and we'd wakened half the building up. Or the story of how Simone had been called in to see the Principal to account for why the number of names on the Annual Official College Photograph didn't match the number of faces. *Who* was the person standing next to her? Not A College Member. She was severely reprimanded, got a warning letter about it. Amy laughed delighted, wickedly and loud, her head thrown back. I told her about how we climbed up over the sloped tiles picking our way across the roof so we could touch the chapel bell. The bell has 1927 written on it, I told her. Wonderful, she said, and I knew it meant nothing to her, and that still, she meant it, it was wonderful.

Is it possible to disagree about everything at the same time as agreeing about everything? Thoughts came straight out of my mouth when I was with Amy, they rose to the surface like air in water and burst out of me. There was no stopping them, even if I had wanted to.

I could actually smell the seasons change. The summers were Rousseau rich, getting hotter every year, heat whiting things out. I put my hand in my jacket pocket one day and my fingers came out coated in chocolate, I had never imagined a bar of chocolate could just melt in your pocket like that. I had never understood before why all those prissy children in English children's stories had to wear hats in the summer. But here one year the spring was so hot that the daffodils burnt up under the sun. I roamed the library looking for her. The heat had broken the main clock mechanism; all the clocks had stopped with their hands at ten to three. I had spent the morning having to make and stick up signs round all the entrances that forbade anybody wearing too little clothing to come in because there had been so many complaints about men in shorts and women too skimpily dressed, bad for the concentration, obviously.

Amy was sitting high in the stacks in the dry sweat smell of old books. I eventually persuaded her to come out into the gardens with me. She was alarmed when I broke through the fence where they were closed to the public. She sat in the shade, straight-backed and nervous, watching in case anyone should catch us where we weren't supposed to be, her book shut on her knee. I lay in the sun on the ground watching the unfurled leaves, hearing a bird in the tree singing, the sound of the leaves lifting. The town hummed in the distant background. I threw cherries into the air and caught them in my mouth, spat the stones out. When I looked to see if she'd seen me catch them, she was learning things out of the book, her lips just moving as the words she read passed in their order into her head. Like that she was cool, cool on the hottest day of the year so far. Just looking at her made me feel cooler, slaked. I told her. She smiled, pleased, as if I'd been a little improper; even her smile was cool, shaded.

There was the time she didn't speak to me for three weeks after I'd said the unsayable, that I thought Virginia Woolf's novels were boring, unbelievable and had no plot. All that death of the soul she loved her she hated her what is the meaning of life stuff, I said, it's nowhere near what's real for most people; real for most people means getting through the boring or horrible day and having enough money to bring home something to eat at the end of it, there's no time for all the sitting around wondering about it. Amy put down her cup, told me coldly that although she didn't expect me of all people to understand, there were standards in art and aesthetics that had nothing to do with mere reality. I said if they had nothing to do with reality then they weren't worth much. Who was it said to me that the English language has hardly any words for anger? With Amy anger was a state of no words, no communication at all. She closed her face like a stone door and didn't say a word to me for nearly a month. Real, very. She was ridiculous. She was patronising and ridiculous. She was patronising, and ridiculous, and so clever that she was stupid.

But when she was suddenly walking beside me under the trees by the river a month later, was suddenly there, from nowhere, at my side and joyfully telling me as if nothing had happened about an aunt and an uncle and a cousin she had who were all going on holiday together and were all making wills so that if the plane crashed and they were all killed their money wouldn't be left to any of the rest of their family, I was so excited to see her again that I could hardly speak. Gold light was breaking on the surface of the river; we walked along past the tourists, we were friends, laughing, and I knew they were watching us, that we belonged to this place and they didn't.

As Amy's rooms got bigger, though, she would more often choose to ignore me on the street. In her eyes the tiniest hint of apology at having to do it, then that too would vanish, and so would I. Once she was sitting at a table with three other women in the library tearoom; it was my teabreak, I'd been up in the tower moving volumes from one shelf to another, I was wearing overalls and my face and hands were smudged with the dirt that comes off books. I pulled up a chair beside her, flopped into it with a loud sigh. Jesus Christ Amy, I said, would you believe it, the History of Art books are heavier than anything else, except the newspaper files and the bloody encyclopaedias, I'm at the end of my rope with it. What are we doing tonight?

Wrong. The wrong language, the wrong place. The wrongness of it settled round me as one of them adjusted her seating, one of them pressed a napkin to her mouth, one of them lifted her cup, another of them waited a moment then carried on talking as if I wasn't there. They were discussing the problematic lightness of the novels of E.M. Forster. One of them was my friend Amy. I took a moment, took a breath. So *that's* how you pronounce Forster, I said. Like Keets and Yeets, isn't it. Kates, Yates. I must get back to my work though. Can't stay here chatting. Otherwise who'll find the books for the likes of you ladies? I pushed my chair back and stood up, smiled at Amy, nodded goodbye.

That was one of the braver days. Mostly I didn't have the chance to talk back like that. Mostly I'd be left standing in the street, one moment there, the next moment air. Here today, gone today.

Like the dream where I'd wake up saying the Our Father and the Act of Contrition, O my God, I am very sorry, That I have sinned against you, Because you are so good, breathing like I'd been running or I was in pain. All the colours in it were washed out, and that eerie nothing where there must once have been sound. First you see an island, you see it from the air as if you're looking out of a plane, so you see the green and the brown of it in the blue Pacific. Then it vanishes. Nothing where it was but water. Then the same dream plays again from a different angle; the island, but this time you're on it, on the beach watching the waves curl into the coast, or sometimes you're leaving footprints in clean sand, and then you notice the people rowing away from you in their canoes, then you're with them in a boat and you look back like they do, watch past their browned shoulders as the island detonates, blows itself high into the sky and shatters, the flash of light, heat, the boat beneath you surges and you have to hide your eyes from the light, you can feel the heat smash past you, and when the boat steadies and you open your eyes and the smoke clears there's nothing there, not even the wreckage of a place, not even the charred bones of its trees floating in the water, or blackened birds that have fallen from the sky, nothing at all to say it was there, just the same whirring silence, the faded moving sea.

It's real. An island did just disappear in the nuclear tests they did in the fifties. The faded colour home movies feel of it will come from when we were small, dad with the whirring camera. A swimming pool or paddling pool, the boys going down a chute into water, and the film of us all the time we went to Yorkshire, on a beach, the red swimsuit, and she has sunglasses on, she has me by the hand, she waves at the camera. They showed them all at the boys' party, and they showed the Charlie Chaplin film at mine, the one with all the people being sick off the side of the boat and the car that goes down the hole in the road and brings the city to a standstill. Patrick put crisps in James's lemonade, everybody laughed, so James knocked my coke into my lap, an accident, everybody stopped laughing at him and laughed at me instead. That's what younger sisters are for, and for ignoring when you're out with your friends, unless you're showing off to them that you're tough and protective.

He's upset about the boys. He's asked me three times since I got here. I keep repeating, they'll be all right, not to worry, leave them till they're ready, they can't be apart for long, it's not the nature of their game. It took me years to understand, and I burst into tears the day I did, they could have told me, there are rules, Ash, and they're not always written down inside the lid with the others but they're there nonetheless. Monopoly, Frustration, Connect, whatever, I thought you just threw the dice and got lucky, or not. When it hit me that Patrick might be being nice to me to get a better handle on the game, or that James might only be being nice to me to get one up on Patrick, I put my hand beneath the Monopoly board and knocked it flying; the money, the little green houses went everywhere. It was like the worst form of cheating I could think of. I was so angry that I walked round and round the block with my hands balled in my pockets, saying all the worst swears under my breath. Karen Milne was leaning over their back gate, she watched me go past twice then she shouted to me what was I doing. She was nine, a year younger than I was, there was nothing to her, bones and skin and bad teeth, but she was wiry, stronger than I was, she'd fought me the summer before with all the older kids round us egging us on to punch each other and she'd beaten me easily. She swung on the gate. She said, at least your brothers don't batter you for no reason, right, mine's always slapping me and Danny just because we're smaller than him.

No, the worst thing they did to me was pin my David Cassidy poster to the shed door and shoot pellets through it with the air rifle. They never hurt me like that. Each other, now, that's a different story.

Melanie just stuck her head up through the hatch. Would I be here or away when she came round again on Monday? I said I'd be away by then, but that she could come and help me with the bonfire if she wanted. She looked so pleased and embarrassed that I got embarrassed. I said it would depend on the weather. Today the rain was even sometimes hail.

Nearly half-past ten. Let me write myself to sleep.

Three days after I'd first caught up with her, Amy finally came to visit my theatre. I found out afterwards that Charles Dickens had once given public readings to huge audiences there. Sylvia Plath, for God's sake, and who knows who else, had traipsed across the stage getting her lines right. I lived there for about a week hidden in a back room sleeping under sheets of canvas that were stiff with dust and age, I spent my nights shivering in the cold, scared of the noises the rats made dragging things about inside the walls. There was a labyrinth of corridors up some stairs; when I explored early one morning I found them, they were packed with clothes hanging on racks. You couldn't go near them during the day, some days there were people in an office up there, but I did manage to steal some quite nice things to wear and some good heavy coats to sleep in.

I pulled the loose board back and climbed up first to show her how, and held the board back for her from the inside. It was very dark, so I took the edge of her coat, hooked my finger through the buttonhole and led her slowly through the rooms, the one where I slept, the one full of the smell of damp rotting boxes, out on to the sudden space of the stage.

I felt her draw breath, and knew she was as amazed as I had been, stumbling into nothing. I let go of her coat, let her stand, so our eyes could get used to the black.

Oh, she whispered, your theatre's a ghost theatre.

Yeah, I said, I think it is.

But it's you and I who are the ghosts, she said. It's you and I who are haunting it.

She took me by the arm. Her grip was strong and sudden, it surprised me how strong it was.

Do you think it can hear us? she said.

I know who can, I whispered back. Listen.

I stamped hard, and the rats under the boards and behind the walls went mad; we heard the scurrying and scuttling of rat panic run right round the auditorium, scraping setting off scraping further and further back. I felt her jump beside me, she made a noise, excited, scared; the noise she'd made echoed out there too and we listened to the silence after it.

They won't come and bite us, will they? she said.

No, I said, they're terrified. If they do come anywhere near us we just have to make a noise and they'll back off.

So we stood on the stage and yelled into the dark. We made ghost noises. We made each other laugh, we listened to the dimensions of our own laughter. We took turns at shouting. We shouted all sorts of things, anything. I called out poems I'd learned at school. Gunga Din, the Burns poem about the mountain daisy. She called things in languages I didn't know, Latin phrases I recognised, cave canem, o tempora o mores, et in Arcadia ego. I sang all of Flower of Scotland and all I could remember of Scots Wha Hae. Such fierce angry songs! she said. I sang Annie Laurie, she said she liked it better. I sang something by Joni Mitchell, I couldn't reach the high notes and had to growl them in a lower key. She purred out poems in French, and announced the beginnings of novels, the past is a foreign country, she called, they do things differently there. I yelled like a football fan, Scotland for e-ver, Eng-land for ne-ver. She sang, and I don't think I ever heard her sing apart from then, she said, I'll sing your song, and she sang that one about the ash grove, or at the bright noon tide in so li-i-tu-ude wan dered a mid the-e da-ark shades of the lone ly ash grove. I laughed at how corny it was, then I listened; she sang it just slightly out of tune, every note just missing where it should be, it made it sound weird, unearthly, I thought beautiful.

Me standing stage left, her standing stage right, as far apart as we dared go in the dark, calling at each other in the rich decay of it, with the dead history in the air.

Can you see me?

No, but I can hear you. Can you see me?

No, but I know you're there.

Outside, years were passing. A new prime minister was working to help rich people get even richer. Someone shot one of the Beatles dead. The Pope got shot, and the new American president, the old movie star. People stopped buying corned beef in Britain and some ships were burning in the sea. There was a new disease, and the word *cruise* had several meanings. A man dressed as a woman was number one on *Top of the Pops*; his song was about how someone was hurting him. People were starving, and a girl tripped up another girl in a race, her screams went round and round the world's television screens. Fame, I'm going to live forever, baby remember my name remember remember remember remember.

The rich eighties were rolling, and we were two girls hanging around in an old rotting theatre, blindly taking steps towards and away from each other like it was all that mattered, like it meant something. We were making our own history, we were friends.

Amy's voice in the dark, saying, where are you now, Ash?

Me following the sound of it, my eyes open, seeing nothing.

I smell of the fire still. On my clothes, on my skin, must be in my hair. Sweet, acrid, I love it. Someone could make a fortune patenting the smell of fire as a perfume or aftershave, potent and nostalgic and sexual for people to spray themselves with in the spring and the autumn, at the hinges of the year. Lancome's Heat of the Moment. Meltdown by Givenchy. Hell by Chanel.

What was her name Miss Mackie bending over the school table and telling the eight-year-old faces. When you die the first thing you see is God smiling at you. And you see Him for just an instant, just the teeniest moment, less than a second. And then suddenly God's face disappears—face the front Andrew—and you're falling away down, it's like you're going down very fast in a lift, like the lift in Benzies, only you go down for miles into the bowels of the earth and it gets hotter and hotter and then the doors suddenly fly open and a huge fire roars in and burns you to a crisp. Yes. Because that fire keeps on burning you to a crisp forever—what can you possibly be finding funny about that, Maria? There's nothing funny about all your skin boiling off all sores and blisters. Is there? No. Just think what it would be like. Think how sore it is if you even just have the smallest wee scald on your finger. And now think about all your skin frying and sizzling on your arms and legs and all over you. Think how sore that would be. And all round you there's a funny smell, like someone's left a chicken in the oven for far too long, and then you realise, it's you that smells burnt like that. And you're so hot, and you're so thirsty, you ask for a drink of water, but not one person, not one person will give you one, and all round you other people are drinking water out of big cool glasses, as much water as they want, and you can't have any. But even worse than any of that. The worst thing of all. Is that you know you will never ever ever see God's gentle face again, Miss Mackie said, slowly shaking her head.

I looked up at Jesus with his nice beard, and with the children gathered round him in the picture on the wall, and He looked so kind. He'd never let that happen. She must have got it wrong. Then I was ten, I was staying up late watching tv by myself one night, black and white, and the man's voice describing, a hell, he called it. I knew then in the sudden long split of a second. People, skin, bone, smoke. This place was what people could do to other people, people the same as them, different from them. I was hiding my eyes behind the cushion, but the man was saying my name, and there was a swimming pool full of grey stuff. All that was left of them, the man was saying, was ash, a pit of ash. I got up with my eyes closed and felt for the button and switched the channel over. Show jumping, a white horse, Flying Wild the caption said, was about to jump the big wall. It cleared it, thank goodness; all the people clapped. I sat down again. I watched the man pat its neck and the horse shake foamy spit from its bit. I thought about the day when she'd shown me, this is what you do, you make a fist, put it on the sand, it's best if it's wet sand honey (she spoke like that, I think she spoke like that) and you put the sand on top of your hand till it's all covered up, that's the girl (her arms round me) then you pat it down like this, smooth it down into the round shape, then just edge your hand out, slide it out slowly, that's it, and look, that's the door. My brothers had run off with the pail and spade. Who needs a pail or a spade now? she'd said from behind me, kissing my ear through my hair. I watched the elimination rounds and the round against the clock and thought hard about the hand houses, we'd made a trail of them all over the yellow beach.

A moment ago. Decades ago.

Now then.

I'm sitting at my table in the dust and the bareness with Amy's diaries piled up over there in the corner; the sleeping bag curled on the floor, it looks as if someone's still in it. But no, there's just me and this book and her books and the moon.

I found the moon book from primary five tonight and we burned it, must have been primary five, it was the nun. Choice for the girls: pets, leaves, making bread. Choice for the boys: transport, flight, the moon. I made a fuss until I got to do the moon, the nun was progressive, she let me. Under a picture of a rocket I'd written TWENTY FIVE THOUSAND FEET PER SECOND!!!, I'd cut things out of newspapers, stuck them in the jotter my father covered in that wallpaper that looked like wood. We made a wall frieze in class. The pitted surface of the moon next to Linda McPhail's pictures of baby animals and someone else's, a boy's, paintings of a postman, milkman, coalman.

Patrick and James and I all watching it on tv, calling each other down from upstairs to see it, till it was on so much and there were so many Apollos that it got boring. But I remember, so clear, Kunta Kinte in *Roots* on his first night as a slave in the new country, lost and bewildered and beaten and he was looking up at it and knowing it was the same moon his lover could see all those millions of miles away in her other world. I read there were civil rights protesters who'd waited at the gates of NASA, they had signs and banners that read Rockets Or Rickets? Feed The Hungry Of America. Even they were shielding their eyes to watch, I'll bet, even they couldn't keep their eyes off it, the fire that was roaring out of it, shaking the ground they stood on that sunny morning men went to plant the flag, play football, jump like excited schoolboys on the surface of the moon. The moon, like an old clock, old wry friend, panda-eyed from staying up all night, a scald scar over the face, the oldest face in memory throwing white half-light on the colours of here. Dragging the dark round, the sea in and out; the physical pull of it hanging there cold in the sky.

Amy's perfume, still hanging in air where she'd just been.

Unthinkable, as unthinkable as sleeping with your sister, if you had one. Inevitable that I thought about it, and stopped myself thinking about it, and then couldn't stop thinking about it. Inevitable that one grey day in the monotony of putting books back on to shelves in the fusty stacks I sank to the floor and closed my eyes and I let myself think all the way through it for the first time, brought it boxed from the cellar stores and carefully peeled back the top, let the beautiful beast of it squint out into the light. I held it at a distance, then I held it cupped in my hands with my eyes shut and felt the smooth beating contours, the innocent solemnity, its milk-breath under my fingers. The strange and the known shape of it. Me. Amy. Pressed together into one. I braced my feet on the shelves opposite, pushed my back into the shelves behind me, felt myself tighten from the back of my neck down to my toes; I spanned in an arc of stretched muscle the satisfying air space between Italian Art of the Renaissance and Orthodox Religions. Two bodies, one. Her, me, yes, that was what it was all about, that was what it had been about all along, wasn't it?

Think of me with my hand in the kittenish mouth of it. Soon it would be big enough for me to put my whole head in. Soon that's what I'd be doing most nights, then twice nightly, sometimes matinees too. From the start I should have known it was savage, it was wild, it would get out of hand, get me like that in its musky jaws. I should have known that even just the thinking about it would leave me bloody, bitten in two.

My. Friend. Amy

: just adored, she just adored a lot of things. Said a lot of things were simply exquisite

: wore thin black wool on the coldest days of winter and the hottest days of summer, as if in disdain of something so common as mere seasonal change

: found it a philosophical dilemma deciding whether or not to put an empty yoghurt pot into the bin. I can't, she said. It's like throwing part of the self away. It brings me literal physical pain. That's just a lot of rubbish, I said. Under her sink was a collection of plastic yoghurt pots, washed out and stacked neatly one inside the other

: said her favourite colour was white

: said I looked good in black

: said her favourite book was *La porte étroite* by André Gide. I could never get through it, I said; she laughed. I adore being with you, Ash, she said, you make everything so refreshingly simple

: said a moment ago inside my head, I think you know I'm less of a cliché than you're inferring, Ash

: was at the supermarket one day; I saw her, she didn't see me. I followed her down the rows; I saw her pick up a tin of something and read the label and think about it for a moment and put it back. I saw her run her hand over the tray of cherries, saw her put two apples in her basket and finger and choose two peaches. I saw how her eyes flicked over the checkout girl in a quick appraisal, watched her going through her purse to pay, watched the straight black line of her back as she waited for her change, the straight swift line of her walk as she left. I stood outside the shop and I found I had a pack of hundred watt lightbulbs in my hand; I had to go back in and apologise and pay the girl at the cigarette desk for them. In my head, the hand, the blind fruit

: had at the age of twelve stopped eating meat and had at one point stopped eating altogether, eating being impure, and had done herself such damage that she didn't have periods for years, just like the medieval saints, as she once pointed out to me

: loved to talk about food and the sweeter and stickier the better. But in all the years I knew her I hardly ever saw her eat anything; grapes maybe, yoghurt, and as I watched her grow into the adult version of herself she was chic, slim, elegant, or like a starved child with her erudite head weirdly oversized on her body (yes, all right, depending on how you saw it, that is)

: let her friendship with me lessen in proportion to a number of things. The more important she became the less we saw each other and the more indecorous, invisible, northern and androgynous I felt myself becoming. Now that she was a Fellow, and after the argument where I said that pain and loss and yearning weren't just romantic, they were something people and sometimes governments had responsibilities to be doing something about, and after I shouted at her about how she should eat more, and especially about how I hardly got to see her any more, well, after that we hardly saw each other at all

: whom I hadn't seen for quite some time, phoned me up in the middle of the night to get me to come over, said on the phone would I mind, she needed me for a moment. I ran down the stairs. It took me just minutes to get there, cycling so fast against the rain that I arrived with my heart battering inside me. When she opened the door her perfume hit me like a wall and the room was thick with it. She was in her nightclothes with her hair down. She looked exhausted.

I'm afraid that there may be no point now to my having called you over here, she said.

She had wanted me to chase two wasps out of her room. But by now both the wasps were just about dead; she showed me one on the desk and one on the floor behind the door, curled and tortuous on their backs, twitching their legs where they lay. I was spraying it at them, she said, but I kept missing the wretched things, I've used up almost half the bottle and now I shall have to buy some more.

She pointed up to the ceiling, to the paper lampshade, to where the perfume had left big grease patches. She sat down. I told her she looked pale. She said she'd been working too hard, she'd been having trouble sleeping.

I went to go, but she hung back, no, Ash, there's something you'd like, surely. Now that you're here. Rain was running down my neck from my hair; a towel was put round my shoulders, her arm brushed my wet back, you're soaked through, she said. Let's go through here away from this; she gestured into the air at the heavy scent.

But the scent was everywhere in her bedroom too. She had slid herself inside the bed and pulled the covers up, she had taken one of my wet gloves and was smoothing it in her hand, passing it from one hand to the other. I sat on the bed, my heart so loud that I thought she'd hear it. But she was speaking over the top of it, she'd said something, I had to stop and concentrate. Ridiculous, she had said, and the word but, and the word scared. You know, Ash. What, she said, if tonight were the night that the random thing happened, say, the random murderer, the random rapist were to come through the window?

Well, he'll look through the window and see I'm here too. So don't worry, he won't be coming in, I said.

She shook her head slightly. It was the possibility of it happening that would make it happen, she said, hugging her knees. It was the thinking of it, the letting it even enter your head.

I said she was being daft, and anyway it was like a car accident or a plane accident or the place burning down, wasn't it; if you thought it would happen, if you went out of your way to think about it happening, then it probably wouldn't.

But what if our thoughts are the only things that are truly real? What if this is how we make things real, make things happen, by thinking about them? she said.

But you know they're not, you know you don't, I said.

And what if. What if, somewhere, there's someone else that I should be, could be, sitting here with now? What if, somewhere else in the world at this precise moment there's someone I've missed meeting, and this other person is randomly meeting someone other than me, precisely because of the randomness of it?

Chill creeping up the back of my neck. Well, I said, still smiling, shrugging it off with a shiver. At this precise moment you got me, didn't you?

What if, she said as if I hadn't said a word, what if our lives have taken the shapes they have, the shapes they've had so far, just by meaningless chance?

She had her hands up over her face with my glove over her eyes. I took it from her, I stood up and pushed my hand into it. Cold, wet. I had been relegated to random, the wrong person one more time, and by the one I'd allowed to tease me into this waiting half-life, into this foreign country, into her room in the middle of the night only to take me by the shoulder and shove me further away, further into the distance. Her face was its blank self but her eyes were scared like an animal waiting to be punished; she was waiting for me to say it, to declare it, but I was angry so I said something else, I said my usual lines, I said:

You're bloody off the head sometimes. There are a thousand more important bloody things in the world that you should be worrying about, and a thousand more even before you get to *that* thousand.

Somewhere I heard a noise, a door or a window slamming shut beyond us; it stopped me in my tracks. She sighed and closed her eyes and tipped her head back against the bedstead. She even looked a little relieved. Yes, she said. It was kind of you to come out, Ash, for such a small thing. I'm so sorry to have troubled you at such an inhuman hour.

The cut-out angels at her side looked down on her, looked out at me, cheap, seductive. I turned on my heel. I cycled home stupidly through red lights with no brakes, skidding in the wet, angry at her pale face in my head and the sense that was spreading through me like ink or blood in cotton, that I'd failed, I'd got the answer wrong. Missed something, missed the boat, missed the bus, missed the point. Worse, when I got home her perfume was coating me. I could taste her even through toothpaste. I threw myself rain-wet into bed, shut my eyes and she was still there, maddening, chemical. What was never going to happen was keeping me awake as usual, working me harder in the dark, mauling playfully at me, playfully shredding the flesh into rags.

I sneaked into the big hall with the rest of the crowd. The notice on the swing doors said The Body of The Text III; I was in the right place, then. I sat on the edge by the steps and as she walked down to get to the platform the smell of her caught in my throat, the expensive invisible promise of it was tracing the air before and after her.

She stepped to the side of the podium; I hid behind the head in front just in case though I knew she wouldn't see me, I knew she was short-sighted, I knew things that nobody else in this hall could possibly know, I knew all about her, and I watched as she did something I couldn't have imagined, bid the hundred heads in the hall turn her way with the barely audible clearing of her throat, and they did. Then her voice, quiet, reasonable, then stretching, witty, almost a parody of the voice I knew, hit the air and soared above the heads and the hands already writing her down. The girl sitting next to me jogged my elbow, she was asking if I needed paper, gave me a piece, I held it in my hand.

Shining like metal turning in light, like thrown knives. Sending arcing into the air words, names, references, long complex quotations in all their languages, like—like what? like one of those plate-spinners who used to be on tv, setting words off one after the other spinning on their points, so many that you couldn't believe she'd be able to keep them all in the air at once; look how good I am, she was saying, and look how reassuring, not one of my spun words is going to fall and smash. She was writing; she flicked a switch on the machine and the words threw themselves on to the wall behind her; she drew connecting lines between them. Words as Act. Supremacy of Text. Textual Intercourse. Textual Texture. Birth of Text. Pure Text. Corruption of Text. But the Text never dies, she said, because luckily for it, it was never alive in the first place! and she made little quotation marks round the word alive with her hand and the girl next to me laughed, charmed, like everyone else, and wrote it down. Then everybody stood up packing books away and when I could see again she'd gone, I couldn't see where she'd gone.

But I remember what she said. That language was meaningless, that words were just random noises. The twentieth century, she'd said, was, more than ever before, the century of testimony, because it was more than ever before the century of questionable meaning. But since language was all an act, a performance, since words were by nature all fiction, words could never express anything but the ghost of truth. *The ghost of truth.* The girl next to me had written it all down; she'd underlined *language not real,* underneath she'd been drawing things on her page; a tree, a dog, a face, flowers, an intricate abstract webbing. She turned to me as she pulled her jacket on. That was fantastic, wasn't it? she said.

I looked at the piece of paper in my own hand; I saw I had written in the margin over and over, like one long word all the way down the page, her name. I put my hand over my paper in case the girl saw. Yes, I said, wasn't it? The girl was looking me up and down, curious. Don't you work in the library? she said. Do they let you come to lectures if you're just someone who works in the library?

At the railway station workmen were gutting the old cafe, hauling a sign with the words QUENTINS BISTRO on it up into place. There was a pile of new chairs made of shiny metal tubing dumped waiting at the entrance. I sat on the ground by the wall, rested an arm on the old sign they'd taken down. CAFE SAND-WICHES HOT SNACKS ICE-CREAMS. I turned my face up to the sun. The workmen's radio was playing Steve Wright In The Afternoon, the insane radio voices yelling at each other or cheering and clapping, and the music veering from miserable cleverness to pastel colours, Morrisey and Wham!, Madonna singing about being touched for the very first time. This one, this is the one, I just have to hear it and it gets me all sweated up every time, one of the workmen called to the other. His friend gave me a lopsided grin, scratched at his dusty chest and upended one of the chairs for me with an exaggerated gesture of friendliness. I smiled back and shrugged no, pushed myself up off the ground, checked the train times to London. I went back to my house, up to my room. I went round opening and closing drawers, putting things into a plastic bag. Then I sat on the bed. Then I took the things out of the bag again and put them back on the table, back in the drawers, back under the bed, sat on the bed again, unfolded the piece of paper in my hand.

Amyamyamy.

I was washing my hands at work and I saw myself in the mirror. I had black circles round my eyes. I sat down at the issues desk again, feeling the ache round them like I'd been in a fight. I looked down at my hand hanging at my side and I clenched my fist. I swung back in my chair, nearly fell off it, got a silent reprimand from Myra, fourth in command. Ignored her. Ignored the tweedy woman holding the book in front of me waiting for me to stamp it. The woman stood there with her book held open, confusion gradually paining her face. Just before she opened her mouth to say, just as its corners twitched, just as her eyelids began that caught-bird flutter, I hit the inkpad with my stamp and stamped her book and slammed it shut, handing it to her with a smile.

It was time to make something of it. It called for a grand gesture. A glorious blaze. It called for me to play my part, be the disruptive heroic rebel of a Scot I knew I was born to be.

After that, when no one was looking, I began slipping one or two books each day back on to the shelves into the wrong places, even, when I was feeling most brave, on to shelves they shouldn't actually be on.

Still the high smoky taste of fire at the back of my nose and mouth.

Barbara said, ah now, this'll be the famous Aisling, oh but you're like your dad aren't you. Come away in, I've the kettle on.

Her front room had the smell of old apples; there was a budgie in a cage, rattling and cheeping. The tea had leaves that surfaced with the milk going in. Now, she said, and sat back in her chair. She looked at me; she didn't smile. That's us comfortable for a wee chat, she said. Now, how long is it you're home for? Oh, that's no time at all. Then it's over the sea, like all the young ones, oh aye, she breathed in. You're a grand one for the gadding about, I hear. But it'll not do. You should see and come home a wee bit more. It's different with boys. But fathers need their daughters. You're not married are you now, Aisling? No, I thought not. Well then.

The fire spat. She bent down and poked the poker through the grate and shook down the embers. I put the other half of the biscuit I'd stopped eating into my mouth, swallowed it down with the tea, I felt polite and bad as a ten year old. She heaved herself out of the chair, oh, old bones, eh, they're no use to a body, she said. She crossed the room and came back with a photograph in a plastic frame. That's us when *we* went to the States, the year before he died, she said, and he'd always wanted to go so it's as well we went when we did.

In the picture she was standing beside a small grey man, they were inside a kind of grey concrete box. Look, can you see, it's liberty, we're inside it, the Statue, you know. We got my cousin to take that one for us, she said. We went right up into the hat and everything. You should go up it if you get the chance, oh, the sightseeing, it's just spectacular. No, you sit right there now Aisling, I'll give Melanie a call for you, she's a good girl, our Melanie, no, it's no bother at all, it'll not take a minute.

Mrs. Ross from across the road, a bit like her, though Mrs. Ross was kind. Get away from those canal banks Aisling McCarthy or I'll tell your father on you. She had me over when I was too small to be home by myself after school, she remembered birthdays when my father forgot, your mother was a good friend to me, she'd say, what else could I do but see you right. Never put money in your mouth, she said, you don't know where it's been. She was a bus conductress till they laid them all off, and she made it clear, she knew money'd been in some pretty fishy places. Before that she'd worked in an aspirin factory in Glasgow and that's what killed her in the end; breathing in and out at her work had burnt her kidneys up. Those big lads in your house, and your feckless father God bless him, they'll be no use to you at all and there'll be nobody telling you anything worth knowing at yon school, she said; come over on Tuesday and we'll have a cup of tea and a girl's talk, your mother would have wanted me to.

I was excited. I wondered what could be so special that girls had the exclusive right to it. But I sat on the edge of her arm-chair pretending politely, after all I knew it all already, I didn't need some old woman to tell me, though she meant well, talking about curses and the laying of eggs like she did, like periods and sex were the same thing, and she wouldn't look at me, only at the ceiling, so I knew it was supposed to be embarrassing and private, only I'd learned more facts from Carolyn MacGilvray bringing the obscene Oor Wullie cartoon into school that we'd passed round at assembly, singing God moves in a mysterious way and craning our necks down the row to see the pictures.

I picked at the clean lacy cover pinned to the arm of Barbara's chair. I stood up and fingered the Venetian blinds apart. Barbara had a view of the mental hospital up the hill, the new housing estates packed round it and behind them the mountains crowded at the back of the town. Still snow on the tops. I could hear her in the hall on the phone. Aye, she was saying. Your new *movie star* friend's here, she came all the way across the road in one of they, what're they called, *limousines,* just to get your phone number. She says to tell you about a fire.

I heard her hang up. I sat down quickly again in case she caught me doing something I shouldn't be doing, something like standing instead of sitting in her front room.

We trailed the school stuff, the chewed-up games, old letters and paper from the garage to down by the compost heap. My father was watching. Are you sure? he was saying. Do you not want these things? You'll want them later, mark my words you will. He picked up a stray piece of paper that had blown into the pinks. For Christ's sake, he said. 1974 Inverness Music Festival Third Equal. You can't burn this. I'm telling you girl, you'll not have it, and that's when you'll want it.

Melanie was poking about at the book boxes in the garage. She'll never let you near those, my father called to her. I had to moor my boat on the loch because of the books. Boxes of the buggers filling up my garage. Some years it was the only thing you'd get. Eh, Ash? You'd not get a letter. You'd be lucky if you got an address. But there'd be bloody books sent home to have to find somewhere for.

I saw his eyes going over Melanie's back and thighs as she stooped over a box of books, so I stood right in his sightline between them. I've given her divine right to any books she wants, I said, and I turned my back on him. Melanie was going through some of the books we had when we were small. Look, she said, the corners are all ripped off this one. And look at this one. And this one, it looks like a dog's had it. She was flicking through some book or other, gaping at the pages torn right back to where the words were.

Tell her, go on, my father said with the laugh catching in his chest. I'll tell her then, he said, coming over and putting his arm round my shoulders. She ate them. She was always eating paper. You had to hide the *TV Times,* it'd be torn to bits. You had to hide *The Press and Journal.*

Wasps eat paper, Melanie said from inside another box, they make their houses out of it. So that's where you've been for the last seven years, my father said, wheezing. That'll be where she's been staying. He stuck his hands deep in his pockets and went out to kick the fire back from the border and the lawn.

I'll bring them back, Melanie said. I'll just take a few now. I'll bring them back when I've finished with them. You can keep them, I told her, you can take whatever you like, there's no use books lying unread in boxes. No, no, she said, I'll just borrow them. After all. What if you got hungry?

Look, she called, coming out of the garage carrying armfuls of books, what are these? What are they? Are they a novel? Are they yours? She put them down on the grass; she picked up the top one. No, I said. She was stroking the marbled cover. Even the paper in them's so nice, she was saying, they're really beautiful, they were just lying in an old bin bag. No, I said, and I gathered them up off the ground and balanced them against me, carried them inside. I put them on the kitchen table. I brushed the grass off the one on the bottom of the pile with my hand.

When I came back down from the loft Melanie was watching the fire, and came and stood by me not saying anything; I was sorry, I thought I must have scared her. But before I could say, from nowhere she said, you know the director of the film you were in? Is it, like, gay films that he made?

Well, I said, that's what he's famous for. At least, that's the label people in the papers and things give his films.

I'm on the debating committee at school, Melanie said. We do debates about things like that, like whether you can be gay or not. Oh, right, I said, and can you? I can't remember what the exact score was, she said, but I think most of the people there thought it was all right as long as it wasn't hurting anybody. But hardly anyone came. It was one of the most poorly attended. It's on at lunchtimes. My mother didn't want me to go to that one but I have to go, I'm on the committee. Last week loads of people came. It was about This House Believes That Scotland Would Be Best As An Independent State. We had real trouble finding people to speak against the motion. Almost everybody except the girl who did speak against the motion's friends voted for yes, that a referendum would be good. Like, you know, they had one, years ago, but it failed.

Yes, I said, I know.

We were told about it at history, she said.

Devolution, deviance. I was watching the burning, running words through my head to the tune of The Locomotion. Love as long as it's not hurt-ing a-nybo-dy. I was whistling it. Melanie whistled along too. That's a hit from the sixties, isn't it? she said. We have that on a record. When is it you go away? I can't wait to leave. Not Scotland, though. I wouldn't like to leave Scotland. Not for any money. Did you hate England? I'd hate it. All the, you know, English people. You know what I mean?

I could see my father at the kitchen window. He was bending at the sink washing or drying something. The time when I'd been off school and been left at home by myself all day, he let me lie in his bed even though I was throwing up, I'd woken up being sick all over mine. He came all the way home from his work at dinner time and came straight up the stairs. I've brought you this, he said, holding out an orange, a big one, big for his large hand. He sat on the bed and peeled it for me then watched me closely as I ate it piece after piece, on you go, he said, all of it, you've to finish it. Now, he said, you're going to feel worse. But you'll feel better soon after that. He took the basin away, brought it back clean and laced with cloudy disinfectant, the sweet safe smell. I lay in bed in the afternoon, sicked the orange up, felt better. My father could do the most amazing things, I remember thinking as I stared at the swirls in the ceiling. He could even make sick taste good.

What could you do with it all? The clothes could go to Oxfam, the books could be given away, the rest, old postcards, old letters, old wage slips, the bland details of days you couldn't remember, burn them. But all this stuff that eddied in your head all the time? Now my father through the window looked like an old man, any old man, one I didn't know. There was the sound of the fire getting going at last. The sound of this girl still talking beside me. There isn't even a Body Shop, she was saying. There isn't even a Pizzaland. It's so crap here. You can't do anything. Her voice pulled at my sleeve. Was it? she was saying. What? I asked. Brilliant, she said. Did you go to a big drama school and get chosen at an audition and have to sing on the stage and that?

I told her. I'd been serving this man, he had a big nose, was wearing a really scruffy anorak but he had a clutch of beautiful people round him at his table, and some of them were asking him things and writing down what he said. I was tired that morning and in a very bad mood; someone had groped me on the tube and then I'd got soaked on my way to work and my hair was still stuck down to my head. I slopped his pasta all over the floor, splashed it on his anorak, and he smiled at me kindly; he said, I wonder if you'd like to be in a film I'm about to make? All the beautiful people turning and looking me over, nodding and whispering things to each other. But he came back to the bar the day after that and asked me again, even after I'd so rudely told him where to go the first time, then we were friends, and then it was made and we never guessed so many people would like it, well, I never guessed, I told her, then someone phoned me from the States. So that's how, by mistake really.

I went into the garage and dug out my copy of *Member of the Wedding*. I told her I thought she'd like it; she put it on her pile of books to take home, will you not need it? she said, will you not need to take it with you? She said she'd never heard of the writer, what was he like? She's really good, I said.

But what's the first film about, the one you've already made, that the nice man in the anorak directed, what's it called again? she asked. It's this story about this girl, I said, it's hard to explain, but she's beautiful and charismatic and magical and attractive. Who plays her? Melanie asked. What do you mean who plays her? I said, giving her a push, she was laughing. And all these people want to, well, they want to take her home to sleep with them, and they pick her up from places, like bus stops and railway stations and night clubs or on the streets, and take her home to have sex with them. But when she gets to their houses she always just falls asleep, and she looks so, it sounds stupid, you have to see it really, she looks so innocent and like they can't touch her, that the people she's gone home with all just leave her lying asleep like that, they lie beside her and fall asleep, or they cover her over with a blanket on the couch, whatever, and they go to sleep themselves. Then when they wake up in the morning they find she's taken their wallets or their money or something valuable from their houses and she's gone. But she always leaves them a message written in lipstick on their mirrors in their bathroom or on the doors of their kitchen cabinets.

Like what? Melanie said.

You will hurt someone if you are not careful. Dare to dream. You will be happy very soon. You can live differently. Your future is happening right now. Those are some of them, I said.

Yeah, and then what happens? Melanie said.

Nothing, that's the end, I said.

That's the end? She just writes the things and that's the end? But what *happens* about the things she writes? Do you not get to find out if they're true?

Well, no, I said, that's the catch, you don't.

That's mad, Melanie said. That's so crap. She kicked at a stone in the grass. That's like ruining it, not showing you what happens, she said.

The fire out there, nearly burnt out. Bright orange in the dark, like the dark has a tear in it and light is on the other side of it.

We were in the art gallery, Simone and I, on a rainy cold Sunday afternoon. I was wandering the stuffy rooms, Simone was somewhere, I'd lost her. I checked my reflection in the glass of a big painting; that morning I'd wakened with a start, not knowing where I was, from leaning over a river and my reflection not being there, nothing but wavering sky and leaves where the face should be. Simone's single bed, too small. I curled into her back, curled my legs tight into her legs; she moved against me, neither of us comfortable. All right? she asked. I dreamed that when I looked I wasn't there, I said. She ran her hand down across my stomach and over my groin, nice. You're there, she said and fell back asleep and so did I.

But all day I'd been catching my own eye in the windows of the shut shops we passed. There I was, and there. Now there I was again on that big painting. I stopped and looked. I saw that my eyes were reflecting in sea, or no, was it hills, I was looking at my face in water that was like mountains, or mountains that could be the white tops of waves. It's home, I thought, it's home, and my heart fisted in my chest and I stepped back to get a proper look.

It wasn't what I expected to see. No realistic landscape with working men in it repairing nets or doing something with creels, no women gathering kelp. Instead the painting was of two angels, they were grotesque and large and ornate, but they were working angels after all, their hair up in a style braided round their ears like those photos of women at first world war jobs. Two angels in heavy work clothes, they were floating with grace and speed over the sea and the mountains. One had more colourful wings than the other, like a higher rank. Between them they were carrying a child, a girl. Was she dead or sleeping? Dressed in white with her hands pressed together like she was praying, she had her legs resting over the shoulder of the front angel. The other one held her small body with hands that were as long as the girl's spine. Two seagulls were flying behind, and down in the sea there was a seal nosing before them. The girl was too pure, too white for the landscape and its birds and seal; she looked more angelic than the angels. The wind which the seagulls rode, which was rough enough to be white-topping the waves, couldn't even lift the girl's long hair out of place.

Simone was downstairs with the suits of armour, slumped asleep on a chair next to a case of Egyptian mummified stuff. Bits of fur stuck out through the bandages; the grey dirt lining the bottom of the glass case was the pure dust of dead deified cats. I woke her, she smiled, rubbed her eye, made room for me on the chair. All these dead things, she said, I couldn't help it, I just fell asleep.

I've found something for Amy's birthday, I said.

Oh Amy Amy Amy, Simone said, her smile disappearing. She stood up and stretched, yawned. Oh all right, she said. Show me then.

Before I knew her, I noticed her, Simone, always coming in to the reading room and sitting at the front table, never reading anything except the big dictionaries, more often using them to prop her arms and head on while she stared into space, or, more and more, I noticed, stared in the direction of my desk. One day when I came out of work she was leaning against the fence opposite on a bike. Three times I walked home, with her following me from a distance. The fourth evening I turned a corner ahead of her, ducked into a garden behind the wall and waited. When I put my head out I could see her past me down the road, balanced on her pedals, confused, until she looked back and saw I'd seen her, put her head down, cycled away fast. Next morning when I came out of the house she was at the bottom of the steps. What is it you want? I asked. She patted the seat of her bike. Come on, she said. There's something I have to show you.

I sat on the seat, she took my hands and put them round her waist, hold on, she said, and she pedalled standing up, past the rich houses, through a housing estate, through a shabbier housing estate with its metal-shuttered shops. She skidded to a halt

248

on rubbly wasteground, left the bike lying on the ground with its back wheel still turning and walked me over to a tall wire fence. Through it I could see train tracks running parallel, curving into each other, some stopping in the middle of nowhere. There was a sidings shed and a train was coming slowly up to it. Watch this, she said. We saw the train go in one end and come out the other, it went in dirty and came out clean. I laughed out loud, I said, is this what you've brought me all this way to see? I thought you'd like it, she said.

We watched it happen several times, a train go in, push through, come out wet and shining with the sun catching on the wet windows. Then she cycled me back to hers and we'd seduced each other within minutes, turning in on each other as soon as she'd closed the door, in among the coats hung on the back.

Simone's mother was a part-time teacher at a university in the Midlands; that afternoon Simone read me the letter she'd just had from her. Two lecturers there had committed suicide, scared of being made redundant; philosophy had closed down, so had music. Simone paced the room. We've got to do something, she said. In bed that afternoon she started writing a play, leaning the foolscap on my back. It was going to be about the miners' strike, about a miner from the north and a tv reporter from London who fall for each other, so that the miner leaves his wife and family to follow the tv reporter and then the tv reporter's embarrassed by him turning up at a posh news party at television centre. I was very impressed with Simone, I thought she was brilliant to have thought that up. I suggested lines that I thought sounded suitably Yorkshire. And a couple of nights later she took me on to the roof of her college, scaling its slant and tightrope-walking along the top in the dark to get to the college bell.

You've got to see things from as many different perspectives as possible, she was saying as she reached down to haul me up. We stood on a thin ledge behind the bell, which was huge. She swung her arm back and hit at it hard with her fist but it made almost no noise, a dull thud like she'd hit a rock. Only money can ring this bell, she said.

This place is over, finished, she told me as we swung our legs off the roof of the college, as I tried not to look down at the far-away ground, the drop appearing beneath us as dawn came up round the bell and the birds all over town began to waken. A dead country, finished, a finished civilisation. You and I, we should be travelling the world, Ash, taking it by storm. Everything's dead here. This bell, this sunrise, even those birds singing in those trees. It's all one big lifeless cliché. We should be doing something different. Something real.

She turned to me, put her arm round my shoulders, she looked with her fierce eyes into mine. You should be out there, Ash, showing them what you can do. You're full of power. You should be doing something powerful with your life, making changes. Making a name for yourself. You will, you know. I have faith in you.

Yeah, I said, not looking down, shutting my eyes, yeah, right, we can do something. If I fell, or worse, if I jumped, Simone with her arm round me like this would fall too. I have this idea for another play, she was saying. You should be in it. You can be the woman whose child gets leukaemia from living next door to the nuclear plant.

Then the bell was deafening behind us. One, two, three, four, five times in a row, the whole world shook.

True to her word, Simone. She did write that play, and we put it on in a double bill with the play about the miner and the reporter, and people came and clapped and some said they had been moved, one man even cried. We had a nice year together doing all sorts of stuff like that. Then I ruined Simone's university career.

But there we are, Simone and I, standing in front of a painting on a Sunday afternoon. You're right, she was saying, your little friend Amy'd just love that. She read out loud what it said on the label at the side of it. St. Bride, John Duncan, on loan from the National Gallery of Scotland.

See? I said. It's just a case of borrowing something that's already on loan.

Simone looked around us to see if anybody had heard; she had just realised what I was asking.

I'll never be able to carry it by myself, I said.

No, she said. It's big. You would need some help.

Of course, we'd never be able to show our faces in here again, I said.

She glanced over her shoulder to see that nobody was watching. She stepped over the ropes and checked behind the picture with her hand to see how it was fixed on to the wall. She rubbed her fingers and thumb together, looked round the room again. Who'd want to show her face in here anyway? she said.

We borrowed the overalls from the cleaners' cupboard at my work; they smelt of pine freshener and made us look like young doctors. Simone arranged to borrow her friend Imogen's Citroen van the day before Amy's birthday. We took the top sheet off the bed. In the van, parked at the back of the gallery, she passed me the screwdrivers.

It was easy, I still can't believe how easy. We just took it, it was as easy as that. We walked into the place and up the stairs and stood in the room. The pictures stared down at us off the walls. They're jealous, they all want to come, Simone murmured.

I began work on the lower half, unscrewing the brackets; Simone stood ready as an elderly woman came up the stairs two at a time. The woman had a whistle round her neck on a string. This one's going back, Simone said pleasantly, it's been recalled. Special exhibition. Oh good, the woman said, I am glad, I don't like it at all, a very odd mixture of the aesthetic and the utilitarian. I wouldn't know, I heard Simone say, all I know is it's got to go back where it came from.

Sweat was running down my back. I was listening for the shrill of the whistle, but no, the woman was gone, she was chasing some foreign students and shouting at them to take their rucksacks off. I couldn't reach the top bracketing, I showed Simone. She stepped into the next room, picked up a spindly-legged chair, slung it over her shoulder. Queen Anne, she said, and stood on it, and she had the fixings loose in seconds; the picture slid down the hessian and I caught the heavy edge of its frame, so heavy it nearly pulled me down with it.

We stood St. Bride on its side and threw the sheet over it. We carried it to the stairs. Then we were down the stairs and I heard Simone behind me calling goodbye to the woman, who shouted back a cheery cheerio. We loaded it into the van, she started the engine, we drove away and that was that. After dark we left the van in the tradesman's entrance to Amy's college, hauled the sheeted picture through the gardens and up the fire escape, across the flat roof; Simone slithered down the drop on to Amy's balcony and braced herself against the railing to take its weight as I edged it over and down.

Amy would be out, I knew. Every Tuesday there was sherry under the gaze of the bearded dead Fellows in the Senior Common Room, and she'd be there, complimenting the older women Fellows on what they were wearing, swapping thoughts on the French Feminists with the younger ones, talking about theory with the boys. The adept murmur of her, nodding and demurring, saying the word dialectic as she fingered doubtfully what she'd chosen from the tray of salty snacks.

So her room was in the darkness I'd expected. I jumped down near Simone, she tore the ivy back and we prised the window open. I hacked at the rust on the catch and got the balcony door to work. Simone pushed St. Bride through. She flashed her torch round the walls of the room. Doing well for herself, your friend Amy, she said. We propped St. Bride against the bed in her bedroom, and Simone unveiled it, whipping the sheet off. That's where we left it in its gold edged frame, dwarfing all the paper thin angels opposite.

Back in Simone's room I fell on to her bed. She shut the door, fell with her back against it. We were both out of breath from running up the stairs.

Brilliantly executed, she said. Done with panache. A work of art.

I undid the laces on my boots. I was suddenly exhausted. Simone was slowly unbuttoning her shirt. There must be easier ways, though, she said, her face thoughtful.

I can't imagine anything easier, I said. I reckon we could do the National Portrait Gallery tomorrow, and the Rothko room at the Tate on Friday, what do you say?

No, I mean easier ways of telling her, Simone said. It's pretty obvious to me. You could just go to bed together. Then there'd be no need to empty art galleries into her room.

I stood up. But there was nowhere to go in Simone's small room so I sat down again.

I don't mind, Simone said. I don't care. You know what I think of your precious friend Amy. I was thinking of you.

Your precious friend. Amy didn't like Simone much either, she called her Simple Simone, had said how she admired Simone's touching enthusiasm. Had said how nice it must be for me to have a twin at last. I pushed my boots off with my feet, shrugged Simone off. It's not like that, it's just not, I said. We're friends. That's all.

Yeah, Simone said, and sighed it away, I could feel her breath warm on my neck. What'll we do next, then, my sweet Ash, my sweet art? she said quietly. What'll we do now?

Do you think we'll get into trouble? I said. Do you think we shouldn't have taken it?

Art belongs to everyone, Simone said, her hands gently, firmly at the small of my back.

Do you think she'll like it? I said. Do you think she'll be pleased?

Well, I would, Simone said, and kissed me. Kissed me all, up and down, the back and the front and the sides of me till we fell asleep on each other, so that I woke up feeling light of heart, light of foot, light of finger, so that I waltzed up the stairs the next day thinking how clever I'd been, and knocked on Amy's door like a bellboy who knows he's in for a huge tip, he's delivering the telegram that says you've won a million pounds stop, or they want you on Broadway stop, or congratulations it's a boy stop, or there is nobody I want in the world more than you stop.

Oh, it's you. Please come in, she had said, and she had shut the door quietly behind me, then she'd walked to the middle of the room and stood with her back to me.

Terribly politely she'd said she would like me to take the stolen goods away. Did I know how easy it would be for her to lose everything she had built up? Did I know how foolish I had been to put her in this position? And could I remove it, if I would be so kind, with the slightest possible fuss and most importantly without anybody seeing me until I was well away from anywhere near her door?

She had spoken in the calmest of voices, but all round her cold anger was sheening the room. The chairs, the couch, the books on the bookshelves. The room had turned its back on me, frozen with fury.

Did you not like it then? I asked.

Silence. I began to speak again, made a sound that didn't come out properly. Amy's hand, which had been down by her side, went up to brush a hair away from her mouth, her cue to herself to cross the room, sit down at the desk, pick up her pen, bend her head. I could see her hand moving as she wrote. I knew there'd be blue ink smudges in the joints of her fingers, the places where the skin folded and creased. I stood in the silence and this small image stuck hopelessly in my head.

Whole minutes must have passed before I dared to try my voice again.

I can't. I can't carry it by myself. You know I can't. I mean, it's huge, I said.

Nothing. The sound of the pages turning. I heard boards creak under my feet as I shifted from one to the other. In her bedroom I saw the dull wood backing of the painting. She must have scraped and clawed it out, wheeled it round on her own body-weight and forced it back in the other way round so she wouldn't have to look at it. Even like that, even like an eye shut on itself, it made the bed and the fireplace tiny, the room like a cheap cell.

St. Bride. Monstrous, getting bigger and heavier each inch I had to drag it, trying not to mark the floorboards or snag the runner of carpet, trying not to knock into anything. I found that if I balanced the weight on my shoulder I could keep the base of the painting off the ground and that if I rammed myself hard beneath it I could get the whole thing on my back. She seemed deep in a book as if nothing were happening round her. But as I grunted past she raised her arm without looking up, pen poised in the air, so I had to stand, wait, see what she wanted.

Before you open the door, she said in the sweetest of voices, I'd be grateful if you'd make sure that there is nobody out there to see you leave.

I put St. Bride down. Leaning up against the couch the picture was garish. There was nobody in the corridor, and when I came back in, St. Bride had given the room an air of the temporary, made it into a storeroom for old unmatching furniture. I hoisted it again, got to the door with it, slid it down on to the floor and I ripped my jumper and my shoulder open on one of the brackets. I swore.

Oh, and Ash? she said as if surprised that I was still there. When you've dealt with this, could you come back? I'll be out at three and I'm teaching all afternoon, but (she consulted her calendar), yes, I'd be available after nine this evening.

I shut her door. I found blood on my fingers from my shoulder. I was angry now. I was at the top of the stairs, I was tipping the weight of the painting on the top step. Any second now I'd shove it hard into the air and it would smash against the banister, shatter open and topple all the way down.

Or I could just kick a hole in it. I could just kick the glass into splinters myself and leave the debris of it here, at her door. That's what I'd do. So I leaned it at an angle against the stair-rail and got ready to jump on it. But then I saw. That the man who'd painted the picture had painted a frame round it, inside the real frame. That the bare foot of one of the angels was stretched out beyond the painted frame. That the wing tips of both angels were too, and even the wing tips of one of the gulls, like they were all about to soar airily out of the picture. One of the angels was turned to look at the girl they carried, loving, solicitous. The other's face was fixed ahead, purposeful, pretty and grim. They were taking her out of the world, or rather, out into it, as if any second now they'd fly right past my head.

I kicked my heels till ten past seven then I couldn't wait any more, I hammered on her door. Amy, open the fucking door, I was yelling, or about to be yelling, when the door opened and I fell through it and she had me by the wrist, pulling me in, shutting the door, pulling me over to the couch. You barbarian, she was saying, stealing a painting, stealing such a beautiful painting.

I took a deep breath, got ready to shout again, I was going to shout all the things I'd been bullishly shouting in my head out there for the last hour and a half in the cold and dark. But when

I looked her face was shining and she was saying. For me. I loved it. It's been the best birthday I ever had. It's certainly the best present anybody ever gave me.

She was so pleased I swear she almost kissed me. You're so brave, she said, her mouth so close to my face I could feel the words. It was so daring of you. Imagine you carrying it here; all by yourself.

Well, Simone helped, I said, shifting away from her.

No she didn't, Amy said, I won't believe that. This was all your doing. You'll get into terrible trouble if they find out, won't you? She sighed admiringly. St. Bride, you know, she said, is actually a form of St. Bridget. St. Bridget started out as a fertility goddess, pre-Christian; she was far too powerful for the Catholic church so they turned her into a saint and declared her to be the mother of St. Patrick. But at her convent in Ireland they couldn't stamp her pagan influence out; little pagan miracles happened all the time. Candles would never blow out. Cows never ran out of milk. You could always tell where St. Bridget had been because flowers grew out of every footprint she left behind her.

Mad Amy was back, dangerously comforting. I sat on the couch, at a safe distance in case she changed her mind again, and let myself listen to the hum of her voice, calm beside me like a neat cat settling its paws under it. I like that, that thing about the flowers, I said.

Yes, I do too, said Amy, and the glow ran down my spine, it always did when we agreed on something. She was trying to open a packet of biscuits, you like this kind, don't you, she said, yes, I thought you did. But she couldn't get the packet open, she gave it to me and I split it at the top with my teeth and gave it back. I love how you do that, she said. She slid down on to the floor, leaning against the couch, snapped a biscuit in half, ate half and gave me the other half. I held it in my hand, away from myself, as if it might bite me, might explode at any moment.

Her feast day's the first of February. That's in some traditions traditionally the first day of spring. Candlemas. Fitting, isn't it? Though I haven't been able to trace what it is the painting actually depicts yet. It's not in any of my saint books. I tried the libraries this afternoon, but I couldn't find anything remotely like it, she said.

The glow that had run like a fuse down my spine had spread through me; it was melting my bones. The cage of my ribs, the thick femurs, the tiny bone connections up through my neck and in my ears, all liquefied. My shoulder was sore. Art shouldn't be so heavy, I was thinking, they should make it easier to carry. The day was peeling away from me. With one move Amy could have me, she could slit the jagged insides out of me like gutting a fish by stripping the ribbing out of it, yanking out the spine. I shut my eyes. I let my head fall back.

You know, I said, I've been having this horrible dream, I've had it three times now. I can't get it out of my head. What do you dream? she said, and I told her about the reflection, the surface of the water. I look and look, I said, but I can't find it anywhere.

Think of it, Ash, she said. You're blessed with a reflection that has a mind of her own. Other people see themselves on the surface of things, but you're lucky. Not only can you see past the mere mirror of yourself. Even more, your reflection is free to go where she wants, do what she wants, regardless of what's expected of her. She's a reflection who is free to choose. She doesn't even have to look like you, she's so free.

I was hooked, I hung on her every word. Are you sure? I said. I opened my eyes. The medieval rafters in the ceiling. The old oak writing desk. My wise ambitious friend sitting at my feet, her in her room, the love affair of it. The richness, old wood, gained space. The books and music, a culture shelved and ordered. The colours tasteful, contained. Streets paved with books and music and the promise of them, the promise of this place radiating out like heat. I looked down and saw the shape of her, I saw the place where her skin met the low top button of her dress and I looked away.

I knew you'd like that fucking picture, I said.

Language, Ash, Amy said, soft, mock-shocked.

They traced the van, and Simone's friend who'd lent it to us got suspended for a term. They never traced me. Simone never told. And even though they found St. Bride safe and well where I directed them to on the phone, exactly where I'd left it, behind the big fallen poplar on the fen with the unbothered cows grazing round it and the first spring aphids settling on the glass over the white-painted girl, even though it was safely back in the gallery by nightfall, Simone still got thrown out, sent down (though her folks lived in Coventry so really she got sent up and across, then sent to Coventry all over again by her parents, as she said in her letter).

But I moved to London, we lost touch. The last thing I had from her was the postcard from India of an ancient temple over-run with monkeys. Dear Ash, I ate a peach I found in a gutter, got dysentery. Feeling better now. It is so spiritual here. When will I see you again? When will we share precious moments? Sending love, your own Simone xxx.

Look at me, though. Stuck in a picture-story plot. Walking around in someone else's schoolgirl jape. The pages of the calendar had a new witty epithet day after day after day in the library. April, blossom ghosting the trees once more along the river. Then August, the leaves a deathly green, nothing they had left to do but fall. I was sitting out my lunch-break in the murderous heat and I felt something. It was a spider, almost too small to see; it had dropped across me and trailed down the side of my face, down to my collarbone like I wasn't there. It blew on to my hand. I thought about killing it, I nearly did kill it, because it was there and I could. The ticklish casual legs of a spider, I was nothing more than a landscape to it, I had nearly slapped it dead anyway without even noticing. Clear and yellow and transparent in the light, it threw itself into the air on an invisible thread off my finger. I caught the thread with my other hand and drew it back up, settled it on my finger again, brought it to my eyes. It scuttled round and over my hand and threw itself off again. I pulled it back up on to my hand. It threw itself off, and this time I let it go, watched it land on a grass blade and spin a new landing for itself, toss itself into the air again and hit the ground and disappear between the close-cut blades as big as skyscrapers.

That was all it took, in the end. I didn't bother going back to work. I left everything behind me, not that there was much. I didn't even pack up my books to send home this time. Maybe she'd come looking for me, after all, and they'd show her up to my room to see the Marie Celeste of my going. The chocolate bar on the sideboard with the one bite taken out of it, slowly turning stale and white where the teethmarks were. She'd sense it psychically, surely she would. She'd wonder where I'd gone. She'd be sorry.

So there I am in London. It's six months later. I am sitting on a wet bench in a small park in a square of town houses and offices darkened by rain. It is so cold that every sound is magnified. The air is full of the horns and engines of cars even though I can't see any. I have no gloves, but the cold is stopping my ragnails hurting. Round my feet there are filthy pigeons, they're after my sandwich. One of them is black with oil. I decide to befriend it. I throw it some crust and there's a squabble as all the pigeons land on top of the one I wanted to feed.

The wastebin beside me has a fresh newspaper stuck in it, rolled and not too soiled. It is starting to sleet again. I take the newspaper out and unfold it and hold it over my head while I try to think of somewhere free to keep dry.

As I unfold it, a photograph catches my eye. I stare at it, then I have to look away. I look at the words instead. In our special historical supplement over the next three weeks we will be commemorating the fortieth anniversary.

It's heavy now, the sleet, shattering in wet dirty lumps on the page of the paper. I stand in a shop doorway. The story is about the city where just one night's bombing sent a firestorm through the streets so strong that people were sucked into it and eaten like air. It tells how people whose clothes and hair were alight dived into the canal to try and save themselves, but the surface of the water was covered in oil from boats that had been bombed, so where the people hit the water the water caught fire and burned them up if they didn't drown. Photos show the burnt-hard bodies lined up afterwards, mummified by heat. People who had simply been standing on the pavements had burned from the soles of their feet up; the pavements, the paper says, were so hot that stone melted.

A woman comes out of the shop and shoves me in the back with her foot. You can't sit here, she says. Move on. There is pavement beneath my feet, I'm walking. I'm sitting on the tube looking at the black outside the window. I'm walking through the sleet and the litter. I'm in the flat and the door's shut. The boy who lives here, who spends what little time I have to endure being in the same room with him when we coincide at mealtimes blushing and looking at my chest, he's out, even he's out. There is no one. I can hear the sound of voices from other people's televisions in the building, and someone in the street below shouting something I can't make out. I sit down. There's a smell of rubbish from the kitchen. I turn the television on but I can't get the thing I saw out of my head. A face, a mouth drawn back into a smile by what has been burnt off it. Two mouths, two faces, two people, holding each other and melted into each other so it is impossible to tell whose face is whose, whose arm that is, whether it is an arm at all; impossible to tell if that was a woman or that was a man, or what they ever were, what they are.

I'm shivering. It must be cold, it's cold, I'm cold. I'm shaking. I shake the paper apart and roll its pages into balls, shove them deep in the fireplace. I scrunch up the photograph of the two people in my hands and push it right to the back. I light a match. As I light the edge of the paper I see the date on it, today's date, February first. In some traditions, traditionally, today is the first day of spring. The match burns into my finger; I let it fall. I have to stamp hard with my foot on the carpet where it fell. Someone downstairs bangs on the ceiling beneath my feet and shouts up: go fuck yourself.

So I do.

I stand outside her door again for the last time, the last time. And I put my hand on the handle and twist it, and under my hand it opens. And I push it noiselessly, and slide into the room, and close it noiselessly behind me, and I can see her at her desk, writing things down out of books. And I take my heart in my mouth and steal up behind her and I'm kissing the back of her neck, the smell of her hair. But she turns like she's been waiting, she turns so fast she knocks a pile of heavy books off the table on to the floor where they lie page-open, she knocks a half-drunk cup of something all over the floor and she doesn't stop to notice, her arms have caught me too tight and she's kissing me back so hard that it hurts. And then we're staring at each other in wonder, and at what our hands are doing, in open mouthed wonder, and her hand is raking through the hair on the back of my head, she's pulling hard and angry, pleased, she's hurting me as she says, where *were* you? where do you think you've *been*? and I'm giving her this look, like that, like I despise her, because for the thin splinter of a moment I do, and she smiles, I'm smiling too and my hand's gone under the wool and caught the curve of her small breast and she's flinching, she says, you're so cold, and I'm saying, no, it's you, you're so hot, now it's me who's flinching, she's finding places to touch on me I never even knew were there, her mouth on me like hot water though she's still keeping me at arm's length so I'm licking at the fine light hairs on her forearm, at her fingers, blue ink, I'm catching the fragments of her words, I don't know what it is she's saying down there into my thigh like that but then she says my name and it's her name I'm saying, I'm saying it like I don't know any word but it, like it's all there is to say, like it says it all.

And it's the sex scene. It's the Act of Union. It's the moment we've been waiting for. I've been waiting so long for this that I can't hold it, if I'm not careful it'll be over too fast, but she bites into me until it all starts again, I'm not letting her away with this, on top of me like this, I roll her over and I'm tunnelling under miles of skirt and working at the straps and fastenings, only she would wear this kind of stuff in this day and age, put herself through all the binding and strapping and reddening of the skin next to silk, a bad fantasy, but my hand's through it all, there, I've found her, and she's ready, the smell of her strong on me and I know so well, I have known so well for so long just what she'll like, and with my tongue with all her heart I have her shouting, holding in her breath, the sounds of pleasure, pain, fear, love.

She's in me. The crowd oohs and aahs. I'm in her. The crowd claps and cheers and roars for more. We're roaring. We're hot and spitting, an obscene fireworks display, sending sparks into the air that spell out the crudest of gorgeous lurid coloured words across the sky for everyone to see. We are at it like dogs, like feral cats, all hair and hiss and teeth and bloody claws. Savage then gentle, stopped and slowed and now slow rolling, slow eddying, we're the laughing earth and all its wonders. The centre of the universe, planets spinning round our heads. The whole solar system in dripping heat and light. We're how you start a fire, and we're burning. We're nothing. The empty husks of ticking insects light as air, I'm gone. She's sent me into oblivion, and given half a chance I'll do the same to her.

We are eating each other alive on the floor of her book-lined room.

And that's enough. That'll do. That's just about all I need, for now.

Afterwards we're quiet, stiff and sore on the floor and she says, look at the depths to which you've brought me, Ash, and I laugh, and friends again we move to the bed, she pulls the covers over us. Those damned angels everywhere. She says, we can call it our lupercalia. Our wolfing it, I say. Our St. Bridget's day celebration, she says, I knew you'd come. I didn't know I'd come in quite this way, I say, yes, quite, she says, though she berates me for the coarseness of it, then she settles down in the crook of my arm. And tells me that story again, all the stuff about the cows, the candles, the flowers in the footsteps. But the most important thing about her is that when she died, at the moment of her passing between life and death, she was changed. She was transformed into a flowering piece of wood. And that way, Amy's voice, hoarse with the force of the love we've just had, is telling me in my ear, the story never ends. It's happening everywhere you look, on every branch that ever blisters into leaf.

At last. Me and Amy up a tree. We kissed all night and we kissed all day. We made love. We fucked. We had sex. We went to bed and we slept, together, fitted into each other, like I always knew we always should have.

Didn't we.

Because the light we'd made of it filtered the shadows of the room all night. If I opened my eyes it was still lit, flickering with the bare movement of our breathing.

Wasn't it.

NO. Of course not. That's not how it was.

Not how it happened, not what it was like. Nothing but fever-heat, word-calescence. Calcinatio of the alchemists, working in a sweat to make gold out of something that wasn't. Caledonian calefaction. Caledonia! stern and wild, nursing the stories of your precious past, the forming of your mountains when your cold earth boiled and cold rock thawed and folded and shifted and thrust its new shape raw into the air. I can't get no, calefaction.

No. This version of things is simpler, sadder, shameful. It chills me just to think about it and it makes my face burn.

I mean, yes I was lost in a cold city. Yes I saw some old photos in a newspaper, yes I freaked out, lost it, crumbled in my own hands like clay. Yes I went running back, past the people asking for money in the shop doorways and the streets, pushing through commuter suits calling for taxis at the mouth of the

Underground, yes I sat on a metal bench screwed to the concrete in King's Cross and watched the rent boys, and the people taking money out of the machines with their plastic cards, yes I held my hand out in front of me and my hand was not shaking, I could read the name of the place on my rail ticket, and when I read it I could think of nothing but her in her room and the air that was holding her. Yes I stepped off the train with a sigh of relief, walked the safe ancient streets that led back to nothing but her with the stride of someone who knows what's round every corner, solemnly taking the stairs to her door and pausing outside it to watch the solemn moment before my raised hand would beat out the rhythm of the beating of the blood along my very bones etc. Yes it was destiny, yes it was fate, yes it was everything. And yes, guess what. No.

No answer, no one there. The jolt of the locked door when I tried the handle. Well. No worries. I'd wait. I'd wait forever. But it got a bit cold sitting on the stairs, so I thought I'd wait forever inside, and after all I was the girl to know how to get in. Up the fire escape, across the roof, I'd wait in the warm till she opened the door to me. What a surprise. Imagine you here. Where have you been. Ripping back the strands of new ivy and shoving the window up, it was tougher to open than before, but I did, and pushed my shoulders through into it, the known air and smell.

I sat crosslegged on the floor and watched the door. I did this for about half an hour. Then I got up, wandered around. I didn't dare go into the bedroom. I ran my hand over the things on her desk, ran my eyes along the shelves. I sat at the desk and picked up her pen, slid it in and out of its cap. I turned the eye and point of the nib in the weak light. Outside someone rattled keys, and I threw myself across the room to get back to being crosslegged on the floor again, get my face ready, my eyes ready to collide coolly with hers. But the footsteps were someone going away growing fainter on the stairs. Then my legs got cramp from sitting like that so I sat on the couch instead. I looked at the beams in the ceiling, slabs of black grooved wood as big as railway sleepers. I stretched. I looked down, and I saw it straight ahead of me, the journals stacked inside. Thought had come out of her head and run down her arm and out of her hand into that cabinet; in behind the glass her secret words flashed and turned and hid like schools of tiny exotic fish.

I sat forward, leaned on my knees. I stood up, crossed the room. I'd just have a look from the outside. I wouldn't touch. I wouldn't open it. It'd be locked anyway. I balanced on my haunches and looked through the glass of the door. I counted the spines, seven. I tapped the glass. I put a finger lightly on the key and the door fell open, so smoothly and suddenly that I lost my balance and landed on my back.

Well, no. Actually I had to turn the key quite hard, actually the lock was pretty stiff. But I got it open, and I read them. Of course I did, who wouldn't? I took one out and weighed it in my hands. Heavy, and cool to the touch. I took them outside on to the roof, out of sight and out of the wind; I leaned against the water tank, I think that's what it was, big hollow metal rumbling at my back as I read them one after the other. I began with the one she hadn't finished yet, and I worked my way back over the years. By the time I got to the last one it was so dark I could hardly see to read. I finished the last pages of the last one, the youngest her, on the petrol station concourse. I hadn't enough money so I was charming to the man behind the counter and he gave me a gallon in a plastic flask, said I could come in and pay him on my way home. I'm so stupid, I said, I never look at the gauge, this is always happening to me, and I'll need some matches. A lethal combination, eh, he joked, I laughed, smoking's not good for you, he said, nothing that's any fun is, is it? Ha ha, I said. Look out, he said as he handed them to me, you've cut yourself. I looked; my hand and wrist were all scratches, I must have done it on my way through the rose garden.

At the base of the cairn I used the big books off her desk, the dictionaries, the primers. I piled them all up against the inside of the door. All the Proust off one shelf, all of Woolf's expensive hardback diaries off another, I hefted them across the room and I threw in some random novels, books I knew she particularly liked. *Hiroshima Mon Amour, A Lover's Discourse,* I splashed the petrol up the door, shook the last of it out over them. As I shut the window after me the room and the night exploded into light.

Self-bound. That's our legacy. We think we have the right to be no different. Sometimes it's too hard to think just how to be any different. I did the first thing that came into my head. As I ran I heard the buckling windows smash, and I was so pleased with myself that it was sore when I breathed. I'd burnt the place down before it entered my head that I might hurt anybody, anybody but Amy, that is. I was on the road out of that small smug town with her diaries under my arm, the fire alarm spiralling behind me, the sting of petrol on my hands.

I had found out that her handwriting got touchingly younger as the years rewound.

I had found out that she wrote beautifully.

I had found out all number of trivial facts, hundreds of forget-table details, the slightest ripples across her surface. I had read the names of people I'd never heard of, and some I had, and I had followed every flicker of her attention round them.

Most of all I had found out something about myself, which was, after all, my main interest in reading them.

Not a word, not a thought, not a syllable. Not once did I get a mention. I wasn't there, anywhere. She'd left me out.

Now I turned and saw the sky was lit up behind me. The sight of it. The smell on the wind. The charred pages. The historic place of burning. I'd done that, me.

That'd get into her diary, then, if nothing else did.

In the newspaper there would be a picture of the building, familiar except for the black fire-bite out of the middle of it, like a jam sandwich in a comic strip. The roof beams burnt to stumps jutting in mid-air. Minor casualties. Miraculously no fatalities. Irreparable. Bitterly destructive. Heritage. Four centuries. The attacker had destroyed literally hundreds of valuable books, including early volumes of philosophical, medical and mathematical treatise stored in the library's special collection. Many original editions from over the last three hundred years had perished when fallen sixteenth-century rafters from the rooms above had burned through the floor into the underground stores. A priceless set of paintings and artefacts had been destroyed, one of the most unusual of which was a lock of Charlotte Bronte's hair, taken from her head just after her death and preserved until now. Countless other precious things had been lost to smoke and water damage. No group had acknowledged responsibility. Police warned about possible copycat attacks.

The boy who lived in my flat had gone out and left six bottles of Mexican Day Of The Dead beer in the fridge. I drank five of them, flipping the bottle caps on to the kitchen floor. He wouldn't mind, I thought, opening the third; he'd be pleased, I'd owe him something. I sat on the floor by the fridge and as the fear haze turned to beer haze I toasted what I'd done. Cheers, to the books that had gone to heaven. Cheers, to the tuft of famous hair, grey and dusty and dead and now frizzled away, singed into life one last time by a final heated kiss. Cheers, to the colour and smoke and the flames that flooded the National Trust serenity of Amy's museum, to the bending and splitting of things, to the furniture burnt back to bones and the fountain pen melted and ashed. To the scent in the fractured perfume bottles spraying the air like flame throwers. The walls wet with fire. The rich velvet curtains shredded by light. The white bed blackened. I cheered the unconcerned faces of the angels in the flames. I cheered my friend. Here's to her, wha's like her. The label on the bottle in my hand had dancing skeletons and red devils on it. I clinked the half-full bottle against the empties; they fell over. The past was past. I would make something of myself. Now I could. Now I had fire cracking my skull, a tongue of fire. Now I could speak the languages of all the beasts.

I don't remember much after that, but I remember crawling round the sticky linoleum, speaking the language of beasts. Then I fell asleep where I was and woke up there on the floor. All the next day I spent throwing up in the filthy toilet, weak as grass. By the end of the day I was throwing up blood. The boy came in to see if I was all right, he made me a horrible milky cup of tea, sat on the end of the bed, looked worried, looked at my chest. I let him touch. It was another wrong decision, another wrong thing to do. It's always a bad idea to sleep with someone you don't actually like, even if it makes you feel better at the time. You can't go much lower. But that's another story.

Gaunt and lost. Flapping in the wind like an empty shirt on a line, an empty skin. Dazed, like a kitten on the edge of a motorway. Everywhere you look, written across the grey sky or blue sky or black sky above the buildings, written above the shops where the shop names should be, written on every blank face that passes you in the street. You are nobody to the one who is everything to you.

But that didn't last long. Romantic crap. It was soon over.

And when I could think about it more, well, dispassionately, it was pure disappointment. How anal, how banal her beautiful words had been, after all. Pages of opinions and speculations on other academics and academic politics, who was going for what job, who discussed Hegel and Derrida and Cixous and Kristeva where, who said which rather clever thing to whom, who gave which seminar paper, who published what and who put down who and what they were wearing when they did. The relentless recording of calories, and of whatever she was working on at the time. Stuff about cross-referencing and indexing. Stuff about headaches and eczema (the doctor gave her hydrocortisone, told her to eat bread). A lot of sub-erotic stuff about someone I couldn't recognise. A piece about the attractive powerplay of teaching. A piece about how very pretty Simone was. And I can't forget a pervasive little fantasy about some girl on the kitchen staff, *her thin wrists and her pale face above the stained white overall, the silent insolence of her averted gaze.*

Words and lines like that one still come into my head by themselves. I opened one diary and the inscription on the first page was a quote: *There is nothing worth the having more than that which cannot be had.* It was one of the early books; she had surrounded it with neat wavy squiggles. And, from a later one, *I do love to play. I love the axial shift of the slightest look or touch or word.* I looked up axial afterwards. And one paragraph I remember studying in particular. Twenty words. *I am reading A Pair Of Blue Eyes. The plot is rather unsatisfactory but the heroine deliciously vague and weak.* I remember it even down to the underlining blue and firm and decisive under deliciously. When I read these words to myself in the failing light up on the roof, they were the only smudged clue I could find to tell me that now I was probably reading about the time she was once on holiday, with her parents, in the Highlands of Scotland.

You never know what sound or smell or word, what barbed little detail you'll have swallowed somewhere along the line. It would be good if you could just hoover your memory out. I thought that writing this would be like that, that I would write it all down and then I could close the cover and it'd be over, out. But it's given me the bad dreams again. Like the one last night where she comes up to me and my face is wet and she kisses each pinpoint of water off my face, saying, be careful, your face is all diamonds, they may cut you, let me take them, I promise to keep them safe for you. She picks each one off with her tongue and as she goes you can see light glancing off their sheer sides behind her teeth.

Write it in the sand and let the sea smooth it away. Write it on paper then hold a match to the corner. Write it in a book and shut the cover. Bury it in the garden or send it through the post to a place that doesn't exist. I read them just the once, that's all, and that's in my power, to choose never to open them again, to put them in a box, seal it shut with parcel tape and leave it behind. As for this one, it's nearly finished now. I've done my confessing. Some time ago I was desperately, blindly, selfishly in love. Luckily, nobody was too seriously hurt.

There.

Or maybe it's much simpler than all the heat and the noise. Maybe we just met on the street and this time I chose to look straight through her, as if I couldn't see her, and we went past like people who don't know each other from Adam. Maybe we ran into each other in the street one hot hot day, and exchanged pleasantries about the weather, and with the shying eyes of people who haven't really that much in common, that much to say to each other any more, looked past each other, at the people buying fruit in the market square, and the people going to pay their electricity bills in the electricity showroom, and said, hot, isn't it, yes, isn't it, well, see you around, yes, and goodbye. Everything held in the one trivial word. That would be the civilised way; you could call that the English way.

Anyway, either way. The Amy part of this is over.

———

His boat is smaller than I thought it would be, just a rowing boat really with a motor stuck on the back. It has the name June on the side, on both sides. I did that lettering myself, he said when he saw me looking.

He steered us out to the middle of the loch and cut the motor. Silence, the smell of petrol, and the sound and thick smell of the water moving beneath us. I watched him tie the fly and the weights on; his fingers were too big but he wouldn't let me do it. Your brother made this one, he said, holding the fly up. You remember that case on the wall in the living-room? It got smashed in the move. They're better on the end of a line anyway. That's what they were made for.

No no, for God's sake girl that's not how to do it, he said. He took the rod out of my hands. Like this, he said. But that's exactly what I did, I said. Yes, he said, but you did it wrong. You don't get the pull on it or the length on it if you do that. Do what? I said. Well, what you did, he said. Now be quiet. You'll catch bloody nothing if they hear you coming.

Miles from land, unsteady on the surface and the midgies gathering. Great. Too early, too early in the morning for me, and I felt hung over, weird to be anywhere near the place again; the last time I was out here Donna and I were busy finding somewhere to hide, so it's perfect, timed just right, when my father starts in on me. You do still go to Mass, now, don't you? I'd be sorry if you didn't. I'd be sorry if you'd let all that go to waste. You need your faith. A help to you. Disappointed. Your mother'd have been. Raised decently. I made sure. I made sure for her. No other woman made me turn my head, even. Nobody ever took your mother's place. From the moment I put the ring on her finger there was nobody for me but your mother.

I couldn't help it, I burst out laughing. The laugh hurt the back of my throat. He laughed too, confused.

Oh yeah, faithful, I said. Faithful, yeah, sure you were.

From the moment I put the ring on her finger, he said again. He was fiddling with the reel. He was looking away across the loch, and he shook his head. He said, well, I'd not expect you to know what it was like.

Yeah, that's right, I said. You're the man who loved and lost. And there's nothing in the world like a hurt romantic man.

He stood up, rounded on me; the boat swayed, dangerous. I think he was shouting, it was very loud. How would you know? How the hell would you know? How the hell would you know what it was like? How could there be anything in your joke of a life that was like anything I had? How? You've no right. They were the happiest years of my life. My whole life.

He sat back down. I pushed my boot as far as I could into a dent in the floor of the boat, into the curve of the planks. One plank had begun to split. He never used to take me fishing. It was always the boys got taken fishing, never me.

As for you, he was saying. Well I'll tell you girl. As for you. I'm ashamed. Your mother'd be ashamed too. What you've done.

I didn't know what he meant. What I'd done. What I'd done. Now he had his reasonable voice on again, the expansive, generous voice. In my day the girl stayed at home in your old age. In my day that was the point of having them. But you live your life. You go and live it. You enjoy it. There's bugger all else to do with it.

This is rich, I was thinking, coming from him, and running through my head the time I made myself a boiled egg and I had to reach up above my head to boil the kettle, stand on the stool to light the gas, put the pan on the cooker, because there was no one else there to do it, and all the crimplene women who paraded through our dinette with their sad excited eyes, but I didn't say, I let the silence fall round his reasonable voice. I could sense his broad back inches away almost touching my own back, and then something else he'd said smashed open in my head; so I would never know, would I, what it was like to love someone like that? The joke my life was, joke, was that what he'd said? Ashamed. He'd definitely said ashamed. Well if he was ashamed, I was too. I was still ashamed, last night seeing his eyes on that teenage girl, and I was going to say it but then I didn't, I kept it burning inside my head as proof that I was right and he was wrong, I heard him make an exasperated noise under his breath and I hunched my shoulders and shifted away to the very edge of the plank I was on. I heard him huff out a sigh. I sighed too. I sat and stared stonily ahead. He was staring stonily ahead too, I could feel it. I looked out over the water at the hills and the trees and the sky clearing, the light over the surface of the loch. A bird was singing, the same few notes, then again, and again, and the mountains stretched round us and down, green and brown, into the water.

We sat in the boat in the beautiful place with our backs turned on each other.

Then from nowhere my rod was jerked nearly out of the boat and the reel was whirring wildly and the whole boat was jolting in the water. Girl, girl, you've got one, my father was at my back with his arms coming round me, feed it, feed it, he was shouting, it's a big one, Christ, it's a beauty, don't lose it now, that's right, that's it, you're doing it. The rod bent like a bow above me, what if it breaks, what if it snaps, I was saying, no no, he was laughing, feed it out and draw it back, run with it, that's the way, that's it, you're a natural, that's it, give and take, play it in, gently, gently, that's the way.

I brought it kicking and flapping to the side of the boat. He swung it in and I shied away as he gaffed it on the floor. He slid his finger under the gill, hung it pink and silver off his arm. Its cold eye was wide and bloody, and slime and blood ran down from its neck. That's a fourteen pounder, he said, see if it's not. See this, see the tail. See how it fans out? That's a wild one. The farmed ones have smaller tails, not like this.

He held the salmon up. You always were a lucky fisher, girl, he said. Look at that, now. Is that not beautiful?

Patrick in the back garden, with a stick, some string, a slice of white bread and a cardboard box from the Co-op. What're you making? I asked. He tied the string around the stick and balanced one edge of the box on it. Then we hid behind the fence and when the bird went inside to get the bread he yanked the stick away and the box fell down over it. He let me look through the top where the flaps didn't quite overlap and I saw the blackbird's eye looking back at me, the yellow ring round the black, before Patrick pulled me off. You could hear it hitting its wings and beak and head off the sides of the cardboard, then you could hear how quiet it went. Sometimes they die of fear, he said, they die of heart attacks. I thought of all the birds flying above all the back gardens; I thought how I had looked one of them right in its prehistoric eye.

Mostly he caught blackbirds or starlings and kept them under the box for a while on the lawn then let them go. We wanted a dog but it wasn't allowed. James said it was because our father had had one when he was a boy and his father had made him kill it. We had the record of Hank Snow singing Old Shep. Shep saves his master from drowning at the old swimming hole, then when Shep is too old his master holds the gun to his head, but he just can't do it, he wants to run, he wishes they would shoot him instead. Once when we were sitting listening to it grinding out of the record player I looked round at Patrick and James and saw they were both crying, both pretending they weren't. If you left the plastic arm off the top of the records then the record player would keep playing the same record over and over. You could kill yourself, Patrick said, and your favourite song would keep on playing after your death. But you wouldn't be able to hear it any more, I said. That's the point, stupid, Patrick said. Anyway, how do you know you wouldn't, James said. He switched on the television. Robinson Crusoe, the waves breaking in black and white on the shore.

Like there was the time in the holidays when he made the boys take me with them for the day; they cycled out the Nairn road with the idea they'd easily get sixteen miles to the beach or the penny arcade, I was trying not to lag behind, and we'd hardly got out of town and the rain started. It was pouring down; they were wheeling the bikes across a field to get under some trees. James saw the shed. Through the window we saw tools and a workbench. The door was open. It was as wide as a barn inside, and half filled with sawdust piled in a hill that touched the roof. How or why I can't really remember, except that I wasn't supposed to play, I was supposed to hide my eyes. Patrick went first. He pulled his clothes off and stood like a statue with his fist at his forehead, his genitals hanging small and curled and compact, whiter than the rest of him and smooth like china, as smooth as his chest. Then James slowly pulled his jumper off, slowly pushed his shorts down over his knees and stepped out of them, and stood naked with his arms hanging by his sides, he was hairier than I'd seen before, hairier than Patrick, his body lumpy and his face serious, I think about it now and he's standing there like the illustration photograph for something in a medical book.

I had to fight for my turn. If I was going to have a turn I'd have to leave my top on, James said. He'd taken *his* off, I said. Girls had to be more private, Patrick said. Anyway, girls didn't have anything to show; there was no point in me doing it. I walked round the side of the sawdust hill and piled my wet clothes up as they came off. I stood where they had, exactly where they had, where the imprints of their feet were still in the sawdust. Their faces, turned away, shy. I stuck my arms out like the women assistants did on the David Nixon magic show, but they still wouldn't look. I wiggled. I did a kind of dance humming the strip tease tune, and their faces were so grave that I began to laugh. I fell over laughing, I was rolling about on the floor of the shed. I ran at the hill, threw myself up it until I was pushing the palm of my hand against the roof. That made them join in. When we'd finished there was no hill left and there was sawdust everywhere on the floor of the shed, flung all round the bench and all over the machines. I had to dig to find my shirt. We were putting our clothes back on again, Patrick was swearing as he put his legs into wet trousers, when the man came back from his lunch and threw us out with a lot of shouting.

Sawdust all over me. In my ears, hair, clothes; small yellow scrolls, paper-thin wood. In my brothers' hair and clothes on the way home, the wind snatching it off them and bouncing it along the road as they cycled ahead of me. There was sawdust on the floor of the bathroom after tea when I was washing my face. Sweet when you held it to your nose. Sweet and rough on your tongue when you tried it to see how it tasted.

James put his head round the door of my room that night where I was reading in bed. If any boy ever messes with you, Ash, he said, you just tell us, and we'll do something about it, we'll sort them out. You just tell me, you hear?

My father said, do you remember the night you were crying your head off when the Irish girl won the Eurovision Song Contest?

The fish was on the floor of the boat; my father had taken a drink out of his flask and offered me some. I could feel it burning all the way from my throat to my stomach. No, I said, choke-laughing, I don't remember that at all. I don't even remember the song.

I couldn't get you to stop, he said. By God I thought you were dying. It was that Irish girl, that one who does the holy programmes now. You remember. You would if you heard it. She came out to sing the song again on the stage after she won, and

I looked round and there were tears running down your face, I said, what's the matter? I thought you must be in pain, you were maybe not well, I said, are you sore somewhere? You went on crying and crying, I couldn't get you to stop. I carried you up to your bed, I was going to call the doctor and you said, it's not my tummy, it's the song. I said, the song? what song? and you said, the song the girl sang. Well, I couldn't work it out. I thought maybe you were angry that Britain hadn't won. I tried to make you laugh, I said, never mind, we'll win next year, and on Monday I'll buy you a copy of that awful song and we'll drop it out of the bathroom window and see if it smashes on the stones. And you said, no, dad, no, I liked that song that won, I liked it. I sat back and I said to myself, well that beats all, she's crying because she likes something.

No, I said again. I don't remember any of that.

He said, do you know, they think that ten thousand years ago this was a jungle paradise under here? I read it in the paper. Scientists took a sample off the bed of the loch, they think it was a tropical paradise with grapes and all growing down there.

He said, we were sailing into Syracuse and the Americans were landing at Palermo. It was midnight, maybe half-past, and I was only young but we'd heard the guns before. There were these gliders in the water. The Americans, see, cut them loose and let them fall and ran off scared of the anti-aircraft, and they were five or six miles off the shore, these gliders, packed with men and stuck in the water. They called to us to pick them up, they were waving. We couldn't stop, you can't just stop the engine like that, we told them we'd pick them up on the way back. The Plain of the Dead they call it. Mount Etna, when Etna blows its top it all falls on the Plain of the Dead, that's why they call it that. Jesus, it was a good name for it that day. Two hundred, three, maybe four hundred of them, and they were all in their gear, all the heavy equipment, they wanted us to pick them up. Well, when we came back, maybe six hours later, half six in the morning and it was a beautiful morning too, there wasn't a man left alive, the gliders had gone down. And I'll tell you girl. You never hear about that on the television. You never hear that on their documentaries, their *World at War*. Nobody says a bloody word about that. Three hundred of them, maybe more, all our boys. Oh it was high summer, we had the time of our life in the harbour swimming and lying in the sun, diving off the side of the boat. One time we were diving off the side and Jerry dropped a bomb, landed on the other side of the boat and never touched us. But after that, ha ha, the officers wouldn't come down into the ship's mess any more in case we got hit. Then we sailed up into the Bay of Naples. Then the war was on the turn.

He said, my own father was in Italy in the First. Got gassed in Ypres, got invalided out, signed up again, got shot in Italy, invalided out, signed up again. He didn't want to come home. He was a gamekeeper for the laird, and the laird was a German sympathiser; he threw all the men off the land when they got back from the fighting.

He said, the smaller house suits me better. Now that you're all off. The birds have to leave the nest. Anyway I wasn't sorry to go. I got up one day and some bugger had put a dead rat in the dustbin. One day they put a note through the door about burning out the bloody Fenians. The Johnstones, I think, a right queer bunch, the Johnstones. Ach, I couldn't be bothered with it, or the business, nothing but a dead weight. I'm better off without it. Years it takes to build it up, and it ends like that, he snapped his fingers, it ends in the blink of an eye. Somewhere else opens with its own car park and there's nobody left for you. Hygena got bought out. Wrighton got bought out. It's all different now. Electrolux, Whirlpool, the big companies bought up all the white electrics. You go into any store and you'll see. Made cheap and sold hard. It's not the same. It's enough to make you wonder what it's all for, girl. And what it's all about, I'll tell you that. Years you give to it, and what have you got?

He said, the first thing was, she fell over in the shower. She said the floor was slippery. A month, just a month, and you could almost see through her she went so thin. When she was on the drugs for the pain she told me I was the colour blue. She said I tasted of blueberries. She said there was a man in the room and a bird in it too. She kept trying to move her head out of the way of its wings.

He held the flask upside down above the water and shook it; nothing came out. He screwed the top back on. He said, the very first time I saw her she had a towel wrapped round her head, she'd been washing her hair. I was working for McIvor then, I was putting a kitchen in an upstairs flat in Telford Street, and I saw this woman with a towel round her head waving to me from down in the garden next door, I waved back, then I thought I'd chance my luck, she was pretty good-looking from up there, and I leaned out of the window to shout, hello, I saw you waving, I shouted. Waving? she said, I wasn't waving, and she had this different accent, I couldn't work out where she was from that first time I heard her. You did wave, I said, I saw you, you were waving like this. Oh no, she said, that wasn't waving, I didn't even know anyone was up there, I was chasing away a fly, like this, and she started to laugh, so I asked her out anyway, and her hair, the colour, like yours it was but it was long, she took the towel off and her hair fell all down and round, well by God I said to her that night when we went to the dance, if I'd known you were a blonde I'd have asked you out even quicker so I would. She was a dancer, you know. Jesus, she could dance. There wasn't anybody could dance like her.

He didn't say anything else. He'd turned so I couldn't see his face. I know, I said. I know, right. Right you are, dad.

I'm sitting up here and I'm wondering about when this house was built, where the bricks and stone came from, who the first people were to bring chairs and cups and carpets into it, and the next people, and the next. If the ground under it remembers what it was like to be light and grass. If the streets and the pavements and the houses and the office buildings and the shops and street-lights, all the things that make up a town, can all be pulled up and rolled back like a carpet. Like for a dance we're too human to know the steps of. If battlefields remember what happened on them. If new buildings hold the ideas, the cores somewhere of the old ones that were there before them. If, the day after tomorrow, I'll have left something in this room I was never in before, more than just old dead skin or the scuffed dust of my moving around in it for a few days one spring.

Nah. It's good to know things can just go, can disappear into thin air. It's good that marks are hard to leave, or if they're left you can't always read what they are. There's a free country in that. We're always hanging on to what we know, what we remember, like it's got the power to make us who we are. Maybe it would be better to hang on to what we don't know, maybe there's a better kind of power in that. There's so much more of what we don't know. What we know compared to it is like, well, I don't know. A leaf, compared to a whole forest full of unknown plants and uncharted trees full of squalling howling chattering silent creeping flying multicoloured living creatures. A speck of sand and Ben Wyvis. A drop in the ocean. A cliché.

But my father, leaning on a formica worktop with the cookers and the kitchens shining round him, their surfaces unscratched, their cupboards empty, waiting, longing to be filled; nothing behind their doors but new-smelling air, unsullied shelves, a little storeroom dust. Schreiber. Hygena. Kandya. Jonelle. English Rose. Grovewood. Peerless. Prestige. Tall Cupboard. Tall Wall Unit. Corner Wall Unit. Standard Wall Unit. L Shaped Worktop. External Drawer Unit. Hob Unit. Single Drainer Sink Unit. Words that from nowhere can conjure a home. Younger, with a pencil stuck rakishly behind one ear, in a shop bright with overhead fluorescent lighting, his tie loose and the top button of his shirt undone and his sure sale smile reflecting in the eyes of the woman he's serving, her pot-bellied husband bored in the background standing winding the handle on a wall-fitted tin-opener and watching the little teeth go round.

I was waiting on the bank as he moored the boat. The whisky was wearing off, he was whistling.

So what about that Barbara, then? I asked.

Barbara? What about her? he said. He sat heavily down beside me, began to pack the fish carefully into his bag.

Well, you know. Have you, well, have you done her kitchen yet for her?

Oh no, he said, she doesn't need it done, it was refitted about ten years ago when she rewired her house. Then he caught on, looked sideways at me, laughed out loud. Why, you fly wee monkey, he said. You wee chancer, you. He laughed for a long time. Oh no, he said. Barbara's not my type. You know me. I like them a bit younger than Barbara.

I think she likes you a bit, though, I said.

Aye, well, that'll be right, he said, that'd be it, right enough. He got up, put the bag on his shoulder and straightened his jacket, looked out over the water. He was smiling.

All the way home he was smiling. You fly wee chancer, he kept saying. Have I done her kitchen yet? Have I done her kitchen? I never heard the like.

I am thirteen, and I am leaning out of the boys' bedroom window looking across the hills one evening in early spring, an evening like this. Birds are singing all over the sky. My brothers are out. Down in the back garden my father is hanging a washing on the line; it must be after he brought home the new whirly washing line and spent a Sunday afternoon making concrete for planting its steel leg in the middle of the lawn. The next door neighbour is in her back garden too; she's taking her washing in. She comes to the hedge and shouts over. He shouts back and goes to speak to her for a moment; they laugh and come back to their washing lines. As I watch he shakes out a shirt that flashes white in the last of the light. He pulls at the legs of the wet-dark jeans to stretch them. He has the peg bag hanging from a belt loop in his trousers, and pegs pinned on the lapel of his work jacket. I can see Mrs. Short crossing her lawn, going into her house with her arms full of dry clothes. I can see my father bending over the laundry basket. He puts the pants neatly together on the same line. He hangs the socks in pairs. He pegs the tea-towel with the picture of the toucan on it upside down. The sky is deep red now, the day is burning up round us. He looks up and sees me, smiles and calls. Get down here girl and hang the rest of this out for me. No way, I say, grinning. I'm busy right now.

I'm there with my chin on my hands, leaning out of the window watching him, and the words I'm thinking are these: I don't know what I'd do without my dad, I really don't.

SO I'm home. I'm home and I'm gone. Seagulls as big as small dogs still stamping on the roofs, still fighting over old fish and chip papers on the river bank, or landing and standing blankly on the stones that break the run of the river foaming past them. River grey and fast between the grass banks and the churches and shops, past the low old houses there since after the Jacobites, past the Highlands and Islands Development Board office blocks, leaving the Old High and the Caley and the castle and the Kilt Shop behind and speeding beneath the bridges, furrowing round their struts, pushing from the hills through the town and out into the Firth, then the wide water that coasts the edge of the country and out beyond land. Smoke of spring fires shrouding the evening town, smoke from the chimneys and smoke rising from the fields, like held breath in the Sunday sky as the town settles in its curve for another night, the houses on the estates closing their curtains, the church spires all along the river fading to silhouette, the washed-out weather-battered bird-shat stone of the streets and the shops and the buildings is changing tone again in the going light, the weak street lights, of just another gone day.

Scenery going dark. Hills to the north, hills to the south, I don't know their names. Mountains that hang at the back of the sky as white as ghosts from the last few snows, and night coming down again over bleak Drumochter, grim treeless gateway to the Highlands. Coming down over the Cairngorms, the forests of Loch an Eilein, the tourist chalets at Aviemore, the German soldier's head carved by the wind in the rockface at the side of the road by Tomatin. Night on Loch Linnhe, Loch Lochy, night over all the places I can't remember or never knew the names of, and all the ones I do. Castle Urquhart, Glen Urquhart, Glen Moriston, Fort Augustus, Fort William, Fort George, Fortrose, the Black Isle, Beauly, Muir of Ord, the north. Blanking out the dual carriage-ways where the cars going north and south throw their pins of light, and the darker tourist roads, General Wade's old road; the silent clan names gashed into the rocks at Culloden, gone dark; dark on deer forests, trout rivers, rocks and pines, and the smoky frozen quartz buried deep inside the mountains. Wind and land and water and the storm-scratched ridges high in the sky, the long Lairig Ghru filling with dark with nobody there to see; rain falling unwitnessed above hills and rivers, sheep rubbing against fences with their feet in stringy heather; night. No line left now between the mountains and the sky. Darkening on calm Loch Ness, over Foyers where the waterfall is, and Dores where the nice pub is and the pebbly beach, over Abriachan and the road west, over the locks and the weirs and up the spine of the canal and over the town and all the houses. And this house, and this window, and here.

Glen Urquhart, Glen Moriston, Glen Livet, Glen Morangie, Glen Campbell, Glen da Jackson, Will Ye No Come Back Aglen. This is my last entry. Entry, what a word. But that's what diaries are, a going into it, where you put yourself in the landscape. As if what you do each day every day, day in day out, matters; look, I'm a contender. This is what I did. This is what I thought. This is what I'll be doing with my day tomorrow, and the next day, and next week and next month.

I'm no Anne Frank; I'm one of the lucky ones. I don't have history to deal with, thank God, and the world has no need of this particular life-and-times. At my level it's wanking. A long slow circling self-important lot of wank.

Though this was never a diary. Vile idea. And at the same time it is one, vile as it is. I'm pressing against all the written pages beneath my pen and I am wondering what it is that I'll have left out, what thing it is that I don't know and never knew. The things we so blithely forget or don't see; the whole selves that can disappear and nobody thinks to report it, nobody calls an inquest. Instead there's this blind obsession with something or someone; a decadence, a kind of adolescent luxury, the self-torture that helps you not see the real torture. I've wallowed in it, swallowed it, rolled in its musk and my own, and I still haven't made sense of it. Well, good. I wouldn't want it to lose its impact completely for me. What would I do at nights without it?

So, soon, I'll close this book. Goodbye. Maybe I'll put it in a box with the other diaries. That'd be good; they'd breed, some sort of hybrid loping guttural creature that's terribly polite, roaming the countries of the world hopelessly looking for where it belongs or looking for someone to rub up against, someone to listen to its story. On second thoughts maybe it'd be better to burn it. The record of one passing week at home in the Highlands, when I was twenty-six years to heaven and nothing much happened.

Now though as the dark comes down I am staring for all I'm worth out of the window at where I live, and it's the picture inside my own head that's still clearest. It's hard to see what's really out there past the scratches that get left on the retina by what you've seen before and the fiddly engravings already etched into the surface of your brain. Apparently the new cells of the body will still, years after the bite, reproduce the shapes of the teeth that bit you all those years ago. Bodies, hoarding what scars them, bodies are the places your memories hog the best armchair, flick the television over from what you're watching to the programme they want, and sit there exhaling the smells of earlier suppers, mince and tatties when you were a child, mm, remember that?

This afternoon I went for a walk. I went up to the top of Tomnahurich, up from the bottom of the hill with its fresh graves waiting, the soil hidden under the bright green artificial grass they use so as not to shock the mourners, and the curved new mounds of earth covered in bouquets of flowers just beginning to brown. I went up past the dead soldiers, the Second World War stones a little whiter than the First World War, the shiny buttons rusting and the regimental fabrics rotting to dust in the black beneath. Up past the stones of the fifties and forties, past the black granite Protestant stones and the ornate Catholic ones with the breasty angels and the stone bibles, running my hand over the fixed pages. Sunday, so it was busy with people bringing flowers, but the further up I went the fewer people there were, soon nobody but me on the path. Back through the thirties and twenties, I went on up past 1915, 1903, all the way to the top, a century ago. I sat where I used to sit, on the granite bricks round the edge. I leaned against the stone. Back then I'd have brought a book, or my made-up dog (sending him off to look for bones, ha ha), later stolen cigarettes from the container behind the birth certificates in the bureau. Lighting the matches just so I could blow them out. Scraping the letters in the stone with the end of the match to gouge the lichen out. Dedicated to the Memory Of   Margaret Ethel Inkster   1839–1877   Beloved Wife of John Inkster   Merchant of this Parish.

The words don't look any fainter than they did ten years ago. The day, sharp and clear, the clear smell of the pointed firs and ferns and earth and old leaves. All the tall trees evergreen, or getting ready for the new leaves. Below me the whole cemetery, green and hard like a damp rock; beyond, the canal slipping along its carved route exactly where the Brahan Seer said it would. I can see ships with furled sails round the dry foot of Tomnahurich, he said, and hundreds of years later Thomas Telford said just the same thing, only he probably made a lot more money out of it.

I shifted down and sat by Margaret Ethel Inkster's feet. Small and dark in her heavy Victorian clothes, her tweeds and shawls and skirts. She'd have been quite well off married to a merchant, of wool maybe, or sheep, or imported goods in a shop. A nice smile, that's how I thought of her when I was fourteen too. Give her the benefit of the doubt, let her have smile lines round her mouth as well as weather lines, and a penchant for giving the poor children who played outside her shop sweets out of the jar so long as they promised to say their prayers. No, let's take that bit about prayers out, make her a woman quietly ahead of her time. Down at the river with the other women, beating their wet clothes on the stones. Rolling newspaper into spills for the fire, stopping to look at the paper in her hand, a picture of a boat, an advert for the boats in the west going to America, thinking of the people, you still saw them in the town, tired with the walking and nothing to eat. And when she was small herself she hit a hoop with a stick, sent it bowling along down by the river, and her grandfather told her stories about the old language, and the people burned out of their houses where the smoke on the hillside was visible for miles, and how some of them carved their names in the window glass when, no homes to go to in the snow, they hid in the church. And took her to see the barges nosing along the new canal, and told her again how they'd been digging it since he was a boy over forty years ago.

Who knows what she was like? More likely she was nothing like that, nothing like it at all. I sat on her grave and I made up my mind not to go chasing my mother's remains in Boston after all, or her mother's and father's, whoever they were. No point now. Smiling so prettily in fading black and white she's a young girl, younger than me now, sitting in the grass in a summer print dress, holding her dress round her knees and bending forward for who-ever is taking the picture so that she's held in the square of paper as if she curled herself neatly in there on purpose, just the right fit. When you look closely you notice the pattern on her dress is a sort of African one, with exotic animals, birds, flowers; you can see a gazelle, a strutting peacock, a tree bearing fruit, falling into place all down her body. Smiling on a lovely summer afternoon, the moment stops. Her face is shadow and light.

That's better than some name on a square of brass in a place I've never been or seen. And Margaret Ethel Inkster's bones, her slim frame of space, will do just as well for last rites; that's what I thought when I was fourteen and she had to do, and that's what I thought now, as I stood up off the cold granite and picked my way between the old hardly-marked places, hoping not to be stepping on anybody, till I came to where you get the best view. There wasn't much to see. Far up on Craig Phadraig cars were glinting between the trees, and there were people on bicycles, small people walking their dogs along the canal banks, the dogs running ahead, stopping to sniff and circle each other with their tails up and running back.

There was even heat in the sun. Warm, but it wasn't going to stay warm for long. Sun falling through the bare branches on to the curve of mossy grass that's Margaret Inkster; I went back and took my jacket off, spread it out and lay down on my back on top of her, thought of her beneath me with her nice smile, she wouldn't mind, and even if she did, not much she could do about it now. I pulled a piece of grass and put it between my teeth; the inside of it was sweet. I was trying to think how to say it; what it's like. I was lying there and I liked the idea that tomorrow, and the next day, and the next, for a while at least, there'll be cars going along that road and people with their dogs going up and down and up and down the footpath by the canal.

Like the way a leaf opens, flattens itself out and you can trace the veins in it. Like holding a leaf in the palm of your hand. Like the brilliant colour it is. Like the thirty seconds that it takes for an earthquake to kill thousands of people, or gas to leak out of a factory and poison and blind thousands of people. Like the story the builder told me when I lived in Hartwell Street, about his daughter, they'd just found out she had something wrong on the inside of her head, he said, he said the word tumour as if it were a word in a language foreign to him that he was determined to get right, she was twenty-two and she was losing her sense of smell and she was angry that the steroids were making her so fat, it's not just that she's dying, he said as he picked at the fireplace with his chisel, and stopped and looked down, and looked round, it's that everything else is so bleeding miserable for her too, you know what I mean? Like the old man on the train who was show-ing the woman opposite him his collection of photos of steam engines, proud like they were pictures of his family, and she was embarrassed, pretended to be asleep when she saw him coming back from the buffet. Like the ferry that went down last month and took all those people with it, or the shuttle exploding, the schoolteacher's children waving their flags at the smoky wreath, a great primeval bird's head drawn on the sky. Like the top of the reactor blowing clean off and leaving the country scorched away for hundreds of miles round it, whole villages blown away, with the news on tv about how reindeer in Norway were ill because of it. Like how, right now, somewhere in the world not far from here, because nowhere in the world is really that far from any-where else, they will be lining people up and shooting them into pits or at the side of the road because they believe different things, or have different nationalities, or are a different colour, or something like that, or something to do with money. Like how people play all day on their computers with money that doesn't exist, like how there are people who can spend £75,000 on silk ties. Like how there are people who can't afford a loaf and have to fill in forms to see if they're eligible for the money for it. Like when what's her name Carmen's friend had to have the abortion and Carmen woke her up the next day with four pancakes piled with ice-cream, ran her a bath, warmed the towels on the radiator for her, what else can you do? I didn't know what else to do, she said afterwards. Like what she said about when she took the tamazepam, how the whole world outside would hurtle through a hole in her forehead the size of a pinprick and expand in her skull, so she felt like her head was going to have to stretch like a balloon and that it would burst if anything touched it; she developed a fear of the sharp teeth of brushes and combs. Emotion recollected in tranquillisers. Like James, last time I saw him. I don't want to think about that. God, yes, like when there were all those kids in a big circle in the playground yelling fight fight fight, and a girl from the class above told me it was my brothers, I didn't believe her till I saw their tee-shirts, the ones with the brown stripes, dressed the same they were vicious, punching and kicking at each other and for the first time ever I couldn't tell which was which until Patrick, he must have been winning, but he looked so scared too, and James so diminished, till the janitor separated them and was dragging them in to see the headmaster, shaking each of them by the shoulder and I saw Patrick even then glance worried at James and even then after everybody had seen, James nodded, you won, with the slow bruised smile coming. Like the endless jokes, why was the beach wet? because the seaweed, like the joke that was so unfunny that it made us fall about laughing, Batman and Robin were walking along the road, and

Batman fell, and Robin laughed, and Batman said why are you laughing? and Robin said because that was funny, like how they used to torture me with that one to get me to laugh if I was crying or in a huff and no matter how hard I tried not to laugh it was impossible, I couldn't not. Like how once the phone went and it was for me and someone said it was the Beatles, it was Paul, just phoning to say hello, and he asked me how I was and what my favourite song was, Yellow Submarine, I said, then the pips went, it wasn't till years later that I realised it hadn't been the Beatles at all, but one of my brothers. Yes, like that too.

I turned over on the grass and lay with my head on my forearm. I turned and the sun sent the spectrum through my fringe, my eyelashes. Like the sun, making you sweat and your heart beat faster, changing the colour of things. Communion wafer through clouds, imagine the sun on your tongue. Bless me Father for I have sunned. Like the first time you kiss someone, the moment before you touch, then the moment when you do, the soft-rough mouths of boys, the smooth insistent mouths of girls and women. The first real kiss, the one you know you've been waiting for because after it you're full of explosive and the tips of your fingers are lit. Like Donna and me, midsummer, hard at each other in that rusted ancient dormobile her parents kept down by the lochside for putting up visitors, we picked the lock and pulled the curtains and pulled off our clothes, tore them off, she still had one sock on, her mouth was all over me, we were miles from anywhere and we could make as much noise as we wanted, then we realised we were rocking the van on its axles like they did in all the films, that was funny, it's blurred now like a twenty-four-hour flu but I can remember the moment of her shoulders, the arch of her elbow and her smooth-haired forearm moving, the fear and then the sheer guiltless pleasure reflecting from my face to hers and back again; light came through the gap in the curtains at two in the morning, it hardly got dark at all, there were birds' cries in the tall trees above us and the sound of water pushing in at the edge of the land all night. Her fine firm hands on me. Yes, like putting your hand fearfully, fearlessly, on someone. Someone else's hand fearless on you. Shocked into a smile yourself at the pure soar of power someone's just sent through you. Like putting a leaf in your mouth. Standing on the middle of Waterloo bridge and looking at the buildings along the river. Watching films with your father on a rainy afternoon, not having to say a word. Like singing, going swanking down the street. Like the days you get to cycle with the wind behind you. Hot days. Sleeping on that woman's roof when the hotel was full in Crete, rocky and furzy like Scotland in heat, nothing but the sky above us, and making up names for the stars we couldn't remember the names of, being wakened by the noise of the bells round the necks of the she-goats the woman was hauling away from their kids up the hill to tether. Like standing with warm sea up past your waist and urinating into it; like when some of Simone's period blood leaked out into the sea and the small fish swimming round her legs fought over who got to eat it.

The sun had moved; it was colder, and I stood up, pulled my jacket on and went down the path, walked home. Like the time when. Like the time. Like. There was no stopping it. All the way down the hill my head was full of the dried leaves I'd kicked into a mess. There was no stopping it and there was no getting near it. You say something's like something else, and all you've really said is that actually, because it's only like it, it's different.

When I got home I saw he'd gutted my fish and left it ready for supper. He's gone out, to the river probably, waiting till it's dark enough for some illicit fishing. I came up here and he'd left me some things on the table, they were folded inside a fifty pound note together, under them a piece of paper saying AT LEAST THIS TIME I HAD ENOUGH WARNING TO GIVE YOU A LITTLE SOMETHING TO TAKE WITH YOU. I folded the money and the note up and put

them in my pocket. The recipe and these other things I think I'll
leave in here.

> Take Frying Pan.
> Cover bottom of pan with Sun flower oil
> Cut up Med. onion or whatever, small,
> put in pan & brown with lid on.
> Dice (Small) neep.
> & 1 large carrot.
> Add to onion Cook for 5–10 min.
> Break up mince on board
> & salt & pepper & mix
> with veg. Put on lid &
> Cook until red is gone
> 1–2 oxo in just half pint boiling.
> put in casserole or pan
> add frying pan mix
> Then
> Put on lid
> Pan simmer for ¾ h
> until brown.
> Put on lid & in oven for 45–1 h
> until brown 180–200c.
> If in pan stir to stop burning at bottom
> When cooked
> 1–1 ½ tablespoon
> Co-op Gravy gran.
> Mix thoroughly.

Prayer to St. Joseph
(printed in Italy)
> *Oh, St. Joseph, whose protection is so great, so strong, so*
> *prompt before the throne of God, I place in you all my*

interest and desires. Oh, St. Joseph, do assist me by your
powerful intercession, and obtain for me from your divine
Son all spiritual blessings, through Jesus Christ, our Lord.
So that, having engaged here below your heavenly power,
I may offer my thanksgiving and homage to the Most Lov-
ing of Fathers. Oh, St. Joseph, I never weary contemplating
you, and Jesus asleep in your arms; I dare not approach
while He reposes near your heart. Press Him in my name
and kiss His fine head for me and ask him to return the Kiss
when I draw my dying breath. St. Joseph, Patron of the
dying—pray for me. (This prayer was found in the fiftieth
year of our Lord and Saviour Jesus Christ. In 1505 it was
sent from the Pope to Emperor Charles, when he was going
into battle. Whoever shall read this prayer or hear it, or
keep it about themselves, shall never die a sudden death or
be drowned, nor shall poison take effect on them, neither
shall they fall into the hands of the enemy, or shall be over-
powered in battle. Say for nine mornings for anything you
may desire. It has never been known to fail.)
IMPRIMATUR. September 25, 1950
Hugh C Boyle, Bishop of Pittsburg

The prayer must have belonged to her, something she left below. I
suppose the pouch thing has the remains of something, or someone, sewn inside it. I can't take it with me. I feel insolent just
reading it. Just holding it.

The woman phoned from New York. She said her name was Jay,
and that someone would be collecting me from the plane. She
said she loved my accent. She said it sounded so innocent. She
said that nobody had a complete script yet, not even her, so, not
to panic, it was kind of the distance thing she wanted to achieve.

We'd be starting with a cool improvisational treatment to give it even more of the distance thing, and she was planning to make it kind of weird, so it looked like a home movie.

I put the phone down and came back up here. I sat on the dusty floor and pretended to phone Malcolm. His phone ringing, him picking it up, his voice deep and ironic in my head. Ash, he said, my fine grey area, it's you. How are you? Are you in the New World yet?

No, I'm still in the old one. You sound so far away, I said.

That's because I am, he said. You too.

What's it like up there, then? I asked. We're all dying to know.

Oh very funny, he said. Well, believe it or not, it's splendid. I feel much much better. As you can imagine. And I do like the clothes. But you, you're in the bleak frozen north, no? And how is it for you, my dear?

He talks like that, *my dear*. He's so English.

It's all right, I said. Well actually, it's a bit confusing. Ghost-ridden. And Malcolm, did you overhear that phonecall? Did you hear what the woman said? It all sounds stupid. I don't know what to do.

No, Malcolm said, I didn't hear a thing about it. Are they paying your fare? Well then, that's it decided. Send me a postcard of the beautiful bridge the poets all write about. And you know how to deal with ghosts, don't you?

Lay them? I said.

It's the thing I always found most charming about you, your ceaseless ingenue sexuality, he said. No, my dear, all ghosts need is a good story. Give them somewhere to live, that keeps them happy.

At least, I think that's what he said. You're sounding fainter, I told him.

You terrible Scots, he was saying, always wading about in the past looking for some old trout to tickle.

Guddle, I said, the correct term is guddling. Hello? Malcolm, can you hear me?

Can you still hear me? he said.

Only just, I said. Did the sores heal?

I can't hear, he said.

The sores. Did the sores get better? I shouted.

What snow? he said. Who is this, again? Ah, yes, fine-featured Ash. Listen, sweet heart, if you're still there. Have a wonderful time across the water. Travel light. Go naked.

Then I'd turn some heads, I called. But he was still talking, far away, his voice coming and going.

(Something) let go, he said. Scatter (something) four winds, and all that. Breathe easy till.

I couldn't hear the rest. Then I couldn't hear or feel anything, nothing there except the sound of the air in my nose and the cold of the air at the back of my throat. So I sat and listened to that, just that, and time went past and when I opened my eyes it was now.

The simplest of things. The in of air, the out. It's like, if you can stop everything else and just listen to that, you can even find the exact place where you first touch the rest of the world, the exact place where it first comes into you. When there's nothing but that you can give yourself room. You can feel your lungs moving inside your rib cage like the opening and closing of wings.

A man walks into a bar. Ouch—it was an iron bar. No, a man walks into a bar and asks for a half and a short. He is in a city he doesn't belong to, he stumbled into this bar to get out of the night and the rain, to dry off before he goes to catch his train. He looks in the mirror behind the bar and sees himself asking for a half and a short. Then he realises, it's not a mirror at all, it's a hatch through to the other bar. Through there someone who looks so like him they could be brothers is staring back at him in disbelief. The man is so surprised he lets the glass at his mouth slip out of his hand where it smashes into pieces on the bar. Sure enough, the other man has done exactly the same thing.

By the time he gets on to the train he's so drunk he can't stop the laughing. He throws himself into a seat, he sees his double in the black of the window and he laughs at that too. People all up and down the carriage are looking at him. He doesn't care. They don't know. He has a stomach full of food, his head is wise with the whisky, and there's a stained beermat in his wallet, in the warm of his inside jacket pocket, with his brother's writing on it.

He knows they had so much he must smell of it. He knows that if someone held a match to his mouth or nose he'd breathe out fire. He closes his eyes, and remembers something his brother said to him, or something he said to his brother, so funny and clever and stupid that there's nothing else for it. His eyes fill with water. He puts his head down on his arms on the table and he chokes sweet chemical laughter into the wool of his jumper.

And an old man is sitting in a boat on the water. He has cut the motor; the boat is beating back and fore as the water moves under it. Spring winds rock him. It is early in the morning, still the colour it is before the sun comes up. It is cold. His hair is white and blown back off his forehead; his stubble is rough and grey. He is waiting; on the end of his line, with any luck, there will soon be the mouth of a fish.

The minnow he's baited his line with is black then scarlet then gold as it turns deep below him in the water. He is handsome, he knows he is. He is nineteen, and his smile can melt butter. He is thinking about girls. In his heart he is nursing an absolute beauty. He will know it as soon as he reels it in.

The boat creaks on the surface, back and fore, back and fore.

And it's high summer. The sun is up. Two friends are watching it rise, hunkered down in a dry grassy ditch in the middle of nowhere. They have just woken up. Soon they'll stand and stretch their arms and backs and walk down the field till they find a road. One of them will flag down a van that's delivering bread to the nearest villages. They'll slide into the van, squashed close together in its high seat next to the gear stick and the handbrake. The man will drive them to a station where two or three hours later they'll get on the first train. Before that, though, one will see the other out of the corner of her eye as she sits in the warm air that's coming through the window, and think how she looks like a different person, her hair everywhere, her face smudged with dirt.

But for the moment, they're still lying there in the dry ditch, keeping out of the night's slight chill under a jacket. One of them has her head on the other's chest.

I can hear your heart, you know, she says.

You can what? the other says, waking more clearly now, so that she is startled by how close they are, so close that she doesn't know where to put her hands; there is nowhere safe to put them. But her friend doesn't move, she stays with her ear pressed against her.

It sounds like a train crossing tracks, she said, muffled against my shirt. It sounds like a horse that's broken into a canter. It's getting faster, she laughed; then she stopped, serious, listened. Wait a minute. I can hear what it's saying.

Saying? I said. What? What's it saying?

She listened. She lifted her head off me for a moment, and then she listened again.

It's saying the words, go on, she said.

Then she asked me to tell her what hers was saying, and I put my ear to her chest and listened.

What does it say? she said.

It's like, like—I said, and I stopped, I couldn't think what it was like, it was Amy's heart, it wasn't like anything else. But she misunderstood me; that's good, she said, like, that's a good word, and she looked so pleased I didn't want to spoil it so I didn't, and then we stood up and wandered down through the grass and fields until we got to a road and caught a lift in a van, in the smell of petrol and sweat and new bread, with the man's radio blasting out that Haircut One Hundred song, where do we go from here, is it down to the lake I fear, and the flatlands spread round us like a flooded desert, we waited in the early morning station for the first train, go on beating inside me, keeping time over and over, and I dared to clean the smudge off her chin with the corner of my shirt, I took her face in my hands and turned it up towards me like a child's and put the corner of my shirt in my mouth and cleaned a grass-dust smudge off her skin with my spit. We sat on one of those old brass benches they'd painted green when they redid all those small stations to make them look like they do in adaptations of Edwardian novels on the television on Sunday evenings and we didn't say anything, nothing out loud, you could hear the summer for miles around us.

That was something. I liked that then, yes, I did.

Dust's quite thick on the surface of this table even after just a week. Write the letters of your name in it with your finger, take a deep breath and blow it away.

I can hear my father coming in the back door. Maybe he caught something. A shred of the wing of a plane that went down in the war. A vine with its tendrils dripping with grapes. A fish to put on the newspaper on the floor of the larder.

I'll maybe just go down and see.

ACKNOWLEDGEMENTS and thanks

Thank you, Xandra.

Thanks to the Eastern Arts Board, and the Scottish Arts Council.

Thanks to Bridget, Catherine, Kasia, Kate, Sheila, Bernard and Philippa.

Thanks to Lennie and Sarah at Virago.

Special thanks to Katherine. Thanks to Mr. Crisp at the Kitchen Association, and to Belinda Arthur.

Thank you, Sarah.

FURTHER ACKNOWLEDGEMENTS

"(They Long To Be) Close To You"
Words by Hal David/Music by Burt Bacharach
© New Hidden Valley Music and Case David
Copyright Renewed—All Rights Reserved
Lyric reproduction by kind permission of Carlin Music Corp.
UK administrator for the Commonwealth of Nations (excluding Canada/Australasia) Eire and Israel.

"Not Marble" by Edwin Morgan
reprinted with kind permission of Carcanet Press
Edwin Morgan: Collected Poems 1949–1987, 1990 Carcanet Press Limited.

"All Kinds Of Everything"
Words and Music by Derry Lindsay and Jack Smith © 1970.
Reproduced here by kind permission of EMI Music Publishing Ltd, London WC2H 0EA.

Quotation from *A Streetcar Named Desire* by Tennessee Williams by kind permission of The University of the South, Sewanee, Tenn., and New Directions.

All efforts have been made to contact holders of copyright. In the event of any inadvertent omission please contact the publisher.

ALSO BY

ALI SMITH

HOTEL WORLD

Five people: four are living; three are strangers; two are sisters; one, a teenage hotel chambermaid, has fallen to her death in a dumbwaiter. But her spirit lingers in the world, straining to recall things she never knew. And one night all five women find themselves in the smooth plush environs of the Global Hotel, where the intersection of their very different fates make for this playful, defiant, and richly inventive novel.

Fiction

THE WHOLE STORY AND OTHER STORIES

What happens when you run into Death in a busy train station? (You know he's Death because when he smiles, your cell phone goes dead.) What if your lover falls in love with a tree? Should you be jealous? From the woman pursued by a band of bagpipers in full regalia to the artist who's built a seven-foot boat out of secondhand copies of *The Great Gatsby*, Smith's characters are offbeat, charming, sexy, and as wonderfully complex as life itself.

Fiction

THE ACCIDENTAL

Each of the Smarts—parents Eve and Michael, son Magnus, and the youngest, daughter Astrid—encounter Amber in his or her own solipsistic way, but somehow her presence allows them to see their lives (and their life together) in a new light. Smith's narrative freedom and exhilarating facility with language propel the novel to its startling, wonderfully enigmatic conclusion.

Fiction

The Book Lover is a treasure trove of what Ali Smith has loved over the course of her reading life, in her twenties, as a teenager, as a child. Full of pieces from amazing writers like Sylvia Plath, Muriel Spark, Grace Paley, and Margaret Atwood, it also has a wonderful selection of lesser-known authors like Joseph Roth, only just gaining proper status now, and Clarice Lispector, a Brazilian genius who's far too underpublished. From surprising figures like Beryl the Peril, Billie Holliday, and Lee Miller to unusual selections from the most prominent writers in history, *The Book Lover* is an intimate, personal anthology that gives readers a glimpse of how writers develop their craft—by reading other writers.

Fiction

ALSO AVAILABLE

Artful
Autumn
Companion Piece
The First Person and Other Stories
How to be both
Public Library and Other Stories
Spring
Summer
There But For The
Winter

VINTAGE BOOKS
Available wherever books are sold.
vintagebooks.com